Special thanks to the following people for breathing life into the Godsverse when I thought its light had been blown out:

Katrina Roets, Pat Shand, Starr, Ernie Sawyer, I'm a Ninja, Logan Waterman, Matthew Johnson, Gary Phillips, Ramsey Church, Phil, Melissa Hooper, Jean Lau, Eric P. Kurniawan, Peter Anders, Collin David, Nikres. Joshua Bowers, Jeff Lewis, Emerson Kasak, Linda Robinson, Susan Faw, Talinda Willard, Courtney Cannon, Dave Baxter, old_fogey@yahoo com, Nick Smith, Charlotte Organ, Chad Bowden, Jason Crase, John L Vogt, Philip R. Burns. Bloodfists, Death's Head Studio, LLC, Daniel Groves, Rodney Bonner. JF weber, Walter Weiss, Mitch Fittler, Stacey Henline. Stephanie, Kathy Ash, Charlotte Ulla Pleym, Ray, Jason Schroeder, Chris Call, Maximilian Lippl, Andrew Rees, Tawnly Pranger, Minarkhaios, Vincent Fung, Dave Kochbeck, and Bob Jacobs.

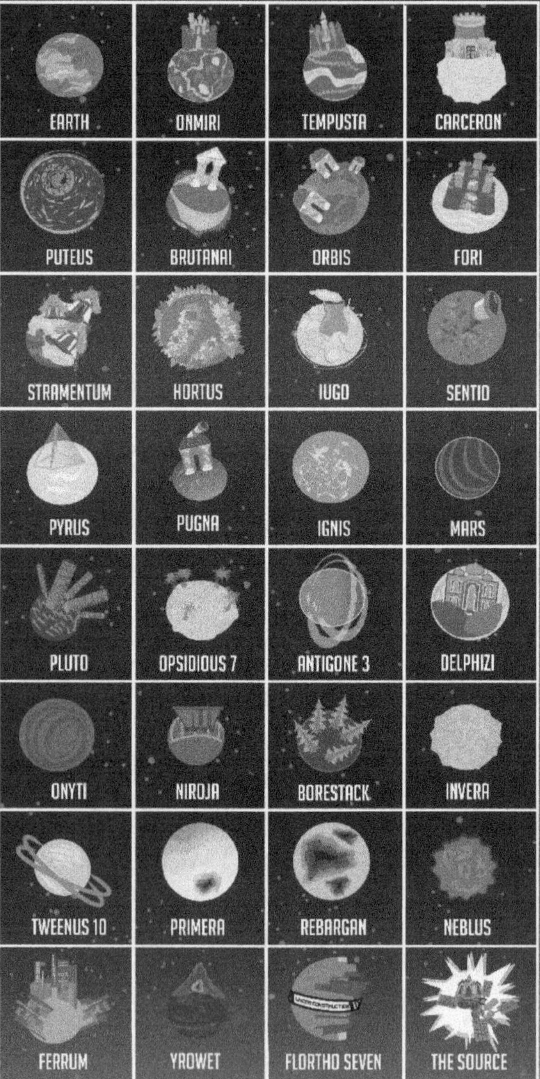

GODSVERSE PLANETS
EARTH
ONMIRI
TEMPUSTA
CARCERON
PUTEUS
BRUTANAI
ORBIS
FORI
STRAMENTUM
HORTUS
IUGO
SENTIO
PYRUS
PUGNA
IGNIS
MARS
PLUTO
OPSIDIOUS 7
ANTIGONE 3
DELPHIZI
ONYTI
NIROJA
BORESTACK
INVERA
TWEENUS 10
PRIMERA
REBARGAN
NEBLUS
FERRUM
YROWET
FLORTHO SEVEN
THE SOURCE

1000 BC – BETRAYED (HELL PT 1)
/PIXIE DUST
500 BC – FALLEN (HELL PT 2)
200 BC – HELLFIRE (HELL PT 3)
1974 AD – MYSTERY SPOT (RUIN PT 1)
1976 AD – INTO HELL (RUIN PT 2)
1984 AD – LAST STAND (RUIN PT 3)
1985 AD – CHANGE
1985 AD – MAGIC/BLACK MARKET HEROINE
1985 AD – EVIL
1989 AD – DEATH'S KISS
(DARKNESS PT 1)
2000 AD – TIME
2015 AD – HEAVEN
2018 AD – DEATH'S RETURN (DARKNESS PT 2)
2020 AD – KATRINA HATES THE DEAD
(DEATH PT 1)
2176 AD – CONQUEST
2177 AD – DEATH'S KISS
(DARKNESS PT 3)
12,018 AD – KATRINA HATES THE GODS
(DEATH PT 2)
12,028 AD – KATRINA HATES THE UNIVERSE
(DEATH PT 3)
12,046 AD – EVERY PLANET HAS A GODSCHURCH
(DOOM PT 1)
12,047 AD – THERE'S EVERY REASON TO FEAR
(DOOM PT. 2)
12,049 AD – THE END TASTES LIKE PANCAKES
(DOOM PT 3)
12,176 AD – CHAOS

ALSO BY RUSSELL NOHELTY

NOVELS
My Father Didn't Kill Himself
Sorry for Existing
Gumshoes: The Case of Madison's Father
Invasion
The Vessel
The Void Calls Us Home
Worst Thing in the Universe
Anna and the Dark Place
The Marked Ones
The Dragon Scourge
The Dragon Champion
The Dragon Goddess
The Obsidian Spindle Saga

COMICS and OTHER ILLUSTRATED WORK
The Little Bird and the Little Worm
Ichabod Jones: Monster Hunter
Gherkin Boy
How NOT to Invade Earth

www.russellnohelty.com

DOOM

Book 6 of The Godsverse Chronicles

By:
Russell Nohelty

Edited by:
Leah Lederman

Proofread by:
Katrina Roets & Toni Cox

Cover by:
Psycat Covers

Planet chart and timeline design by:
Andrea Rosales

BOOK 1

"Every Planet Has a Godschurch"

CHAPTER 1

I woke up with a vicious hangover, rolled over in my bed, and popped two aspirin. There was a finite supply of aspirin left in the city, and I hoarded as much as I could. When a new shipment came to the hospital, I made sure the orderlies held back a crate just for me.

Most of the thieves went for the morphine or other addictive drugs they could flip on the streets, but not me. I didn't need the money. I got paid a lot for doing my job, and so I was happy with bags of saline, clean needles, and aspirin, which all went to cure my daily hangovers.

I trudged across the room and hung a bag of saline from the coat rack, right next to the floor-length leather coat, which had become my calling card after the war. The needle stuck in its familiar place on my arm, and the saline did its job rehydrating me.

Back in my old life, things were simpler. Back then, I might've complained about living in a crappy apartment above a dive bar, but if the last twenty years have taught me nothing else, it's to never take anything for granted, and I never do; not anymore. I've rolled with the punches, and they've come hard and fast enough to knock out everybody I ever loved, leaving me alone in this world, living in a derelict apartment in the slums.

People left me alone in the slums. That's why I lived here. In the better parts of the city, there were way too many rules. In the slums, nobody cared what anyone did, and as long as you could take care of yourself, nobody messed with you.

The problem with living here was that the water wasn't clean. Brown liquid belched out of every sink, so I made sure to keep lots of clean, natural water around, boiled and purified for my drinking pleasure. There was a guy named Jack down at the water treatment plant, and in return for a screw every now and then, he delivered me more water than I ever needed.

Yes, we still screwed, even in the worst of times. It was about the only thing we did for fun, but we had to choose our partners carefully. You couldn't just screw anything that moved. Some of the demons got into the prostitutes, and if those prostitutes screwed one of your lays, you could get a series of diseases that—well, let's just say you didn't want. That's why I vetted my men carefully before letting them lay the pipe to me.

***

After the saline drip finished, I turned on the purified water filter for a shower. I stripped off my clothes and caught a quick glimpse of my naked body in the mirror. Dark, jagged scars cut up and down my torso, and a wide gash slit across my face, a constant reminder of the time a demon saved my life from the Horde, only to be vaporized in the process.

Twenty years ago, the Horde descended upon us. They were a race of disgusting bugs of all types—ants, millipedes, spiders, flies, and more. If you could name it, they existed in the ranks of the Horde. Armed with blasters that could disintegrate a person in an instant, they set out to destroy us. It was a nightmare.

Within hours of their arrival, they leveled most of our major cities with lasers from their massive spaceship stationed above the atmosphere. Before they even touched down on Earth, we'd lost billions of people. Then they released their invasion force, which blotted out the sky and turned day into night, and by the end, we lost a few billion more.

Every inch of me was the memory of the great battles from that war, the scars of which reminded me I was still alive when so many other people—better people—died. I lost one of my eyes in the war and had it replaced with a mechanical red one whose wires spread across the left side of my face and caused my cheek to involuntarily spasm. It wasn't pretty, but it gave me two eyes and depth perception, which was important in the new normal. Some might even say it's why I can be so accurate with a gun because I have a cyborg's eyesight. I think it's because I practiced for a long-ass time.

***

Every day in Thebos started out the same. I walked down to the bar under my apartment and waited for orders to come. One of Piggy's disgusting lieutenants came to the bar under my apartment by around eight am and gave me a list of chores for the day.

The chores changed daily, but they all involved using violence in some way or another. They might be collecting money, offing somebody, or sending a message with my fists. It didn't matter what it was, I was supposed to do it, and I did, every day, crossing off my missions as I accomplished them.

Sometimes it took an hour. Sometimes jobs went late into the night. It all depended on the day. It didn't matter to me. It all paid the same, whether I had ten tasks or two. Once I crossed them all off my list, I ended up at Matt's bar again to drink it off.

I heard everything that went on down there through the floorboards, which is how I knew that Matt was up, cleaning the bar from last night. After I was dressed, I walked down the creaky stairs.

"Morning," I said, walking through the door.

It was the only place in Piggy's quadrant that didn't pay protection money to him. That's because I personally protected the bar from hooligans, and in exchange, they let me drink for free. Honestly, with as much as I drank, they would have made out better paying for protection.

"We're not open yet," Matt replied, brushing dirt across the floor with an old broom.

I sat down at the bar. "That's what you always say. Whiskey, neat."

"I'm serious this time. We ain't open."

I spun around on my barstool, making sure he knew I didn't care. "I don't want to pull rank on you, Matt, but this was the deal."

He didn't bother looking at me. "You aren't worth it. You're drinking me out of business."

"I don't see anybody messing with you. That's more than I could say for most of the businesses in this town, so I think I'm plenty worth it. Of course, if you don't think so, I could stop protecting this place altogether and see what happens. I don't like your odds, though."

Matt stopped his sweeping with a sigh. He couldn't argue with me. He also knew a threat when he heard one. "Fine. One drink."

"No, as many drinks as I damn well please."

Matt walked over to the bar and poured me a glass of whiskey, straight up, no ice. Whiskey was the one drink still readily available in Thebos, and everybody left chugged the stuff like water. It was the only drink you could guarantee wasn't contaminated, the bonuses being that it made you forget your problems, and if you drank enough, you'd die, which was always a plus.

"Here you go," Matt said.

I knocked back the drink in one shot. I didn't taste the bitterness of the alcohol, but then I couldn't taste anything. A gun backfire during the war made sure of that.

Matt leaned himself against the bar and rubbed his finger on my hand. "Did you know we've never had sex before?"

I smiled at him. He heard me having sex with other people—those floorboards worked both ways—and it always stuck like a craw in Matt's side, but I was adamant that I couldn't protect his bar and sleep with him at the same time. Since I didn't want to find a new bar, we couldn't bang. I moved my hand. "Did you know I've killed people for less?"

He leaned in closer. "Please. You don't have the stomach to kill me."

My jacket flew open, and, in a flash, my pistol dug into Matt's forehead. "You have no idea what my stomach is capable of, my friend."

After a second of tension, we both laughed. In a different life, decent people wouldn't have laughed at a legitimate death threat. But we've all learned something in the past few years; laughing about it is the only way to survive.

I holstered the gun, still chuckling. "Next time I pull my gun on you, I'm gonna shoot you with it."

Matt wiped the tears out of his eyes. "That'll be the day."

The bell chimed over the door, and a fat, oafish demon walked into the bar. The only demon up before ten am was my handler, Odahai. He was disgusting, with a face like an ogre and breath ten times worse. Yes, I said demon. They lived among us. It's part of what made life such a miserable experience for all of us.

We weren't ready for the Horde War. When they came from the sky, we didn't know what to do. I still have nightmares of their unyielding forces. Earth quickly became a nightmarish Hellscape—and I mean Hellscape in the most literal way possible. When the Horde attacked, it triggered an Apocalypse.

Yes, a biblical one.

I know it sounded crazy, but that doesn't make it any less true.

Rifts to Hell opened all around the world, and monsters of every type entered our world. Demons, ghosts, dragons, orcs, and more rose from Hell and scattered along the Earth. I heard stories about Hell on Earth eons ago but seeing it with my own eyes was wholly unbelievable.

Even more unbelievable . . . it turned out they were on our side. The army of the damned took up arms alongside us to drive back the forces of the Horde. The Horde's forces were endless, but so were those of the undead. Together, we held off the armies of the Horde and drove them back—and eventually, we won.

After the Horde Wars, nothing was the same. People who once clung tightly onto their last shred of hope abandoned it and stared dead-eyed into the ether, waiting for the sweet call of death. We had all been through so much and somehow survived. We lost our loved ones, our souls, and our reasons for living.

Yet, we were still very alive, and we dared not take that for granted. So many of us didn't make it out of the fight that killing ourselves, well, it felt downright selfish. So, we plowed along. This was the new normal, and we were determined to get along, even after we'd lost everything.

On top of the shit burger that was our lives, some genius decided it was a good idea to let the demons stay on Earth if they wanted. I guess I kind of understood it, in theory. After all, humanity would have been wiped out without them. Whoever made that decision really screwed us, though, because demons like Odahai didn't play nice.

Odahai's knuckles dragged behind him as he hobbled into the bar toward me. He was broad enough that all but the widest doors forced him to enter at an angle. He reached into his pocket and handed me a slip of paper.

I unfolded it and looked over the note quickly. It only had three tasks on it. "Is this it?"

Odahai chuckled to himself like I'd made a joke. "That's it."

"What's so funny?"

But he didn't have to answer. I scrolled my eyes down the list, and my stomach dropped when I got to the last item.

Goddamn it. Sometimes my job really sucked.

CHAPTER 2

Ten years before the Horde descended on us, Earth was pulled into a black hole. It happened in an instant. We were minding our own business, living a pretty decent life, when the sun collapsed upon itself, creating a black hole and sucking Earth through it. We called it the "Sun Incident."

It sucked. My head felt like it split right down the center. A million screams bellow from the edges of your brain while every color in the rainbow tries to flay you alive.

Every one of us prayed for death at that moment, and most people had their prayers answered. Eighty percent of the human race died—eight billion people. Dead. In an instant. I can't even imagine that many people.

Those of us that survived wondered what made us special, but we knew in our hearts the answer was nothing. We just got lucky.

Somehow, I survived that ordeal.

Eventually, Earth was pulled back into our universe as fast as it was sent away. The sun returned to normal, and the world kept spinning as if nothing had ever happened. Scientists studied the phenomenon for years with no results until they threw up their hands and shrugged, chalking it up to a thing that happened sometimes. There were rumors that Apollo himself sent us into oblivion and pulled us back out again. I don't know if that's true, but it wasn't the craziest thing I'd ever heard. Not even close.

I trudged through the streets of Thebos, dreading everything I had to do that day. There wasn't a lot of time for dread in my life, and certainly not for pain, but some tasks managed to pierce through my thick outer shell. I had never failed to deliver on anything Piggy asked of me, and I wasn't going to start now. Some of his errands truly tested my patience, though, like the last one on my list. Every task I accomplished moved me closer to it. Usually, I didn't mind working for demons, but today I loathed it.

It was hell trying to live with them. No matter how much humanity wanted to work together and rebuild ourselves, the demons had their own ideas. They lived for the chaos. During the war, the demons had a purpose—something to slaughter. They directed their overblown sense of rage toward the Horde and were both effective and efficient on the battlefield. Their bravery and zeal for winning could not be overstated.

When the battling stopped, their anger had nowhere to go except toward us. Demons were already used to taking their aggression out on humanity since it's what they did down in Hell. They were our torturers and our wardens. After the Horde Wars, they decided to do what came naturally and lord over us again.

Once they beat us down, the demons battled each other for control of a world that wasn't much worth fighting over. They developed their little fiefdoms all over the world. Eventually, those fiefdoms turned into kingdoms, and we had no choice but to serve our warlords unless we wanted to pay the ultimate price.

***

The first job on my list was to pick up protection money from a bodega in Little Kenya. A group of African refugees were stranded in Thebos after the Horde War and set up a community together. Until two weeks ago, they used Piggy's men for protection, just like everybody else, but that changed. They thought it would be a good idea to use their own people as protection. Piggy had a problem with that—a big problem.

If one community could get away with protecting themselves, then more would surely follow, and the need for Piggy's services would vanish. It was my job to show them the error of their ways, starting with one shop and working my way up to burning the whole town to the ground if necessary.

It was a charming store, with colorfully painted walls and little statues carved into the wood lining the counter. The smell of turmeric and ginger filled the air as I walked through the aisles. I found the owner filleting a chicken behind a glass case full of exotic meats.

Piggy could have picked any store on the block to teach a lesson, but this time it was this guy's store. He had no idea what was coming for him. They never did. The fickle finger of fate pointed to him, though, just like it pointed to everybody at some point in their lives. For the unlucky ones, it pointed their way again and again. Life was heartless and cruel. Most days, you escaped the odds, but some days, some days, you rolled snake eyes and crapped out.

"Mr. Mwangi?" I said with a warm smile. A smile was disarming. It made people take down their guard, and it worked with him, too. Mwangi turned from his work with none of the tenseness that would have been appropriate, based on my appearance—and my reputation. Instead, he showed a bright smile that showed off a nice set of teeth.

"Yes," he said cheerfully. "How may I help you?"

"Well," I said, gesturing at the shop around me. "This is a lovely store you have here. It smells so alive, you know. Most stores I go into smell a little like death if they smell like anything at all. But this one? It's almost overpowering, honestly. Almost like an old-time marketplace."

He puffed out his chest with pride. "Well, thank you. I try to keep it pleasant and inviting, like home. Most of my customers don't have a good memory of home anymore, and I like to think this is like going into a little slice of Kenya."

It didn't matter where you were, people loved to be complimented. Compliment somebody enough, and you would surely get into their good graces. That was a guarantee.

"A little slice of Kenya." I ran my finger across the deli window. "Damn, if that isn't beautiful. How long you had this place?"

"Next month will be my fifth year," he said, placing his hands on the counter.

"That's not bad. Most of these businesses, they rise and fall overnight. But not you. You lasted five years. That's quite an accomplishment."

"And hopefully another five more."

"Hmm," I said, looking down at a picture of Mr. Mwangi surrounded by seven children. "Well, that's where things get interesting. See, Mr. Mwangi, I would love it if you could last another five years. I really would, but it's dangerous out there. Thebos is full of thieves and scoundrels."

His eyes were wide, and he nodded solemnly. "Oh, I know. I have been very lucky."

"Lucky. That's one way to put it, Mr. Mwangi. But I think you have a guardian angel looking out for you. Yes, I do, because nobody is that lucky. At least, not in my experience."

The smile on his face faltered. "What do you want?"

I put my hands in the air, pretending to be nonchalant. "I'm just trying to have a conversation. You have kids, Mr. Mwangi?"

Mwangi pointed at me with his meat cleaver. "I think you should leave."

"Whoa," I said. "That's not very nice, Mr. Mwangi. I'm just trying to be pleasant. Don't you want to be pleasant? Just answer me, do you have any children?"

Mwangi folded his arms across his chest. "Two children."

I picked up the picture of him with his children. "This picture here shows seven kids. Let me guess, the other five died in the war?"

"You should leave." His voice fell hollow.

I placed the picture back down carefully. "I get it. I lost people in the war, too. A lot of them. Every person I ever cared about, actually. It's good you have two kids left, Mr. Mwangi. It really is. Most people, they have no attachment to this world. It's good you still have some left."

"Get. Out."

"In a minute, Mr. Mwangi," I said. "I see it in your eyes, you just want me to get to the point. Well, here it is. I have a favor to ask you."

"I know your face. I recognize you. Your eye gives you away." Mwangi laid his hands on the glass case. "Tell your pig boss I will not pay."

I strolled toward him, shaking my head. "That's not very nice. He doesn't call you names, Mr. Mwangi. And he could since you haven't paid him his money for the last two weeks."

"And I won't."

I chuckled. "That's where you are wrong, Mr. Mwangi."

I grabbed a metal rack that held a collection of spices and thrust it to the ground. My steel-toed black boots were perfect for inflicting damage on glass without breaking my foot. I used them to round-house through his meat rack.

Mwangi jumped back. "What are you doing?"

"I'm showing you that life is dangerous!" I shouted. "We can all use protection, Mr. Mwangi."

"I can handle you myself!" Mwangi said, lurching forward with his meat cleaver.

I held up a warning finger. "This is not funny, Mr. Mwangi. I have no time for your nonsense. You will pay my boss today, or I will burn this shop to the ground."

Mwangi rushed around the counter and swung at me. The trick to fighting somebody that owes you money is hurting them badly enough that they bow to your superior strength without fatally injuring them. You don't want to kill them. Heck, that would make it easy. It's much harder to wound somebody than to outright kill them.

Mwangi swung again. I shot up my arm to block and clasped my hand onto his wrist. I spun him around to the floor, and he dropped his knife, whimpering in pain.

"Mr. Mwangi, that is not nice."

"Please!" he said. "Please stop."

"I didn't want to start with you, Mr. Mwangi, but you left me no choice. Now, you will pay me what you owe, and you will tell every other shop owner on this block that the only protection in this town comes from me, or I will take everyone you ever loved, and you will watch them bleed out in your arms. Do you understand?"

Having loved ones is a liability. I used it as a bargaining chip every chance I got. Our own lives don't hold much value, but when you love somebody, you put a value on their soul. And that cripples you. If this poor shop owner had no loved ones, losing his shop and his life would mean nothing, but once I threatened to take away the things he loved, he became putty in my hand.

"Fine!" he shouted. "I will pay! I will pay!"

I let go of his wrist. "I knew you would, Mr. Mwangi. I knew you would."

CHAPTER 3

I left Mr. Mwangi's store with all the money in his register. He whined about not being able to make rent that month and that his children would starve. I didn't care. Starvation was a far better fate than getting their throats slit. Besides, it wasn't my fault he still had loved ones. That was just bad planning on his part.

"Hey!" I heard a young man shout to me as I rounded the corner away from Mr. Mwangi's store. "Hey! I'm talking to you!"

I turned around to see a dark-skinned young man pointing a gun at my face. Behind him, four others pounded crowbars and baseball bats into their palms. They tried their best to seem intimidating, but they clearly didn't have any clue what horrors I'd seen. Nothing they did could frighten me.

"I'll be takin' that money, ya see?" The boy with the gun waved it in my face.

I placed the wad of money in my coat pocket. "No, you won't."

"Dis is our neighborhood, ya see?" the boy with the gun said. "We protect it, and we profit from it. Ain't nobody gonna pay if we just let ya walk."

"Yeah," I said, taking a step forward. "That's the point."

The young man wobbled as he backtracked a step. His stance was all wrong. He didn't know what he was doing. "Don't cha take another step."

I lunged forward as the young man's bullets whizzed past me. I grabbed his arm and slammed his face into my knee. The gun slipped onto the ground when I broke his trigger finger.

"You broke my hand!" he whimpered.

I kicked the gun away and pulled out two revolvers from the gun belt under my coat. "Now, listen here. This isn't your neighborhood. It's Gliporg's. Leave, forget this ever happened, and he'll let you live whatever miserable life you have left."

"Get her, boys!" the young boy screamed just before I put a bullet between his eyes. The four others charged forward. I ducked the first crowbar and fired a bullet into its owner's belly. His friend reared back to strike me, so I spun on my heels and shot him through the neck.

Two gang members left, and I had my two guns trained on them. "Don't make me kill you."

The boys looked at each other, then rushed toward me as if I couldn't shoot them both at once. They were wrong. I blew a hole in both their chests and watched as each one flew backward, dead before they even hit the ground. One of them bounced off a parked car.

Mwangi ran outside his shop, visibly shaken, and I turned my guns toward him. "This is why you need me for protection, Mr. Mwangi. There are hooligans about. You're lucky they didn't land a blow on me. Otherwise, I would have no choice but to follow through with my threat to burn down your shop."

"I'll see you next week, Mr. Mwangi." I kicked the boy's gun into the gutter. "This town is very dangerous. I think the price of your protection just doubled."

Mwangi had no choice but to nod as he watched the blood of five young boys bleed into the sewer in front of his store.

***

I crossed the first item off my list as I waited on the roof of a dilapidated, tenement high-rise pointing an M-2400 sniper rifle at the mansion across the street. The building used to be two hundred stories tall, but now it sat a pathetic, dilapidated structure. I climbed up four stories of rotten, wooden stairwell and found a perfect sniper perch. Nothing but a ruin, really. An ideal place to lay in wait.

The mansion I aimed my gun at belonged to Piggy's biggest rival—a demon named Ctumiti—who ran the southwest quadrant of the city. We all called him "Itty" behind his back. He was self-conscious about the fact that he was the runt of the warlords, but what he lacked in size, he made up for in viciousness.

Ul'brem had forced an uneasy ceasefire between Itty and Piggy for the last year, but last night one of Piggy's best lieutenants, Ylgur, defected to Itty's band of mercenaries, and Piggy didn't like that one bit. Piggy demanded loyalty and paid top dollar for it. If one of his own crossed him, they had to die.

I'll be honest, I wished that I had more trouble working for demons, but I just—don't. At all. I've had a lot of horrible bosses over the years, and demons weren't the worst of them. I worked for whoever paid the most. When there was still a government to speak of, they needed help disposing of despots. After the Horde War, it was demon warlords who controlled huge tracts of land and fought each other bitterly for more.

The thing was . . . they were both equally bad, but the demons paid more and paid faster. It truly didn't matter who I worked for; murder was murder. I was always good at rolling with the punches. Psychologists would call it moral ambiguity, but I don't care for big words or headshrinkers. I just know I'm a survivor.

Before the war, I was a naïve little girl who loved creature comforts. It didn't take long for me to figure out that if I wanted to live, I needed to be ruthless and cunning, tough as stone and sharp as a razor's edge. I spent all of my waking hours training my body to fight like a champion and my mind to abandon all emotion. I also took the time to develop a unique set of skills which kept me in high demand long after the war was over.

I became a sniper. I could fight well enough, but my real gift was sitting in dark crevices, planting, and waiting for bugs to pop their heads up so I could eliminate them one at a time. I preferred the elegance of a long-range kill over the brutality of a close one. It was less taxing on the muscles if you didn't mind extreme boredom, which I didn't. The life of a sniper was boring, but I enjoyed the tedium of sitting in wait. It gave me time to clear my head and think. I was a prodigy, really, and after the war, demons enlisted my services to kill each other.

I was a deadly accurate shot and a compassionless killer, two traits highly sought in the chaotic aftermath of the war. Business was good in Thebos until things settled and Ul'brem emerged as its king. After that, snipers weren't as much in demand. Still, I enjoyed jobs like these that gave me the chance to dust off my skills.

After an hour of waiting, a long, black Humvee limousine pulled up in front of the house. Out stepped two of Itty's guards, followed by the traitor, Ylgur, a demon dressed in a three-piece pinstripe suit and decked out in gold chains. He always was a flashy one. It made my job easy.

I steadied my breath and peered through the sight. I couldn't use a laser for guidance. Not with so many guards around. The wind blew from the southeast, but the demon charges fired straight and true even in a tornado. I only had one shot. If I wasn't perfect, Ylgur would scurry underground and never emerge again.

I took one more breath and held it. Then I slowly squeezed the trigger until the sound of the demon hunter whizzed through the air and blew Ylgur's head into a hundred pieces. I pulled the gun down from the ledge and crossed number two off my list.

Only one item left, and that's when my dread kicked into high gear.

CHAPTER 4

Getting out of the building was easy. That's the nice thing about an assassination—everybody's so confused and startled in the hustle and bustle that they forgot to look around and find the shooter. I packed up the sniper rifle, walked out of the building and into a cab without anybody even noticing me.

Once I was back at the bar, I placed the case next to me and sat down on my regular stool. It was evening now, and the place was crowded, but there was always room at the bar for me. That was part of the arrangement I had with Matt.

"Rebecca!" he shouted at me, slurring his words. "Come sit down!"

Matt liked to drink with his customers, and tonight was no exception. He saw me sit down and shouted over the bar, "I'm going to get you a shot!"

"Make it two," I replied.

Matt's was my favorite bar in Thebos, and not because I lived upstairs. I lived upstairs because this place was my favorite. Every sorry thief and scoundrel made their way through the front door at least once a week. It was a murderer's row of scumbags, and they didn't ask questions and who you worked for or what you did. Your job was your business.

Outside these walls, it mattered whose side you were on, but inside you were just a human trying to get pissed and forget your problems. You could shoot somebody's mother, and they wouldn't take it out on you in this bar. They might slice you open for it later, but in these walls, every beef was squashed.

Matt brought a shot glass over to me, and I pounded it down. He grabbed the bottle and poured me another. "Did you know," he said, pointing at me, "that we've never had sex?"

I chuckled as I downed another shot. "Yes. I knew that. I'm a drunk, Matt, but I'm not that much of a drunk."

"I hear you up there just about every night." He gestured down the bar. "We all hear you. And I gotta ask… why not me?"

I grabbed the bottle and took a long chug. "I don't shit where I eat, Matt. I actually like this place. Seriously, you should take it as a compliment."

Matt grabbed the bottle from me and took it to the head. When he was done, he slammed it back on the table. "I respect that. I do. But I have to tell you . . . I am pretty good."

I laughed. "All right, Matt. Prove it."

Matt started to laugh before he processed what I said, and his eyes went wide. "Wait, really?"

My face dropped. "Really."

***

He was right. The sex was good. A little sloppy at first, but he found his form, and his stamina wasn't bad either. I'm happy if I get to cum once, but he got me off three times.

That was nice; what came next was a shame.

Matt fell asleep after banging me, which is for the best. He didn't need to be awake for the next part.

I rolled over in bed and pushed myself to my feet. The floor was cold and hard. I knew every creak of the wood, and I danced around them to avoid Matt waking up. I walked over to my coat and pulled out the paper Odahai gave me earlier in the day. I scanned past the first two tasks that I had completed earlier in the day and lingered on the third.

Kill Matthew Perez. Crime: Failure to pay for protection. Harboring known enemies of Gliporg. Serving unsanctioned liquor without a license.

I grumbled under my breath. I had never failed Piggy before, and I wasn't going to start now. If I suddenly grew a conscience, it would be my head on the chopping block.

I would have to move after killing him, of course. Luckily, I didn't need much, and I didn't keep much. Things tied you to a place, and I couldn't be tied anywhere.

My revolvers were in their holsters in my coat on the chair. I pulled one out and spun the chamber. Six bullets. I reloaded it after fighting those boys in Little Kenya. They weren't bad kids, but it wasn't about that, was it? They had to die, and I was the one who delivered them to their end.

The world is cruel. It has always been cruel, and it will always be cruel.

Matt was a dead man, but at least I could give him one final moment of bliss before sending him off to the great beyond. Hopefully, he would end up in a better place than this—he deserved that much. I took a swig from the bottle of whiskey Matt and I brought up from the bar, then crept over to the bed.

The pale blue light from the sign outside Matt's bar illuminated my naked body as I slid along the hardwood floors. If he woke up, then he would know that I betrayed him to protect myself. He would beg for his life. I didn't want that to be my last memory of him. Without making a sound, I picked up the pillow from my side of the bed and stuffed the gun muzzle tightly into it. I dropped the gun down to Matt's face and pulled the trigger.

He never cried out. He never knew. That was my gift to him. Blood oozed out under the bed and dripped down onto the floor. No doubt it would seep through the cracks and into the bar below me. Somebody would see it, but it wouldn't matter. Down there, nobody asked questions. Even in Matt's death, they would honor that.

I tossed the pillow on the table and dressed myself. There was still work to do. I grabbed the bottle from the table and poured its contents around the room. I pulled a lighter out of my pocket, along with Piggy's instructions, and crossed off the third thing on my task list. There was only one thing left on the note—

Burn the bar when you are done. Then, come to the mansion. 10 pm a car will meet you outside.

I picked up the sniper rifle case and walked toward the door. My guns were the only thing I would need now. I tossed the lighter on my way out. I wouldn't need this place anymore. It was too bad. It was the first place that felt like home in twenty years.

Oh well. Life is cruel. It has always been cruel. It will always be cruel.

***

The fire consumed the bar while I waited for Odahai to pick me up. Screaming patrons poured out and ran off into the night. A few caught my eye and gave me a knowing look. I had destroyed their safe space. I would pay for it later, but out of respect to Matt, their retribution would wait. One day, somebody would double tap me in the back of the head, but it would not be tonight.

The fire raged from my building to the next. Before long, this whole block would burn to the ground, all because Piggy wanted to teach a lesson to one obstinate bartender.

A black limo pulled up, and Odahai rolled down his window. "Get in."

***

I hated the sound of shoes on marble. Really, I just hated marble in general. It echoed, and echoes were the worst enemy of an assassin. Of course, that was the exact reason Piggy's entire mansion was built with white marble from a quarry outside Rome. Footsteps bounced off every surface. He would always hear trouble that way.

Odahai led me through the foyer. The walls were mostly blank except for a huge, tacky mural depicting Lucifer in a victorious battle over Heaven—a demon's wish that never came true. Piggy adored Lucifer and talked about him at length, explaining in painstaking detail the raw deal Lucifer received by revolting against Heaven itself.

Piggy's hooves clomped down the spiraling marble staircase. He loved silk and was dressed in a purple silk robe and nothing else. His cock would have swung low if it wasn't stuck up behind thirty layers of fat and nastiness.

He waddled toward me with a sneering smile, sweat glistening on his bulbous body. His big eyes narrowed to dots as I reached into the pocket of my overcoat and pulled out a wad of money.

"Here," I said, handing it to him.

He snorted loudly as he flipped through the roll. "Can I trust you that it's all there?"

"I don't know," I replied. "Does it look like I want to get fed to your dogs?"

Piggy's dogs were legendary in Thebos: Three-headed Hell hounds with piercing yellow eyes and voracious appetites. Their diet consisted mainly of people that displeased Piggy. He loved to hear their agonized screams while they were eaten alive.

"I suppose not," Piggy said, looking me up and down. "Still."

Piggy handed the money to Odahai, who unfurled the bills and flipped through each one in turn.

"I'm embarrassed for you, really," I said. "I thought we were past this. How long until you finally trust me?"

He shot me a dark look. "You tried to kill me once, little one. I doubt I will ever fully trust you as long as I breathe."

It was a fair point. In fact, I only worked for Piggy because he offered me ten times my price not to kill him. The offer was too good to pass up.

Odahai handed the money back to Piggy. "It's all there. Every last dollar."

"I told you," I said, straightening my jacket. "Do you really think I would have come if I didn't have your money?"

Piggy snorted. "And what about the rest of it?"

I handed Piggy the briefcase with the sniper rifle in it. "You should have gotten word that the traitor you sent me to kill is dead."

Piggy smiled, showing his baked bean teeth. "Yes. You made it quite the spectacle. And the third thing."

"The bar is gone," Odahai said. "I watched it burn. The whole block should be ashes by morning."

"Good, good," Piggy said, relaxing his arms. "It must have been hard for you, pulling that trigger."

"No harder than any other," I replied, swallowing hard. "A mark is a mark."

"But this was a friend, and one under your protection. How can anybody trust you again, now that you have killed somebody under your watch?"

Suddenly, the reason for Matt's death became clear to me. It wasn't about sending a message to somebody else. It was about sending a message to me.

I needed to get out of there and quickly. I turned to flee. "I didn't think—"

"No!" Piggy barked the word. "You didn't think."

Odahai grabbed my arms as I struggled to free myself. I kicked and screamed, but demons are strong. His muscles rippled against my coat, boxing me in.

"Did you really not think I would see you skimming off the top, Rebecca?" Piggy said casually.

I snarled at him. "Skimming off the top? I was helping a guy in exchange for free booze!"

"Ah, yes, but that booze is money in my pocket. That money should have gone to me, my dear. It should have gone to me."

There's a reason I wore a bulky coat. It helped intimidate my enemies since it made me look bigger, but it also helped me escape holds like Odahai's. The coat was so large on me I could wriggle out of almost any bind. I yanked my arms, and the jacket gave just enough so I could free myself.

With my arms free, I shoved hard on Odahai's chest and flung myself at Piggy. My legs wrapped around his neck as I pulled the demon hunters out of their shoulder harnesses. I dug the guns into Piggy's head until the fat on his face nearly enveloped them.

"I think you forgot who you were dealing with," I said. "Now, I could put two charges deep into your brain, or we can forget this little incident ever happened. Which do you want it to be?"

The blood drained from his face. Odahai lunged forward, but I dug my guns in deeper. "I can't hear you. Do I pull the trigger, or do we forget this whole thing?"

"Give!" he shouted. "I give."

I slid off his back and rolled along the floor, standing with my guns still pointed at his chest. I had no love for life, but I certainly didn't want to die. There was too much up in the air for me if I did. Frankly, I assumed I would end up in Hell being tortured by somebody worse than Piggy.

My hands trembled as I tried to hold the guns steady. "Do not question my loyalty again, Piggy or I will not be so kind the next time."

"Don't call me that," he grumbled. He hated that nickname. I'd never used it to his face before, but I needed to prove a point. I needed to show I wasn't afraid of him, even though he petrified me.

"You are in no place to call the shots," I replied. "Now, toss over my coat."

Odahai looked at Piggy, who nodded. He tossed me my leather coat. I placed one of my guns back and used my free hand to swing the coat around my body.

"You can put the gun away," Piggy said, smiling. "You've passed my test, Rebecca."

"No way that's true. I know you. When you don't like somebody, you stop at nothing to hunt them down."

He took a small step forward. "That's true, but I like you. I very much like you. I just had to know something about you."

"And what's that?"

"Just how far you would go to carry out my wishes. And now I know. You would burn down everything. It's not every day that you meet a soldier with such loyalty, even if they sometimes aim a gun to your head."

I cocked the gun again. "It's still aimed, Piggy."

"Yes," he said, "but you haven't pulled the trigger. I respect that."

I pulled my other demon hunter out of its holster. "Don't give me a reason. Well, another reason."

Piggy picked up the sniper rifle case off the ground. "I don't want to hurt you. I want to offer you a job. A job I can only entrust with the best of the best. Somebody who would never dream of messing up and feeling the horrible extent of my wrath."

"Go on," I said. Part of surviving in Thebos was going with the flow. "I'm listening."

"There is a target, a very special target, that I need you to take care of for me. If you do this for me, I will pay you enough to retire twice over."

"I like what I do."

Piggy laughed. "Of course you do! Which is why I love you. Please, please, take this job. Let me pay you a king's ransom, and whether you retire or not, it will be entirely up to you."

"Who's the target?" I asked, stowing my guns.

Piggy took a manila folder from Odahai, opened the rifle case. And placed the folder inside. He snapped the briefcase shut and handed it to me.

"You'll find out once you get to the location. Don't open it until then."

"This sounds like a setup."

Piggy snapped his fingers, and fifteen red dots appeared on my chest. "My dear, if I wanted you dead, I would have told them to fire ages ago."

CHAPTER 5

The streets of Piggy's quadrant were rough and coarse. I felt every stone and pebble as Odahai drove me through the streets of southeastern Thebos. Deep potholes made most streets undrivable, but that was how Piggy liked it. And really, it was why we thieves and scumbags liked Piggy's quadrant so much.

He was always preparing for an ambush, and his terrible roads prevented anybody from rolling through and attacking. If somebody wanted to start trouble, they would have to survive hellish conditions for miles for the privilege, leaving them tired and weakened in the process. Nobody liked coming to Piggy's territory, and that gave us a sense of security.

Driving over the bridge that led into Itty's territory, that all changed. The roads leveled out. The streets were clean. Soldiers armed with machine guns patrolled the sidewalks.

Itty's main source of income was drugs, and those clean streets helped him move product fast. Everybody wanted to forget about their problems, so he made money hand over fist, which gave him plenty of capital to hire people. That's why Piggy hated him. Piggy drew the short straw when it came to territories. Itty got drugs. Logbar got the church. Tjigbal got prostitution. Piggy was stuck with us, the misfits and rejects.

We passed through Itty's territory quickly and cut northeast into Logbar's quadrant. I hadn't been into the northeast quadrant in years, and frankly, I could have never stepped foot in it again and been happy.

Logbar valued religion over everything else. Churches were all over the city, but the biggest, most beautiful ones resided in his quadrant. The religious class erected a church, mosque, or synagogue on every corner and paid Logbar for protection, which meant the demon was well funded and got a piece of every tithe. Even if you went to church in Piggy's quadrant, everything funneled back up to Logbar eventually.

And everybody went to church. Some people went out of obligation, others out of devotion, but we all went. It's hard to keep your head in the sand and say there isn't an afterlife when you witnessed Hell on Earth. I dealt with demons all the time. Gods roamed the countryside, and tales of angels granting miracles filled every drunkard's stories.

I stayed out of Logbar's part of the city since—well, since Teri's funeral. She was the only person in my family to make it through the Horde Wars. My other sister died fighting alongside me. More specifically, I put a bullet through her eyes after a grenade blasted her in half. She was suffering, and I didn't want her to suffer. She begged for me to do it, so I did.

Teri was a lover, not a fighter. I mean that literally. After the war, she couldn't fight anymore. It took everything out of her, and there aren't a lot of choices in Thebos if you don't want to use your fists. So, she became a prostitute. You could make good money as a prostitute if you were connected right. She was—or at least I thought she was.

I thought she was careful. She *said* she was careful. She wasn't, though. She got the wrong john on the wrong day, said the wrong thing, and he slammed her into a table so many times I couldn't recognize her face when I claimed her body.

She'd made it through another universe and back, then the Horde Wars, but she couldn't make it through Thebos.

The church she went to tried to sell me a big funeral. I couldn't deal with any of it. I cremated her body and dumped it into the ocean, and was done with it.

Teri was the only thing that tied me to the world. I used to worry about her when I was on missions, worry when she took in a john. After that day, I stopped worrying.

"Are you crying?" Odahai said, looking back at me. "Don't tell me you have emotions. Emotions are bad for business."

"Just drive," I said to him, wiping my eyes.

And I did. I choked my emotions down and hid them away, and a second later, I was back to myself.

***

Odahai drove further north than I had been since before the war, past the light and pollution and into the Badlands. It was the only place to escape the light pollution of Thebos.

All around our car, the Earth worked to retake its land from humanity. Vines grew over every inch of the dilapidated buildings, all of which were covered in a thick layer of dust.

The Badlands were beyond the protection of the city, where even Ul'brem's reach couldn't touch. I didn't think there was anything of value in the Badlands. Nobody respectable lived there. Finally, Odahai stopped in the middle of an overgrown town. It might have been a bustling town once, but after the war, it faded into ruins.

On one side of the street, an office building sank into the dust, the casualty of time and neglect. A relic of a bygone age, just like me. A derelict church stood on the other side of the street, forgotten by time. The painted façade cracked and flaked. With a collapsed roof, the rain had turned the tiny building into a run-down rind of its former beauty. The cross on the top of the church hung rusted, swinging with the wind. Under it, somebody splattered an Egyptian all-seeing eye on the wall. I caught my reflection in the car mirror. My red, cyborg eye stared back at me, and I felt sympathy for the buildings.

"Why are we here?" I said.

"This is it," Odahai replied. "Get out."

"This is nowhere. Are you bringing me out here to kill me?"

Odahai shook his head. "No, not to kill you. I'd like to, but I can't. I just drive where they tell me. Get out. Now."

I slowly opened the door and stepped outside the car. There was nothing around for miles. It wasn't a place for a hit, but it was the perfect place to stash a body. "Are you sure?" I grabbed the sniper rifle case and walked toward the old office building. I was confident they wanted me to die out here but also knew that Piggy underestimated my will to live.

Odahai rolled down the passenger window. "Third floor. End of the hallway. Wait. Aim toward the church. Your target will appear eventually. Call me when it's done." He tossed a cell phone out the window. The car spun its wheels and turned away, speeding off toward civilization.

The rotten carcass of the building smelled of mildew and soggy blankets left out in the dark too long. I stepped inside and found the crumbled floors from ten stories lying bare on the floor, stacking toward a hole left from a mortar shell.

Or maybe it was a bomb dropped from a Horde ship.

Whatever made the hole had torn through every floor of the building and left a crater in the floor below, blocking my path. Only a thin walkway remained, and although it creaked as I stepped my foot upon it and shifted my weight, it held for me.

I walked around the crater until I reached an emergency staircase made of concrete. It stood up better than the rest of the building, though the concrete split every few stairs, and little cactus buds peeked out from them.

***

I lugged the sniper rifle case up the stairs until I reached the third floor and walked out into the hallway. The floorboards creaked under me as a reminder they could snap at any time and leave me tumbling to my death. This wasn't my first time in a condemned building.

I walked lightly and tested each foothold before I stepped.

As a sniper in the Horde Wars, I often perched inside buildings for days waiting for my prey. While I walked through the rubble, I listened for anything that could indicate somebody was coming, but only wind whipped through the gaps in the walls.

I made my way to the end of the hall and turned into the room that faced the church. A gaping hole remained where the window would have been, no doubt the result of some bombing raid by the Horde. Fortunately for me, it looked out directly over the church,

I dropped the sniper rifle case onto the floor and flipped it open, slipping the manila folder under the case for safe keeping. I never looked at who I was going to kill until it was time for action. The name inside could give me pause, and I didn't want any reason to back out of the job at hand. I'd killed holy men, presidents, and dignitaries that, in better days, I would have dubbed righteous. I might have had second thoughts if given the chance to collect myself.

Once the gun was locked and loaded, though, it was all business.

***

Twenty minutes later, the gun sat fully assembled on a tripod overlooking the ramshackle church. I checked the sights to make sure it was in focus and then picked up the manila folder. Nobody worth killing ever came out into the badlands, so I couldn't imagine who they'd lined up for me.

I flipped open the folder and found a picture of the god Velaska staring back at me. My target was a god—a real god. People told tales of demon hunters taking out gods, though I had trouble believing them. I'd always assumed that gods were immortal.

If there was a god more deserving of assassination than Velaska, I'd never heard of them. Velaska made a name for herself as a sympathizer to the Horde's cause during the war. She gave them intel on our troop movements, and she cavorted with them out in the open. Two hundred thousand deaths could be directly attributed to her dealings with the Horde. She played both sides against the middle. In short, she sold us out with the hope the Horde would protect her. Once we won, she went into hiding, only emerging for fancy parties where she could be sure it was safe.

Velaska was the prissy sort. She liked the finer things in life and was known for lavish parties and extravagant formals. Thinking of her slumming it here, of all places, in the Badlands, was laughable. Thinking that I was the one to put a bullet in her head made me giddy.

There was a lot of talk on the front lines about what we would do to Velaska, traitor to humanity, if we could ever lay our hands on her. A billion men died fighting in her war, and I looked forward to being the one to carry out their will by putting a charge between her eyes and blowing her pretty face away.

A bright blue light flashed inside the church. I looked through the eyepiece on the gun. A wrinkled old man, dressed in an elegant, red, glowing robe, shuffled out of the church's entrance. He wore a golden medallion carved with an all-seeing eye, inlaid with diamonds around the inside of the pupil.

It was time. Whatever was happening was about to go down. I placed my human eye on the eyepiece. I never used my cyborg eye to shoot. It might have helped, but I never got used to the feeling.

In another flash of blue light, a woman appeared. Her hair was yellow and flowing, and she wore a white gown. She turned her face toward me as she smiled at the man. I would recognize those big, blue eyes anywhere. It was Velaska.

I breathed deeply through my nose and steadied my hand. I looked through the eyepiece again, leveling my gun, and followed Velaska as she floated toward the door. This was my only chance at this. Placing my finger on the trigger, I took one final look at my target and squeezed.

At the last moment, my hand jolted forward, and the gun lurched. It had never happened before . . . but I missed. The bullet ricocheted off the wall of the church. Velaska turned and spotted me instantly.

I tried to run, but it was too late. She snapped her fingers, and the sound echoed off every wall. Heat flooded the room and ate at my skin. The last thing I felt before passing out was the searing pain of burning flesh.

***

Over the next several hours, I woke up in agony multiple times, each foray into consciousness lasted only for a moment before the pain knocked me out again. I don't remember much except for the excruciating pain. I'm pretty sure I made it to a hospital, where I heard doctors screaming for an open operating room, and I believe I felt the tug of my skin peeling from my body.

What I remember vividly was being lifted out of my body when the blast went off. I was floating upwards into the sky, where a beautiful warm, white light shone down on me. Beneath me, what remained of the dilapidated building collapsed to the ground. Velaska sauntered over to my corpse, and then I didn't care anymore about what happened to my body. The bright white light called me home, and I yearned to enter it.

In another moment, the light was gone. A great force jerked me back to my body with a thud. Pain shot through every limb. Two scratchy male voices took bets on whether I would live to make it to the hospital, and then I was gone again into unconsciousness.

It was Heaven they pulled me away from as they worked to save my life. I knew it. For so long I'd been sure I would end up in Hell. But then I died, and I went up, not down. I still had a chance at Heaven, even after all I had done.

And it was taken from me.

CHAPTER 6

I drifted in and out of consciousness for some amount of time, maybe a day or maybe a year, but eventually, I came out of my lazy haze and back to reality. My eyes fluttered open, and my vision sharpened. The pain had subsided from unbearable to simply excruciating.

"Oh, you're up, are you?" I heard a smooth, feminine voice in the corner of the room.

I tried to turn my head, but even moving myself an inch burned so deeply that I nearly passed out from the pain. I opened my mouth, but my cracked lips delivered no voice except a deep moan.

"Don't worry," the voice said. "I'll get up."

A chair creaked and slid backward. Then, two feet clipped delicately across the floor. Slowly and daintily, they made their way toward me until the shadow of a goddess fell over my face, followed by the goddess herself.

A golden crown lay upon Velaska's head, the enormous emerald at its center shimmered as she peered down at me. A halo of pure light radiated around her, illuminating her face in an ethereal radiance. Her crimson lips parted, and her perfect lips sneered at me.

"Why did you try to kill me?" she asked.

I tried to protest, but all that came out was another low, guttural moan. I was suddenly consumed with terror, remembering the vengeance gods bestowed on their enemies.

"I'm waiting," she said, tapping her foot. "You know, I am surprised you are still alive, truth be told. There aren't many who could survive a blast from a god like that. You must have a strong will to live."

A slow breath escaped my lips. It seemed natural for me to fight death. I'd fought against it because the alternative—death and then an eternity in Hell—seemed a heck of a lot worse than this. But now I wasn't so sure, now that I'd seen that bright light.

Velaska smiled as she watched the wheels turn in my head. "I like people with strong wills to live. They are so few and far between these days. Most people just want to die. It's quite a bore, truth be told. I used to so enjoy you humans on this planet and your tenacious grip on life. You humans would do anything, and I mean anything, to live longer. Now, well, I mean, just look at you all, moping around, crying about like there's not a big, bright universe out there to explore."

A big, bright universe. What was she talking about? Were we living in the same place? As far as I could tell, the universe was filled with disgusting bugs bent on destroying humanity and gods who sided with them. My muscles tensed at the memory of Velaska's betrayal and sent spasms coursing through my body.

This again made Velaska chuckle. "I would be lying if I said seeing you in pain didn't make me happy, at least a little lit. After all, you did try to kill me, but this . . . it just won't do. It's like talking to a brick wall, albeit a moaning, screaming brick wall."

Velaska raised her hands into the air and snapped her fingers. Across the room, the sink turned on, and she pulled a flood of water into her hands. When she took a deep breath in, the water pulsated with a light blue glow.

"Don't move," she said, then winked at me. "Forgive me my jokes. I am old and have little in the way of fun these days. You humans are quite the dour bunch."

Velaska brought her hands to my throat. I thought I was dead for sure, but her touch felt cool on my aching flesh. Papery flakes of my skin fell away with a crackle. My neck muscles pulsed, but there was no pain.

"There," she said, raising her arms and releasing the water back into the sink. "Now talk."

I opened my mouth, expecting nothing but air, but when my lips parted, I heard my voice. "Go to hell."

Velaska cracked a smile and then guffawed. "My, my, my, you really are a strong-willed one, aren't you? I mean, go to hell? So original. You know, I spent plenty of time in Hell already, and I have no intention of going back. I'll pass."

"You betrayed us," I whispered. "I have nothing to say to you."

"Betrayed? My dear, I think you have your words confused. You are broken and wounded. I understand. I think you mean saved. Saved is not betrayed."

I tried to laugh, but the pain was too great. I whimpered instead. "No, I think you are the one who is confused."

Velaska pointed her finger lazily in my direction. "Now I see why you tried to kill me. You are so misguided. I can enlighten you if you help me."

"I wouldn't help you do anything but die."

Velaska smirked. "I like that. That's very, very good, but I feel that you will sing a different tune when the pain sets back in."

"I'm already in all the—"

Velaska's smile turned into a sneer. She dug her thumb into my stomach. The agony seared through me like a lumbering freight train. I screamed out in pain, but Velaska snapped her fingers, and my lips sealed shut.

"Now, as I said before, I need your help. I tried to do this the polite way, but I will do it the hard way if need be. You will tell me who hired you, or I will kill you right now. I don't care how strong you are; I guarantee you have no idea what it is like to come face to face with a god's wrath!"

She pulled her finger out of my stomach. Flakes of my burnt skin fell off. "Ugh. That just won't do."

Velaska walked over to the sink and washed her hands. After she was done, she walked back over to me, her hands pulsating with a shining blue light of water again. "Now, I am not wholly unreasonable. If you help me, I will cure you of all this horribleness. It will be like it never happened."

I tried to speak, but Velaska's magic still held my mouth shut. She saw me struggling and giggled. "Of course. I forgot. I would lose my head if it weren't attached." Velaska snapped her fingers, and my lips parted.

"I would rather die."

"Would you, though?" She raised an eyebrow. "You have had so many opportunities to die already, and yet you are still alive. Something tells me you shift your allegiances with the wind, and honey, right now, the wind is howling for you to help me. You don't have to like me, of course. I doubt you liked anybody you've worked for in the past, but you do have to be loyal to me, which means helping me, so I can help you. Work for me, work with me, and you will not regret it. Deny me, and I will make you suffer."

It was a job offer. A job offer like I'd never had before. It wasn't for money or glamour. This job offer was a simple trade for my life, which was hilarious to me because my life was worthless. Still, if there was a Heaven, I wanted to get back there and helping a god couldn't hurt my chances.

"I accept," I said hoarsely.

Velaska smiled. "I knew you would because you're a survivor."

She was right. I was a survivor.

Velaska's hands flowed in a circle as more water pooled in her arms. "When the water surrounds you, my dear, take a big breath. Just inhale and let the water do the work. It's going to feel like you're drowning—and that's because you are, you see—but it's all a necessary part of the process."

The glowing water flowed from her hands and encased my entire body. I rose from the bed and floated toward the ceiling. The frigid water eased my burning wounds. I took a deep breath, and the water poured into my lungs until they nearly burst.

I couldn't breathe. I gagged for air. Involuntarily, my throat tried to retch up the water, but when I opened my mouth, only more water entered my lungs. I held my hands up against the water, but Velaska smacked them away. "Don't move. It will be over in a second."

And in another second, it was done. The water drained from my lungs. It slipped down my throat into my bloodstream, where it expanded into every inch of my body. The fire that surged through my body was replaced with a soothing chill.

"Now," Velaska said with a smile, lowering me back down to the bed. "About that name."

I had made a deal with a lot of devils in my day, but none made me feel as uneasy as I did at that moment. Something about the grin spreading across Velaska's face, the way that her lips curled with delight, like a hunter springing a trap, took me aback.

I was used to demons lording their brute strength and power over me. They were not subtle about it, but Velaska was a different animal altogether. She had all the power of a demon and more and combined it with tact, cunning, and pure ego.

***

"I didn't know you were pretty," Velaska said with a snicker.

Frankly, I didn't know I was pretty, either. Yet, I was. I had been staring at my naked body in the mirror for the better part of an hour, confused at the face that looked back at me. For the last decade, whenever I looked into the mirror, all I'd seen was a hideous scar down the middle of my face and that bulbous red, mechanical eye looking back at me.

Now, they were gone, replaced with a smooth face and a genuine, non-cyborg, emerald green eye. I forgot that I had emerald eyes, bright and striking, and now I had two of them. My nose barely stuck out of my face. I wondered how I could even breathe out of a thing that was so small. My lips were plush and red like they had lipstick on them, even though I never wore the stuff.

"I don't mean to rush you," Velaska said. "Except that I do mean to rush you. Time is wasting."

I couldn't stop touching my face and feeling the smooth contours of my skin. It was as velvety as a baby's bottom as if it never felt the sun or the rain. I didn't recognize this person. It was some stranger staring back at me, but one that I somehow knew from years past.

"I'm sorry," I said. "I'm just freaked out."

Velaska nodded. "Yes, the gods' magic is powerful stuff. Frankly, I think I overdid it. I didn't intend to fix all your deformities, just make you passable."

I smiled, and it startled me. It was brighter than it had ever been before. "Thank you."

"Don't thank me. Before, you were wholly unremarkable, like every other person on this gods forsaken planet, and now, well now I've made you into quite the attractive thing, haven't I? Yes, I've done quite the job."

I turned from the mirror. "I feel like I need to get punched in the face to rough it up a bit."

"I can make that happen." Velaska smiled, rubbing her hands together. "Now go put on some clothes. I'm sick of looking at your naked . . . well, all of you. I took the liberty of picking something up for you."

Velaska snapped her fingers, and a pair of folded jeans appeared on the bed, alongside a black t-shirt with the words "Don't screw with me" scribbled on it. A long black trench coat lay on the chair next to the bed, and under it were a pair of steel-toed black boots. A shoulder holster with two demon hunters lay on the desk, with two silver revolvers propped up against it. I dare say it was perfect.

I slid the jeans over my bare legs. They fit nicely. "Why are you being nice to me?"

Velaska chuckled. "Nice? My dear, this isn't nice. They had to pick pieces of your jacket out of your skin. It took eight hours. Lucky that you were unconscious. This whole…*ensemble*, if you can call it that, is simply a reminder that I can kill you with the snap of my fingers."

I shrugged, then threw the t-shirt over my head. "Say what you want, but I know kindness when I see it. I don't see it often, so it sticks with me."

She waved a hand. "Call it whatever you want, my dear. As long as you help me find the people who tried to kill me."

"You aren't going to like them."

"Of course I'm not, dear. They tried to kill me, but they were not the first, and they will certainly not be the last. Now, chop-chop."

***

Velaska floated toward me after I was dressed and placed her hand on my forehead. "Show me where we should go."

I closed my eyes and thought about Piggy's mansion. She snapped her fingers, and we were there. Gone were the guards that once held vigil over the wrought iron. The gate itself banged in the wind, left ajar by a careless somebody. The front lawn was empty. Usually, a half-dozen guards patrolled the grounds.

I pulled my demon hunters and inched forward into the yard. Something was wrong. Maybe a trap or the aftermath of an ambush. Perhaps this was the result of Itty's retribution for killing his informant—except that there weren't bullet holes sloppily strewn about the compound, which was one of Itty's calling cards. In fact, there were no bullets at all. It was as if everybody had just vanished into thin air.

Walking up to the front door of Piggy's house, we should have come across a dozen guards, but I didn't see even one as we entered the door, nor were there any snipers in the trees or roof to prevent a long-range attack.

"Is this normal?" Velaska said, walking forward as if nothing was amiss. "I know my share of demons, and they are usually much louder than this."

I studied the grounds with a cautious eye. "I've never heard it this silent, personally. It's usually raucous."

"Raucous is a three-dollar word. I didn't know any of you humans knew three-dollar words anymore."

I pushed open the front door slowly. "If you spent more time with us instead of your Horde pals, maybe you'd know we are full of surprises."

Velaska peered around the door. "You have a grudge against me, that much is clear, but it might interest you to know that everything I did, I did for the betterment of humanity."

Careful to look out for any tripwires or laser grids that might spring a trap, I took a step inside the mansion. "Whole platoons were slaughtered because of intel you gave to the Horde."

"Casualties are a reality of war." Velaska raised an eyebrow. "Do you have any idea how many battalions I saved by giving away that information? For every soldier killed, I saved a hundred more by funneling information back to the Devil and our generals in the field."

I stepped quickly across the foyer where I'd held a gun to Piggy's head the last time I saw him. "So, the ends justified the means? My friends died out there fighting the Horde, and you sent them to slaughter."

"Yes, the ends justified the means. You are too myopic to understand the full scope of what I did for you. It's just like you humans to ignore what is best for humanity. Connie was the same way."

"Who is Connie?"

Velaska smiled. "Why, your Devil, of course. She took over for Katrina, who took over for Thomas, who took over for Lucifer, who took over for me."

"I've seen pictures of the devil. He doesn't look like a 'Connie' to me."

"So myopic. Of course, the demons of Hell wouldn't admit to being led by a woman. They are testosterone-filled and stupid. It was the same in my day. I took over from Hades, but do you think anybody ever talked about me? No. It was always Hades this and Hades that. And then, after I left, they only talked of Lucifer. Always Hades, then Lucifer, even though Hell has been ruled by women much longer than by men."

Velaska studied the smiling picture of Lucifer, clad in armor, with big, red horns coming out of his maroon head, staring down at her. "What a twat."

I saw a shadow in the darkness. I raised my guns toward it as I flicked on the lights to the room. There, at the center of the room, was Piggy, tied to a chair, beaten and bruised, oozing green blood from his nose. A hole burned through his forehead from a demon hunter charge. His eyes peered out at me blankly. He wasn't going to be any help to us.

"That's a dead-end," I said.

"Who else might know who hired Piggy to hire you?"

"If I had to bet, it was the person who probably did this to him. Itty."

"Show me."

Velaska placed her hand on my forehead, snapped her fingers, and we were gone.

CHAPTER 7

We reappeared with a flash in front of the iron gate that guarded Itty's complex. Two confused guards raised their guns to us, but Velaska was too fast for them. She snapped her fingers, and their guns vanished into thin air.

A third, bird-like guard flapped up to the gate, sneering through its long beak. "What do you want?"

Velaska's eyes narrowed. The timbre of her voice dropped. "I need to see your boss."

"I really shouldn't be here," I whispered into Velaska's ear. "I'm at the top of their most wanted list."

Velaska scoffed. "Nonsense. They won't even recognize you. I barely recognize you. Nothing will happen to you so long as you are with me. Understood?"

I felt more confident. Velaska talked in a way that brought ease to the most absurd scenarios.

The guard scowled at us. "Go away."

"I am trying to be polite, but if you would prefer, we can do this the hard way." Velaska snapped her fingers, and the guard exploded in front of us. Guts and blood splattered everywhere. The guard's intestines landed at my feet, and a piece of his liver fell onto my coat. I flicked it off without a second thought.

"I don't know why everybody insists on doing things the hard way," Velaska said, pushing open the locked iron gate.

Three dozen guards pointed their guns at us as we stepped through the courtyard of the mansion toward the front door. Velaska waved her arms, and the guns rose into the air. The guards forgot about us in their struggle to catch their floating weapons.

"I don't think they know anything," I whispered to Velaska.

"What makes you say that?"

"Look at them. They're on high alert, like they expect an ambush, even though their biggest enemy is dead back at his mansion. Why would they be so worried if they were the ones who carried out the raid?"

"Interesting."

Velaska pushed open the front door to Itty's house, and we started down the hallway. Unlike Piggy's sparsely decorated mansion, Itty's house was lived in and homey. There were paintings hung on every wood-paneled wall, depicting—of course—Lucifer in all his glory. Velaska grumbled at the sight of him.

"Do you see this?" Velaska said. "All I want is a little respect, but can I get it? No. I was the Devil for thousands of years and not one demon will acknowledge it."

I knew the layout of the mansion from when I'd worked for Itty and also knew that he mostly confined himself to the kitchen when he was home. I could hear his ravenous chomping as we neared the kitchen.

The kitchen was filled with every toy that a chef could want, from big stoves and cast-iron pots to fancy knives, appliances, and every type of gadget under the sun. Itty snacked on a meal of roasted pig at the long end of a wooden picnic table.

"Itty!" Velaska said. "It's been a long time!"

He was more a rat than a demon, with his long snout and coarse fur. The overbite completed the look. His dead eyes barely registered Velaska before he resumed gorging on a pig leg. "What do you want, Velaska?"

"A little respect would be nice," she replied, gliding toward him. "You know I was your boss for thousands of years, right?"

"Then you weren't. Things change. Get lost."

Velaska snapped her fingers, and the food in front of Itty vanished, including the leg he held in his hand. "That is not nice, Itty. I never did anything to you. I wasn't going to bring up how rude it is that you don't have one painting of me up on those walls."

"Bring it back!" Itty shouted, scouring the table for any morsel of pork Velaska might've missed.

"When you help me, I will give it back."

Itty wiped his rat-like mouth and stood up. He scurried over to Velaska, looking like he was going to scream into her pretty face, but he was halted by my presence. "I know you. Who are you?"

"Nobody," I said. Velaska was right. He didn't recognize my new face with two good eyes in my head, and I was happy to keep it that way.

"I know you from somewhere," Itty said, pointing at my face. "Did we bang?"

I gave him an innocent smile and shrugged. "I just got one of those faces."

Velaska snapped her fingers, and Itty turned to her involuntarily, as if a giant, invisible hand grabbed him, pinning his arms and legs in its grip. "You are being very rude. I'm trying to ask you questions. She is inconsequential. Now, help me, and you'll get your food back. Don't, and I'll flay you alive."

Itty grimaced, trying to break free of Velaska's hold. When he tired of struggling, he finally sighed. "Fine! What do you want?"

"First," Velaska said, "why is everybody so on edge out there?"

"That's none of your business," Itty hissed.

"Hey," Velaska said, snapping her fingers. The invisible hand squeezed Itty like a sausage. "I thought we agreed you were going to answer my questions."

"All right! We sold a guy, a group of guys, some weapons we stole from a Horde ship we salvaged. Demon hunters that could vaporize somebody on sight. Stuff we haven't seen since the war. They paid top dollar. Then, we heard Piggy was ambushed, and we figured they'd be back for us to tie up their loose ends."

"Who were these people?" I asked, unable to contain myself.

"I don't know," Itty cried as the grip around him tightened. "They wore masks. They paid in cash. We didn't ask questions."

Velaska placed her hand on Itty's forehead. Her eyes lit up a bright blue. "He's telling the truth."

"I know I'm telling the truth!" Itty squealed, kicking his feet in the air.

"Next question—who put out the hit on me?"

Itty bobbed his head from side to side. "I don't know that, either. Probably those same guys, and now they want to clear their tracks since the hit clearly went south."

Velaska's invisible hand squeezed tighter around Itty's body. "Who would know why I was targeted?"

"Ow! Ow! Ow!" Itty pleaded. "Please stop. There's only one guy. Only one demon."

I sighed. "Ul'brem."

"Dat's right!" Itty shouted. "He's the only one that would know. Now please, let me go."

Velaska snapped her fingers, and Itty slammed to the floor. The food reappeared, and he skittered over to it, hiding behind the table and shaking.

"You know where this Ul'brem lives?"

I nodded. "He was my first job in Thebos. He's the one who assigned me to Itty in the first place."

Velaska placed her hand on my forehead. "Take me to him."

"Hey, why didn't you just do that mind thing to me to get the information you needed?"

Velaska scoffed. "Because this was more fun."

***

I have only met the big Boss of Thebos twice in my life. The first time was after I ruthlessly butchered a demon who plotted against him. He brought me in to congratulate me on a job well done. The other time was when he assigned me to Itty's squad. I wasn't supposed to leave Itty's side, but I did when Piggy offered me more money.

We arrived at Ul'brem's castle after the sun set, and the street lights turned on. It was a massive structure sitting atop a hill overlooking everything else within a five-mile radius. Humanity originally built the castle to be a house to showcase magic in all its glory. That's why Ul'brem targeted Thebos in the first place—he thought it sat on a hotbed of magical activity. It wasn't until after he'd taken the city that he discovered the palace contained nothing but parlor magic. That pissed him off good. He no longer had the troops to win another city, so he was stuck in Thebos, ruling over us.

When I first met the Boss, he had grown content to rule over a large but unpowerful fiefdom. Nobody cared enough about Thebos to attack it. To other demons, Thebos was a city that shouldn't exist, built in the middle of the desert, surrounded on one side by a salty ocean, and filled with broken humans.

There was no money in Thebos, really. Some were rich, but in cities like Aukta or Reboulde, there was real wealth, which could buy and sell Thebos many times over. The only thing Thebos had going for it was a nearly unlimited stock of people. They were the Boss's only resource after the war, and he could leverage them, sell them off, to keep money flowing into his coffers. The slave trade was the only real commodity of Thebos, at least where the other cities were concerned, but nobody talked about it. Often, people would go missing, though, and all we could do was look the other way.

"Why are we here?" I asked as we rematerialized in front of the gates to the Boss's castle. "Or I should ask, why am I here?"

"I need you to show me where to go."

I stopped in my tracks. "No, you don't."

She gave me a searching look and then a smile. "No, I don't. You're right. You know what, I could probably do this on my own, even if it took more time, but here's the thing—for some reason, you lived."

"Excuse me?"

She pointed to my button nose. I dare say it was cute. "You lived. When I snapped my fingers and blew you up, you wouldn't die, and that is . . . curious to me. It shows you have great fortitude of will, and with people trying to kill me all the time, it's helpful to have that sort of will by my side. These are unsavory times we live in, my dear. Besides, it is nice not to have to figure this out on my own."

I didn't believe her, but Velaska was very good at playing her cards close to the vest. She strolled toward the gates of the great magic castle on the hill, and I followed behind her. It was one of the true relics left from before the Horde Wars and one of the few structures that stood even after coming back from the black hole. Some called it majestic. I called it an eyesore.

The four demon guards at the gate pointed their weapons at us as we approached. "I don't have time for this. I'm not stopping," Velaska shouted, snapping her fingers. The guards floated into the air. "I want to see your boss."

"Why are you making a scene?" I asked, trying to keep up with her.

"Do you know many powerful men? They treat women like garbage unless they fear us or believe you can do something for them. Since I don't plan on doing any favors for Ul'brem, I have no choice but to make him fear me— again."

"Was he another one of your demons?"

"Was he ever. Pain in my ass is what he was, always scheming to get more power. I can see why he took to this place after the war. He didn't stand a chance of holding power in Hell, but here he created a nice little fiefdom for himself. Lording over humans is so much easier than gaining a foothold with demons, except possibly the sniveling cowards and sycophants I've met so far who run this city. Be lucky you live here and not somewhere controlled by a demon with gravitas."

Velaska stormed up the steep driveway toward the entrance to the house. Twenty men lifted their guns to open fire on her, but they didn't shoot. They just stood there, dumbfounded, wanting to shoot but not being able to stop staring at the god walking past them.

She came to a stop in front of the house and called out with a booming voice, "I'm not stepping foot into another tacky demon mansion today, Ul'brem. Come out and face me."

CHAPTER 8

We stood on the front lawn of Ul'brem's castle for the better part of ten minutes, and still, none of his guards moved from their positions, their guns trained on us. I studied their faces and saw their desire to shoot at us, but their fingers wouldn't pull the trigger to carry through with it. Velaska had control of them all.

"Why aren't they shooting?" I asked her.

"Because my countenance shines down upon them. They couldn't fire on their goddess, whom they have just realized is the most beautiful being in the universe."

"That's quite the power trip, my friend."

Velaska's eyes fluttered. "Are we friends now? That's nice. But this isn't a power trip. It's just something that happens when people are around me, the most beautiful of all the gods."

"Isn't the most beautiful god Aphrodite? That's what they say, anyway."

"Piffle," Velaska replied, screwing up her mouth. "Aphrodite couldn't hold a candle to me, and she knows it. If I was in the pantheon, then people would know my name. They would know my beauty."

"What is the pantheon?"

"Why, it's the gods you know and love. Think of them like the spokespeople for the gods. They are everywhere, which is why they have stories written about them on every planet in the cosmos. They are the ones that you worship. Every once and a while, we lowly gods get a temple or two, but it's like pulling teeth and a pittance compared to those in the pantheon."

"I don't worship anybody," I replied.

"Not you, you, the royal you. All of humanity. I've been trying to get into the pantheon for eons, and Aphrodite has always blocked my application. Of course, she does, though. She's jealous of my beauty." Velaska gestured to the guards around us. "I mean, look at what I can do to men and demons alike."

"It's a really good trick. I don't deny that." I also couldn't deny how human Velaska seemed. She had all the flaws of humanity and needed more validation than any human I'd ever met. It was almost as if being a god amplified the worst flaws I saw in myself.

"You know, I could destroy you with just a thought," Velaska said flatly.

"I know. You've already tried it once, though, and it didn't work," I replied with a smile. I couldn't believe that I was starting to like this terrible god who betrayed us during the war, but she had a way about her that I couldn't put my finger on. Also, in the back of my brain, I kept thinking about that moment I almost made it to Heaven after I died. I wanted to get back there, and she was the best chance I had for salvation.

Velaska held up her arms and the demons around her lifted their guns in the air. "I'm sick of waiting, Ul'brem! Do not make me come in there after you. That would not be a good look for a warlord."

Velaska moved her finger in a circle. The guards spun their guns around and stuck them in their mouths even as they fought it, even as their eyes bulged out in terror, even as their muscles trembled. "You have ten seconds, or I will make all your guards shoot themselves with their own weapons."

I was all the way up to "nine" in my head when the front door to the castle swung open and out lumbered Ul'brem. His distended belly dragged behind him as he walked toward us on all fours, his beady eyes glistening in the light from the streetlamps.

"What do you want?" Ul'brem snarled through two mammoth tusks protruding down from his upper lip.

"Careful," Velaska said, dropping her arms. The men dropped their guns and leveled them at Ul'brem.

"Do you think a few guns are gonna scare me, Velaska?" Ul'brem let out a deep laugh. "Don't forget, I was down in Hell with you the day you scammed Lucifer into taking over as Devil because you couldn't take the heat anymore."

"It's not that I couldn't. I just didn't want to."

"Spoken like a true coward."

Velaska snapped her fingers, and one of the guards shot Ul'brem through the leg with a demon hunter charge.

Ul'brem fell to the ground. "You bitch!"

Velaska raised one finger, and two laser sightlines appeared on Ul'brem's forehead. "I know you don't have much of a brain left, but with one more snap, I could send it flying across your pretty castle, and then somebody would have to clean it up. It would be much easier if we could just be friends."

Ul'brem snorted angrily. His shaggy fur was sopping up his green blood. "What do you want?"

"It's simple. I want to know why you tried to kill me."

Ul'brem gave another deep laugh. "That's rich, Velaska. I don't want you dead. I don't even think about you. Ever. You are a nothing in my life."

"I can assure you that after this, you will be thinking about me for years to come." Another snap of her fingers and a demon hunter clipped Ul'brem's kneecap. He grit his teeth, but he refused to scream. He refused to show pain— that's why he was the boss.

"Don't count on it," Ul'brem said, stumbling to his feet. "I have a lot of enemies with a lot more power than you."

"We'll see about that." Velaska went to snap her fingers again, but I held her hand.

"Wait. Ul'brem, listen, man," I said. "I get that you are powerful and need to save face, but she's really going to kill you."

Ul'brem wasn't as stupid as Itty. He recognized me immediately. "And you would know death, wouldn't you, Rebecca? It's a shame you have changed sides and for such a pathetic price as beauty. You were my best assassin. I look forward to roasting you over a spit and eating your heart."

I stared deeply into Ul'brem's eyes as he spoke, past the sneering and bravado, and into his soul, and saw something I didn't expect. "I knew it. You are scared."

"I am not!"

"Yes, you are. I can smell the fear on you, Ul'brem. It's wafting off you like you bathed in it this morning."

Velaska's gaze went from me to the Boss. "Is that true, Ul'brem? Are you frightened of me?"

Another laugh from Ul'brem echoed through the night sky. "Of you? No. I fear something greater than you. I fear the greatest power the universe has ever seen."

"Hello!" Velaska said, pointing to herself. "I am a god. I am literally the most powerful thing the universe has ever seen."

"Once, perhaps," Ul'brem said. "But now, I fear a power greater than you. It came for Piggy. It will come for Itty, and eventually, the reckoning will reach me, too."

"Give me a name, Ul'brem," I said, pressing my foot on the demon's gunshot wound until he screamed out in pain. "Give me the name of the person who called in the hit, and this will all be over."

"If I give you a name, then it will all be over anyway."

"Good. Then you'll just be in the same place you are now. Tell me a name."

"Yunter Haus."

***

It wasn't hard to track Yunter to the northwest quadrant of Thebos. He used to drink at Matt's bar until I burned the place to the ground. Actually, he was the last person out of Matt's bar the night I torched it, so he knew what I'd done. I put him at the top of the list of people who wanted to double-tap me for razing Matt's bar. I destroyed something beautiful, something pure in a world where everything was coated with a thick layer of grime, and Yunter would make sure I paid. That's if I didn't find him first.

The northwest quadrant of the city was run by a demon named Tjigbal. It was its most peaceful quadrant because she ran all the prostitution rings in Thebos, and she wouldn't let you have sex with anybody if you caused a problem. Men and women alike respected that. The prostitutes respected that even more, especially my sister. Teri put her trust in Tjigbal, and she paid the ultimate price for it.

My sister still had a good reputation in the quadrant. She was one of those people who liked everybody. People remembered her and liked her. Not just johns, either. Everybody from the madams on down to the jizz moppers reminisced about her like she was a sea of sunshine in a land of misery. Because of the deep love people had for Teri, they talked to me. That's how a cheap trick named Doris turned me on to a quaint little whorehouse in the middle of the district where Yunter was staying for the week. A sizeable payment to the front desk got me his room number.

"Now," I told Velaska as we walked up the stairs. "The reason they gave me this information is because they know I'm not going to mess it up and cause a scene. You cannot screw stuff up in this room, do you understand?"

Velaska nodded. "I understand, even if I don't agree with your primitive human customs."

We reached Yunter's door at the top of the stairs. The bed creaked inside, and a woman gave the slow moan of a fake orgasm. I pulled my revolvers out of their holsters and swung open the door.

"Yunter Haus," I shouted with my guns drawn on him. "I have questions for you."

The woman, a bosomy redhead, screamed and rolled off Yunter, who stood straight up with his manhood still erect and scrambled for his gun. Velaska snapped her fingers, and Yunter froze in the air, the god's invisible hand squeezing around his chest.

"What is happening up there?" the front desk woman shouted.

"Nothing, ma'am!" I said, slamming the door closed. The redhead was in the corner whimpering, and I showed her the revolver in my belt to convince her to shut up.

Yunter wouldn't have been an attractive man in the best of times, but he was ugly even by Thebos's postwar standards. Half of his face had been blown off by a bomb in the Horde Wars, and the other half wasn't doing him any favors.

"Now, you listen to me," I hissed. "I don't know what you're mixed up with, but you can tell my friend—"

Yunter didn't even look at me. "I know you. I can smell your stench anywhere, Velaska."

"Ah, so you've heard of me," she replied.

"Yeah, we've heard of you," Yunter replied, struggling to break free as the invisible hand tightened its grip. "But you already know we put the hit out on you, or you wouldn't be here, would you?"

Velaska walked around Yunter Haus, holding him in place with her invisible hand. "And who are 'we?'"

Yunter chuckled. "You know who we are. We've come for you and your brethren. Your day of reckoning is at hand. The gods of old will rule us no more. We have tried for years to find a way to take you down, and now we have the means to destroy you. The Horde gave us that gift."

I walked toward the nightstand and picked up Yunter's wallet. I tossed a wad of money at the prostitute. "For your troubles."

I sifted through the wallet and found a card. It was black. Engraved on its surface was a red plateau with a Greek temple on it, slashed through with a big x. On the backside of the card was scrawled "All gods must die."

"Have you ever seen this before?" I asked Velaska, holding up the card.

"Bring it to me." She held out her hand without taking her eyes of Yunter.

I handed her the card, and she looked it over. Her face turned red, and she growled under her breath. "So, it appears you truly are one of them." The words were hardly distinguishable, her jaw was clenched so tight.

"We are the Godless," Yunter replied. "Your kind has lorded over us for eons, and now it is time to send you back where you belong."

"You bore me," Velaska said, snapping her fingers.

The invisible hand squeezed Yunter so hard he exploded, covering the room with his entrails and blood. The red-haired woman screamed while Velaska casually walked out of the room.

CHAPTER 9

"I specifically told you not to cause a scene!" Two paramedics sprinted into the whorehouse while we ran just as fast to get out. "Blowing somebody up is the exact opposite of not causing a scene!"

"I did not blow him up, love; I squeezed him like a zit. But, I see your point." Velaska scurried along the street, picking up her pace with every step. "You can go. I release you from your duty to me."

She tried to snap her fingers, but I lunged for her hand and caught it. "Stop! You can't leave me here. I have nowhere else to go. I've literally pissed off everybody that I worked for and burned every favor I have left. If you leave me here, I'm as good as dead."

Velaska dropped her hands and came to a stop, fighting back tears. "You don't understand. I can't protect you. I can't even protect myself. Not anymore."

"What are you talking about?"

She looked down at the ground. "The Godless . . . they believe that the universe would be better off without any gods."

"Well, they aren't wrong."

Velaska grit her teeth. "I am a god, mortal. Watch your tongue."

I threw up my hands. "Sorry. It's just . . . you haven't done a very good job around here, have you? I mean, look at this place."

She shook her head. "No, we haven't done much better with any of the other civilizations which we've managed, either."

"Other civilizations?" I said, confused.

"Yes, of course. Did you think you were alone in the whole universe?"

I cocked my head to one side. "Kinda?"

Velaska sighed loudly. "Of course you did. Typical mortal. Thinking this whole universe was built just for you."

"So…you're saying it wasn't?"

"There are thousands of civilizations just like yours. Some more advanced and some less so. Some older and others much younger. But they are all undoubtedly human."

I looked up at the sky, hazy with smog, but beyond it, there were millions of stars in the sky. "Thousands of civilizations, planets, just like this one?"

"Yes, and these Godless, they have been a nuisance for thousands of years. Nobody knows where they began, but I heard stories of Godless agents even when I was the Devil on this planet."

"Really?"

"That's right, but they were little more than a whisper until recently. The Godless took hold on the worst planets in the lot of you. Planets that fell into disrepair, that were abandoned to time, that fell through a black hole into the void."

"Wait, you mean . . . the same black hole that Earth fell through?"

Velaska sighed. "Well, yes, my love, the same one this Earth fell through, except that instead of staying for a few days, some of them remained there for a million years or more."

"A million years beyond the void. How did they survive?"

"A lot of them didn't. Those that did hung on just barely. A few thrived in the other universe, but not many. When they returned to this universe after Apollo closed every black hole in the universe, those planets were . . . well, they were confused, mostly. Their civilizations rose and fell without ever knowing the stars, and for some of them, being pulled back was like us stealing them from their home. They were pissed."

"Rightfully so."

"Maybe, but many decided that the gods should be punished for their actions, and the Godless were there to welcome them into the fold. Then, when the Horde attacked with their god killer weapons, the Godless finally had their means to bring down gods. They united against us. A few terrorists at first, but soon there were tens of thousands to their name across the universe. I wanted to believe they hadn't come here, that somebody else was responsible for the hit—I have many enemies, you know— but if I'm on their list of gods, I'm as good as dead."

"How is that possible? You are so powerful."

"Do you remember the Horde?" Velaska asked, expanding the gap between her hands. "How they blotted the sun out like locusts with their numbers? The Godless are no different. We may be powerful, but they are numerous. When we stamp them out, they come back with greater numbers."

"And they are all intent on killing you?"

"Not just gods, my love, but anybody that has helped us, too, and now that includes you."

"What!" I shouted. "I didn't even want to help you. You forced me."

"Yes," Velaska nodded, turning away. "They don't seem to handle nuance particularly well. Now, I really must be going."

She tried to snap her fingers, and I grabbed them again. "Wait. Take me with you."

"Are you sure, love?"

I nodded. "I have nothing here."

"Very well," she said, interlocking her hand in mine. "Let us away, then." She snapped her fingers, and we were gone from the street in a flash.

***

We reappeared in front of the worn-out church where I had tried to kill Velaska. Across from it was the old office building that had crumbled when she blew up my sniper perch. While Velaska walked toward the church, I pulled my hand away from hers and headed straight for the rubble of the building.

"Where are you going?" Velaska asked.

The rubble pile reached far above my head. I knelt in front of a charred piece of cinder block, black from the explosion and broken into a hundred pieces. "How did you find me in all this rubble?"

"It wasn't hard, love. You were the only mangled carcass in the wreckage, and you moaned and groaned so loudly you were hard to miss."

"And you—you just decided to save me, right then and there?" I asked, choking through my forced words.

Velaska made a face. "I didn't want to save you, at least not in an altruistic sense. I wanted to make you suffer, and in death, you would stop suffering, at least for my enjoyment. There was more to it than simply pleasure, though. While it was fun to watch you moan—you deserved it, after all—but I needed answers. I tried to place my hand on your head and get the answers I needed about who hired you, but you—well, some people with extraordinarily powerful wills can prevent me from seeing their thoughts, and you were one of them. I needed you alive. I acted rashly, as is my way."

I pressed my fingers on the blackened building, and the charred blocks broke apart in my hands. "I do deserve to suffer."

"Oh, *tut-tut* and all that. Is that all you got from what I said? If that's the case, then we all deserve to suffer, my love. That is the universal condition."

"You mean the human condition," I said lowly under my breath.

"No, if I meant the human condition, I would have said the human condition. I mean the condition which all of us are burdened, even me. We were meant to cause suffering and to suffer. That is how the maker made us, and thus, how we made you."

"The maker?" I asked, turning to her. "But you're a god."

"We all have a maker, love." Velaska reached out her hand. "Now come, let us go. It's not good to dwell on the past."

I placed my hand in hers and rose away from the rubble. I knew it was folly to think about my own mortality, but I couldn't help it. Being blown up was the closest I had ever come to death. It was the closest I had ever come to Heaven.

"We all die, my pet," Velaska continued. "But that doesn't mean we stop fighting death. Often, we can fight it for eons, but it will catch up to us eventually. I mean, look at me. I should be immortal, and yet, my mortality keeps catching up with me."

A white flash came from the derelict church, accompanied by a choir of angelic voices. "Is that Heaven?" I asked. "Is that where we're going?"

Velaska laughed. "You wouldn't want to go there. Heaven is a silly place, and your god keeps it far too cold for my liking. No, we are going somewhere better. To the nexus of the universe."

The door to the church opened, and a figure stepped forward, wrinkled and folded upon himself; he was more a ball of flesh than human. His skin drooped over his eyes until nothing but little slits remained, and his mouth was nothing but a little oblong crack in his otherwise amorphous face. Covering his body was a long, maroon robe that shimmered like glitter in the white light from the church. Around his neck he wore a medallion of the all-seeing eye with a dozen gems glittering in its pupil.

"Velaska," the man said coldly. "I didn't expect to see you again so soon. I thought we told you—"

"I'm sure you have many lovely things to say, Angus, but things have progressed since our last meeting. I found the sniper who tried to kill me and have recovered this from the wallet of a man who put a hit out on me."

Velaska handed Angus the Godless card that Yunter kept in his wallet. I didn't mind that she didn't give me any credit for helping to find it. She was a god, and that was the sort of thing you had to expect from a god.

Angus lifted the flaps over his eye and examined it for a moment. "Yes, this is most troubling. Very well. In light of this new evidence, the Godschurch welcomes you, Velaska."

The wrinkly little man held out his arm and pointed toward the door of the church.

Velaska beckoned me forward. "Come on now. Don't keep us waiting. Angus isn't pleasant in the best of times, and he hates to be left waiting."

I frowned and took a hesitant step toward them. "I don't understand. What is the Godschurch?"

Velaska pushed me to the threshold of the door. "I'll explain in due time, Rebecca, but for now, just hurry up."

The white light shone from the open door at the church's entrance. As I neared it, a coolness enveloped me and tingled through my body. I watched my arms and legs vanish inside of it, and suddenly I felt at
peace in a way I had only found once before—in the moments after my death, before I was cruelly returned to the world.

CHAPTER 10

When I rematerialized, it wasn't inside a run-down shithole of a church. It was inside an ornate cathedral with hundred-foot high ceilings and stained-glass windows that shimmered onto the wooden pews below.

Each window was a work of art unto itself. I had seen books as a child, filled with images of beautiful stained glass, but words escaped me upon seeing them in person. The churches in Thebos were rudimentary by comparison. The artistic merit of the people left after the Horde Wars was...lacking.

The walls themselves stood a hundred feet high with hand-painted murals of humans, animals, monsters, gods, and angels on every surface. A soft angelic voice reverberated throughout the church and melted the tension away from me.

Walking through the entranceway, I rubbed my hand along one of the many tall columns. The domed ceiling depicted a great battle between angels and demons, fighting each other atop a mound of dead people bleeding out. It was as beautiful as it was horrific.

"What the hell is this…?" I asked.

"Please," Angus said. "Language."

"This is the Godschurch, Rebecca. Every planet has a beacon to the Godschurch like the one we just used, but this is where it rests, here at the center of the universe, amidst the stars, feeding off the power emitted from the nexus point of the universe."

"So, you're saying that we're out in the middle of the universe?"

"That's what I'm saying."

"Bullshit."

"Language!" Angus shouted.

I had to see where we were for myself. No way did I believe we were in the center of the universe. Turning around, I grabbed for the heavy, wooden door. Cherubs and gods pointed to the wrought-iron doorknob twisted elegantly in the shape of a spiral.

Velaska stayed my hand. "I wouldn't do that if I were you."

I brushed her off and opened the door. Gone was the rubble across from the church . . . gone was Thebos altogether. Instead, millions of stars twinkled across the expanse in front of me. A meteor whizzed by, and I tracked it as it rocketed across the bow of the church. A giant orb of energy pulsated below us, sending rings of light out into empty space for hundreds of miles in a rainbow of colors.

Velaska slammed the door in my face. "That's about enough of that. We have business to attend to."

I was still in a daze. "Where are we?"

"I told you, the nexus. This is the convergence of every piece of energy in the cosmos. The Godschurch acts as its protector, and since the gods created all of this, and we are critical for its continued existence, they protect the gods, too."

"Which is why the name—"

"Precisely." Velaska nodded.

Above the altar was a twenty-foot-high golden statue of the all-seeing eye, and inside its pupil danced a thousand gems of every size and color. It looked like a much larger version of Angus's medallion. I pointed toward Angus, plodding up the aisle between wooden pews toward an altar at the front of the church. "And what's with this guy?"

"Angus." He burped.

"Angus. He's the one who protects you all?"

Velaska chuckled. "Lords, no. He just works here."

"Come, come," Angus said, his voice a nasal whine. "They are waiting."

Every step Angus took felt like a grand expense of energy. He breathed deeply out of his mouth as he lumbered forward, one foot in front of the other. "Please," he said. "Do not touch *anything*."

I looked around the church once more, at the stained glass etched in the windows. Great battles waged, and beautiful maidens twirled and danced. Everything did look exquisitely expensive. "And what's with the stained glass, and the paintings, and the bloody battle on the ceiling?"

Velaska took a moment to study the paintings. "It depicts our whole history. Everything notable from every god since the dawn of time is enshrined in these works of art."

"Are you in any of them?"

Her face darkened. "No. And it's a real stick in my craw. I've brought it up several times. They have it 'under review.'"

Marble vines snaked up every column and blossomed throughout the church. I could almost smell the fragrant bouquet they gave off as I followed Angus down the pews toward the altar.

He pointed at the walls as he walked. "The entire edifice was constructed some three million years ago by the cherubs themselves. They did it all by hand. It took them two thousand years to carve all the walls. I think the work speaks for itself."

"It certainly does," Velaska said sportingly. "Doesn't it, Rebecca?"

"Art never really did it for me—" Velaska elbowed me in the ribs. "But this—it's…pretty nice."

The wrinkles on Angus's face mushed together as his mouth creased into a smile. "Why, thank you. Now, come along."

In front of the church, underneath the all-seeing eye, sat three thrones, made from ornate gold with red velvet backing and inlaid with hand-carved depictions of the gods. On each chair sat an old man. They had all aged better than Angus, but that wasn't a high bar to meet.

It was impossible to tell them apart. All three were salt and pepper-haired, wearing dark red, shimmering robes and sporting a scowl that caused their aged faces to lag even lower on their wrinkly bodies.

The only distinguishing feature of the three came from the chair in the center, which loomed over the others from a raised pedestal. He was clearly the leader because he was the only one that spoke.

"Velaska," he said, his words dripping off his tongue. "Why have you come? I thought we banished you last time."

"Yes, you did, Master Jamil, but these are desperate times."

"Quite," he replied. "You have always been good at desperation. And you brought a human whom we have never seen before, to what, parlay with us? Can you please send her away? I don't have time for this."

"I would rather stay," I growled. After everything we'd gone through, this guy just didn't have the time? I already didn't like the Godschurch.

Velaska grumbled under her breath before turning to me. "My love, can you please sit in the pews while I talk with the masters?" She forced me down into one of the long, wooden rows. I didn't like it, but since I didn't know what was happening, I didn't fight her. With me seated, she turned back to the old men in their golden chairs.

"I'm sorry for that outburst, masters of the Godschurch. Please accept my humblest apologies."

The men looked at each other and nodded, but only Master Jamil spoke. "This is your third time in front of this council in as many months, and each time we have given you the same answer. As we currently only acknowledge you as a demigod and thus a junior member, you do not receive the full protection of the church and thus cannot receive a personal security detail."

"But this is different," Velaska said, pulling Yunter's card out of her pocket. "This time, I have proof that the Godless are targeting me. You can't just dismiss it as conjecture anymore."

Velaska handed the card to Angus, who waddled it up to Master Jamil. He looked it over for several moments before handing it back to Angus. "Yes, yes, this is troubling. Most of the targets for the Godless have been . . . important gods. Their numbers must be growing to widen their focus like this."

"Of course, it has grown!" Velaska shouted, forgetting herself for a moment. She shrunk back down and comported herself. "You have done nothing to stop them in all these many years. Why should they not have the confidence to expand their reach across the galaxy?"

Master Jamil stood. "We have seen them expand their reach for months, but we did not think it had reached your…pathetic *sector.*"

He said "sector" with a seething hatred I usually heard only reserved for demons. Something in his blood-red eyes made me cringe in disgust. He moved his eyes from Velaska over to me and then back to her.

"I suppose you give her as an offering?"

An offering? What did he mean by an offering? I didn't have time to collect my thoughts before Velaska spoke again.

"She is a worthy fighter. She was contracted to kill me, but she has helped me more than any other mortal on her planet has in a generation."

"Girl!" Master Jamil shouted. "Come! Let us see what kind of offering you are?"

"What are they talking about?" I whispered, leaning toward Velaska. "What is an offering?"

"I am not a true god, not by their standards, and so I am not eligible for the personal protection they provide to those gods targeted by the Godless. However, if I bring in somebody who can become an officer of the church, then I'm not using their resources, and thus, they will look into my case. I need their resources. Don't you understand? *You* are my bargaining chip."

I couldn't even be mad. I just had to laugh. "This was your plan all along."

"Well, not all along, just since I fixed you up and realized how pretty you really are. The masters love pretty girls."

"And you blew up Yunter Haus because you knew it meant I could never go back again."

She shrugged. "Maybe a little. Mostly I did it because he was so awful, but that doesn't change the fact that there is nothing left for you on Thebos. If you play your cards right, you could have a new life here." She looked over at the masters. Jamil hadn't moved an inch. "They are aggravating, granted, but the Godschurch does good work, and officers curry great favor with the gods."

It was her last statement that caused me to perk up. "Curry favor...you mean, like, they have a better chance at Heaven?"

Velaska frowned. "Well, Heaven is merely a concept—foreign to most of the universe, at that. So, no promises there. But it does mean special treatment, that is for sure."

I thought for a moment. Working with gods couldn't be any worse than working for demons, and the chance at Heaven made it a tempting offer.

"So, what? I'm going to be a monk?"

She laughed. "Not exactly, but that's all I can tell you until you accept."

"You don't give me much choice," I told her with a grumble. "Fine. I will do it. What do I have to lose?"

"Quite literally nothing."

"Very well," I said to Master Jamil. "I guess I'll join your church."

Master Jamil retracted his finger, scowling. "That is an excellent attitude for an initiand. So much enthusiasm, but you are mistaken. It is you who is auditioning for us, not the other way around."

I laughed. "Trust me, any test you give me I'm going to pass, unless it's to act like a pompous—well, like you. I'm not going to do that."

Master Jamil ruffled his robe. "You will learn respect."

"Better men than you have tried, master. Most of them are in a body bag."

Master Jamil turned to Velaska with a raised eyebrow. "This would be the type of impudent swine you would bring us, wouldn't it?"

Velaska held out her hands. "She's a little rough around the edges, but trust me, when push comes to shove, she'll make a fine officer."

"Let us hope so."

CHAPTER 11

I didn't like Master Jamil, and I hated the tacit endorsement the other two masters gave his rampant dickheadedness, but Velaska wasn't wrong. I needed something new in my life. Thebos had kept me stagnant for more than two decades and sucked the last vestiges of humanity from my bones.

During my time in Thebos, I worked for, killed, or pissed off every powerful person I came across, all the way up to Ul'brem himself. If I ever went back there, I would be shot on sight.

Even if I left Thebos to try my luck in another city, it would be no different. Every city was run by thieving demon warlords. It would be a different street and a different castle, but at the end of the day, I would be running hits on people just the same.

Plus, there was the matter of Heaven. Realizing there might be a chance for me to get into the good place after all made me eager to cash in as many favors as possible to get there. If I could work with gods instead of demons, then maybe I had a chance to escape Hell altogether. I didn't know much about the Godschurch, but they weren't on Earth, and there weren't demons. For the moment, that was enough for me.

"What is this place?" I asked Velaska as we followed Angus toward a heavy, wooden door in the dark, dank corner of the church behind the masters. "Can you tell me yet?"

"The Godschurch . . . think of it like the eyes and ears of the gods. We can't be everywhere at once, but the Godschurch can."

Angus finished pushing open the door and disappeared into the darkness. I followed him. "So, they're like your own secret police force?"

Velaska cocked her head, considering this as she walked through the door. "Yes, that is quite like it, but I like the Godschurch better. It sounds—official—less scary."

"Sure, it sounds all honey pots and rainbows, but the truth is that you're probably doing the same shit I do right now."

"Language!" Angus lit a lantern which illuminated a long, spiral staircase.

"Well, of course, it's the same stuff you do now," Velaska said. "How do you think I knew you'd be a good fit?"

I stepped onto the staircase, brushing the damp cobblestone walls with my hands as I descended the stairs behind Velaska. "I guess I would be."

It was a nice thought that I would be doing something different with my life if I joined the Godschurch, but a fleeting one. My hands would be just as dirty, but for a new master—though this was one that had a pipeline to Heaven.

"They wouldn't be that dirty," Velaska said. "I mean, the Godschurch is very clean, for one. More so than that Thebos."

"So, can you read my thoughts, then? I thought my will was too strong to have my thoughts read by you."

In the darkness, I couldn't see her shake her head, but I heard the jingling and jangling of her jewelry as her head swayed back and forth. "That's true, but when I fixed you, I may or may not have given myself a backchannel into your mind. A strong will is nice but dangerous for a god like me.

You understand, dear, don't you? I can't have your thoughts shut out from me. Not after you tried to kill me."

"I guess."

Angus grunted against another door at the bottom of the stairs. It opened slowly, and light flooded into the hallway. "Come, now," he said. "Don't be shy. There is so much to do."

I walked out of the hallway that held the spiral staircase and into another world. While the church upstairs and the stairs below it felt ancient, this new room was as modern as anything I'd ever seen—clean and a perfectly crisp white.

A row of windows looked out onto the universe. I walked over to them and marveled at the scope of infinity. The nexus spiraled and swirled below me, and I was transfixed by the spinning of the great ball of energy.

Velaska beckoned me forward. "Come on, now!"

"What is this place?" I asked, walking toward the center of the room. I wondered how many times I could ask the same question.

"Command center!" a short woman barked from the middle of the room. Her black hair was tied up in a tight bun, and her furrowed brow made her beady eyes look even smaller. She held a tablet in her hand with a vicelike grip.

Surrounding her, a hundred workers dressed in clean, white suits typed into monitors. Their keyboard clacking created a pleasant sound, like waves crashing into the shore. All the workers wore headpieces and mumbled under their breath. Behind her, three dozen monitors displayed maps of the galaxy, times of day on different planets, and showed camera footage of various streets and buildings.

"Come now. There isn't much time," the short woman said, marching toward me. "Angus told me you were coming, and there is so much to do." She looked me up and down. "There was a time that the Godschurch had standards, you know, but I suppose those went out the window, didn't they?" Raising my arms and inspecting me more closely, she pointed to the demon hunters around my chest. "You won't be needing those anymore, no you won't."

She reached for my guns, but I smacked away her arm. "You can pry them from my cold, dead hands."

The woman smirked. "Yes, well, that is probably what will happen anyway, now, won't it?"

"I don't know about you, but I'm planning to live for a while longer."

"Of course. We all plan to live for a long time, but the universe makes its own plans for us. It planned for you to be here today, and it has planned for your death as well."

"I take exception with that plan," I grumbled.

She looked down at her tablet. "Clearly, a sparkling conversationalist. Shall we get started?"

"I don't even know what I'm doing here. So, no. You tell me what I'm doing, and then we can get started."

The woman rested the tablet against her chest and crossed her arms over it, giving me an even stare. "You are in training to become a probationary agent of the Godschurch. We must test your reflexes, your aim, and your general temperament, to see if you qualify. I suspect you don't, but as I mentioned, the rules have gotten quite lax recently since our agents keep showing up—well, dead."

"Comforting."

"It is, in a way. In death, they return to the Source for us to do it all again. It's marvelous. Well, let's go." The woman stalked down the maze of monitors, and a door opened in the glass in front of her.

I stole a glance at Velaska. "She's charming."

"It gets better. Just go with it. You'll be fine."

"Aren't you coming with me?"

"Oh no," Velaska responded, scrunching up her nose. "I have much better things to do—like anything."

***

A doorway shuddered open in front of us, and the woman led me down a long, glass corridor. All around me, stars and nebulas twinkled and glowed. It reminded me of the desert outside Thebos, which I thought had the most stars I would ever see in my life, but I was wrong. The glass bridge put that desert to shame.

"Please don't slow down," the woman said. "We have a lot to do."

I hurried to catch up to her. "What's your name?"

The woman walked faster. "That will be inconsequential unless you pass the tests."

"Well, I'm going to pass the tests, so you might as well tell me, you know?"

She gave me a sidelong glance. "You can call me Tress, as in Miss Tress."

"That's very good," I said, walking across the bridge as a glass door opened in front of me, then closed behind me. "Has anybody ever told you that you're funny?"

A sly smirk came across her face. There isn't a person alive who didn't like compliments, a trait we must have gotten from the vain gods like Velaska that molded us from the primordial ooze.

"Why yes, in fact, they have. Get inside."

Tress led me into a stark white room where the only object was a handgun. She pointed to it. "Pick it up."

"I would prefer to use my own."

"The world is tough, and we rarely get what we want. Now pick that gun up, soldier."

I did as she commanded and lifted the sight to my eye. It was heavier than I expected, yet the trigger was light as I pulled down on the grip—I accidentally depressed the trigger, and a laser shot across the room and scalded the wall.

Tress took note of it in her tablet. "Minus one for accidental discharge."

What is wrong with me? It was the first time I had ever accidentally misfired anything before, which got me to wondering. Was I really that nervous…for something I wasn't even sure I wanted?

Tress gave me a stern look. "You will come across many new guns on missions. You won't have time to get acclimated to them all. Are you expected to shoot from the hip with every new weapon in your arsenal? I should think not." She scribbled a few notes on the tablet and muttered to herself. "We wouldn't get very far as a secret society if our soldiers blew up everything that moved now, would we? No, we would not."

"I'm sorry," I said, contrite.

Tress snapped her fingers, and I shut my mouth. "There will be targets that show up in front of you. Some will be innocents. Some will be victims. Some will be the enemy.

It is your job to figure out which should be shot and which should be left alone. Are we ready?"

I held up my gun and steadied it with my free hand. "When you are."

I had played this game in the army more times than I could count. I didn't enlist in the army until the Horde Wars started, but I was a quick study, and I enjoyed the structure...for a while. Five years after the war, the government disbanded officially, and the demons overran everything, including the army, and I was on my own again. I missed it, sometimes, but I didn't enjoy being yelled at and treated like a child, which was what Tress was doing.

Just like Tress, the army liked to pretend there were innocents, but the truth was that you shot anything that moved and asked questions later. Of course, I knew that wasn't what the Godschurch wanted to see. They wanted to see that I valued human life, at least those that mattered, so when the first four people appeared to be innocents, I didn't fire.

After them, three enemies popped up, and I shot them through the head as I made my way across the room to angle my shots better. When it was all over, my face was shiny with sweat.

Target practice was never an issue for me, especially in an enclosed space. With no wind in the practice room, every shot went straight and true. That never happened on the battlefield. In practice, well . . . we like to pretend practice estimates real battle, but anyone who's been there knows it doesn't. Real battle was a hundred blasts firing around you and trying to take out the enemy while your platoon scrambled into the crossfire.

Tress smiled at me. "Good work. You've gotten a ninety-nine percent. Nearly perfection, except for that misfire. Next is a test of your mental skills. Follow, follow."

She scooted out of the room, suddenly imbued with an energy I hadn't seen on her before like my shooting made her giddy.

***

Tress brought me into a sterile white room and laid a puzzle on the floor for me. My job was to figure out how the puzzle fit together, even though all the sides were smooth and all the pieces were white. There were several dozen scenarios which could have been correct, and I tried them all. The first was a square, then an oval, then a triangle. I tried a duck, and a pig, and a squirrel.

Each time I thought I finished, a big red light flashed through the room, and an airhorn screamed in my face, echoing off every wall. With each incorrect answer, I became more frustrated, but I knew what they were doing. This wasn't my first time getting tested for my nerves. By the time the bell went off a fourth time, I was sure that there was no right answer. They were just trying to see how many answers I could give before I snapped and screamed.

The military gave the same test during sniper training to gauge our problem-solving and concentration, but it was really about testing our temperament. Temperament was incredibly important for a sniper. Often, we had to lay in wait for hours—sometimes days—perfectly still, waiting for our target to emerge. Enemies would sometimes pass within inches of our position, and if we flinched for even a moment, they would spot us. If we didn't have a strong will and a lot of discipline, we would never survive.

Most people snapped during the intense pressure of this test, but I thrived. I wasn't one to let my emotions get the better of me. People said that made me callous and cruel—prone to psychotic tendencies, even—and while that wasn't without its merit, I was also incredibly effective. I never let emotion get in the way of a job, which is why I'm still alive.

It's also why Tress couldn't break me. She could try, but she would fail because I had a will of iron and nerves of steel. Yes, it was true that my hands shook faster putting together the puzzles each time a loud noise belted forth, but my constitution never wavered. I played mind games with myself, trying new ways to stack the pieces on top of each other to make a mountain, then a skyscraper, and finally a swan.

After an hour of repeated failure, the lights turned off, and Tress walked back into the room. "That was . . . well, you're done."

"Great," I said, smiling. "What's next?"

The frustration nearly bubbled over into Tress's face when she realized that she couldn't break me. Her eye twitched, and her head jerked, but she kept her composure. I got her to lose her cool for a second, though, and that was satisfying.

CHAPTER 12

"There really was a correct answer," Tress said, walking me down the hall. "To that puzzle, I mean."

"I'm sure there was. How many people have ever gotten it, though?"

"Three."

"Out of how many applicants?"

"More than you would like to know. Most go crazy after the first twenty minutes and start flinging the puzzle pieces at the wall. One man smashed his head against the wall so hard he gave himself brain damage. I suppose, aside from getting the right answer, lasting an hour is the best I could have hoped for."

"I told you I was going to pass your tests. You should just let me into your little club now."

A door slid open, and Tress beckoned me inside. "It's not over yet. Inside, please."

"Out of curiosity, are you being so horrible to me because you dislike Velaska or because you hate me?"

She smiled. "Can't it be both?"

I stepped through the door. "Walked right into that one."

Inside the room, ten identical men—black-haired, bearded, dark-skinned—stood in a semi-circle, dressed in combat boots and camo pants with green tank tops and black bandanas. They looked the same, dressed the same, and moved the same. They even held the same six-inch, serrated knife in their right hand.

I stared each one in the eyes as I moved around the room, sizing up each man in turn. Tress walked to the middle of the semi-circle and held up her tablet.

"One of these men has the key to disarm a nuclear bomb," she said. "The other nine are decoys. Your job is to—"

"It's the one in the center." I pointed. "Fourth from the left."

"How did you—"

"He moved his eyes away for just a split second when I looked at him. That's a clear sign of hiding something, to me. If you turn out his pockets, you'll find the key in the . . . front, left pocket, where he's been pawing since I walked through the door."

"You really are quite cocky. Did you know that?"

I folded my arms. "I've just been around the block a couple of times."

Tress stepped aside. "Very well. If you are so confident…prove it."

I strutted up to the man. "Hold still. I am going to reach inside your pocket and grab the key you have hidden there, all right?" When I reached for his pocket, the man grabbed my hand and spun me around. I leaped into the air as he spun me and landed on my knees. He fell to the ground when I kicked his legs out from under him, where I knocked him out with a quick punch to the forehead. The other nine men scrambled toward me. It had been a while since I took on nine men at once, but it wasn't the first time.

"How much violence can I use?" I called out.

"Maximum," Tress replied without looking up, jotting notes down in her tablet.

I moved into a corner so that they couldn't surround me. From there, I ran forward and bicycle-kicked the first charging man in front of me. He landed on the ground. I smashed my hand through his face and grabbed his knife. One sliced at me, and I grabbed his arm, flipping him over my shoulder, and slammed him into the wall with the full weight of my body. Another man charged, and I took his knife arm and stabbed another one of my attackers through the throat with it.

Tress didn't seem to care about the death of her soldiers, which led me to believe this was all a simulation. That meant I could be even more aggressive with my last six attackers. I held tight to my knife and jabbed it through one of the men's eyes, then used his knife to slit the throat of one more.

Four more soldiers stood upright, and I pulled out my revolvers.

"No guns!" Tress shouted.

I flipped over the guns in my hands and used them to smash the nose of a charging soldier, sending him spurting blood all over the walls before he fell to the ground. I danced around the room with the last three attackers as they took turns swiping their knives at me.

I didn't have to be hasty. I needed to find an opening, and finally, one of the attackers gave me one. He swiped high, over my head, and I uppercut him in the throat. He dropped his knife, and it fell into my hand. I sliced open his neck and kicked him into his comrades. Then, I flung the knife through the temple of one of the last two remaining soldiers.

There was only one soldier left, but he attacked as furiously as if there were ten. I was getting tired, but he hadn't broken a sweat. Using what remained of my strength, I rushed forward and slammed him into the wall. He stabbed at me, and I avoided his blow, grabbed his wrist, and dragged him to the ground before punching him in the face until he blacked out.

With all the soldiers incapacitated, I walked over to the first soldier I'd confronted, shuffled through his front right pocket, and pulled out the nuclear key.

"See? I told you," I said breathlessly, handing the key to Tress as the soldiers twitched under my feet.

"It seems you may be of some use to us yet," Tress said, begrudgingly.

"What were these? Android?"

"I wish." She nudged one with her foot. "No, they were just your average clones. Much cheaper that way."

***

"So, did I pass?" We were walking back across the glass bridge to the central control room, where I'd first met Tress a few hours ago. Time sure crawls when you're having alarms blare at you and clones attack you.

"Yes, you passed."

"Cool," I said. "What does that mean?"

I followed Tress through the door to the command center. Velaska and Angus gazed at the wall of screens in the middle of the room.

"It means that you are on probationary status as an officer of the Godschurch. You must be accompanied by a full agent of the Church during your probationary period. If that agent approves of you, then you will be granted full access to the church."

"Actually," Angus piped up in his nasal whine. The sound of his voice made me want to punch him. "She isn't to be given any partner for this mission, as she's not technically helping a god of the pantheon."

"I am a god!" Velaska said. "Just because I'm not in the pantheon doesn't mean I should be denied any privilege of a god."

Tress looked down at her tablet. "Have you paid your dues?"

"As a junior member." Velaska's voice dropped a few decibels.

"Hmm. Well, as a junior member, you get junior member privileges, which doesn't include a full officer of the Godschurch for protection. You don't want to be caught abusing your privileges again, do you?"

"You know I can destroy you in a snap, right?"

"Yet, here I stand," Tress said. "Un-blown up."

I admired Tress. She stood up to Velaska like she was her equal, if not her better. Yet, there was nothing about her that showed she was anything but a human.

"So, are you a god?" I whispered from behind Tress.

"Heavens, no," she replied without missing a beat and with a little giggle.

"Then . . . how can you talk to gods like that?"

"Simple. They have entrusted me to protect them, so they treat me with a level of respect appropriate to somebody in my position. It is one of the advantages of being me."

"I didn't think there was anything cool about you, but that's pretty cool."

She puffed out her chest and straightened her shoulders a bit. Yup, it didn't matter where in the universe. Humans loved to be complimented.

***

After listening to Velaska and Tress bicker for five straight minutes, I'd had my fill. I walked over to the windows at the edge of the command center and looked out into the universe. Somewhere out there was Earth.

"It's on the other side, actually," Velaska told me, strolling up behind me. "But honestly, they all look the same. You could call any of them Earth, and it wouldn't really matter."

"I'm not really that obvious, am I?"

"Well, yes, but that one was a gimme. No matter who I bring here, they always want to know about home."

"So, I'm not the first person you brought to the Godschurch?"

"Sorry to burst your bubble, but over thirty of the people in this room are ones I personally brought to the church. Even Tress over there. She's one of mine."

"Then why do they treat you so badly?"

Velaska cleared her throat. "I may or may not have tricked them into coming here to achieve my own ends."

"Yup. That sounds like you."

"That's not the only reason they dislike me, though. I don't fit into their perfect definition of a god. I like to do my own thing, and gods, well, the gods hate that. They want everything conformed and rigid. I mean, look out on that room. If I didn't tell you over twenty-five sectors were represented there, would you even know?"

I gazed out across the control room, and while there were black, white, Asian, and every color under the sun, they were all distinctly human. I could have walked into any one of them on Thebos and had no idea.

"No. They all look—they all look like part of the same race."

"And they are the same. Sure, their planets are different, but they are all created in our image. A thousand galaxies filled with plain old god-looking humans. And that's the way the gods think about everything, boring and plain, so when somebody comes along and doesn't play by the rules . . . well, they don't like that."

I really felt sorry for Velaska. I couldn't believe it, but I felt sorry for her. Her eyes dropped to the ground, and I could tell it pained her to be such an outcast, like I was an outcast, trying desperately to survive in a universe that didn't want us.

"I'm sorry," I said, placing my hand on her shoulder.

Velaska placed her hand over mine and squeezed lightly. "Oh, it's okay, my love. Today is another day, and tomorrow is one, too. We all, every one of us, have our burdens to bear. This is mine. I have tried very hard to conform to their ways, but . . . well . . . it just doesn't seem like it's in the cards for me." She took a deep breath, and her voice lowered. "And that . . . that's all right."

I knew that it wasn't all right. Velaska wanted to be loved like a little puppy wanted to be loved. The way she was neglected and cast aside had a profound effect on her. I also knew that sometimes it felt good to save face, so I let her have that one. I walked away.

***

My thick steel-toed boots echoed through the halls as I made my way around the halls of the Godschurch. The outer wall of the walkway was glass, which meant I could see the universe in every direction.

Each star and nebula was breathtaking, but I spent the most time looking down at the Nexus, swirling in space as the station spun around it slowly. I hadn't let myself be awed by much in the last two decades, but the idea of a universe bigger than Earth's made my stomach flutter. To think, there were whole worlds where the Horde didn't destroy everything, ones that never fell into a black hole. Maybe there was an Earth with another me, whose mother and sister weren't dead, and who grew up to become a teacher, or a lawyer, or a housewife.

"You're the new girl, right?" a deep, masculine voice said from behind me. I turned, and sure enough, there was a man dressed in the same camo and tank top as the clones in the simulation. I had just killed him ten times, so seeing him again made me instantly think he was out for revenge.

"I am the new probationary officer, yes, and I do happen to be a woman."

For me not wanting to be called a girl, he sure looked boyish when he blushed. "Sorry. I didn't mean girl like that."

"I know," I said, scowling. "Nobody ever means anything like the way they said it, at least not after people take offense to it."

He held up his hands. "Look, I come in peace. My name is Dean. I'm just coming to say hello. I'm sorry I offended you."

"Didn't I just kill you a bunch of times, Dean?"

"Guilty. That was me. I promise I'm a much better fighter than my clone army." He held out his hand, expecting me to shake it. "That's kind of weird to say."

I stared at his outstretched hand but didn't accept it. "What planet are you from, Dean?"

He pointed out the window toward a small sector of space which, just like Velaska had said, looked just like every other sector I had seen. "Hecate. It's in the Antigone galaxy."

I stepped forward, and his hand accidentally grazed my side. My heart gave an involuntary flutter. He was cute, I had to admit, and the adrenaline still in my system from the fight earlier made him look even better. "Are you from a peaceful planet, would you say?"

"Define peaceful."

"Have mutant bugs ever destroyed everything you love? Do demons roam the earth fighting each other for domination? Have you ever fought alongside a zombie and watched its head get blown off, only to feel sorry for it? Any of that happened to you on your planet, Dean?"

He shook his head. "Fortunately, no."

"In that case, I would say you live in a peaceful world, Dean. That must be nice for you."

He chuckled nervously as I grabbed his thigh. "Well, we both ended up here."

I was close enough to smell Dean's musk, and his aroma was intoxicating. I don't remember a time when I didn't have to get past the stink of sweat on a man before bedding him. Usually, their faces and bodies were mangled by war, but Dean, there wasn't a scratch on him. He was a perfect specimen of a man, and I was ravenous.

I stepped closer to him, whispering in his ear. "Let me ask you something, Dean. Are there beds in this place?"

"Y-y-yeah."

“You should take me to one. Now.”

Dean gulped. “This is very weird.”

“Get used to it.”

CHAPTER 13

It wasn't that Dean was a bad lover. He was just . . . "tender" might be the right word for it. He kept asking if I was all right. Maybe that's how it's done on his planet, but I'm not used to gentle. He even tried to kiss me and look me in the eyes while we were banging. Those were two big no-nos on Earth. You took what you wanted, got what you could, and when it was over, you were on to the next thing.

"So . . . was that good for you?" Dean asked as I came out of the bathroom and put on my shirt.

I was up minutes after he was done, ready for the next thing. You couldn't stay too long in the lap of coital bliss on Earth because that's when they make their move against you. Just like I did with Matt.

"It was fine," I replied. "Why, wasn't it good for you?"

"No, it was great. I don't think it's hard for it to be good for a man, though. It's kind of thrust, thrust, thrust; then you're done, you know?"

"That's a true statement. Men are ruled by their . . . cravings in a way that I have never been."

"And yet you are the reason we are here."

"Yes, well, this has been an odd day overall, and you were . . . smooth."

Dean laughed. "I'll take that as a compliment."

"Good, because I meant it as one."

The loudspeaker squawked to life. Tress's voice screeched over the intercom. "Lobdell! Control room! Now!"

***

I ran into the control center, where Velaska and Tress stared over a computer screen. A petite, black woman with a loose ponytail and furrowed brow typed furiously into the computer under their watchful eyes.

"Are you sure that's correct?" Tress said.

The woman nodded. "Yes, ma'am. I checked it three times."

Velaska looked up when I entered the room. "Ah, Rebecca, my love. It's so nice of you to join us. You look…flush," she said with a knowing smile. "Did you enjoy your nap?"

I tried to ignore her look. "It was a nice stress relief."

"Yes," Tress said. "You have been through a lot, and so I let you sleep, but it's time to work."

"I'm ready," I said, walking toward the console.

On the screen, a dozen dots zigzagged across a continent that didn't look dissimilar to America, assuming, of course, a drunk fifth-grader drew it with a crayon. This continent bulged out in the center and then quickly narrowed into a tiny point on either end, smaller than the state of Rhode Island as if they'd squeezed America like a balloon at the top and bottom.

Tress pointed toward the computer screen. "Carol here has been studying the card that you brought us, trying to find out where it was manufactured."

"I just assumed that they printed it at the local Wal-Mart."

Wal-Mart was the only company that survived both the pull through the black hole *and* the Horde Wars. If you had a regular job, then it was probably at a Wal-Mart.

"That would be inaccurate," Tress grunted. "Carol, tell her what you've found."

Carol gave a polite nod. "First, I analyzed the paper. While it was made up of mostly oak, there was a residual of a tree unique to a specific quadrant of the galaxy."

"Hang on. I thought that every planet was basically the same," I said.

"Yes, ma'am. Every planet is basically the same, but there are slight inconsistencies between planets depending on where in the universe they are made. Sometimes it's a slight change in the makeup of the planet's crust or a floral species which can only grow in one part of the universe. In this case, the tree is only present in sector 124.591."

"Which god controls that sector?"

"None, ma'am. It was once controlled by Hypnos but was abandoned three million years ago when he was arrested for crimes against the gods."

"This sector has been without a god for three million years?" Tress asked.

"Yes, ma'am," Carol replied.

"What human-inhabited planets are present in that sector?" Velaska asked.

"Just one. Cambrial. Apollo pulled it into the void three million years ago when Hypnos was arrested, and it stayed there until twenty years ago when Apollo pulled it back, but Hypnos never returned to reclaim his planet."

"And where is Hypnos now?"

"I don't know, ma'am. He's not checked in since being freed from Hera's prison during the Horde Wars."

Tress looked at Velaska. "That seems like the kind of place that the Godless would choose. It's remote enough that we wouldn't look for it, and without a god, they could build their cult in secret."

I pointed to the screen. "Great, so what's the plan now? What do all these little dots mean?"

"That's what we're going to find out." Tress smiled. "We can't go in guns blazing until we know that this is the right place, and we can't know it's the right place until we get an operative on the ground."

"You want me to sneak around and figure out where the Godless are hiding out?"

"Gods, no. You would be a disaster," Tress said. "I'm not sending a probationary officer to take down the biggest threat to the universe. Not in a million years."

"I can help. I know I haven't been here long, but I've survived a lot worse than the Godless."

"She is very good," Velaska added, trying to be helpful.

Tress sized me up and typed furiously into her tablet. She flipped through what I can only assume were my test scores, gritting her teeth. "Her test scores were quite good, and we're running out of agents. Very well, but I will not let her go alone."

"Fair enough," I said.

"I'm assigning you to partner with our best officer. Even though Velaska technically doesn't qualify for a team, finding a Godless base is too important a mission to leave to any single agent. I'll have him paged now."

I didn't even have to ask who that officer was—I just knew. I knew deep down in my bones that irony was a cruel bitch.

"Officer Dean Hendrix!" Tress shouted over the loud speaker. "To the control room!"

Yup. Irony was a cruel, cruel bitch.

***

"I'm not going to sleep with you again," I said to Dean as he walked me into the weapons locker. Thousands of guns, swords, and knives were arranged inside the translucent cases that filled the room.

"I'm not expecting to sleep with you again," Dean replied, pulling a demon hunter off one rack and a Beretta off another and stuffing them in the holster he kept around his waist.

"Good," I said, a little disappointed that he wasn't more disappointed.

He looked at me. "All I want to do is my job, and my job isn't to have sex. It's to find the Godless and put a stop to them. Are you cool with that plan?"

"Very cool with it."

"Good," he said, raising an eyebrow. "Now, when we get back, that's another matter."

I chuckled under my breath. He was funny. "Men and their bravado. When I say I'm not going to sleep with you again, I meant ever."

Dean grabbed a set of knives off the wall and stuffed them into the sheaths strapped to each of his legs. "That's a long time, my friend. Life is too long to say anything with such certainty."

It was a precious sentiment and one that I certainly didn't agree with, at least in my experience. In my experience, life was short and miserable. The only thing that made it bearable was the thought that death would be worse.

"Let's just keep packing."

"Fine with me," he said, stuffing a can of pepper spray into his belt. He noticed that I wasn't loading up on any new guns. "You know, we have more advanced guns than the ones you're using."

"Do they shoot any straighter or kill any faster?"

"No. Just later models."

The newer demon hunters held a charge longer and fired faster than mine, but they were also prone to jamming at inopportune moments and overheating quickly. A side effect of shooting faster was that the guns became white-hot after a minute of firing. If you didn't give the guns a chance to cool, then you risked frying the circuits inside, and in the heat of battle, it was easy to forget to take your finger off the trigger. Dozens of good soldiers were mowed down in the Horde Wars because of a gun jamming or overheating. I wasn't going to let it happen to me.

"Mine'll work just fine," I said, holstering my revolvers before kneeling to pick up a box of bullets and four new mags of Demon Hunter charges. "I will take these, though."

My guns weren't the latest and greatest, but I knew every nook and cranny of them. I knew how to push them past their limits without breaking them and when to pull back. I knew one gun fired slightly to the left, and the other's sight was off by two millimeters. I could correct for those imperfections because I knew them so well. New guns took time to break in, and I didn't have any time to spare.

***

Dean and I walked back into the control room. He was suited up with more guns than a small squad of super-soldiers, but I didn't say anything. I figured he felt I was underprepared, so together, we made one perfectly prepared team.

"About time!" Tress called to us from the control console in the middle of the room. "Your mission is simple. Find the Godless complex if it exists, infiltrate, and gather information. Do not destroy the complex or engage with the hostiles within. When you have the information, report back here for further instructions. Am I clear?"

Dean nodded. "Crystal."

"What about you, Rebecca? Do you understand?"

"I understand the scope of the mission, yes."

"The most important part for you is not to blow anything up," Velaska said. "That's what the Godschurch is here for if you find anything. Got it?"

"I think I can handle that," I replied.

"I'm trusting you," Tress said. "I've never sent a probationary officer on a mission this important before. Don't let me down. This is our first real chance to find a Godless compound, and I don't want to mess it up."

"Yes, ma'am," I said.

"Follow Angus," she said. "He'll get you situated."

I turned to Velaska. "Wish me luck?"

She shook her head. "I don't do that, and you wouldn't need it anyway."

***

Angus walked us up the cobblestone staircase leading back to the church.

"When was this church built?" I asked Angus.

"Oh, I am not good with time," he replied. "So many different worlds with their own definition of time and years. I would say it was built before I can remember, and I can remember a long way."

"Does that make you a god?"

Angus made a noise that I think was a laugh. "No. I'm not a god. Not that I know of at least, but living out here in space, well, it halts a lot of the aging process, not to mention my mother was a fairy, which brought along its own natural long age."

"A fairy?"

Angus heaved open the heavy door which would bring us back into the church. "Of course. I know they are small creatures, but my father didn't care. They fell in love and had me, their little half breed."

We walked through the church, and my feet reverberated through the rafters. The masters were no longer seated in their chairs at the front of the church, though I felt a shudder of contempt just thinking of them.

"Wait by the front doors," Angus told us before disappearing behind a red, velvet curtain.

"Where is he going?" I asked Dean.

"Every planet with a human population has a Godschurch. Some have several, but they all have at least one. It's up to Angus to triangulate the location of the Godschurch closest to our intended destination."

"So, we just walk through those doors . . ." I indicated the big, wooden doors at the front of the church.

"And we'll be somewhere else in the universe entirely. The same way you ended up here. It works on the same principle gods use to make their way to Mount Olympus, but since we can't harness the power of the gods and disappear at will, we need an anchor on the planet to make the transports work."

I furrowed my brow. "I don't understand anything you just said."

"That's okay," Dean replied, walking toward the front door. "All you have to know is that we walk through that door, and we'll be on Cambrial, where our contact on the planet will pick us up."

"Okay!" Angus shouted through the curtain. "Ready!"

Dean beckoned me forward. "Come on. It's time." He opened the door, and a bright light flooded the room. I walked forward and watched my arms and feet disappear into its beams. Behind me, Dean and the church faded from view.

CHAPTER 14

I drifted through the ethereal white blur until I saw structures forming. I moved toward them, and suddenly, I was in another place—a place I didn't recognize. Instead of tall skyscrapers like we had on Earth, the structures on this planet were domed, and each one was covered in grass and flowers. The same was true about the church. The only thing that I recognized about the church was an all-seeing eye above a wooden door. The rest of the building was covered in plants.

Behind me, Dean emerged from the door, and then it closed. Hundreds of citizens bustled through the streets, which were paved white and filled with hover cars.

"How did this place fall through a black hole into another dimension for three million years?" I asked Dean. "It has so many people. It has such strong architecture. It's like they didn't miss a beat."

"I don't know," Dean replied. "I've been to a lot of planets, but none that fell through the black hole. If I had to take a guess, I would say that in the three million years they were in that other universe, they rebuilt themselves stronger and prouder than they were before. Human ingenuity is an incredible thing. I learned never to underestimate it."

A hover car blasted its wind-powered jets down onto the ground and came to a rest on the street next to us. A thin, slight man with a beard and dark skin opened the passenger's side door and waved at us.

"These are our guides," Dean said.

"Do they work for the church?"

"No," Dean replied. "They are just . . . allies."

"Are you Mister Dean and Miss Rebecca?" he asked with a thick accent.

Dean walked to the car. "That's us."

"I am Avrid. I will be your guide. This is Bob. He will be your driver. Excuse me, but he doesn't speak your English."

"Nice to meet you," Dean said before turning to me. "You coming?"

***

"We have tracked down the printer of your card, Mr. Dean," Avrid told us after we got airborne. "They are just outside of town. We should be there very soon. Just sit back and relax."

Avrid whispered something to Bob that I couldn't understand. Dean pulled out a pair of glowing headphones with a neon blue cord that fed into his jacket and put them into his ears.

"What are those?" I asked.

"Universal translator. Avrid speaks English like us, but most of these people speak languages and dialects you've never heard before."

"Can I have one?"

He gave me a long look. "Avrid! Can you give Rebecca here your universal translator? She seems to have misplaced hers."

"They never gave me one, actually." I was annoyed having to defend myself.

"Of course," Avrid said, opening the center console between him and the driver. "It would be my pleasure." He pulled out a long set of headphones connected to a small square box, no bigger than a silver dollar, and handed it to me.

"This is it?" I asked.

Avrid nodded. "Every language from every human dialect in the known universe. Of course, there are some languages from non-gods-sanctioned worlds that aren't recorded, but you probably will never have to deal with that—at least I hope not."

"What is a 'gods-sanctioned-world?'" I asked.

"The gods," Avrid replied, "in their infinite wisdom, create every world that has human life. They cradle it and nurture it. They make sure it can sustain life. Those planets are sanctioned by the gods, but there are also planets that aren't sanctioned by the gods, and there grow all sorts of horrible creatures, like bugs ten feet tall, and—"

"I get it. Planets like the Horde."

"Ah yes, the Horde. Terrible beasts and completely unsanctioned, which is why they are so evil. They have no god to guide them."

Dean tensed up, and his jaw clenched. "Of course, just because a planet doesn't have a god doesn't make it evil. After all, this planet has no god."

Avrid nodded his head. "It is a great shame to us, I promise you. We would like for nothing more than to have the countenance of the gods shine down upon us again, which is why it is so embarrassing that the Godless may have taken up residency here."

The car tilted skyward, and we rose above the cityscape. For the first time, I noticed the unfettered sky, tinged red, above the domed buildings. The car turned, and my eyes grew big as saucers. In front of us, fifty times bigger than the moon, sat an orange planet in the sky with a thousand rings around its core. It was like Saturn switched places with the moon.

"What is that?" I asked.

Avrid smiled. "That is Ishtar, our sister planet. Since we came back from the black hole, it has moved in perfect rotation with us."

"Is it safe for a planet that big to be that close?"

"Oh yes. In fact, many of our citizens have taken up residence there as our planet's population has grown so rapidly since coming back to this universe."

"How?" I asked. "How is it possible that there are so many people? The trip through the rift killed most of our citizens. It nearly killed me too."

"Yes. It was hard, but we survived—somehow."

"I can't imagine growing up in another universe," I said, staring at the great planet Ishtar with its thousands of rings. "What is it like to be back here?"

Avrid tried to smile as he stared back over the horizon, but his mouth sunk. Ishtar grew closer as the car bowed toward the planet below. "Most days, this still does not feel like my home. I feel like an outsider, but for so long we have dreamed of coming back here that I feel guilty not being grateful every second of every day."

He fell quiet after that, and I decided not to press him. Back on Earth, we didn't talk about the Sun Incident. We made a silent pact to pretend like it didn't happen, except in our memory. Still, I knew what it was like to have to make due in another universe. Even though this is where they'd started out, so long ago, it wasn't home anymore. These people had come here as outsiders and were expected to make this strange place their home.

I studied Avrid's face as he looked out over the horizon, watching the great planet Ishtar expand across the whole front windshield. He made me wish there was something I could say to comfort him. More so, I wanted to bond with him. Not many people in this universe understand what it's like to move through a black hole, and it was something we both shared. It connected us, even across millions of light-years.

There were so many things to say, and yet I said none of them. I looked over at Dean, but he was deep in thought as well. All I could do was stare out of the window and enjoy the ride.

***

It took another ten minutes to make our way to the print shop on the outskirts of the great city. The wind whipped up the sand around the building, obscuring everything except the broadest details. We could barely make out the dome of the print shop as we landed next to it. The neon sign that read "Action Print Co." acted as a beacon. Bob fought to keep the car steady against the sand and wind while trying to land the car, which shook violently.

"This used to be great farmland back in the other universe," Avrid said. "Now, it is a desolate wasteland. Still, some people are stubborn and refuse to leave, like this shop and the surrounding town."

Once the car touched down, Avrid ran out of the car and opened the door for me. The sand blew into my face before I'd even stepped out. I covered my face with my coat as protection against the scalding wind whipping at my face.

"We will wait for you here!" Avrid shouted.

"You're not coming in with us?"

Avrid shook his head. "I am just a guide. I would do you no good inside."

Dean tapped me on the shoulder, gesturing. "Come on! It will be fine!"

We walked away from the car together. The sand blew so violently that I lost track of the car in a matter of seconds. Dean continued onward, following the blinking neon light to the entrance until we made it to the door.

***

Inside, the building was nearly silent. Except for the occasional rap on the front door from the wind, you wouldn't even know that a sandstorm blew violently outside. We walked through a pair of glass double doors and ended up in front of a receptionist desk. The woman sitting behind it was wide-eyed and frazzled. Her thick glasses had a thick layer of filth on them.

"*Cambliti mao ilttit?*" she said in a high-pitched voice. The inflection at the end made me believe it was a question, but otherwise, I just stared at her blankly.

"*Imli riblo nostom,*" Dean replied.

"How are you doing that?" I asked.

Dean pointed to his headphones. "Put yours on."

I dug into my jacket and pulled out my headphones. I placed them in my ears and pressed the power button. My brain might as well have melted when the earbuds pulsated through my ears. Just as the pain became unbearable, it stopped. My ears rang loudly for a moment, and when it died into a low hum, I could hear everything around me in perfect English.

"Yes, we would like to talk to somebody about this," Dean said, handing her the Godless business card.

"Just one moment," the receptionist said, picking up her phone and dialing. Surprisingly, the device seemed to work the same way it did on Earth. "Yes, somebody is here about the thing."

I studied her, still surprised I could understand her. "Can I ask you a question?"

She smiled a fake smile. "Of course."

"How do you live out here with all this sand?"

She stood and brushed out her polka dot dress. "It only whips like that for about an hour at a time, then it subsides. Then it gets bad again, and then it dies down. You just kind of get used to it, I guess."

"Sounds horrible."

"It's okay," she replied. "Follow me."

***

"I don't know what you are implying," a fat, burly man with a bald head and undersized, tweed jacket shouted at us. "But I don't like it."

His name was Ted, but I really wanted to call him Fat Teddy. He sat behind a desk in a chair that was too small, in an office that barely fit him, staring out from a pile of papers that could have easily crushed him. His bushy mustache twitched, and his red face pulsated in anger.

"I'm not implying anything," Dean replied. "We are outright stating that you printed these cards for the Godless, and we want to know the shipping address."

"That is proprietary information," Fat Teddy said, shaking his jowls. "I don't see any warrant or badges, so I don't have to care at all."

"You're right, sir. You don't have to give us anything." I stood up. "Of course, if you don't, we'll make life a living hell for you."

He slowly leaned forward in his chair, trying to act like he was tough. "And what do you think those nice gentlemen will do when they find out I talked to you?"

"Probably the same thing they'll do whether you help us or not. Let's be fair, the Godless aren't known for their mercy." I had no idea what the Godless were known for, but I knew their type. "They'll see you as a loose end one way or another after this, and they'll take care of you."

"She's right," Dean added. "The Godless are ruthless about cleaning up their messes. If you help us, though, we'll protect you."

"Can't nobody protect me from the Godless, fella," Fat Teddy replied.

"Well, then we can die trying."

Fat Teddy thought for a moment. His bushy mustache twitched to either side as his fingers strummed his desk in rhythm. "All right, fella, I'll help you. Not her, though, cuz she's a little bit awful, but I like you, so I'll help you."

I wanted to reach across the table and rip him in half, but we needed him, so I just had to bite my tongue and nod slightly.

"It'll take me a while to find the records," Fat Teddy continued. "We do things old school here, with good ole paper. None of this newfangled computer crap. You head into town, and I'll give you a call when we have it. Sound good?"

Dean nodded. "That'd be just fine."

"There's a place called the Two Pillar Motel. It's not the best motel in town, but the owner knows me. Tell him that Teddy sent you. Ask for room fifteen. Got me?"

"Thank you."

They shook hands, and when Fat Teddy turned his hand toward me, I just walked out of the office and down the hall.

CHAPTER 15

"I can't believe that piece of garbage," I said, sitting inside the little motel room we rented in the little town that adjoined the print factory.

"I'm not defending him," Dean replied. His calm tone was infuriating. "But you are ignoring the facts of the situation."

"I'm not ignoring them. I'm allowed to complain for a minute, though, aren't I?"

"Sure, as long as you understand that right now, he's the only person who can help us figure out whether the Godless are still on this planet."

"Of course, I understand that Dean, but we both know they're on this planet. That's why Fat Teddy was acting shady. If you just let me knock his teeth in, we would have the answer by now."

"Maybe, or maybe I've been on more of these cases than you, and you'll have to just trust me on something . . . gods know you don't trust me on everything."

I shook my head. "I do trust you, Dean, because you're my superior and because Tress told me to trust you. But there's a deeper layer to trust, built on getting your partner's back, over and over. It comes with time, and I don't have that y—"

Before I could finish, Dean tackled me onto the ground and laid on top of me. Red dots from laser sights appeared on the walls across from me. Then, the firing began. Bullets tore through the window of the room and ripped the bed to shreds and the wall along with it.

"Shit!" I shouted. "They sold us out! I'm gonna murder that—"

"There'll be plenty of time to deal with him later!" Dean said, reaching into his pocket for a phone. "Avrid! Avrid! We're pinned down! Get over here!"

Avrid and Bob were getting food at a diner down the street. They wouldn't get to us for at least five minutes, and it would all be over by then. I army-crawled over to the table and pulled my demon hunters from their holsters.

"Cover me!" I shouted.

"What?"

I tossed one of the demon hunters to Dean. "You want to earn my trust? Then cover me!"

Dean rose and fired my demon hunter into the street, exploding a hover car parked in the lot. It blew ten feet into the air and gave me some cover to run outside and down the hallway of the motel.

I needed the high ground, and that meant getting onto the roof. Two rooms down from ours, I'd noticed a ladder next to the ice machine, and I ran toward it. The firing began again just as I made it up the ladder.

Across the roof, I found the first of the shooters and headed over to him. My stealth failed me, though, and the crunch of my boots alerted him to my presence. He swung his gun toward me, but I was ready. I blew off his head with my demon hunter.

I looked over the edge of the roof and counted four more shooters staggered throughout the parking lot. The closest one was right below me, and, with one shot, I dropped him to the ground. Within moments, I had gunned down each one of the gunmen with a precision shot to the chest.

Years of sniper training allowed me to focus in even the worst conditions. The demon hunters helped. Usually, the demon hunter charges were too precious to waste on humans, but their lasers weren't affected by the swirling eddies that whipped through the motel. I had no choice but to use them if I wanted to stand a chance against a squad of men with automatic weapons.

I looked down at the shooter below me and saw that he was still moving. I bent my knees and leaped toward the ground. It was only a one-story fall. The man let out a high-pitched shriek as I used his jacket to drag him into one of the rooms.

I threw the man on the bed and pulled off his mask, only to realize it wasn't a man at all, but a woman with long, blond hair. And she was wearing a laser-proof vest.

The rest of the gunmen must have been wearing them too, and I'd shot them all center mass. They were all very much alive, even if stunned for the moment.

Pulling the demon hunters back out of my holsters, I ran back outside just as the soldiers stood up, ready to fire again. I took a deep breath and took four shots, and the gunmen's heads vaporized instantly.

***

"Tell me where your hideout is," I said calmly to the woman bleeding on my bed as I plugged my universal translator into my ears. The vest prevented my demon hunter from being a kill shot, but it still hurt like hell and left a gaping wound in the woman's stomach.

"I won't tell you anything, Godschurch scum."

I pressed on her stomach wound. Dean leaned over until his shadow covered the woman's face. "Tell me where the Godless are, or my friend will make you suffer."

The woman stared deep into my eyes. "She doesn't have the balls."

I looked over at Dean, who nodded at me, a tacit acknowledgment that I could continue turning the screws, which I did.

"Now, listen closely," I said, sneering at her, "and trust the words I'm saying to you. If you don't help me, I will dismember you one piece at a time until you scream for death, but death will never come. Tell me, do I have the balls for that?"

The woman dropped her eyes. I could see the fear fill them. "Fine. I will tell you. The—"

Before she could get out the sentence, a bullet flew through the window and nailed her straight in the head. I spun around and pulled out my demon hunters just as a second group of soldiers rushed forward into the lot.

From above, a machine gun fired at the soldiers and sent them rushing backward. The sound of our hover car boomed from the sky. It landed on the ground and stopped, thrusters blasting underneath it. Avrid was in the back seat, blasting the machine gun out the window. He turned to us. "Hurry!" he shouted. "Get in!"

Dean and I ran out to the car and fell into the back seat as the bullets whizzed around us.

Avrid handed me the machine gun, and I laid down cover fire while we rose into the air. Enemy bullets pinged off the undercarriage of the car as the thrusters kicked in and pushed us forward.

***

We settled down again in front of the print factory. Dean was shaking his head. "I don't like this, Rebecca. You're not a soldier anymore. You're an officer of the Godschurch."

"Not yet, I'm not. I'm still in training, remember? But even if I was, I've been a soldier for a lot longer than I've been with the church. You asked me to trust you, but now I need you to trust me. They are going to burn down that factory and every piece of evidence in there."

"Even if you're right, you were a sniper, Rebecca. You aren't qualified to take on a militia."

"Yes, I was a sniper, but that wasn't all I was. I've run enough extraction missions to know what I'm doing. I know you don't believe me, but please, just trust me."

"Fine. Then I'm coming with you."

I placed my hand on his shoulder. "I appreciate that, but have you ever been in combat before?"

Dean shook his head. "No."

"Then you'll be a liability in there. I know what I'm doing, okay? I will find the location of that base and take down any Godless scum I find."

I flung open the door to rush out, but Dean held me back by gripping my forearm with his strong right hand. "Be careful."

"That's not really how this works, Dean, but I'll do my best."

I shook him off and stomped out of the car. I'd refilled Avrid's machine gun cartridge before we landed, and between those, my demon hunters, and the revolvers, I felt like I could take down an army.

I kicked in the front door of the print shop and was greeted by the same receptionist as before, except now she had a bullet in her head and blood streaming down her face.

I smelled the gasoline before I even got past her desk. They weren't expecting me to live through the gunfight, so hopefully, they were taking their time lighting the place on fire.

Fat Teddy was in his office, his throat slit open. In his hand, he held a slip of paper. I pulled it from his fingers. It was a phone number as near as I could tell, but I would ask Avrid to make sure.

I made my way out of the office and turned toward the front door just as one of the Godless soldiers ran out of a nearby cubicle holding a lit Molotov cocktail. He didn't see me, so I had the element of surprise. I rushed up and placed my machine gun to the back of his head. "Don't move. Tell me where the base is, and I'll let you live."

"Either way, I'm dead." The soldier dropped the cocktail, and the fire spread quickly. "At least now you'll come with me."

Two more soldiers ran out from the back room, firing at me. I rushed down the hall as the hail of bullets embedded into the walls on either side. I smashed through the front door and rushed toward the hover car. "Move move move!"

The car lifted into the air just as I jumped inside. The soldiers rushed out of the building, and I picked them off one by one while Dean and Avrid laid down cover fire.

"I told you it was a trap!" Dean shouted.

"Yeah," I said, holding up the scrap of paper. "But I got this."

***

The Godschurch has amazing resources, let me tell you. It didn't take Avrid ten minutes to triangulate the phone number that led us to a hydroponic farm three hours away from the print shop. It was a different world than the desert we had just left. While the print shop had us dodging sand in a desert, this farm was set inside a lush forest with high grass and trees surrounding it.

"We're not going in half-cocked this time," Dean said.

"Fine, fine."

Dean exited the car first and pulled a Beretta out of the holster on his leg. I chose to use the machine gun for better cover fire. We snuck toward the house. The domed farmhouse was illuminated by the light of Ishtar glowing orange against the red, dark sky. My job was to hold back in case this was also a trap and make sure nobody escaped.

I wanted to go first, but Dean refused. I already pushed him previously when I'd gone into the print plant without him, and I couldn't argue with him again. Not so soon. Dean needed to assert himself as the leader of this mission, which meant he went out front—even if I thought it was a stupid idea.

The dewy, high-grass rose all the way to my thigh. I waited silently while Dean crept up to the front door of the farm and held up his arm for me to hold. That's when I saw the black-clad figure in a dark hood rushing out of the side door and across the field behind the house.

"Stop!" I shouted, but it was too late. I heard three beeps, and I knew it was a trap. "Dean! Move!"

But it was too late. Dean clicked the doorknob, and the house erupted into a fireball that knocked me backward. I cracked my head against the fiberglass of Avrid's hover car, and I was out.

***

I woke up to the sound of gunfire. A scream ripped the air above me, and Avrid fell next to my face, dead and bleeding out of his eye. The other eye stared at me blankly.

His blood pooled around my head, and I rolled to avoid it. Another flurry of fire, and Bob dropped beneath the car's undercarriage. I peered around the car and saw a silver ship in the distance. A squad of soldiers, all dressed in black, was rushing toward me.

Then, my vision blurred again. I felt the back of my head. It was my own blood that had been pooling around me, seeping from a nasty gash. Everything went white, and then I passed out again. The last thing I heard was the sound of the soldiers' feet to tell me I was screwed.

CHAPTER 16

I woke up to shaking and jerking all around me. Through my blurry vision, I could make out the back seat of a hover car where two hooded figures sat in front. I struggled to swing my hands free, but thick rope dug into my arms and legs. I screamed out, but my mouth was gagged.

"You can't escape," one of the figures said with a thick Russian accent. It couldn't be my translator because I'd left it in Avrid's hover car. The man must have spoken English.

I struggled to speak again but just ended up chewing on the gag in my mouth.

"If you promise not to scream, I will take off your gag," the Russian voice said. "Agreed?"

There wasn't much choice. I glowered at him with whatever venom I could muster, but then I nodded my head. Even though I was still bound with rope, at least with the gag removed, I might be able to bite off their fingers.

"Very good," the man said as he reached back to pull down my gag. "I know you don't like me much already, as I've kidnapped you, but this will all go a lot easier if you don't yell."

"I don't need to yell to tell you what a piece of scum you are."

The man smiled. "Me? You don't even know me."

"I know your type."

"My name is Dimitri, by the way, not that you asked."

"I don't care."

"I know, but I am a human, just like you. I have hopes and dreams. The last thing I ever thought was that I would be working with the Godless."

"Then why are you?"

"We do not always have a choice. My whole family died when the gods sent us through a black hole. Most of my friends died when they brought us back on their whim. There was nothing for me on my home planet, but the Godless, they gave me a new family—a new purpose—a new plan."

"A plan to wipe out all the gods."

He pulled a gun from his shoulder holster and pointed it at me. "Yes. I know. It sounds ridiculous, but I promise it's as good a plan as the gods have, for one. I can tell you are from Thebos, yes?"

"How do you know that?"

"Apologies, I looked through your wallet. I am from Moscow, on Earth, just like you. I fought in the Horde Wars. I assume from your age that you know it."

"I fought in it, too."

"I assumed as much, and what remained of my life was destroyed by the Horde."

"Then why aren't you mad at them instead of the gods?"

"I am mad at them, but they were right, you know. The gods, they don't care about us. They work for their own ends, not ours, and expect us to worship them. We are playthings to them. Don't you remember how bitter you were at the gods after the Horde Wars ended?"

I did remember. "I hated them."

"I know. This is why I ordered a hit on Velaska. She is the worst of them."

"You? It was you!" I struggled against my ropes. "You are the reason I am here! I got hired for that hit, and it nearly killed me."

"I did nothing except let you carry out my greatest wish, to kill a god. Anybody left on Earth would have relished that possibility, which is what the Godless have provided me. Do you not still wish that on them, death, for what they did to your family?"

I didn't have a good answer. The truth was that until I met with Velaska and promised to help find the people that tried to kill her, I felt the same way Dimitri did. The Godschurch offered me a way into Heaven, which was what drew me to them, but if the Godless had tried to recruit me themselves just a week ago, I would have happily joined.

"What happened to Dean?" I asked.

"He died, I'm sorry to say. A good man, but misguided. So full of bad ideas. He would protect the gods. I hope you are not as stubborn."

"Perhaps the same could be said for you," I said, trying to wriggle out from my ropes.

"Perhaps. I was never a good man, though." He sniffed. "Even before being sucked into the black hole, I was a drunk who cheated on his wife. She deserved better than me, but the gods had no right to take her away."

"You aren't much of a terrorist, I must say."

Dimitri took a deep breath. "I have been told I talk too much, that I have too much sympathy for those we kidnap. I cannot say whether that is true or not. I can say that you are not my enemy. You are confused. Hopefully, I can show you the way."

The planet Ishtar grew in the windshield with every passing moment. "Where are you taking me?"

"Ishtar. The base of the Godless, at least on this planet."

"How many bases are there?"

"How many worlds are there? Hundreds? Thousands? We have grown in number beyond anything the Godschurch could imagine. For now, sit back and know we are not the enemy—the gods are."

"I don't believe you. I don't believe you would tell me anything or speak to me at all if you weren't already intending to kill me, so I couldn't tell others."

Dimitri laughed. "You are too cynical for your own good." He turned the butt of his gun around in his hand and, in one motion, cracked me over the head with it.

***

When I woke up again, I was being dragged down a long, concrete corridor, a long line of cells on either side. Scraggily-looking men and women sat behind electric force fields that hissed and popped when they neared the edge of the cell.

Some cried out at me, begging for help, but for the most part, they just sat, resigned to their fate. None of them looked like fresh prisoners. They looked like they had been there for months, or even years. At least that meant the Godless didn't kill quickly. That would give me plenty of time to plan my escape.

I craned my neck backward to see two burly men dragging me down the hallway. My arms ached as they jerked me forward.

"Where am I?" I said.

"*Umalg!*" one of the men said in a low, guttural tone.

I didn't have to speak his language to understand that meant to shut up. We reached the end of the hallway, and the man put his hand on a keypad. Behind me, an electronic forcefield lowered, and they chucked me inside.

***

The guards came for me an hour later and hauled me into a room, dimly lit by the bare bulb above a metal, bolted-down table. They shackled me to the table and left without a word.

I had been interrogated before. I had been tortured before. I had survived before. I knew what they wanted. They wanted to know how to get into the Godschurch. If they could infiltrate the Godschurch, then they would be able to bring it down, along with every agent in the universe. With the Godschurch gone, they had free rein to kill every god.

Or maybe all they wanted was data.

Maybe they wanted the tracking information we had on every god in the cosmos. That would certainly make things easier for them to hunt and find the gods if they knew where they were.

I don't think they understood who they were messing with, though. Yes, I was new to the Godschurch, but not to torture methods. I was not new to pain. The longer I withheld the information they needed, the longer they would keep me alive. The minute I gave in, they would shoot me . . . like a dog.

Dimitri walked through the door and slapped a folder on the table."I want to tell you a story."

A common interrogation tactic. Start by being the good guy—the nice guy—and try to catch people off guard.

"I'm all ears. It's not like I have a lot of choice for entertainment here, and I love a good story."

"It's the story of a girl. She had a mother, father, two sisters, and even a cute little dog. She lives on the thousandth floor of a high rise in one of the nicest areas of the biggest city on her planet. Things are good for her. She has a nice life, a nice apartment, and she doesn't have to worry about much. Sound familiar so far?"

I pressed my lips into a smile. "It sounds like me, a thousand lifetimes ago."

Dimitri smiled. He had nice teeth. His face was kind, too, not like the guards who threw me in the cell. I could see why they used him for breaking prisoners. He looked like the kind of guy that didn't want to hurt me.

"Then you know the rest of the story. One fateful day, Apollo snapped his fingers, and the sun imploded into a black hole, sucking you and everything you love through it. Your mother died instantly. Her head collapsed from the pressure. That was merciful compared to your father's death. He took weeks to die after a rebar rod punctured his stomach, and it got infected. The doctors tried to help him, but there were just too many people to aid and not enough time. That's sad."

"It was sad, but I got over it."

"Of course you did," Dimitri said. "You are a survivor. That is what is clear from this file. You are a survivor. Even after the Horde Wars, you survived. Even after you shot your own sister in the head to prevent her suffering at the hands of the Horde, you still survived. Do you know how many survived the Horde Wars?"

"Not many."

"Twenty-six million, out of two billion before the Horde Wars and ten billion who fell into that black hole. The odds of you surviving were literally one in a million. How did you do it? Survive so long?"

"There are a lot of us that survived."

"Yes, but how did you do it?"

I looked up at him. "I move with the wind. When somebody offers me a better opportunity, I take it. That's how I've survived."

Dimitri smiled again. His perfect teeth shone through even in the dark room. "That's what I hoped you would say because I want to be your friend. I want you to join us."

"Join you?"

"Become one of us, the Godless. You would be an amazing asset. Fight back against the gods that have imprisoned you."

"You are the one who has imprisoned me."

"And this is your way out," he said, placing his hand on the dossier. "I will leave this here. Read through it. Remember what the gods did to you, and then, join us. We are a far cry better than either demons or gods."

***

I studied my file after they brought me back to my cell and removed my shackles. It laid out my entire life and every way the gods screwed me. It made special mention of Velaska being a traitor to humanity by working with the Horde, but it covered all the greatest hits, including dossiers on every god they could find and a list of their crimes.

"Hey," I heard from beyond the cell. Out of the darkness, a raggedy, white-bearded fellow wearing a toga crawled forward.

"What do you want?" I whispered back.

"What planet are you from?"

"Earth."

"No kidding? You know, I used to rule Earth back when I was a real god who didn't get locked up all the time."

"Come on. You're telling me that you are *the* god."

"No, really. I'm just Bacchus, one of many gods. I *was* the god of Earth for a while until Apollo arrested me, of course."

"You!" I shouted, jumping out of my cot. "You are the reason. You are the reason we fell into a black hole."

"Guilty. I mean, I was never tried, but yes. That's right. But before that, I watched over you guys pretty good."

"Except you set off an Apocalypse and left us living with demons."

Bacchus waved his arm dismissively. "No. That was Katrina. I set off a different Apocalypse."

"A *different* Apocalypse?"

He shrugged. "It was a long time ago."

"Why are you telling me this?" I snorted. "It's not making me want to help you."

"They said you were from the Godschurch," he replied. "Is that right?"

"In a manner of speaking, yes."

"You gotta get me out of here, man. I've been trapped here for years. I gotta get out of here."

"How much information have you given them?"

"As much as I know, man. I don't know that much. I wasn't really a big player when they were making stuff, you know. I liked to drink, and that made me forget things. That's why they put me on Earth to begin with, so I would be out of the way."

"Did you tell them where the Godschurch is?"

Bacchus shook his head. "No, but that's because I couldn't remember. I knew it was near a swirling thing. I told them where every entrance on Earth was, though."

"Great. They must have passed along that information when they hired me to kill Velaska."

"You were gonna kill Velaska? Why would the Godschurch want to kill Velaska?"

"They didn't. I was hired by the—you know what, all you need to know is that I'm a very new recruit."

"That's tough, man. Tough, but fair. So, can you help me?"

If I helped him, I was throwing my lot in with the Godschurch. It would be much easier to become a member of the Godless, live here, fight gods . . . but I couldn't get past the idea that I owed the gods something, even if they'd never given anything to me.

"I'll think about it," I said.

"What does that even mean?"

It meant I needed to think. When it came to working for demons, they were all the same, but now there was a battle raging between the gods and humanity, and those were two very different things. On the one hand, the Godless were my people, humans, and I felt a kinship with them. On the other, the Godschurch could give me eternal life. The Godless could fulfill my desire for revenge, but the Godschurch offered a new path, where I was better than what I had been for the last two decades—where I had a chance for redemption.

CHAPTER 17

I sat up throughout the night, thinking about whether I would stay loyal to the Godschurch or join the Godless in taking the gods down. I weighed the pros and cons of both, and honestly, they were just about even by the time the sun came up. However, I did come to one decision: if I was going to join the Godless, I had to be asked by the man in charge of the organization first.

When I flipped from Itty's gang, it was Piggy that convinced me to take the deal, not some peon with a nice smile. Next time I was dragged out of the cell, I would give Dimitri my demand.

My chance came the next morning when the burly guards dragged me into the interrogation room, chained me up, and once again, Dimitri sat down across from me.

"Have you made a decision?"

"No," I admitted. "But I have a deal for you."

"You have a deal for me?" Dimitri said, laughing. "This should be good. I would love to know what negotiating power you have."

"None," I replied. "Except that you want me to join your little organization, so you must see something in me, and that gives me a little bit of leverage."

Dimitri raised his eyebrows. "Go on."

I placed my palms flat on the table. "If you want me to work for you, your boss has to ask me himself."

"That's not how it works. The Godless don't have bosses. Everything is built on a decentralized network of power nodes that—"

"You can save it, Dimitri," I replied, flicking my hands at him. "Everybody's got a boss. None of this decentralized power crap. If you want me to turn on my employer, then drag me down to the boss and have him ask me or let me rot in a cell forever. Either way. It doesn't matter to me."

Dimitri thought for a second before he stood up without a word. He didn't have a smile on his face anymore. Instead, he wore a deep scowl.

***

The guards led me back to my cell and threw me inside. They hadn't gotten more than a hundred feet away before Bacchus crawled out of the darkness toward the edge of his cell.

"What are you waiting for?" he said. "Save me."

"That's not really my job anymore," I replied.

"You're a member of the Godschurch, aren't you?" he sniveled. "Your job is to save the gods, and I am a god, so save me."

I opened my file and started reading it again. "I might not be a member of your church for very long, and either way, I've only been an agent there for a day, so I think you are tugging on the wrong strings there, buddy. I have no special love for you."

"Money? Is it money you want? I have money. I can give you as much money as you want. Power? I can make you powerful. I can grant you any wish you desire!"

I slid the folder below my eye line and stared at him. "I want my family back. How about that? Can you make that happen?"

His eyes sunk low onto the floor. "You would not want them back, even if I could give them to you. Trust me on that."

"Buddy, I don't trust you at all."

***

I was rereading my file for the twentieth time when a pair of feet clipped toward me. These weren't the slow, plodding steps of the goons who dragged me down the hall. No. These were rapid-fire stomping. It was Dimitri rushing down the hall to see me.

"Come with me," he said, placing his hand on the keypad.

The electric field came down, and I walked toward him. "Aren't you nervous I might kill you? Don't you want to put the cuffs on me?"

"Trust me," Dimitri said, turning on his heels. "You couldn't kill me if you tried, but if you tried, there would be a hundred men on you in a second. Follow me."

Dimitri walked fast down the hallway. I struggled to follow behind him. "What's the rush?"

"You don't want to keep the boss waiting, and you are keeping him waiting. He's prone to order executions for tardiness. Of course, I wouldn't be surprised if he ordered you shot just for demanding an audience with him."

"Well, if he does, then we'll be in the same place we are now, and at least I won't have to wait. I hate waiting."

Dimitri turned the corner and led me into a massive room filled with black-hooded soldiers staring up at a screen that was raised high onto the wall. Below it, the symbol of the Godless, red plateau with a Greek agora on it, all crossed out with a giant X, was painted on the black wall. The screen was pixelated and grainy, but I could make out a shrouded figure on the screen, standing tall.

"Ah, Dimitri," the voice said in a tinny, high-pitched voice that grated on my ears. "Is this *she* who would make demands of *me*?"

Dimitri bowed. "Yes, sir."

"Come, child," the voice said. "I hear you have something to ask me."

The hooded figures surrounding me chanted in low tones as I walked into the dimly lit room toward the screen. I didn't know why they chose to wear robes now when they hadn't during the rest of my visit, but it was creepy.

"I don't think it's what I have to ask you," I said, walking up to the screen. "It's what you have to ask me. I heard you would like me to join you, and I want to hear it straight from your mouth."

"I like you," the figure replied, deadpan. "But I do not ask for disciples. They come to me. They beg me for salvation from their wretched lives, and they find nourishment in my bosom."

I chuckled. "I don't care about any of that. I care about money. My loyalty is as solid as the money that it's built on. If you can pay me better, I work for you. Otherwise, I don't."

"Is that all you care about?"

"It's not all I care about, but it's a good start. It's kept me alive this long. I must bring something to the table for you to call all your—whatever these are called—to gather here, wearing hoods. So, what'll it be? Can you pay me what I'm worth, or do you shoot me in the head?"

"I did not call them, child. They heard I would be here, and they came to show their reverence for me."

"I don't have any of that. I just want the money."

The figure hesitated for a moment, deep in thought. "Money it shall be, then. My countenance shines down to all in whatever way they require."

"I just had a god offer me all the money I could want if I set him free, so I'm eager to see your offer."

But the offer never came because that's when the bombs dropped.

The screen cut out as the building quaked around me. Suddenly, three explosions rocked the inside of the building, dropping the ceiling into the room and crushing the television. The hooded figures screamed and ran toward the exits, but too late. The building collapsed around them. I was already running down the hall, away from the assembly room.

"You!" Dimitri shouted at me. He was right on my heels.

I smashed him in the face as he went for his gun. He collapsed below me, which sucked because I needed his hand to save Bacchus. I pull his unconscious body through the halls back to the prison. Bacchus rushed to the front of his cell when I reached his cell at the end of the corridor.

"Were you serious about your offer? All the money I could ever want?"

He fingered his beard anxiously. "Yes. Yes. All of it!"

I placed Dimitri's hand on the keypad, and the electric gate came down. "One thing first. You have to free the rest of these people."

"Done!" Bacchus shouted.

The electric forcefields turned off at the sound of his voice. The prisoners screamed with joy, and they rushed to Bacchus to hug him. Just in time, he grabbed my arm, snapped his fingers, and we disappeared.

***

We reappeared outside of the building. The prisoners that had managed to latch onto Bacchus before he snapped his fingers released their grip. Now they were free, and they ran away from him, the building still crumbling to the ground behind them.

Surrounding the building were a dozen ships with the Godschurch's all-seeing eye symbol on them, firing lasers at the roof and walls. As the hooded figures of the Godless fled out the building, agents ran forward and arrested them.

Tress stood in front of it all, hands on her hips, enjoying her victory. When she saw me materialize with Bacchus, she marched toward me. "Agent Lobdell. Good to see you alive."

I nodded. "It's good to be alive, ma'am. I'm sure you know Bacchus. He was once the god of my home planet."

"Good to see you again, Bacchus. We thought you were dead, or worse."

"Worse?" he asked.

"Helping the Godless," Tress replied as the laser exploded on the roof of the Godless compound. "That would be a fate worse than death, in my estimation."

He nodded solemnly. "Yes . . . that would be bad."

"How did you find us?" I asked.

"Agent Dean—before…he planted a tracker on you just in case."

"He was a brave man," I replied. "He will be missed." Was he brave? I didn't know. It was just something you said in moments like this, no matter if they were true or not.

"Yes, he will." Tress pointed down to my hands. "Is that one of them?"

I looked down. Dimitri was unconscious at my feet. I had forgotten I had hold of him when we disappeared. "Yes, ma'am. This is one of them. Second in command, I think."

"And the leader?" Tress asked, placing handcuffs on Dimitri. "Is he here?"

I shook my head. "No. He was on a video feed, not in person, but we'll find him."

Tress whistled, and two agents came to drag Dimitri away. She turned on her heels and walked away as well. "Yes, we will."

"Don't worry," I said to Bacchus. "They'll never know you helped them."

Bacchus smiled. "And they'll never know you almost joined the Godless."

"Almost . . . but didn't. Two very different things."

"Exactly."

***

They held Dean's funeral the next day. I didn't know whether he was a good guy or not, but he covered my back when things got tight, and where I'm from, that was what really mattered.

The funeral was a short affair. We gathered at the front of the Godschurch. Dean had been laid in a casket, and the masters pushed him toward the center of the universe swirling around us.

"May the universe carry you back to the Source," Master Jamil said. "May you be absorbed back into the center of all creation."

The masters turned from the door, and the funeral was done. Everybody else went toward the altar of the church to descend into the command center, but I stayed, watching the casket fall into oblivion. After a moment of silence, Velaska placed her hand on my shoulder.

"He was a good agent . . ."

"And a good man? Usually, they say, 'and a good man.'"

Velaska shrugged. "I have no idea if he was a good man or not. You would know better than I. After all, you slept with him."

"He was as good as I've known a man to be."

"Yes, I'm sure he would not have offered his services to the Godless in a moment of weakness."

I couldn't argue. "Can you blame me, though? They are way more my speed. I don't even know what I'm doing here."

Velaska flashed me a smile. "Sure you do. The Godless give you a sense of vengeance, which is all you ever wanted, but here, you have a purpose, which is what you need. Vengeance has gotten you this far, but purpose, real purpose, that will get you everything."

***

Velaska followed me down the old stairs to the Godschurch headquarters, where Tress was already back to barking orders from the command center.

"Ah, Agent Lobdell," Tress said, turning to me. "So nice of you to finally join us, agent."

"I think you mean probationary agent."

She shook her head. "No, I mean agent. If you still want to join, that is."

Velaska whispered behind me, "I didn't tell her. If you are going to stay, then stay. One hundred percent. Full commitment."

I looked back at Velaska, then down at the shield, and finally back at Tress. For the first time, I wanted something. I really wanted something. I wasn't just surviving, I wanted to thrive.

Crap. Now good things were happening to me. That couldn't be a good sign.

BOOK 2

"There's Every Reason to Fear"

CHAPTER 1

I rounded the corner of the bazaar, pulling my revolvers from their holsters. Thousands of people and vendors milled together on the cramped streets. "Get on the ground!" I shouted. "I'm not going to say it a second time."

The man in front of me grinned like he was playing a game. This was no game, though. He was a scumbag terrorist determined to detonate a bomb, but if I had anything to say about it, he'd soon swallow those teeth. His greasy hair and thick beard blew in the thick gusts of wind that weaved through the merchants selling their wares.

The scumbag was a bomber named Fezzick, a known affiliate of the Godless, who were a group of radical terrorists bent on killing every god in the universe. He'd been hired to take out the god Persephone on the one day of the year she descended from Mount Olympus to walk among the living. I was assigned to keep her safe, and I was currently failing at that mission since I didn't know where Fezzick was going to strike. I locked eyes with him as he stood motionless across the bazaar. He hadn't moved in thirty seconds, except to raise his arms above his head.

"I have something to tell you," he said in perfect English. This planet didn't speak Earth's English, and I didn't have my universal translator in since the earbuds fell out whenever I ran, so he must have learned the language of my home planet somehow.

"I don't care." I squeezed the handle of my gun tightly, doing everything in my power to prevent myself from pulling the trigger. "All I care about is where you planted the bombs."

"That's what I'm trying to tell you," he said, opening his hand to reveal a silver trigger with a red button. "I have placed one in this bazaar. If you don't let me go and stop following me, I will blow it up and disintegrate all these nice people, including you."

I took a step forward. "You think I believe that?"

Fezzick's beard twitched, then the sides of his lips curled. "Look into my eyes and tell me if I am lying."

Detecting lies was my strong suit. It's how I had brought down three Godless terrorist cells, each on different planets, in the past six months. I single-handedly stopped five assassination plots against gods initiated by the Godless. Now, staring deep into the bomber's bright blue eyes, I detected no lies.

"You'll never pull the trigger," I said. "You will be vaporized with us. Then you'll die."

"That's where you're wrong. My life is meaningless. If it serves the cause, then I would gladly die for it."

Fezzick's thumb twitched. I fired one bullet from my gun and blew it off. I was a crack shot, and even in the wind, I could shoot through the center of a silver dollar from a quarter mile away.

"You crazy bitch!" he shouted, dropping to his knees. Blood spurted across the bazaar as men and women fled from me. They didn't know I was the good guy, the one who had just saved all their lives. All they knew was that I pulled the trigger.

I stepped carefully toward the bomber with my gun drawn. "Drop the detonator."

"As you wish."

He opened his mangled hand, and the detonator fell to the ground. I leaped for it, but it was too late. The detonator landed on the trigger, and the red button clicked down. For a moment, an intensely long, silent moment, there was nothing. Then behind me, a green wall of fire exploded through the bazaar, vaporizing half a block of innocents in an instant.

He had done it. He ran up the street past a line of weeping peasants who were screaming out at Persephone for help. I had two options: calm the citizens or catch the bomber. At that moment, I was woefully unprepared to deal with the citizen's grief, but I could make sure the bomber didn't get away. I could make sure Fezzick paid for what he did to the poor people in that bazaar.

***

I've killed a lot of people in my day. I've fought in my share of wars. I've looked men in the eyes as they begged for their lives and then blown their heads off. You must be cold, callous, and resolute in the idea that your bullet will end the life of the person you are looking at—but bombers don't have that problem.

Bombers could be a thousand miles away, watching TV, when their bomb exploded. They could set a bomb to detonate when they aren't even in the same country. I've seen bombs discharged decades after the coward who made them died.

For that reason, I've always found bombers weak, even when I fought alongside them in the Horde Wars. They didn't have the force of will to look their target in the eyes before they took their life. There was no honor in that.

I spent much of my adult life as a sniper, sitting in silent areas waiting for the perfect shot, and people often compared us—snipers and bombers—because we were both so far removed from our victims.

The job descriptions couldn't be further apart. As a sniper, I waited for hours, days—sometimes weeks—to get the perfect shot. I knew everything about my target. I knew their hopes, their dreams, and their goals. I knew when they slept and how they took their coffee. I knew them better than their best friend, and still, at the end of the day, I pulled the trigger.

That took an icy resolve.

Bombers? They mixed chemicals together and blew stuff up. They didn't care who they killed, as long as it was enough people to make a statement, and that made them weaklings. There was some dignity in being a sniper, but none in detonating a bomb.

Everyone rationalized their role in life, though. We tried to make ourselves the protagonist of our own story—the good guy. The Godless thought they were the good guys. They thought the universe would be better without gods, and maybe they're right, but they were willing to kill innocents to get there. That's where I drew the line. That's what separated the good guys from the bad guys—whether or not they valued life. I didn't always if I was being honest. For years, decades even, I didn't, but that all changed.

I haven't always been the good guy, but I was trying to be better than my baser instincts.

***

It wasn't hard to follow Fezzick as he snaked through the narrow streets of the bazaar. After all, he was bleeding profusely from his thumbhole, and that left a trail through the sinewy streets. A streak of blood on a vendor's table told me to turn right, and another told me to turn left down a tiny alley.

Even with the trail, Fezzick moved quicker than I could follow on the crowded streets. After taking three more turns—fighting the avalanche of people along the way—I finally broke free into a large square, where hundreds of cars and thousands of people zipped one way or another.

Usually, the streets of Zetaria wouldn't be so busy, but today people were making their final preparations for the festival, which would occur at sunset, where Persephone would emerge from the great tunnel, like a child from its mother's womb, and greet her adoring subjects.

It was the perfect day for a bombing. Tonight was the holiest night of the year, and at sunset, there would be a jubilant celebration. Until then, the streets were packed with people trying to buy their last bits of food and find the perfect presents for their children.

Because of the traffic, I lost Fezzick's trail. I looked down at the dusty ground, but the throngs of people had buried any droplets of blood under the sand.

There was only one thing to do. I'd have to tell Persephone the truth.

***

"What do you mean you lost him, Rebecca?" Persephone yelled from her bathtub. The people of Zetaria spared no expense to make sure their god was treated lavishly when she descended from Mount Olympus. They showered her with the finest luxuries in the world. She bathed in a marble tub in the middle of a room with vaulted ceilings and detailed murals covering the walls. Two handmaidens brushed out her long, red hair while another fed her pomegranate seeds, and two more filed her nails.

It was this kind of pampering that so angered the Godless. They believed humanity had evolved beyond the need for gods. In my short time with the Godschurch, I'd traveled all over the universe, and I hadn't seen anything on any of the worlds I'd been to that made me think humans aligned with the Godless's ethos. As far as I could tell, humanity was as infantile and directionless as the day we'd emerged from the primordial ooze.

"I mean, I had him for a moment," I said meekly from the corner of the room. "And then an explosion went off, and I lost him."

Persephone smiled. It was the kind of smile people only used to cover up their seething anger—the kind I rarely saw among the paupers but often experienced among the elite and powerful.

"So. You not only failed to capture the bomber, but you also let an explosion go off in my bazaar. Tress told me you were one of the best she had. I hope that is true."

Tress was my boss and leader of the Godschurch officers. The Godschurch was the church of the gods— every god in the universe—and its mission was to protect them from harm. While there was a religious order to the Godschurch, the officers of the church did the nitty gritty work. We live in a base underneath the church, which rotates around the nexus of the universe.

The nexus of the universe—where Cronus first emerged into this universe and birthed the stars, which birthed the planets, which birthed life, whose evolution created the need for the first gods—was a great ball of energy that spun the entire universe around its axis. It had existed since the beginning of time itself.

Information on the gods flowed to us from every corner of the universe, and from the nexus, we captured and processed it all. We kept tabs on every god in the universe and assigned protection details to them as needed. Eons ago, the Godschurch protected them from a range of dangers from the big, like Bifrost giants, to the small, like a small sect of nonbelievers with plans of world domination. Now, though, every threat came squarely from the Godless, who infected all the corners of the universe with their anti-god philosophies.

"I am one of the best, ma'am." My words shook in my throat. I didn't believe what I was saying. I had only been a member of the Godschurch for six months, and while I was the first officer to take down a Godless compound and had captured more Godless terrorists than the other officers combined, the truth was, I hadn't even made a dent in the millions of members of the Godless. No matter how much I fought against them, their numbers kept growing.

"I fear for the Godschurch," Persephone said, "if you are their best and brightest."

The truth was that the Godschurch didn't have many agents left, but I kept that to myself. For every successful raid on a Godless compound, there was another that ended up with entire teams of officers killed. Maybe I was their best officer, but that was only by default. There simply weren't that many agents left.

"You don't have anything to worry about," I said, refusing to let the fear show in my voice. "I have a plan."

Persephone let out a deep sigh and threw back her head. "Oh, you have a plan, do you? Is that what you told my poor mother?"

Persephone's mother, Demeter, was my biggest failure to date. I'd set up a sting to expose a Godless splinter cell on Gilpeia, a planet that was flourishing under Demeter's guidance. She trusted in the Godschurch to protect her, so she agreed to be the bait in our sting operation. Everything went as planned . . . until we walked into a Godless ambush that killed Demeter with a shot to the head. She disintegrated on the spot, and the ensuing battle killed ten more of our best officers. I barely escaped with my life.

"That won't happen again, ma'am. I promise."

Persephone laughed a bitter, sarcastic laugh. "That's rich. As if a promise from you means anything."

"Do I still have your support?" I asked. "Or would you like me to return to the Nexus?"

"I don't have much choice, do I, Miss Lobdell? I don't see any other officers around to protect me."

"No, ma'am. You have two choices. Go back up to Mount Olympus or stay here and receive the praise you so richly deserve . . . under my protection."

I learned long ago that flattery quickly endeared you to humans, and it worked even better on gods. They were vain, selfish, and egotistical creatures, even more so than the humans they created.

"Very well," Persephone said. "But remember, my safety is on your head."

"I accept that."

I heard the ting of the grenade landing in the bathhouse before I saw it roll along the floor. I launched myself over the tub, knocking it over, spilling the water all over the room and covering Persephone as we slid along the floor. The explosion from the grenade vaporized the handmaids instantly. As the green flames cascaded through the room, Persephone snapped her fingers, and we disappeared from sight.

CHAPTER 2

Every god is bestowed with the ability to disappear at will with the snap of their fingers. When they disappeared, they did so in a flash of light that they call—unoriginally, I might add—"the light." They can disappear and reappear anywhere on a planet with just a thought, though interstellar travel taxes their body.

Persephone used her light to disappear from her bathing room and reappear on the street in front of the smoldering building. The taste of pomegranates lingered in my mouth. It was no secret that every god had a different taste to their light, and Persephone's tasted like pomegranates dipped in sugar.

A small crowd gathered around and stared at the goddess who had appeared in front of them. Though Persephone was one of the most accessible gods in the universe—she made an annual appearance, even—none of the inhabitants of her planet had ever seen her so close . . . let alone dripping wet and naked as a baby. Her yearly sojourns to the planet were a source of contempt for many gods, seen as a great weakness that she needed such adulation from those she governed, but those gods never left Mount Olympus nor spoke to humanity at all, so I gave her credit for intermingling with her people.

Persephone looked down at the puddle of water pooling in the sand underneath her. With another snap of her fingers, her body turned from naked to clothed in a long, ornate golden toga, her face covered with flawless makeup.

"If you could do that . . . why even take a bath?" I asked.

"It's nice to be pampered," she said matter of factly. "Also, who are you to ask me anything?" She pointed to the smoldering wreckage of the bathhouse. "Do you see what just happened to me in there? I could have been killed."

"But you weren't killed, ma'am, because I was there to save you."

Persephone stared at me for a long moment, then another. The wheels turned in her head, wondering if she should flay me alive or walk away. Finally, in a snit, she pulled her finger slowly up to my face.

"This is unacceptable. UNACCEPTABLE, Rebecca!"

"I know, ma'am, and we are working on it. Trust me."

"Trust you? Trust you! You almost got me killed!"

I tried to pay attention, even if I didn't like being harangued like a child, but my eyes wandered from her finger to the street behind it. When my eyes focused, I saw Fezzick staring at the wreckage before he spun around and turned up the street.

"Yes, ma'am," I replied, not knowing what she just said. "Now, if you'll excuse me. I have to—"

I didn't wait to finish my statement. I bolted down the street to catch the bomber as he disappeared around a corner and out of sight. This time I wouldn't fail. This time, I would be bigger, faster, and stronger. This time, I would catch the bastard...

...Except, when I turned the corner, he had vanished again.

I pulled the universal translator out of my pocket and plugged it into my ears. All seventeen million human dialects and languages from every corner of the galaxy were contained in the device, which was no bigger than a silver dollar. Flipping the switch, a blue glow emanated from the device and crawled up the headphones until my earbuds pulsated a neon blue hue.

I walked up to the closest vendor. "Excuse me," I said when he turned to me. "Have you seen a man missing one thumb?"

The vendor, a short, pudgy man with a bristled beard, shook his jowls at me before a customer caught his attention, and he turned to help them.

I inched forward down the street. Fezzick didn't know I had seen him, and I wanted to keep it that way. I scanned the vendors haggling their wares under cheap awnings, selling everything from exotic fruits and meats to cheap rugs they tried to pawn off to tourists as originals. I could barely hear my own thoughts above the din of the market, but I kept my eyes and ears sharp to capture anything out of the ordinary.

Of course, I was on a planet that I had never visited before, so everything seemed out of the ordinary for me. The gods, in their infinite wisdom, started every planet the same way. They created the water, and the life, and the microbes, and then let it grow into humanity. While a planet was first booting up, all the gods chipped in to govern until it became sustainable.

They seeded humanity with the knowledge of the gods, then most of them left to start a new civilization, leaving one god in charge of each sector. These gods are called God. They are praised. They are exalted, and they are tasked with keeping things running in the way the gods would approve.

On some planets, like this one, the God did a good job of ruling. On others, like Earth—well, it was a bit of a shit show. We got Bacchus, who hadn't done us any favors. Each planet had its own unique flair, that's for sure, and different traditions grew on every planet, just like they grew in every culture around the world.

For instance, while I walked from one end of the street to another, examining every face I passed, I overheard two men bartering a child for an expensive car. In the back of my head, I disapproved of this trade, but it wasn't my planet nor my customs and had nothing to do with the pressing task at hand. And then I spotted those bright blue eyes. Fezzick was strolling pleasantly along through the streets as if he didn't just blow up a bazaar and try to kill a god.

This time, I knew better than to spook him. I crept slowly, using the people walking through the streets as cover until I was right behind him. I pulled my gun out and dug it deep into his head. "I've got you now," I whispered into his ear as I yanked his arms behind him and locked them in a pair of electric handcuffs.

"Yes. It would appear that you have found me. If only I didn't have ten pounds of C-4 strapped to my body."

"You're bluffing."

"Feel for yourself."

I patted down his back and chest. Sure enough, I felt the outline of a bomb vest. I ripped open his coat and saw ten packs of C-4 bricks strapped to him, all wired into a wireless detonation trigger under his chin.

He watched my face as I studied the explosives. "I don't return in ten minutes, my friend will blow up my vest with me in it."

"That's not a very good friend."

"Contrary, we are doing humanity's work. The only work that matters in the universe anymore, and there is no greater aim than dying to defend it."

I spun him around and glared right into his heartless eyes. "Take me to him."

He shook his head. "No. And if you force me to take you there, I will get us lost until we blow up. I have no fear of death, you see. I know what awaits me. Do you?"

I did fear death—specifically because I didn't know what awaited me. It's one of the main reasons I joined the Godschurch. I was a horrible person when I lived on Earth. I thought for sure I would go to Hell, but after being caught in an explosion, I saw a glimpse of Heaven and realized I might have a shot at going there, even if I had been a sinner for most of my life. The Godschurch allowed me to redeem myself from all the horrible things I had done during my darker days, with the slim hope I might win enough brownie points to gain everlasting peace upon my death.

I spat. "I fear nothing."

"Then you and I are the same. Now, you have two choices. You can let me go, and hope that the tracker you place on me will find its way to my friends. Or you can hold me here and wait until my friend blows us both up. I promise you, I find either way acceptable."

I let go of his collar and spun him around. I wanted so badly to watch him explode, but I couldn't afford to waste my only lead. I unfastened his cuffs and stuffed them in my pocket, then placed a tracker on his jacket, just like he said I would. As a secondary measure, I dropped another one into the heel of his shoe.

"You watch yourself," I said to him, pushing him off into the crowd.

***

"So, you're telling me that you let the terrorist go again, Miss Lobdell?" Persephone was standing at the back of her float, where artists had arranged a fifty-foot-high garden of flowers shaped like her face. It was the final float in the parade that snaked its way through the streets in her honor.

"Yes, but I have a plan."

The parade had already begun two hours earlier, and there was still an hour left before she exited the tunnel and made her appearance for all the world to see. Marching bands and hundreds of floats would line the streets before her.

"Yes, you've said that, but look me in the eyes and tell me that your plan isn't likely to get me killed."

I tried to look her in the eyes but couldn't. Instead, I looked at the floor. "I can't, ma'am. All I know is that if you are down here on the planet's surface, those terrorists won't leave. They will keep trying and keep trying, but if you leave, so will they, and we'll have missed our chance to find the sons of bitches that killed your mother."

I didn't know if these were the exact people who killed Persephone's mother, but the Godless were responsible for that attack, and I could tell by the softening of her face that my words landed with her. She paused for reflection, her big, green eyes narrowing.

"I will give you one hour and no more. If you can find the terrorists by then, I will stay and finish out the day. Otherwise, I will be gone. I'm sorry, but I am not as trusting as my mother. I am no lamb for you to send to slaughter."

My eyes still on the floor, I nodded. "That is fair, your grace. Thank you."

I pivoted on my heels and ran out of the tunnel where they kept the last of the floats. Outside, the entire city had turned out in celebration. Thousands of people threw flower petals, which floated down from the buildings onto the street and created a soft layer of beautiful red, pink, and white.

I stomped over the petals as I pulled out my GPS tracker. The bomber thought he was smart, telling me exactly what I would do, but I made a bet that he didn't think I would follow through and place a tracker on him—people typically expect you to change tactics when they call you out. Even if he did find the first tracker, the one he predicted, I bet he wouldn't find both.

My device beeped when it turned on, and sure enough, it showed two trackers in two different locations around the city. Hopefully, that meant he only found one and not the other. It was time to find out.

***

I followed the first tracker in a sewer underneath the subway line, where a rat munched happily on the edges of its metallic frame. Clearly, Fezzick found that one, which might have led to him finding the other one, but I suspected he was so proud at finding the first tracker, he didn't even think to look for the second.

The second tracker led me to a house on the edge of the city that hadn't seen a kind hand in a long time. The windows were broken, the paint chipped. Weeds and thickets grew in the front lawn. The rusted gate around the property bowed and swung open, smashing against the iron in the breeze. I heard a group of at least half a dozen people talking and laughing inside.

Since joining the Godschurch, I spent most of my days hunting humans. My revolvers could shoot a man dead, no problem, but when I didn't have much margin for error, I called on my demon hunters. Demon hunters had been designed and used by the Horde army to kill gods. A single charge could disintegrate a god in an instant. I was there when it happened to Demeter. Since we'd defeated the Horde army, we took their weapons and modified them, using them to kill the demons who terrorized us. The Godless had taken to using them the old-fashioned way—to assassinate gods.

My guns ready, I crept up to the door. If the bomber had friends inside, then this was a job for a SWAT team, but Tress didn't give me one. She told me to handle it myself. There were too few agents and too many gods to protect.

Fezzick I needed alive, but the rest were nothing. I closed my eyes and took a deep breath, then kicked the lock off the door and smashed through it with all my might. Inside, seven men watched the parade on a screen.

Fezzick smiled at me. "You are just in time." He pointed at the screen, which showed the decorated tunnel Persephone would be coming out of any minute. I wasn't going to make it back in time to prevent her from returning to Mount Olympus, but at least she would be safe.

I had hardly finished that thought when an explosion rocked Persephone's tunnel. It collapsed in on itself, and green flames plumed out into the street. Screams echoed as the smoke cloud covered the camera, and the screen went dark.

CHAPTER 3

The Godschurch sent me an extraction team to help me bring Fezzick and his friends back to our holding cells. Our base and the jail cells located within it rested under an eons-old cathedral dedicated to the gods. It took ten thousand cherubs two thousand years to finish and housed the Masters of the church along with every sacred text, tapestry, and shroud accumulated by the church over its eons working for the gods. The only entrance to our base was through the cathedral.

Every planet with human life had an entrance to the Godschurch. In fact, most of them had several. Persephone's planet was no exception. The closest church entrance to Fezzick's house was through a rundown mosque in an unused square on the outskirts of town.

To enter the Godschurch, Angus had to grant you permission. Angus was the kindly, old bag of wrinkles who acted as steward of the church. If he deemed you worthy, he sent down a beam of light to your church which connected directly to the Godschurch's home base.

We waited at the entrance to the Godschurch for an hour until the old man finally sent a beam of light to retrieve us. This light was different from the gods' light, but it was based on the same magical principles. Angus had initiated it rather than the gods, and it used some sort of technology I would love to explain but never understood fully. Anytime Angus tried to explain it to me, I dozed off before he got very far.

We floated through the ether until the door to the Godschurch opened on the other side. In front of me, a hundred feet high, stood the interior of the gothic

Godschurch, painted floor to ceiling with reliefs of the gods in great battle. Hundreds of pillars rose into the balconies, hand-carved with ivy and flowers through billions of hours of tedious labor. Stained-glass windows shone down on the mahogany pews beneath them.

Several dozen members of the Godschurch slouched in the pews and listened to Master Jamil speak. The other two masters of the Godschurch sat behind him on golden thrones with an expression of utter solemnity on their faces. The masters, including Jamil, all looked the same, with strong jaws and salty black hair adorned in red robes which covered their frail frames.

The extraction team trudged into the church behind me, carrying the bombers. We headed toward the command center entrance located under the gem-encrusted totem of the all-seeing eye, hanging behind the masters against the back wall. Nobody took notice of the dozen armed guards in full battle fatigues stomping through the church. Instead, the worshipers' eyes remained transfixed on Master Jamil.

I turned to Angus, who waddled up to me in his red crushed velvet robe, smiling under the folds of his fat and wrinkles.

"Were you successful, Rebecca?" Angus said to me.

"I found the bombers," I replied, trying to obfuscate. "If that's what you mean."

"And Persephone?"

I placed my hand softly on his shoulder. Angus was friends with all the gods and took it particularly hard when one fell. To me, this was a job, but to him, it was a calling.

"I'm sorry, Angus."

His lip quivered, and he turned away from me. It never got easier to tell Angus one of his friends was dead, but I felt it my duty to be honest with him, even if he hated me for it.

I walked down the center aisle of the church. Master Jamil glowered at me from under the bejeweled and gilded all-seeing eye, which hung twenty feet high behind the altar.

"And with that," Master Jamil said. "Let us pray."

I slid into a pew, bowed my head low, and closed my eyes. I wasn't a religious person, but the gods brought it out of me sometimes. After all, Heaven and Hell were real—I knew that for a fact—and I worked for a church that protected gods, so it was hard not to have a little religious zeal seep into my bones.

"We do not pray to any one god, but to the Source itself. We give back to it what we put into it, and we protect it the best we can with all the days of our lives."

The Source was the essence of all the power in the universe. It's what Cronus used to create the universe, the gods, and every human in existence. There is only a finite amount of energy in the Source, and when we die, our energy replenishes the Source for a new generation.

"Open your eyes," Master Jamil said. "And look upon your fellow parishioners. Take them in, and know they want the best for you, and we want the best for the universe."

I smiled at a couple of faces I recognized: Velaska, the god who brought me to the Godschurch originally, Doctor Palmer, who headed up the medical division—her kind eyes and inviting smile were a pleasant change from Tress, who glared at me from her pew in the front of the church.

I was in for trouble.

***

"So, what you are telling me, Agent Lobdell," Tress said while the rest of the parishioners filed away, some to their rooms and others out the doors to their respective planets around the universe, "is that you let another god die?"

"That's one way to think about it," I said, rubbing my neck.

"I know we're understaffed. I know you're undertrained, but you can't keep letting gods die. It's literally antithetical to our mission statement."

"We found a Godless cell and captured it."

"That cell is useless now, Lobdell," she replied. "They outlived their usefulness the moment Persephone died."

"They might have valuable information—"

"No, they won't," Tress said. "You don't get to weasel out of this botched shit show of—"

"Language!" Angus said, sweeping the altar. "Language."

Tress gave Angus a sour look. She didn't like being interrupted, but he didn't care. Nobody knew how old he was, but, as of yet, I couldn't find anybody who was a member of the Church before he started, including the Masters, and for that—simply outliving everybody else— he earned respect.

"Just find the main base, Lobdell." She spoke through gritted teeth. "Otherwise, Persephone is just another death in vain." Tress stormed away to the back of the church and down the spiral staircase that led to the command center.

"She's not wrong, you know." I heard Velaska say behind me. I turned, and her bright blue eyes calmed me for a moment. Velaska wasn't a calming force in my life, but there was no doubt her smile radiated warmth.

"Of course she's not," I exhaled in a huff. "'Don't let gods die' is kind of our mission statement."

"It's also the reason I brought you here in the first place."

"I thought it was so you could use me as leverage with the Masters to get what you wanted?"

Velaska stumbled for a moment. "I—well, yes. That is one reason. But I am one of the gods you are supposed to be protecting, and I can't say that I feel very safe."

My eyes narrowed. "I promise you that I am doing all I can."

She placed her hand on my chin, gently. "Yes, my love, that is what I fear."

* * *

"Tell me where the Godless base is!"

Fezzick just stared at me with dead eyes. The interrogation room was hot and cramped and smelled bad, being right next to the jail cells. I had already gone through his friends, and none of them gave up any information. I doubted they had any information to give. They were willing patsies for Fezzick's plan, but he was clearly the mastermind.

Finally, he laughed at me. "There is no base. We work in a decentralized system, each operating independently from each other."

I punched him in his ugly face, and his head snapped back before smashing into the table. I'd roughed him up once already while arresting him and his friends, and he seemed to get off on it. Still, I couldn't help myself. His face was so punchable, and the demand for results loomed over me more with each passing hour.

Every day Tress pressured me more insistently to bring down the Godless, as more gods died due to their actions and our negligence. I was the only person who'd ever taken down a Godless base, and for that, I became the de facto head of the task force. It was nearly impossible to protect the gods these days. Since I'd started, over two hundred gods across the universe had been murdered by the Godless. And as more people joined the ranks of the Godless's terrorist network, they were able to send out more and more splinter cells to carry out assassinations and massacres.

We used to receive a tip a day from our informants about a new splinter cell forming, but in the last few months, we've received one an hour, every hour, for weeks. Meanwhile, there were only seven thousand agents of the Godschurch in the field, and another five hundred as administration staff, so our numbers were stretched thin. While a Godless splinter cell could be made up of a rag-tag group of idiots with bombs, every Godschurch officer was an elite soldier and one who believed in the church's methods, which wasn't easy to find.

I slammed my fist on the table. "I talked to your boss on a video screen a few months ago, the leader of the whole thing, so don't jerk me around. You know something, and if you tell me, things will be much easier on you."

He laughed again, this time more maniacally than before. "You think this is about my comfort. I serve the Godless because the gods took everything from me and turned a blind eye when I begged for help. Now, my wife and child are in the underworld, suffering, while the gods have parades."

Heaven was a strictly Earthen concept, thanks to Bacchus bastardizing his version of Mount Olympus. He made Heaven more than just his dwelling place, but a place where "good" people could go after they died. This concept was foreign to almost every other gods-led civilization in the universe. Everywhere else, everyone who dies (which is everybody) ended up in some form of Hell, having their sins tortured away so they can return to the Source as pure energy. That's where Fezzick's family was, and I understood why it ate him up inside.

"The gods did nothing to you," I said.

"No," he replied. "They did nothing for me, either, and they will pay for it."

I couldn't help myself. I balled up my fist and smashed it across his face, again and again and again, until Fezzick collapsed on the floor unconscious and bleeding from every hole in his face.

CHAPTER 4

Fezzick didn't die. He eventually came to and was just as gleefully unhelpful as he'd been before I knocked him out. Feeling defeated, I returned him to his cell. He wasn't going to reveal any secrets even after I'd beaten him senseless—at least not until he had time to recover.

I wasn't surprised by his lack of cooperation, just disheartened by it. I had interviewed dozens of people just like him over the past six months from star systems across the universe, and it always turned out the same. They joined the Godless because the gods were to blame for their rotten life. They never wanted to take responsibility for their own actions, and lashing out at the gods seemed like the righteous path. There was a time not long ago I would have agreed with them.

I could admit that, for the most part, people who joined the Godless did have a rough go of it. Some had been subjected to torture, or rape, or watched their loved ones die in the most despicable way possible, but most of their suffering had nothing to do with the gods or the gods' part in their lives, because, well . . . frankly, the gods don't care about humanity.

It was true. I knew people wanted to imagine they were important to the gods, and in a way, they were. Humanity, as a collective, was like their pet project. The gods believed the continued survival of the human race was their greatest mission—that's why they kept creating us in their image on planets across the universe. With so many humans out there, the odds of any one god caring about any one single person were extremely rare.

Humanity wasn't any different. A person might care about their own dog or dogs as a concept, but nobody had the energy to think about every dog in the world, every minute of every day. That would be crazy.

The same was true with gods. Gods loved humanity and enjoyed humans, but they didn't have the energy to reign their countenance down on every individual human all day, every day.

The problem was that humans were more self-important than dogs. Dogs didn't care that the universe was unfair. They lived in the moment, finding joy in every interaction. They didn't blame their masters if something went wrong in their lives. Unlike humanity, which blamed the gods for everything.

Basically, dogs were better than humans—by a factor of about a million.

That's something I only remembered after I joined the Godschurch. Back on Earth, I was in a constant struggle for survival. My hands committed atrocities that still made me lie awake at night to avoid seeing them in my dreams. I lived with demons—literal demons that came from Hell—and worked for them as well. They made me do unspeakable things. And I did them because that was how I survived.

I compartmentalized. That's the only way I could live with myself.

But when I came to the Godschurch, things changed. I changed. I no longer had to dedicate my whole life to survival. I could let down my guard, at least in the comfort of my room . . . which led to me remembering how much I loved dogs.

Before the Sun Incident and the Horde Wars, back when things were good, I had a dog, a little Pomeranian named Noodle. She slept with me, licked my face, and, like all my loved ones, she tragically died too young. I never had time to mourn her. I never had time to mourn my parents or my sisters—or anybody, for that matter, but for some reason, that stupid dog hit me the hardest.

Then, one day I was chasing a terrorist down a back alley on Schooma, a world governed by the God Eleos, when I tripped over a tiny, squishy rock. My momentary stumble allowed the terrorist the escape my clutches. I was beyond angry like I always was when a perp got away and turned around to curse out the rock. That's when I heard the rock whimper. It turned to me with the biggest, saddest puppy dog eyes I had ever seen.

In that moment, I got a flash of Noodle in the tiny dog's eyes that looked up at me, and my heart melted. I picked the dog up and cried with it in my arms for forty-five minutes as the sadness of my lost family poured out onto the dirty asphalt below.

I couldn't let that dog go, so I didn't. I brought it back to the Godschurch with me, and little Noodle has stayed with me ever since that day. She never complained, never yelled, and she never judged me. My little Noodle.

***

The Godschurch jail cells were small and confined. They were not meant to keep prisoners for long. Most prisoners were held off site in facilities around the universe, where they could be interrogated for their knowledge and kept from endangering society for as long as necessary. Soon, I would transport Fezzick and his friends to one of the off-site prisons and let them rot for several decades while I hunted for new terrorists.

Another fruitless interrogation session led to another bloody nose for Fezzick, but he still didn't break. I was nearly at the end of my patience with him.

With a press of my hand on the entrance to the jail cell, it slid open for me. I pushed Fezzick through the metal door and dropped the electric force field to his cell.

"Bleed out for a while," I said to him. "Maybe then you'll talk."

I tossed him inside and raised his forcefield until the blue hue of the electricity shone on his beaten face. He crawled into the cot and turned his back to me. I heard him sob softly to himself, finally able to break down. In time, he might crack, but it wouldn't be soon enough.

"Don't count on it," I heard from the cell behind me.

Dimitri, my first arrest, was grinning at me when I looked over my shoulder. Long gone was the perfect smile he had when we met on Cambrial, and I arrested him during my first successful raid on a Godless sect. He was the de facto leader of the sect and the closest I ever got to finding the leader of the Godless. For some reason, the Godless liked to say that there were no leaders and that everything was run by independent organizations around the cosmos, but the thing was, humans were little more than lemmings. They needed to be led, and because of that simple fact, everybody has a boss. Every organization had a leader.

"Why is that?" I said, strolling casually toward his cell.

Dimitri was a smug one who had always relied on his appearance too much. His looks had given him confidence and swagger, but now, when he smiled, four gaps appeared where teeth should have been. One of his once-piercing eyes listed to the left after one too many punches to the face. Still, I couldn't take it all from him. Even after six months, he still had a bit of that swagger left.

"Because we don't value our lives, Rebecca," Dimitri said from his cot. "When will you understand that? We are nothing compared to the cause."

"I know you say that, Dimitri," I replied. "But you are only human, and humans want to live, no matter what they say. They value their life more than they value their cause."

"Then why have none of them broken? Why don't you have any information?"

"It only takes one."

Dimitri shook his head. "No. It only takes the right one. One who knows the information you need. And everybody who knows anything of value would rather die than tell you. That boy, over there," Dimitri pointed. "He is a pawn. You might break him, but he knows nothing."

"Maybe that's true. But you know something, and it's only a matter of time before I break you."

CHAPTER 5

Almost all the officers of the Godschurch lived on the base. A few lived back on their home worlds, but our schedule was demanding, and there was no time for family or loved ones, so most went without any semblance of a life outside the church. I was one of them.

The barracks for the Godschurch officers was built on the other side of the complex from the jail cells. You had to pass through the main command center, get yelled at by Tress, and pass through the training center across a transparent sky bridge to get back to your bunk, walking through ten glass doors as you went from one end of the base to the other. All the while, the Nexus spiraled under your feet.

Living in the church was a welcome change, and it got me out of having to find a place on Earth where I'd always be looking over my shoulder. I took up residence in one of the bigger rooms on base, which was made available after two of its residents died in a Godless bombing incident. Until then, I had been shacked up in a bunk-style room with three dudes.

I didn't like that. I wasn't much for socializing, and they talked constantly. When they stopped gossiping, they complained some more, at all hours of the day and night. They also liked being naked more than I cared to see— completely comfortable blabbing about nothing for hours with their floppy penises hanging out. The male form has its uses, but I didn't care to see it swinging around for the world to see.

When a big room became available, I petitioned them that I needed more space. I was one of the newest members of the Godschurch, and they normally didn't give single rooms to newbies, but after I explained that watching penises flop around all day and night was offensive to me as a woman, I got my way. I hated playing the "female card," but every once and a while, I had to use it.

After all, the room wasn't for me. It was for Noodle. She needed a place all her own, and when I got her, I needed to make sure she could just chill out all day until I got home, assuming I ever got home. If not, I had a contingency plan.

The moment I walked through the door of my apartment, the excited barking started. Noodle didn't so much bark as, well, I guess you would call it "aroo." She was so happy to have me back that she arooed in a very long and sustained manner—at least a minute and a half. A few times, after I'd been gone for a few weeks at a time, she would sleep on my face for two days to make sure I knew she missed me.

Noodle ran toward me, so excited she wagged her tail sideways. I took off my gun belt and shoulder holster, along with the thick leather coat which had become a signature part of my look. With a relieved sigh, I bent down to untie the steel tip boots I wore and tossed off my socks as well. Noodle liked to lick my toes, but I picked her up before she could try.

"I know, girl. Did you miss me? Did you miss me?"

She licked my face, and I didn't even mind. I should have minded. It's bad puppy training to allow them to lick your face, but I didn't much care. She was more excited to see me than anybody else in the world, and some days I needed to feel that excitement from something, even if it was a tiny pupper.

"Did you have a good day, girl? Did you?"

She shook with excitement in my arms and turned over to expose her belly to me, completely unguarded. I would never open myself to anyone in the way she did to me. Even in my most intimate moments, I was always ready to protect myself should the need arise.

Not Noodle. She trusted me with every bone in her doggy body. There was something to be said for that level of trust. I appreciated it in a strange way. The last thing that trusted me so much—well, I shot him in the head as he slept.

The doors to my quarters opened, and I turned to see a blast from the past smiling at me. "Oh, hey. I didn't know you were back yet. I was just about to take Noodle on her afternoon walk."

The voice came from Dean, my old partner . . . my dead partner. Except, this wasn't him. Not really. He had the same high cheekbones, dark hair, and beard as the man I once slept with, but it wasn't really him. It was his clone.

Dean was the Godschurch's best officer, so they developed a clone force from his DNA to train recruits. Tress hated holograms, as she didn't think they responded correctly in battle and wanted something more authentic. They were only shells of Dean, not really him, but they did have all his memories—at least the ones from before his last mission.

It was his last mission and my first. Dean opened the wrong door and got himself blown up. Until he died, none of the clones lived outside of the training simulation, but lots of people couldn't stand the thought of him being gone. Dean, I found, was much beloved in the Godschurch, and his presence was missed.

Tress allowed the clones to go around and do chores for people, including walking my dog. This Dean, who I named Dan because I am wholly unoriginal, was quite helpful, if not a little daft.

"I told you," I said, as Noodle licked my finger, "I would be back by tonight, and I didn't need your help walking the dog."

"Okie dokie," Dan said, smiling. "If you need anything, you know where I am."

He turned to leave, and my stomach tightened. "Wait. Can you stay for a minute?"

"Sure. What can I do for you?" Dan gave me a vacant expression.

I pointed to the bed. "Just sit down."

With somebody else, there might have been innuendo in my words, but Dan saw none. He wasn't the sharpest tool in the shed. However, he was kind, and while I didn't think that he would understand my plight, I certainly hoped talking to him would make me feel better.

"Persephone died," I said with a sigh. "It was my fault."

"That's not good at all," Dan replied, almost robotically.

"It's not good, Dan. More and more gods die every day, and I can't save them all. I can't even save the ones I'm supposed to protect."

"I have no opinion on that matter."

"I know. How could you have an opinion? You really aren't Dean. You're just a facsimile of him."

"That is a true statement," Dan said. "I am only what I am, a collection of my own neurons and synapses that simulate his memories."

I stared absent-mindedly as Noodle gnawed on my finger. "I know, Dan. I just wanted to ramble for a second and tell you that I'm really sorry I got you killed."

Dan laughed and cocked his head. "I am not dead."

The clones had Dean's eyes, but they were hollow and soulless, without a hint of my old partner behind them. I sighed. It wasn't the same. I hadn't even known Dean very long, but he was the first thing that grounded me to this place, and after six months, I still didn't feel like I fit in without him.

"I know . . ."

Noodle got carried away and chomped down on my finger hard enough to puncture the skin. "Ow!" I shouted, standing up. "Bad dog!"

The blood wasn't much, but I didn't have any bandages in my quarters. "Can you keep an eye on her while I head down to sickbay?"

Dan nodded. "Okie dokie. Noodle, do you want to go on a walk?"

Noodle arooed. I wished I was as excited for anything as she was for everything.

***

Sickbay was at the furthest end of the Godschurch from my room, behind the Command Center and across from the jail cells. By the time I walked back to the command center, it was the night shift. There wasn't much of a night at the Nexus—it was either always night or never night, depending on how you looked at it—but there was a time when most of the staff went to bed. When I passed through the center, there were only three data analysts on duty and no Tress.

They looked up from their computers when I walked by. One of them returned my smile with a wave. I had never bothered to learn their names, but they were always pleasant when I saw them.

Sickbay was quiet, for the most part, and soothing. Unlike the rest of the base, which was built for and made for agents and criminals, sickbay was designed to heal people, and the people who worked there were healers, not blunt instruments like me.

I walked in with my bleeding finger, feeling a little self-conscious about coming to them for something so minor. Sickbay was simulating night, and the room was mostly dark. The only light came from blinking monitors and the dim, overhead light.

A dark figure sat writing on a tablet in front of the only bed with a patient in it. The patient was hooked up to a respirator, beeping away in the darkness. The figure shifted in its seat and turned into the light. It was Doctor Palmer, the head doctor at the Godschurch, smiling pleasantly at me.

"Good evening," she said, standing up. "How can we help you, Rebecca?"

I held up my finger. "Noodle got into my finger again."

Doctor Palmer walked over to me, holding a small tablet in her hand. "That dog. It loves you something fierce. Let me see."

"I think fierce is right."

Doctor Palmer took my hand and scanned my finger with her tablet. A blue beam danced across my finger at first, then a small, red beam fired from the middle of the tablet and cauterized the wound. She patted the finger. "I think you'll live."

"I'm not sure, Doc," I said, giving my best wince. "This is the worst wound I've ever gotten."

"I'm sure that's not true."

"You're right." I thought for a moment. "This one time, a bullet ripped through my shoulder and out the other side. I needed forty stitches from a field medic."

I rubbed my left shoulder. The scar wasn't there anymore, of course, not since Velaska healed my wounds and left my body as smooth as a baby's bottom, but I still felt the phantom pain as I rotated it slowly.

"That was a pretty bad one, but Noodle is a vicious attack dog," she replied. "Count yourself lucky. I think you should be good now."

I looked down at my finger. It no longer bled. There weren't even any puncture wounds. It was like the bite never happened. "I need you in the field, Doc. You would be very useful in a pinch."

Palmer smiled. "I'll take my chances in the Godschurch, thank you very much. It's much safer inside these walls."

"Maybe, but doing what I do out there is how you keep safe in here."

"I know, and I appreciate it. You are a fool for doing it, but I appreciate it."

I pointed to the bed. "Who's the victim?"

She shook her head. "That bomber you interrogated earlier, Fezzick. You left him pretty banged up. After you brought him back to his cell, he started having seizures. He's fine now, but he's been going in and out of consciousness for hours."

"I need him to live, Doc."

"Then stop being so rough, all right?"

"No promises. I never learned how to play nice."

***

I crossed the hallway into the jail cells. Dan would walk Noodle and feed her afterward. He was good like that, always helpful with the dog, so I never had to worry when I was on a mission. I wondered, often, if Dean would approve of my dog. I thought he would, but really, I didn't know him very well when he died.

The honest truth was that, while I wanted to feel guilt for what happened to him, he was the one who opened the door to the greenhouse and got himself blown up. Back on Earth, I wouldn't have given his death a second thought. He was just one of a thousand I watched die in horrific ways. More often than not, I was the instrument of destruction.

This wasn't Earth, though. It was the Godschurch, and I could be better here. Dean's death nagged on me, mostly because it could. Down on Earth, there wasn't time to mourn a life, but here, sometimes days went by when I wasn't called for a mission, and all I had to do was wait in my quiet room and think. There was only so much training I could do, and the alcohol options were sparse on board. Unless you liked sweet Communion wine.

I walked through the cell block and stopped in front of Dimitri's cell, watching him as he slept. Most of the criminals we caught couldn't sleep a wink for ages, but not Dimitri. He slept like a baby from the minute we brought him into his cell.

That's what made him so difficult to crack. He was comfortable here. He didn't mind prison. He was used to violence and loss, too. After all, he was from Earth and had survived the Horde Wars just like me, so he knew suffering. He knew pain. He knew survival. Compared to that, the Godschurch cells were a pleasure cruise.

"I can hear you breathe," Dimitri said to me with his back turned. "I can always hear you breathe."

"I wasn't trying to be stealthy," I replied.

Dimitri turned over. "Well, then you succeeded. I know I'm pretty, but you must need something pretty bad to end up back here, talking to me, almost every night."

I shook my head. "I don't need anything. You'll break eventually. But I do have a question for you."

Dimitri stretched his arms over his head, managing to look smug even with half his teeth missing. "Of course you do."

"You fought in the Horde Wars, right?"

Dimitri nodded. "They never took Moscow. I like to think that was in part because of me."

"Then how did you end up on Cambrial, working for the Godless on the other side of the galaxy?"

"I could ask the same of you."

I shook my head. "No. I used the power of the gods to transport myself, but you are a human and worked with humans. I've not seen any technology that leads me to believe you can move between worlds, so how are you growing so fast?"

For a moment, I seemed to have him stumped. I saw him rolling around excuses in his head, crossing them out one by one.

"If you are going to lie to me," I said, "don't even bother."

He grinned. The gaps in his perfect teeth drew my eyes like a magnet. "If I wasn't allowed to lie, then we would never talk."

***

After an hour sitting on the floor in silence with Dimitri, I stood up and walked back toward sickbay. It was time for coffee if I was going to get through the mountain of paperwork I had to do that night.

I wanted to bring Doctor Palmer a cup, too. They didn't have great coffee in sickbay—or anywhere in the Godschurch—but there was a slightly better option in the mess hall behind the prison. I picked up two coffees from the machine and carried them to sickbay.

"Doctor Palmer," I said, walking into the room, "I got you some decent coffee for once. Not that piss you swill here."

The room was empty, or at least I thought so, for a moment. The bomber was gone from his bed, and Doctor Palmer was bleeding out on the ground.

I dropped the coffees and lunged forward. "Doctor!"

CHAPTER 6

I propped Doctor Palmer up on an exam table and pulled one of her tablets from the wall. I had never used one of them before but didn't think it could be too hard. When I pressed the big red button on the screen, an array of blue lasers shot out from the bottom of the tablet and scanned the doctor's face.

There didn't seem to be anything wrong that I could see, so I flipped her onto her stomach. Blood seeped from a wound on Doctor Palmer's head and matted her hair together. When the tablet's blue lasers scanned her wound, she let out a loud moan. The tablet went dark for a moment, then a small red beam shot out. It burned into her skull as it cauterized her wound. It was over in a minute, and then the tablet turned off.

Doctor Palmer's eyes fluttered open as I rolled her back over.

"Doctor, can you hear me?"

She nodded slowly. "Yes. Yes. What happened?"

"I was hoping you could tell me."

Doctor Palmer winced as she went to shake her head. "I'm sorry. I—wait, the bomber, Fezzick. I remember hearing him move . . . I turned . . . then it all went black."

I patted myself down but realized I had left my guns in the room with Noodle. "Do you have a gun in here?"

"Yes." She pointed to a cupboard across the room. "Combination is two-seven-three-one."

I ran over to the cupboard and pulled open the gun drawer. All she had was a .45 caliber semi-automatic. I didn't relish the idea of using bullets in the Godschurch since the slightest puncture in the hull could kill us all, but I didn't have much choice. I pulled the gun out of its case and checked that it was loaded.

"Stay here," I told her. "Don't move."

***

I stumbled across the hall into the jail block, sure that Fezzick would try to take Dimitri out of his cell. Except he didn't. There Dimitri sat on his bed as if nothing had happened.

"Come back for more?" he said with his best devilish charm. "You can't get enough—"

"Shut up." I had exactly no time for games. I considered heading back to the mess hall, then thought better of it. Fezzick wouldn't go back there. There was nothing back behind the prison but administrative offices. They had no strategic value.

The Command Center, on the other hand, had all sorts of strategic value, and at this time of night, was nearly abandoned. Only three people on shift, as I remembered it. If he wanted to infiltrate the station, they would give no resistance.

Gun at the ready, I crept toward the command center. The door slid open, and I saw a dark figure typing away at a computer in the middle of the room.

"Let me see your hands!"

If anything, he typed faster and louder on the keyboard.

"Did you hear me?" I said. "Reach your hands in the sky before I blow your head off."

Fezzick might not have taken me seriously, but everybody understood the click of a gun hammer, so I cocked my gun. "I will not ask you again! Raise your hands."

After hitting three more keys, he stopped and raised his arms. I walked down the stairs into the command center, assessing the situation before me. Two night-shift data analysts lay bloody on the floor.

"Do not move!" I stepped over the puddle of blood. "What are you doing down here?"

He smiled at me, the kind of cocky smile Dimitri often gave. I looked down at the console he was using, and my jaw fell to the floor. The computer was transmitting the location of every god and agent in the Godschurch. Instinctively, I slammed my hand on the keyboard, but the damage was done. A dialog box popped up that read *Transfer Complete*.

I stuck my gun in Fezzick's face. "What did you do? Where did you send these files?"

He laughed and didn't stop until I broke his nose with the butt of my gun. I pressed my hand on the intercom. "Security! I need security at the command center now! Tress and every agent! I need you now! Just—if you work here, get down here *now*!"

***

It only took moments for the Godschurch officers to descend on the command center. I stood on Fezzick's back until the security detail dragged him away, but the damage was done.

"Oh, my gods!" Tress shouted, looking over the data breach. "How did this happen?"

"I don't know, ma'am," a meek woman said from her seat below Tress. "These codes are changed every twelve hours with five-thousand-twelve bit encryption. It would have taken ten years to break through . . . unless he had the codes."

Tress looked at the woman with pure venom. "So, you're saying that somebody with clearance gave this bomber the codes, Evelyn? Right under our very noses?"

"That's what I am saying, ma'am," Evelyn replied. "There is no other way. It was probably somebody like Rebecca, truth be told."

I laughed. "Yeah. Probably was me."

But Evelyn didn't laugh. "I mean, it would be the perfect scheme, right? It's not like you weren't a mercenary on Earth."

I snarled at her. "You should shut up before you catch a beating. Can you believe this, Tress? I don't even know her."

"Well, I know you," Evelyn said with a hefty bit of snark.

Tress held her hands up between us. "Both of you, calm down. Tensions are already high. I'm not going to have accusations flying around on top of everything else that's happened." She turned to me. "You're off the hook, for now, but you're confined to quarters until we finish our investigation."

"That's crazy!" I shouted back. "I need to be here, helping you figure this out."

"You need to be where I tell you to be."

Two security officers grabbed me by the arms and led me away. It was humiliating and frustrating in equal measure. I shook them loose and continued walking in front of them.

"You can leave me alone now," I said as we walked across the glass bridge that separated the command center from the barracks. I tried to shake them off, but they didn't let up.

"Seriously, I will mess you up if you don't leave now."

The guards sighed and turned away while I kept on walking down the hallway. The glass door slid open in front of me, and I walked into the hallway. The outside hull of the ship was made of transparent aluminum, which allowed me to see for miles in any direction.

I watched the nebulas dance with the galaxies and meteors shoot across the universe. Then, I saw something I didn't expect—the long tail of a comet. Headed right for the ship. A moment later, the comet turned slightly, and I noticed it wasn't a comet at all . . . it was a missile.

I turned back to the command center and ran as fast as I could toward the glass door. The security guards met me at the entrance and held me in place.

"No! Let me down!" I kicked into the air.

"You are confined to quarters," one of the guards said.

"You don't get it! Let me down! There's a missile coming! There's a missile!"

Tress waved a hand. "That's crazy talk. If there was a missile coming toward us, our system would have warned us."

Just then, the lights turned red, and the intercom started screeching, "Missile incoming!"

"I told you!" I shouted, kicking at the security guards until they dropped me.

Every monitor flipped to an image of the missile shooting through space. "How did they find us?" Tress asked.

"It's easy!" I replied. "They have our position now. You have to blow that missile out of the air!"

"This isn't that kind of ship," Tress responded. "We don't have weapons. We thought this was—"

"Then what are you going to do?"

Tress clenched her hands tight. Her lips pressed together into a line. "Evacuate. Now! How much time do we have?"

"At the rate this is flying," the woman said to Tress. "Eight minutes, maybe?"

Tress smashed the intercom button. "Listen up! Evacuate the church. Everybody. Evacuate now. We only have eight minutes. Leave everything and go."

I sprinted back toward the barracks ignoring the warnings that Tress barked out. I couldn't leave, not yet. I had to get Noodle. Crossing over the bridge, a wave of people slammed into me. I couldn't get through. I couldn't do anything. Outside the ship, the missile came into stark focus.

"Noodle!" I cried out, but she couldn't hear me. She would be dead soon, and I couldn't save her. I was a survivor, though, and if it meant leaving something behind to save myself, that's what I would do. My old instincts were still there, even if they were buried deep.

I did an about-face and made my way back into the Command Center. The stairs up to the Godschurch proper were flooded with people rushing the door. I pressed against the lumps of flesh over and over again but couldn't get through.

Then my arms started moving faster than they ever have before. I pressed through the meat pile and suddenly found myself inside the hallway.

I turned back to see how I weaseled through the clogged doorway and saw a trail of gold following me. My arms were vibrating so fast all I could see was a glowing, golden light under me as I shoved my way toward the stairwell.

The walls were crammed ass to ankles with bodies, and I couldn't wait if I wanted to live. I latched onto the guard rail and leaped up the stairs and from railing to railing as the denizens of the Godschurch cried out in vain. Never have I moved so fast or jumped so high. Every time I looked at the next ledge, it felt like I appeared there without even trying.

By the time I made it to the top of the stairs, the cries of agony and pain grew to a fevered pitch. Everybody knew they were dead, and the scared whimpers in their voices turned to bawling as they thought about the lives they left unlived. I leaped over the guardrail and squeezed into the church as the lucky ones who made it out of the stairwell hurried for the door.

Angus poked his head out from the church balcony. "Open the door. Open the door! It's ready!"

A burly man opened the door, and the white light enveloped members as they ran through. A massive explosion rocked the church. The missile had hit, and it hit hard. I looked back down the stairs to see a fireball rip through the people there. The Godschurch floor cracked and bowed, sending the great all-seeing eye above the altar crashing onto the floor.

I leaped forward as the floor below me snapped. There was no way I should have been able to survive the jump, and yet I landed on top of the pews on the other side, leaving a trail of golden streaks behind me. I jumped from pew to pew as the universe gobbled up the slower people behind me.

The floor of the Godschurch fell tile by tile, destroying in a matter of moments the work that took angels thousands of years to complete. Gathering the last of my strength, I leaped from the pews onto the foyer of the church. Angus's balcony collapsed onto the floor beneath it. The wrinkly, old man had died saving us, and I wouldn't let that go to waste.

I leaped into the whiteness just as the last of the Godschurch crumbled into the nexus point, along with everybody I knew—and the only thing I still loved.

CHAPTER 7

I rolled out the door of the Godschurch and into a city like I had never seen before. Instead of beautiful, stacked agoras and flowing togas, the people on this world lived in thatched-roof homes. Their men wore bushy beards, red like fire, and covered themselves in thick furs above their tight, leather clothing. The women wore long dresses that nearly touched the ground but stopped right before they got dirty from the mud.

The city stretched in either direction as far as I could see, and right in front of me, an immense dock housed boats fifty feet high. Dozens of fishermen walked their catches into town.

"Excuse me," I said, trying to flag somebody down. Somebody had to be able to help me out. "Excuse me? Does anybody speak English?"

A little boy pulled at his father's cape. "*Njiol reemojor.*"

I reached into my pocket, trying to find my universal translator, but I'd left it inside my coat, which was back at the Godschurch, along with my weapons and my boots. I was unarmed, standing in the bitter cold air wearing nothing but my jeans and a thin T-shirt.

Wait, I thought. Where are all the other people that came through with me?

I couldn't have been that far behind them. I took a few steps into the square where merchants in wooden huts sold their wares, but nobody there looked out of place.

Having no luck anywhere else, I walked back to the old church and pulled open the doors. There was nothing inside except a set of old wooden pews and an altar rotting at the front. Didn't look like it'd been used in generations.

Dust kicked up on my way in, and I slumped forward on one of the pews. There in the echoing, dismal silence, I dipped my head down low, and I cried. I had mourned my father and my family, and my—oh, my poor Noodle—but I'd never cried for people I barely knew. Not like that. I lost so many. Maybe, just maybe, I would find a place that wouldn't rip my heart out, but that place doesn't exist. Everything I tried to build would be gone sooner or later. Why even bother to—

"Excuse me?"

The voice had a slow cadence to it. It belonged to a handsome, older gentleman who had crept up behind me. He stared at me with big, blue eyes beneath matted, blond hair.

"Can you speak English?"

He held up his finger to his ear, where a universal translator was glowing. His headphones pulsated a neon blue as he smiled at me.

"I know a few words," he said.

"Do you work for the Godschurch?" I wiped my eyes and tried to pull myself together.

"A long time ago, in another life. I am still the caretaker here, though."

I looked around. "Seriously? This place has a caretaker? No offense, but you aren't doing a great job."

The man shrugged. "I am old. My bones won't let me work like I want them to, and with us being—well, let's say that the Godschurch favors Zeus's seed more than the Odinson lineage."

"Odinson, like Norse Odin. There's Norse gods?"

"There are many pantheons of gods in the world—most left Zeus's side long ago."

"Zeus isn't alive," I said lowly. "They have all left his side."

"That is truly interesting," the man said. "Now come. We have much to discuss."

"Wait," I said. "Where are the others? The ones that came through on the beam with me."

The man thought for a moment. "There have been no others in quite some time. You are the first I've seen come through in ages. The Godschurch does not like to come here."

"The Godschurch is gone. Blown up by a missile not ten minutes ago."

"My dear, that is horrible. You are the bearer of much bad news."

"That's what they say about me." I bit my lip to avoid the sadness overtaking me. "I need to speak to the god of this planet."

He nodded. "Then, let us go. I am Bjorn."

***

We trudged through the mud of the fishing village. It felt good between my toes, even if it was cold. Dozens of men and women walked through the muck in thick leather boots, but I only had my bare feet. The sky was dark, a torrential storm on the horizon.

"How long have your people been a civilization?" I asked.

"The gods blessed us with life a million or so years ago. We oozed up from the muck and the mire faster than most. If you'll excuse me for a moment," Bjorn said, taking the universal translator out of his ears as he walked up to a man selling pelts and other assorted leather goods.

I took a seat on a log and looked around the town. It was beautiful in its simplicity. I'm sure there were diseases that decimated the population from time to time and wars that killed too many young men, and lack of asphalt on the roads would get to me before too long. However, it was calm and peaceful, like I've never allowed my life to be, and I liked that. In the calm, I almost forgot the crippling pain of losing the entire Godschurch and being stranded on a planet I've never known, with no information about any of the other survivors.

"Here we go," Bjorn said, tossing down a pair of bear skin pelts and leather shoes. "I think you will be much more comfortable in this."

***

Bjorn was right. When I wiped off my feet and put on the leather shoes, I suddenly felt warmer and warmer still as I put on the leather breast plate and the fur pants customary in the village. Finally, I wrapped a thick, bear pelt around my shoulder and felt ready to fight the universe. I wasn't dressed like any other woman in the village. I was dressed like a warrior.

The outhouse where Bjorn brought me to change stunk something fierce, but I appreciated the privacy. When I walked out, Bjorn handed me two leather bracers for my wrists.

"May I help you put them on?" he asked.

I held up my forearms. "Thank you. Why didn't you bring me a dress, though? It looks like the women in this village all wear dresses."

Bjorn chuckled as he laced up my bracer. "You are not from this village, and I see it in your eyes. You are a warrior."

"Are the women not warriors in this village?"

"Some are, and those that are, wear these," Bjorn said, lacing up the other bracer. "Those who are not, wear dresses or simple slacks."

"And what about the men? Are they all warriors?"

"At one point or another, but many of them choose a simple life when they have the choice. Being a great warrior sounds more thrilling than it is, I'm afraid."

"And what about you?" I asked Bjorn. "Are you a great warrior?"

He stared at me for a moment. In his younger days, those deep blue eyes would have cracked open my heart. "Not anymore."

"I fear you won't have a choice soon."

He nodded. "Perhaps. But until then, I will keep my life simple. Now come. I will take you to our god."

***

Walking through the streets of town was a lot easier with shoes on, and a might bit warmer with a bear pelt wrapped around my shoulders.

"Where are we going?"

Bjorn pointed to a wooden structure in the distance. "There."

The structure was like nothing else in the town. Pillars surrounded the great building like the ancient agoras I saw in most of my travels, except these were made of wood, not marble. None of the other buildings in the town stood higher than a single story, and they were made with thatch. This one towered over the others like an ancient, wooden pagoda, fifty feet tall and shaped in a layered triangle, with slanted roofs stacking up to a giant tower in the center. Across every face of the tower, the gods' all-seeing eye stared out across the town.

"It is the Temple of Thor," Bjorn told me as I stared up at it. "Come."

I jogged up the steps and into the temple. Inside the room, a hundred wooden columns held up the ceiling, intricately carved with scenes of great boats on the ocean fighting kraken and other monsters of the deep. Where the Godschurch had its cherubs, here there were mighty elk and fierce bears. The taxidermized heads of great kills lined the walls, and the altar in the front of the room was constructed from antlers. A massive, wooden throne sat on the altar, crafted with whole oak trees. On each side of it, a stone wolf howled into the rafters.

"Is this another Godschurch?" I asked.

"No," Bjorn said. "This is a temple devoted to Thor, the god of this world. There are dozens of temples to the gods of Odin's line throughout the city, but this is the grandest, so that Thor may look down on us and answer our prayers."

Bjorn walked me up the steps of the altar, where a great all-seeing eye was carved into the wall. After rummaging through his pocket for a moment, he pulled out a small coin. The ground began to quake once he placed it in a small, empty slot near the eye. The door to the church slammed closed, and the building itself began to pivot on its axis. As it did, the wooden slats of the floor opened to reveal a staircase that spiraled into the tower above.

He laid another token into my hand and closed my hand around it. "Keep it safe. People have asked for centuries the secret of entering the tower above the church. Now you know and must keep its secret safe."

"I swear it."

***

The spiral staircase was tight and steep. It led up into the wooden rafters of the temple and finally into the small tower above. It reminded me of the spiral staircase I walked up every time I had to leave the Godschurch, and moments of my old life flashed in front of me. I remembered Noodle, Tress, Velaska, the Masters, and everybody I lost in the explosion.

Stupid, Rebecca. I'd been trying so hard to start a new life I forgot my most sacred maxim. The world is cruel. It had always been cruel, and it would always be cruel.

Things were finally going well, at least for me, and I didn't want to believe that things were the same as they'd always been. Fate was cruel. It had always been cruel, and it would always be cruel.

It will always be the same, but I did not want to be the same.

I liked the human I became after I joined the Godschurch. It was a human that cared about other people; a human that tried to do the right thing and liked things. Yes, I was still the same human who put her life first, forsaking everything else, even Noodle, when the going got tough, but at least I felt guilty about it now, and a little guilt eating away at my soul—I think that was just the human condition.

"Watch your head." Bjorn turned the metal wheel that opened the hatch to the tower. "There's not much room."

I followed behind as he made his way into the cramped tower. He slammed the hatch closed after me, and I was squeezed tight against the black wall chiseled with iridescent, blue runes. In front of us was a small tide pool with crystal blue, glowing water flowing through it.

"This water is from a glacier at the edge of the world. It was personally blessed by Thor and provides a conduit for us to communicate during times of need."

Bjorn dipped his finger in the water and swirled it around until he created a whirlpool in the center of the pool. "Great Thor. Please hear our prayers. This is our hour of need. Please, come to us."

The whirlpool spun faster and faster until it created a vortex that lifted the water high into the air. The water expanded flat, and a long-haired, blond warrior with a great beard and long, flowing cape smiled at us.

"Bjorn, son of Olbrecht. It is good to see your face. It has been too long."

Bjorn bowed his head. "Much too long, my god Thor. I wish I came to you in better times."

"Speak to me, friend. What has happened to depress you so?"

"I believe that it is best to talk of this in person. May we please enter Valhalla?"

Thor nodded. "If you request it, I will make it so."

He snapped his fingers, and a bright light, like the one from the Godschurch, flashed through the tower, and we were gone. I tasted salty trout as we left the earthly plane.

CHAPTER 8

When we rematerialized, it was in the middle of a rocky bridge. On the other side was a thousand-foot-high castle sitting on the edge of a great waterfall. Two stone Viking warriors guarded the entrance to the castle, and spires lining the outside of the castle kissed fluffy clouds. Men and women appeared around us, trudging toward the entrance to the castle. Bjorn and I walked past them.

"What is this place?" I asked. "Who are all these people?"

Under us, the waterfall fell into the expanse of the sky, and all around us, trees and mountains protruded above the clouds.

"They are the dead," Bjorn responded. "Come to take their place at the tables in Valhalla."

"Valhalla? But what about Mount Olympus? I thought that's where all the gods lived."

"It is, for most, but you don't really think every pantheon operates like your gods, do you?"

Until about ten years ago, I didn't even know there was any god at all, let alone dozens of them. "Yes, I guess . . . I mean, no? I don't know the right answer here."

"The main point of contention between the lines of Zeus and Odin was that Zeus and his gods walled off Olympus to humanity. Odin didn't like that."

"What happened to them?"

Bjorn pushed his way through a group of men holding their own heads. "Long ago, all the gods came together to create a habitable planet, that much is true. However, the gods of Mount Olympus saw things differently than the other pantheons . . . honestly, they disagreed on many things. Eventually, they separated. Some went with Zeus. Others went with Osiris. Still more went with Odin and his sons Thor and Loki. Each group created its own mythology and its own lineage. Each respected that only Zeus could create life, but that did not mean that they could not take over planets where he had already created life."

"Like a war?"

"You could say that. Odin and Thor were more violent than your average pantheon god, but nobody really wanted war. After all, the gods were family. They managed to forge an alliance of sorts. Zeus agreed to split the universe into several parts, each to accommodate a different realm of the gods."

"Then why did the Godschurch send me here?"

"All of the gods are protected by the Godschurch. They serve the entire universe. It's just that the Greek pantheon uses it the most."

"How come I've never heard any of this?"

"It's not something that the pantheon likes to talk about, and Odin would just as soon let the past be the past. But now is the time that the gods must band together to stop this threat."

We reached the end of the great stone bridge. Wanderers and warriors waited outside the great double doors, standing a hundred feet tall, a great bear carved into each side, screaming down at the warriors below.

Bjorn walked past them and nudged forward the door. "It's really much lighter than it appears. The worthy can open it with little effort. Those that are not worthy must stay outside until they become so or fall into the realm of Helheim."

Bjorn wedged open the door and pushed me inside before disappearing inside himself.

***

"My friend!" Thor shouted as we walked into the hall. In every corner of the great hall, men and women squished into hundreds of wooden tables, shouting, eating, and drinking from large, pewter, beer steins. The entire room was sloshed out of their minds, and none more so than Thor, the God of Thunder, who stood from his wooden throne at the far end of the hall and stumbled toward us.

"You have made it, worthy chum. I am glad you have come. Ha! A rhyme as well. Excellent! This is a great moment."

Thor slapped Bjorn on the back as they embraced in a mighty hug, then picked Bjorn up into the air and spun him around for a moment before returning him to the ground. With one final slap, Thor released Bjorn, whose smile evaporated.

"I wish I was here under better circumstances, my friend."

Thor's face turned down to match his friend's. For the first moment since we entered the hall, he didn't look gregarious, and the entire room took note of it, stopping their laughter to turn and stare at him.

Thor furrowed his brow and placed his hand firmly on Bjorn's shoulder. "What is it, my friend?"

"I believe Rebecca would be better to tell you."

Thor turned to me and held out his hand. I placed my hand in his, and he clasped it with his other hand. "A friend of Bjorn's is a friend of mine. Tell me, sister, what has happened to cause my friend such pain?"

I bowed my head to him. "I am sorry to tell you, but the Godschurch is no more."

Thor gasped. "Heresy! It has stood since I can remember. What happened to cause this?"

"A missile, directed at us from who knows where blew up the Godschurch this very night." I dropped my head. "There were few survivors and those that did survive…I cannot find them."

Thor wasn't happy about what he heard. The news caused his lip to quiver. "That is horrible news. And what of the other gods? Have they fallen victim as well?"

"It has been a very bad year for the gods, Thor. A group called the Godless has made it their mission to kill every god in the universe, and now they have the last known locations of every god in the cosmos, making their job much easier, which is why you must leave Valhalla. It's not safe for you here."

Thor laughed. "Nonsense! I have lived here for a thousand eons and plan to do so for a thousand more. If the Godless want a fight, bring them on. I have the finest warriors in the universe with me. We shall destroy all who seek to destroy us."

"I don't think that you understand—"

"Do you dare speak to me like I am but a child?" Thor's eyes flashed when he roared. "I am the god of thunder, and my might echoes through the universe."

There was no arguing with stubborn men. "Do as you like. I need to find a way off this planet. Do you have a ship or something I can use?"

Thor was going to roar some more, but he stopped, laughing. "A ship? I've never used a ship in my life. I decide where to go, and I will it."

"Yes, but we are not all gods."

"A pity, that. No, no. There is something else. Aranya! Come!"

From the back of the hall, the sound of chain mail clanged against the stone floor. A woman with dark skin and angry eyes trotted forward, dressed head to toe in battle regalia, with a long sword at her side. When she reached Thor, she removed her metal helmet. It was adorned with wings on either side, matching the wings that trailed the floor behind her.

"This," Thor said, slapping Aranya's shoulder, "is my best Valkyrie."

"Back on Earth, we called them angels."

"Ha! An angel?" Thor scoffed. "Please. An angel is no match for the power of my Valkyries. Right, Aranya?"

Aranya nodded without smiling. "That's right, my Lord. What do you ask of me?"

"Aphrodite once told us of a way off the planet that led to a sanctuary apart from the Godschurch. Do you remember where that was?"

"Yes, sir. In the hills of Tijor. It leads to a Godschurch bunker they would use in case any catastrophe befell the gods."

"Excellent," Thor screamed. "Then you will take this human there while I toast with Bjorn and my new friends."

I realized that for the entirety of our conversation, the men and women sitting in the hall were silent, but at the word from Thor, they held up their glasses and screamed into the air, resuming their bawdy conversations.

"Sir," Aranya said. "Are you sure this is wise? I have not left your side in one hundred thousand years. Should anything happen—"

"Should anything happen, I have the finest fighters in all the world with me here. We will be fine, and this is an order, Aranya, not a choice."

She nodded solemnly. "Consider it done, my Lord."

***

Aranya stomped out of the halls of Valhalla and passed the men and women begging for entrance into the hall. "You do realize that this is a fool's errand, yes?"

"Most are," I replied.

"If the Godschurch was destroyed, it's only a matter of time until whoever is responsible for it comes here, and when they do, Thor will be better served if I am here, not escorting you around the world looking for the entrance to a bunker."

"Hey, I don't need you to come with me. Just point me in the right direction."

She gave me a level stare. "That's cute. I was tasked by my god to make sure you arrive safely, and that is what I will do."

"Just as long as you're aware that you won't be doing me any favors."

She turned back to the castle with a wistful look in her eye. "I have not been away from this place for ten thousand years."

"Then I'd say you're due."

As we looked at the clouds cresting over the castle, a whistle screeched through the air. A comet cut through the clouds and left a trail behind it. Except it wasn't a comet. I knew what it was. The missile flew right over our heads and crashed into Valhalla, exploding it in a cloud of green vapor. The fire plumed outward across the great stone walkway, burning the people who were trying to get into the palace.

"My Lord!" Aranya's armor clanged as she tried to rush forward.

I pulled her back. "There's nothing we can do here! We have to go, or we'll die too!"

"No!" Aranya shouted, but she turned away from the fire just as it overcame us. She yanked a glowing blue vial from around her neck and mumbled some words under her breath. She snapped her fingers, and we disappeared.

CHAPTER 9

We rematerialized in a meadow atop a group of rolling hills. In a valley before us, a great lake extended into the horizon. Aranya threw me off her and screamed.

"THOR!"

She collapsed under the weight of her pain and cried big, ugly tears, the kind of tears I cried after I lost the Godschurch. Even the greatest warrior in the world can't stand the thought of losing everything they had built. It's too much.

I knelt and rubbed Aranya's back, trying to comfort her. I wasn't very good at it. "Hey, buddy. It's okay. It's okay."

"Nothing is okay," she said through gritted teeth. "My home, my god, everything is lost."

"The universe is cruel. It has always been cruel. It will always be cruel. There is nothing you can do about that."

"Want to bet?" Aranya said, shaking off my hand. "I can murder every person who had anything to do with the destruction of my home. What did you say they were called? The Godsmiths?"

I shook my head. "The Godless."

"What a stupid name. I will hunt them to the ends of the cosmos and make them scream out in pain." She unsheathed her sword and pointed it at me. "Do you understand, human?"

I held up my arms. "Whoa. I am not the enemy here. All I want is to find this entrance to the Godschurch and be done with it."

She lowered her sword, nodding. "And we shall, but first, I must see the aftermath of my home's destruction."

"That's not a good idea."

"I do not care. I must see it. It is not a choice." She rubbed a glowing, blue vial around her neck. She closed her eyes and started to hum. "It is my duty to see if there is anything left which can be salvaged. If there is, I must do what I can."

"Are you just going to leave me here?" I said.

"You are welcome to come with me. Otherwise, you can find the entrance on your own, here in the hills of Tijor, or wait for me to return."

"I have no idea what I'm looking for."

She stared at me with an icy, cold glare. "That is not my problem."

I didn't want to fight anymore. I latched onto her, and we disappeared in a flash. I tasted the same flavor of salty trout I had when Thor first brought me to Valhalla.

***

The stink from burned flesh wafted into my nose when we arrived back at Thor's palace. The bridge had collapsed in all but a couple of places, so Aranya lifted me by the arms and flew me over. Charred, black marks dotted the planks where men and women once stood.

"This place has always been a beacon to the worthy since before Thor was chosen as its god."

In front of us, the rubble of a castle should have sat smoldering in a heap of wreckage, but there was no remnant of what the gods built. Not a single brick to show that anything had ever existed there in the first place.

Aranya lowered me down to the ground, then collapsed on the blackened remains of Valhalla.

"Everything I've ever known," Aranya said, "gone in an instant as if it never existed. My people. My Lord." She looked out at a line of people on the other end of the bridge. "The dead still come. They will forever come, and there is nothing for them."

"There is nothing you can do for them here. All you can do is fight to bring them justice."

Aranya sniffed and brushed away a tear. "You are right. There is a time for grief, but it is not now."

***

We reappeared in the hills of Tijor. I had rarely seen so much grass in one place before. Back on Earth, I lived in Thebos, which was one massive construction project lacking green of any kind. We'd long ago paved over the last of our natural world. You had to get a hundred miles outside the city just to see the stars.

Even if you could get out of the city, Thebos was situated on a desert, which meant green wasn't the first thing you saw anywhere. It didn't rain or snow or really have any weather— except the occasional sandstorm if you got lost in the Badlands.

This place, however, felt different. When I breathed in the air, it was almost like I felt the water fill my lungs. I hadn't been on a planet that had such lush greenery. I bent down and touched the clover in my hand, shaking off its morning dew. Thousands of flowers spotted the clover fields. They looked like the tulips and roses of Earth, though I was sure they were called something different on this planet.

"Follow me," Aranya said, hovering in front of me.

Damp dew attached to my legs as we walked through the field. I crested over a hill and looked out on the entire valley below me. Every hill looked the same, full of life but devoid of any marker that would help us find the Godschurch.

"What are we looking for?"

"The all-seeing eye. It will guide us to the location of the bunker."

Of course, it would. That eye. Every time I went to a new world, that eye followed me, marking destinations and showing safe havens for the Godschurch. The all-seeing eye knew all and saw all. However, I didn't see it anywhere.

Except…then I did. Looking across all the hills, I noticed that the tip of each one had a different color flower, just like the all-seeing eye inside the Godschurch, which was encrusted with different colored jewels throughout its pupil.

"Aranya," I shouted. "Can you go further into the air and see if you see a pattern in the grass?"

She didn't respond, except that she flew higher into the air until she disappeared. A few moments later, her speck grew as she flew down. She was pointing to something in the distance.

"It's just one big eye, the whole hill, and the tip of the eye points over there."

Aranya walked down the hill toward a point I couldn't see, and I followed her toward it.

***

We flew forward, Aranya carrying me until we reached a smooth, sheer side of a cliff. This was where the all-seeing eye led her, Aranya told me. She leaned forward into the sheer side of the cliff and listened for a moment.

"This is it. The earth here is hollow."

"Great," I said. "How do we call the Godschurch?"

Aranya pulled back her arm and slammed it through the hollow cave opening. She pulled back and smashed through the earth again with all her might. Each time, the dirt exploded into a thousand pieces, and I ducked as it flew over my head.

When I stood again, Aranya had blown a massive hole in the hillside with her fist.

CHAPTER 10

I expected to step through the hole in the ground and be immediately transported to wherever we needed to go, but that's not what happened. Instead, the hole led us into a dingy fallout shelter which looked like it hadn't been used for ages. A small, ethereal light floated in the middle of the room and illuminated the dusty walls. Aside from a painting of the all-seeing eye along the far face of the room, though, all the light showed was more dirt.

"This looks like a dead-end," Aranya said, looking around.

I felt it too, but I didn't say anything. In moments of panic, when all hope is lost, one person must keep their cool. Palpable tremors echoed in Aranya's voice, and I knew if I didn't keep hoping, everything would fall apart.

I placed one hand on hers, running my fingers along the craggy walls of the shelter with the other. "We'll figure it out."

"What are you doing?" Aranya said to me as I moved to another wall.

The truth was, I didn't know. What I did know was I couldn't stop. I felt myself faltering, and if I gave in to that instinct, I would crumble into a heap on the floor. I wiped my hand over the all-seeing eye, and that's when I felt it—a circular hole in the wall.

"Come here, Aranya. Feel this." I pulled Aranya's hand to mine and pressed it against the hole.

"What is it?"

"I don't know, but it's too perfectly circular to be manmade. Back when I first got here, Bjorn placed a coin inside a hole in a temple wall to allow us access to Valhalla."

Aranya nodded. "In the old days, the gods had to pay for things with coins. We had our own currency. We've long since grown past those sorts of things, but coins are still often used for ceremonial purposes."

I knew what I had to do. I rifled through my pocket and found the coin that Bjorn had given me. I turned it over in my hand. The all-seeing eye glared at me from one side, and on the other was an infinity symbol, signifying the immortality of the gods.

The coin fit perfectly in the hole in the wall, and the moment I placed it there, the whole room shook and quaked. I grabbed onto Aranya for support, instinctively, and she let me fall into her. Her chest rose and fell in rhythm and comforted me for an all too brief moment.

In front of us, the wall gave way, pushing deeper into the cave, then slid away to reveal a reflecting pool with shimmering blue water. The water swirled around and created a vortex. A spigot of water shot from it and took the form of a tall, bearded man in a toga, youthful and strong but dignified and regal.

The figure spoke. "Great Odinson, generations ago, we made a pact that your father would be allowed to govern a part of the universe as he saw fit. However, should trouble ever come upon you, the Godschurch would open its arms to help you. Fall into the vortex, and you will be brought to the safehouse of the Godschurch. By my power as Zeus, I guarantee your safety. Welcome, brother."

The spigot streamed back into the water and a portal of white opened at the bottom of the vortex. I looked at Aranya, who shrugged before she jumped into the water, disappearing into the blinding whiteness at the bottom of the pool. I took a step forward and jumped in after her.

***

The vortex spat me out inside another room, drab and windowless. I heard laughter and merriment coming from down the hallway, which confused me. It was something I hadn't heard since, well, I'm not entirely sure. Certainly, long before I fell out onto Aranya's planet. And this wasn't just happiness, mind you, but pure, unadulterated joy.

I opened the door to the room and walked slowly down a tight hallway as the laughter built into an uproarious guffaw. I turned the corner, and tears sprung into my eyes at the sight of the Godschurch in front of me, or at least a miniature version of it.

There, in the middle of the room, was a command center, with a dozen workers typing on computers. There were tubes and other fancy gizmos that made it feel like the church's command center, but more importantly, there were people, people I recognized, standing around and hugging Aranya.

Among them all, in the center, was Velaska, who smiled and waved before coming over and wrapping me in a warm hug. "I thought we would never see you again."

I buried my face into her shoulder. I couldn't speak. I had so many questions, and yet, all I wanted to do was enjoy the fact that my friend was safe. After a long moment, I looked up at her. I tried to speak but only blubbered my excitement.

Velaska smiled at me. "Come. I have a surprise for you." She walked me to the back of the room, where cryogenic tubes glowed with different aged versions of my old friend Dean, waiting to be thawed. "Wait here," she said.

Velaska disappeared into the darkness, and that's when I heard the faint aroo from down the hall. I didn't have to see Noodle before I knew she was there. Her collar shook and jingled as she ran toward me, the pitter of her nails echoing along the concrete floor. She jumped into my arms and licked my face, and for the first time ever, I understood true joy. I understood how you could be happy even in moments of great pain—how you could feel joy for the few good things that remained while still mourning all that was lost.

***

I played with Noodle for the better part of an hour. There were better things to do, more important things to do, but I was just so happy to see that dog it was like everything else in my life melted away.

Velaska came over to check on me several times, but I brushed her off. She wanted me to be involved in whatever they were scheming, and I simply wasn't quite ready. Not just yet. The moment I looked away from Noodle, there would be responsibilities heaped on me—important responsibilities—but none of them seemed to matter.

Finally, Velaska knelt in front of me. "My love, it is time to come and talk to the group."

I ignored her words, asking instead, "How did you find her?"

"Well, I had a feeling I would see you again, and I knew you would be devastated about that dog, so in the snap of my fingers, I went down to your room, found her, and snapped away. There really wasn't much to it."

I smiled. "That's where you are wrong. There was everything to it. I thought I lost her forever, and you brought her back. That means everything."

"I am happy to see a smile on your face, but truthfully, there is about to be an all-out brawl over there."

I watched a pretty woman with short, brown hair and a leather coat grab Aranya by the chest plate and hoist her into the air. I should have cared, but I didn't. I was too content sitting with Noodle and letting the universe move on without me.

"Why do they need me?" I asked, tickling Noodle's outstretched belly.

"You have an intimate knowledge of the Godless's mode and style of attack, having witnessed two of them first hand and being the first person to spot the missile launched on the Godschurch. Aside from that, you've interrogated more of the Godless than the rest of us combined. Are those enough reasons? I could go on."

"Where are the others? I watched at least a thousand people fall into the whiteness and disappear into the universe. Where are they?"

"Angus scrambled the coordinates of each jump. Most haven't made it back yet. They might never find a way back."

"And Tress? Jamil? The Masters? The other agents?"

"This is everybody we have. Hardly any have field experience. Most were off church at the time. You know more about the Godless than all of them combined."

"Fine." I stood up and tied Noodle to one of the cryogenic tubes that held a clone of Dean. "Stay here, Noodle."

The dog whimpered as I walked away from her toward the group of gods and members of the Godschurch, most of whom I didn't know.

"Katrina!" Velaska shouted at the brown-haired woman tussling with Aranya. "You are a god. Act like it."

"Why?" Katrina said. "Gods are boring. This one here thinks I should be happy staying down in this bunker when there's a madman loose bombing gods. No, I'm not staying put."

"Noted," Velaska said. "However, you are a god, and that is a Valkyrie. You won't get very far beating up on the people who are sworn to protect you, now will you?"

Katrina dropped Aranya and brushed herself off. It was hard to believe the scrawny woman was a god at all—she looked more like a human playing god. She held none of Velaska's poise or radiance.

"I know what you are thinking," Velaska said. "But she truly is a god. In fact, she is not just a god, she is your god. Well, I guess that's not quite right since you took up residency on the Godschurch base before it was summarily destroyed. She is the god of Earth, anyway."

Grinding my teeth, I took a step toward Katrina. "Oh really? So, you're the one responsible for letting demons roam the Earth, huh?"

Katrina folded her arms and stepped even closer to me. "That's right. They served Earth well and deserved a reward."

"Don't you think maybe we had enough to deal with rebuilding our whole planet, without having to add on demons, too? We were trying to rebuild society, and you— you screwed us."

"I saved the planet," Katrina said, balling up her fists. "Earth was toast without me. Do you have any idea what I had to do to save you from the Horde? How about some respect?"

Fire shot out of her eyes, and Velaska stepped in to break us up.

"Yes, yes. You are very powerful. So powerful you are picking fights with a human. Is that how you want to be portrayed?"

Katrina flung her arms in the air. "Who is this woman, anyway? What does she know?"

"I've told you before it is very bad down on Earth. While I respect your decision, I've never agreed with it." Velaska tried to put her hands on Katrina's shoulders, but Katrina shrugged them off and stuck her finger in Velaska's face.

"Watch yourself. You do not want to be banned from my sector, too."

"And now you're threatening me. Really?" Velaska let out a sigh and turned to me. "As you can see, I've been able to gather just a—great team together to help sort this all out and find the Godless encampment. Any thoughts you have about how to proceed would be very helpful."

"Thoughts?" I scoffed. "I *think* we couldn't find the Godless when we were at full strength, and now we're what? Fifty people, maybe?"

"Seventy-three, by my count."

"What happened to the other agents? We've got over a thousand agents, and they weren't all on that base when it blew."

"I . . . don't know. They haven't answered the call."

I held the sides of my head and groaned. "I say we all get gone and understand the reign of gods is over."

"That sounds like pussy talk," Katrina said. "I didn't know there were so many pansies in the Godschurch."

I wheeled on her. "I just watched every friend I ever had blown up. Aranya watched her god, and everything she's ever loved, destroyed in a second. These people, they have technology I didn't even know existed. I haven't seen anything like it since—since—"

"You can say it," Katrina said.

I let out a slow breath. "Since the Horde."

She nodded, raising her eyebrows. "That's all it is. Super-charged Horde tech, there's no doubt about it. It's powerful, yes, but it's also flawed."

"How?"

"Horde tech is unstable, especially when heated. They need a location far enough away from civilization that if the plant explodes, it won't destroy them. Not to mention that Horde tech is hard to keep cool, so they'd need a place that could keep them cool."

My eyes went wide. Katrina actually had a thought that wasn't stupid. And it reminded me of another idea. "Tress and I were working on a theory to trace the Godless using info from weapons facilities built after the Horde War. Lots of companies were trying to develop Horde tech for military uses. At least a dozen blew up trying to use Horde Tech—blasted whole countries out of existence. Our researchers traced the problem back to the extreme heat needed to run the facilities. Working with human souls in that high a quantity requires incredible cooling power. The only factories that survived were built in extremely cold places, and their heat signature . . ." I scanned the faces of the Godschurch in front of me. "Did Ruby make it through the destruction?"

Velaska pointed to one of the consoles in the Command Center. "One of the few."

A petite Asian woman typed away and looked startled when I ran over to her. "Yes, ma'am?"

"Ruby! Do you still have that overlay of the universe with the heat signature map we made?"

Ruby nodded, typing away at her console. "Yes, ma'am. Let me pull it up . . . we pinpointed over three hundred locations across the galaxy as possible plants for the Godless, but never had enough officers to make a sweep happen."

I looked around the room at the ragtag collection of gods and officers. There weren't enough of us to do a sweep. Not enough at all. Noodle barked, and it broke my concentration.

"What do you want?" I growled at her.

She looked so excited and proud of herself. I walked over and petted her and then looked up at the rows of Dean clones. It gave me an idea. A bad idea, but an idea nonetheless.

CHAPTER 11

It took several hours to flush the clones out of their cryogenic tubes, reanimate them, and get them dried off. Once all that was done, Velaska used her powers to clothe and arm them.

When we finished, fifty-five Deans stood in front of us. Velaska and I divided them into teams and interspersed them among the other officers and gods. All told, there were sixty-four different two-person teams to cover over three hundred hot spots around the universe.

I sat on the floor in the back of the room as the Deans mingled, each talking about the exact same experiences, each with the same memories. None of them had the memory of Dean's death. Only I had that. Aranya sat next to me, petting Noodle.

"Are they ready yet?"

She nodded at me. "Yes. It took a long time, but worth it in the end as it's the best chance we have of finding the butchers who murdered my people."

"And mine."

"Both our people," she said in a solemn tone. Noodle, oblivious to the tension, gnawed on Aranya's finger.

Velaska walked over to us. "It's time to send the troops off to battle."

"You mean to their death. This is a suicide mission, after all."

"That's harsh," Aranya said. "We might survive yet."

"I've sent dozens of officers to fight the Godless, and they almost always end up dead. Now, we are sending them to locate the weapons plants themselves, where they make the weapons they use to slaughter us. It's like sending them into a viper's den."

"We have always survived, Rebecca," Velaska said.

"We always survive," I said, rising to my feet. "Until we don't."

"Yes," she replied. "Quite."

"Why me again? Why do I have to rouse them to action?"

"You think I'm going to send them on a suicide mission? This sort of thing is too messy for me. Besides, Katrina will be there to help you. She likes this kind of thing."

One hundred and twenty-eight men, women, angels, cherubs, and gods turned to me as I strode in front of them and cleared my throat. "I'm not going to lie to you. There aren't enough of us to effectively scour the universe, and we don't have time to wait. We don't even know if there are more Godschurch out there, frankly."

"Your earpieces serve two functions: they communicate with your partner in the field and, should the worst happen, they'll send a beacon back to the Godschurch." I pulled out a tiny earbud from my pocket and clicked a button on its side. "Click it like this, and it will send us a homing beacon. We don't have extraction teams or anything like that. Velaska and a small squad of analysts will stay here to coordinate in case anything goes wrong . . . and I am quite sure everything will go wrong."

Any joy or confidence in the room faded with my words. "Sorry to be the bearer of bad news, but that's our situation. If you're headed to a planet without a Godschurch, Velaska will send you there with her magic and pull you back. I have no idea what you'll find on these planets, if they're inhabited, and by what. Could be a legion of Horde waiting for you, could be asphyxiation from a hostile atmosphere—"

"But it's not all bad news," Velaska tried to chime in, smiling.

"Yes, it is all bad news!" I shouted. "We are the last hope for the gods and the universe as we know it. We've targeted three hundred and twenty-three facilities, and we have sixty-four teams. We've just picked the hottest planets, and pray luck is on our side. We don't know anything else."

I looked around at the stone faces of the Godschurch. "If this mission fails, the Godschurch fails. The Godless will have their way, and there will be no gods left. We're fighting for life as we know it." I took a step back. "Now, Katrina will tell you what we're looking for on these planets."

Aranya handed me Noodle when I stood next to her. She must have known I'd need to pet the dog. I had just bummed everybody out, myself most of all.

Katrina stepped forward while I moved to the background. "The Horde weapons are powered by huge vats of green, gelatinous goop. This goop is the essence of human souls, and they use it to power the weapons. Those Demon Hunters you guys love back on Earth? The charges they use—well, you're shooting concentrated human soul out of those guns."

I thought back to how many times I'd fired my demon hunters. Every time I shot my weapon, I was using a part of a soul. How many errant shots did I take? How many souls wasted by an itchy trigger finger?

"It's why Horde tech has such hot heat signatures. Human souls are incredibly hot because they're struggling against the Horde's tech, trying to return to the Source—never mind any of that, though. What you need to know is that we're looking for weapons facilities, and they're going to be somewhere cold—somewhere cold that still radiates heat. Could be a volcano, could be Horde, could be Godless. We're flying blind."

One of the Deans raised his hand. "How long is a sweep supposed to take?"

I spoke up. "We have no idea. Some of these planets have multiple hot spots, and you'll have to check them all. You're there until you exhaust your search. This is your only mission. We must find the leader of the Godless, erase every piece of data he has on the gods, and destroy every facility he uses to construct his weapons."

Katrina started to talk over me. "If you find a facility, get every piece of information you can from it, then destroy it."

I frowned. "That's going to alert them to our presence."

"But it will prevent them from making more weapons."

"That's not the—"

"How are we supposed to destroy the facility?" another Dean asked.

"The Horde goo is unstable. A single grenade will blow it to kingdom come. If you can't find a grenade, find a Horde blaster and slice through it. It will explode after five seconds, and you can use that charge to blow the rest of the base."

"Won't that kill us?" A frightened, young woman said from the back.

I didn't like where this was going. Setting Noodle down, I walked back toward the front. "Quite possibly.

That's why I wouldn't advise blowing anything up unless it's absolutely necessary."

"If it takes down a Horde facility," —Katrina glared at me— "If it prevents them from killing a single god, then it will be worth it."

I held her gaze, glaring back. "If you want to take over, that's fine, but my mission, my rules."

Velaska broke us apart as we stood locked nose-to-nose. "That's enough. I need to speak with these two. The rest of you, go about your business."

***

"You two need to get a hold of yourselves," Velaska said after dragging us into another room behind the clone tanks. "Those people out there are counting on us."

"Fine with me," I said. "Tell her."

"Watch it, plebe," Katrina said, rolling her shoulders. "You are a human. I am a god. Don't forget that."

"Does that make you better than me?"

"No," Katrina said. "Just more experienced."

"Listen, I don't care who leads this mission, but one of us has to take control. If it's me, we're not blowing up the depots until we have the leader. We can wait and gather intel, but that's it."

"And how many more gods will die by then?"

"A few," I said. "I'm sure more than a few, but we'll save thousands more. If they could just hang low and stay out of sight—"

"Yes, because gods are so good at staying out of sight."

"These bombs are interstellar, probably fit with some sort of warp drive so they can move quickly across space.

That takes a lot of machinery and money. I'm just not convinced the Godless have a massive stockpile of them, and if I'm right, then the gods will be safe for a little while they build out their arsenal."

"And what if everywhere you targeted is a weapons depot for the Godless? That's three hundred different manufacturers across the universe. They could have a stockpile of weapons the likes of which we've never seen."

"That's my gamble. I gamble that they don't. She gambles that they do." I turned to Velaska, who had been bouncing back and forth between the two of us while we argued. "You break the tie, Velaska."

"I'm not good at this," Velaska said. "I like you both. I respect you both—but I'm sorry, Rebecca, I've been through too much with Katrina to deny her now."

I slammed my hand against the wall. "Fine. Then we'll blow every facility we come across, but I want no part of it. Any deaths are on you now."

"Fine with me."

***

I stormed off into the dark recesses of the facility, behind the now-empty clone tanks, while Katrina continued the briefing. Noodle followed me until I bent down to pet her excited face. She struggled to lick my hand even while I was petting her.

"You need to cut Katrina a break," Velaska said. She must have followed me. "You have no idea what she's been through."

"She has no idea what I've been through, either. Not that any of that matters. This is a military operation, not a hair braiding party."

Velaska sat down next to me and gave Noodle a pat. "The two of you are a lot alike. Did you know Katrina lived with monsters and demons on Earth during her own apocalypse, the one caused by Bacchus?"

"So, she went through all that—then decided to leave demons on Earth after she caused her own apocalypse? That's balls."

"She was doing the demons a favor. They did just help her stave off the Horde army, if you remember."

"I remember that. Trust me. If there's one thing I remember, it's the Horde army."

"She also moved Heaven and Earth to rescue you from that black hole. I'm not saying she's perfect. I'm just saying—maybe cut her some slack."

I stood up. "You cut her some slack. I've got enough on my plate already."

"Please," Velaska said.

I sighed. "Fine. I'll try."

***

After the briefing, I walked up to Katrina. I wasn't much of a talker. I was a doer. But I decided to attempt deference, something Velaska was always trying to beat into me.

"Are they ready?"

"Ready as they'll ever be," Katrina responded. She was staring at some papers on a desk and didn't look at me. "I don't think anybody is ready for this."

"There's a lot I was never ready for, but I got through it. We'll get through this. Not all of us, but some of us."

"Enough of us?" Katrina asked.

"I don't know," I said. "There's one thing that keeps nagging at me—that night in the command center."

"When the Godschurch blew up?"

"Exactly. I understand that once the bomber got the code, he could transmit our location, but how did he get the codes in the first place?"

"I would be lying if I wasn't worried about the same thing." Katrina looked around the room, then leaned in toward me. "Do you think somebody here is a spy?"

I frowned. "I don't know. It doesn't make sense that a spy would come back here after getting everything they wanted, but I still have an uneasy feeling in my gut, like there's something here I'm not catching, and if I could put it together, then it would solve everything."

"I have felt the same way, many times before." She reached out and put her hand on my shoulder. It was awkward.

"Please don't touch me," I replied in my nicest voice. "I do not like to be touched."

Katrina chuckled and pointed her finger at me. "You know, we're more alike than you realize." She turned to walk away, back toward the analysts, so she could finalize her plan.

"Hey," I said.

"Yeah?" Katrina looked over her shoulder.

"It really was shitty what you did, leaving the demons up on Earth. It ruined everything."

She nodded. "A lot more alike than you realize," was all she said. Then she turned back to the command center.

CHAPTER 12

I couldn't stay in the bunk another minute. The wait was killing me. Waiting for my suicide mission. We had a monumental task to carry out, I knew that, but if we were about to go through Hell, I needed a moment of peace and calm. Normally, I was used to going from one harrowing situation to the next, but the last few days had taken their toll on me.

I asked Velaska to send me somewhere—I wasn't very nice about it, either—and she sent me back out into the fields of Tijor on Aranya's home planet. It was the last time I'd felt peace anywhere, and I wanted to feel it again, if only for a short time.

I also wanted to take Noodle out on a walk outside the Godschurch, into real fields and meadows, where she could play and frolic like a dog should. I loved her dearly, but I wouldn't call myself a good mother. A good mother wanted what's best for her children, and I really wanted Noodle around for my own sanity, not hers.

The minute we walked out of the bunker and into the fields, the little dog's eyes lit up, and her tail wagged furiously. She stared at me for a moment, begging to run wild. I gave her a little nod, and she was off, chasing butterflies and dashing through the grass, rolling and jumping as she went.

I took off the leather shoes Bjorn had given me and walked through the dewy grass toward a lake at the bottom of the valley. I envied the lake for its ignorance. It didn't know that Thor was dead, and it didn't care. It just kept on being a lake, just like Noodle kept on being a dog.

"It is beautiful," I heard Aranya say behind me. "I don't think I ever appreciated this place until I left it."

"Are you following me?" I said, turning to her.

"No. We can both individually want to come to this place. For me, it is my connection to home, the closest I can get to Valhalla without having to see all those souls stuck waiting for Thor to anoint them worthy."

"On the plus side, they can't be sent to Hell, either."

Aranya sat down next to me. "We call it Helheim."

"And you are a Valkyrie, but that's kind of the same thing as an angel or a cherub, right?"

"We're related in concept, anyway."

"Do Valkyries get scared?" I asked, looking out at the water.

"Yes. I am afraid for my people and my legacy. There is great fear when the stakes are high. But at times of great fear, the brave fight on anyway."

"Like now."

"Very much like now." She turned to me, and her emerald eyes glistened with the reflection from the water. "I wish I knew how this will all turn out."

I stared back into her eyes, and an endless forest stared back at me. "What would be the fun in that?"

My stomach fluttered as Aranya reached forward and brushed the hair out of my eyes. I stayed her hand with mine. "I have a bad habit of sleeping with my partners and them winding up dead."

Leaning in a bit closer to me, she whispered, "I'll take my chances."

And then we kissed, and it was good. A spark of energy shot through my mouth and went through every limb of my body. I wanted more, so I took it, and she gave to me willingly as we rolled into the verve and covered ourselves with nature's dew.

***

I'm not saying that sex cures everything, but it definitely got my mind off my troubles for a second, and sex with an angel—Valkyrie, whatever—was out of this world. Seriously, she did things to my body nobody has ever done, things I didn't even know could be done.

Though I guess I couldn't say that Aranya was a she. After all, she had both parts down there and knew how to use them both . . . effectively. I have never cum so hard, so long, or so many times. Noodle must have been very scared for her mother, screaming at the top of her lungs like that, echoing across the lake.

"I'm going to guess that was good for you?" Aranya said, putting back on her clothes.

"I've had worse," I joked, my cheeks flush. I didn't even mind the piercing cold on my body as I wrapped myself in my bear skin.

"That's about the best compliment I could ever expect, given the source."

I grabbed her hand. "Don't die now, okay?"

"I won't. You don't die either, all right?"

I gave a chuckle. "Don't try to control me."

I wanted to stay there forever but knew I couldn't. When we reentered the bunker, Velaska would send us on the most dangerous mission of our lives. By now, the other teams were already gone. Velaska started shipping them off hours ago. I had asked her for another favor—to be sent out last. It was worth it. It's not often you can curry favor with a god, and what better way to use it than delaying your death?

"It's time to go back," I said, taking one last look at the crystal-clear lake as the sun set over it. "I don't suppose we'll ever see this place again."

"We might yet," Aranya said, grabbing my hand and pulling me up. Noodle barked at us, leading the way.

***

Once Noodle put it together that we were heading back to the bunker, she barked incessantly, pulling against the leash as I dragged her forward, desperate to stay one second longer in paradise. She'd seen Heaven, and I was taking it away from her.

I knew the feeling. For one rapturous moment, I had been on my way to Heaven—until it was stripped away from me by the paramedics who "saved" my life. I knew what it was like to chase that feeling. I chased it to the Godschurch and beyond. I chased it on every planet and with every god I met. Yet nothing, not even Aranya and Valhalla, could beat those few rapturous seconds after my death.

The white light that transported us back to the bunker came close, though. Even if its effects weren't as strong as they once were, it was the only thing besides sex that eased my troubled nerves.

"Did you have fun?" Velaska said when we reentered the bunker, blood trickling out of her nose.

I smiled. She knew me too well. She knew my innate humanness and didn't hold it against me. After all, my human qualities and my human needs had been given to me by the gods, and that meant the gods had them, too.

"My gods, Velaska," Aranya said. "What happened to you?"

Velaska's eyes were sunk into their sockets, and her cheeks caved into her mouth. Her skin was pasty and white as she leaned against the console, barely able to stand.

"I'm fine. I've never had to transport so many people such long distances before. I'm not built for it."

"You need to rest," I said, putting a hand on her shoulder.

She batted my hands away. "No. This is more important. I can rest soon, once you are away."

"But—"

"Do not talk back to your god!" Her deep voice echoed through the bunker.

"Fine," I said, feeling like she'd slapped me. "I'm ready. What planet did we pull?"

"I saved the best just for you. Eratus. It's an old mining planet the gods created two hundred thousand years ago and then abandoned shortly after, well before humanity emerged as the dominant life form."

"You just left some planets before they developed—to what, wither and die?"

"Yes," she said, her voice softer now. "Often, actually. Some planets just didn't take to life, or at least human life, so they were abandoned. Interestingly, a human civilization did find it habitable. They came to it ten thousand years ago on an intergalactic cruiser and set up shop mining ore from the planet's core."

"Why is this the best one?" Aranya asked.

Velaska smiled, her radiance dulled by the pain quaking through her body. "I'm glad you asked. This is the civilization closest to a hostile planet. A known Horde planet exists just twelve light-years away."

"So, there's a good chance that this colony has contact with the Horde," I said.

"Yes, and more, they are remote enough that no god has claimed this planet. They have independence and likely have a good handle on Horde tech, plus, they have three hotspots for you to check out. Of all the models we ran, this one is the most likely to have the Godless on it."

I tilted my head with a mock smile. "And you are giving it to me? How sweet."

"Mm-hmm." Velaska decided to ignore me. "Actually, it's because if there are Godless on the planet, there is no better agent to handle them than you. You have the most experience and the most—well, let's call it a violent temperament—when it comes to the Godless."

"I'm comfortable with that," I said. "Let's go."

"In a minute," Velaska said. "First, you look . . . just ridiculous."

She was right. I was still in the clothes that Bjorn bought for me. Leather chest plate, bear skin fur around my shoulder. I looked like an Amazon, not an agent of the Godschurch.

"What? I like it," Aranya said.

"You would," Velaska replied. "It's unbecoming an officer of the Godschurch. And really, it's just ridiculous."

Velaska snapped her fingers, and my clothes were suddenly more familiar to me. Instead of Bjorn's leather shoes, I now had on my thick steel-toed boots. My pants were now my more comfortable stretch jeans, complemented by a ratty old t-shirt. Slung around my shoulders was a holster with a fully charged demon hunter under each arm; two revolvers hung around my waist. Best of all, I was back in my leather coat—the one I used for years on Earth and had been replaced by Velaska once before after she blew me up.

"Thank god. I was so sick of wearing pelts."

"I thought you might be."

"What do you think?" I asked, turning to Aranya. "You've never seen me like this."

She shrugged. "It's okay. I like the fur better."

Velaska took a deep breath in. "Are you ready to leave now?"

"Oh yeah."

"Then I wish you two happy travels, but not too happy. And if you find the Godless, give them hell."

Velaska snapped her fingers, and just like that, we were gone, leaving her in a room full of analysts and the hope that we would find the Godless base before more gods were murdered.

CHAPTER 13

Exhilaration coursed through my veins as I gripped my demon hunters again. I knew the charges were pieces of human soul, and I should find that abhorrent, but I didn't care. I had lost them in the Godschurch explosion, and Velaska gave them back to me, just like she gave me back Noodle. For the first time in days, I felt whole.

I reappeared in a flash of white light on the outskirts of a giant chemical plant. Green light shone from underneath the complex and gave it an ominous backlight, causing its already imposing metal construct to loom even more darkly over the chasm.

Aranya appeared next to me and took a position behind the wall of the rocky cavern that protected the plant on every side. My hands shook as I gripped the guns tight. This trip was harder on my body than usual. Gods aren't powerful enough to leap people between planets, but Velaska harnessed the power of the bunker to amplify her abilities at the expense of her own health and mine.

That is why the Godschurch was initially set up, actually. The gods could not communicate with each other, and they needed access to different points in the universe without expending all their energy.

"First place, and we already found the Horde."

"All right," Aranya said, pulling me toward her behind the rock. "What's the plan?"

Two termites with massive tactile Horde machine guns strolled past as we crouched behind the top of the cliff face. When they passed, I looked down the narrow bridge which would be our only entrance to the plant—that is, if we were traveling by foot.

"Do you think you can lift us above the cliff and drop us down at the top of that spire?" I asked.

"I can drop you down there, but I was not built for stealth. I cannot go inside the plant without sounding the alarm."

She pointed to her wings, which extended several feet behind her. She was right. She couldn't risk being seen until we had an idea of what we were dealing with inside.

"All right. Drop me down there, and then wait for me to signal you. Hopefully, I won't need you, but if I do, come in hot and ready to fight."

She smirked. "I can do that."

***

Aranya flew me to the top of the plant and left me on the spire, the highest point on the plant, and I climbed down to the roof from there. I ran into a Horde centipede and a fire ant guarding the roof with more Horde tech and confirmed my suspicions that this plant wasn't run by the Godless. Still, the Horde were creating weapons, and nobody creates guns without the intent to use them. Destroying even one facility would set back whatever plans they had—all without announcing our presence to the Godless.

My demon hunters evaporated the guards on the roof before they had a chance to alert their comrades. I once thought that we had destroyed the last of the Horde during the Horde Wars. How naïve of me. We destroyed an armada of ships, sure, but the Horde had invaded the whole galaxy, with thousands of planets under their control.

Their defeat on Earth set back their plans, though, but from the looks of this plant, they would be back to full strength very soon—which meant I couldn't leave this facility standing. Even if I could only destroy one plant, it would make a dent in their arsenal.

I pressed the earpiece. "Testing. Can you hear me?"

Aranya's voice rang in my ear. "Loud and clear."

"Wait for further instructions. I think I saw a big glass skylight on the roof. If I need you, I will signal you there."

"Copy."

Green goop pulsated through the halls under the slotted walkway beneath my feet. A metal hatch granted me access to the facility. I spun open the wheeled knob to open it, then dropped inside to the main plant. Katrina warned us that the layout would be confusing, but if we could follow the green tubes on the wall, they would eventually lead to the main tub of green goop at the center of the plant. Placing a charge there would destroy everything.

I expected the place to smell like charred flesh, but it didn't. I can't say it smelled pleasant, but it was more a stale smell like a musty grandmother's house.

The bright green liquid swirled through the tubes above me as I skulked along, using the darkness as best I could to avoid the creeping, crawling Horde guards slithering past every few seconds. Eventually, the tubes led me to the center of the facility. Just like Katrina had predicted, a gigantic vat of green goop pulsated in the center of the room. Above it, two mosquitos worked the controls of a robotic arm, making it scoop up the green goop and place it on a conveyor belt. I wondered how many humans had been slaughtered to make these Horde weapons.

"*Fedhkfinjeroi*," I heard across from me on a metal walkway. "*DFhwdkfj kljdf!*"

A fire ant was above me, pointing a gun at my chest, screaming at me. I was found out. I looked past the ant and saw a skylight above the reactor core. A dark figure with wings silhouetted against the sky, and I hoped it was Aranya.

"I need you," I said into the earpiece.

Within seconds, Aranya crashed through the skylight. I used the distraction to fire a demon hunter charge at the ant, who vaporized instantaneously. I rushed over to the ant's position just as a squadron of pill bugs descended on me.

"It's always an adventure with you," Aranya said, landing at my side.

I picked up the ant's gun and drew Aranya's sword out of her sheath. "Get ready to fly."

I slashed the ant's gun in half as the bugs fired on us, then flung the pieces over the side of the railing toward the vat of green goop below. We only had a couple of seconds before the gun exploded.

Aranya picked me up and dodged the lasers whizzing by us as she flew us out of the plant. The gun exploded below us and set off a chain reaction, vaporizing the vat of goop and eradicating the plant from existence. We managed to get high enough into the air to avoid being vaporized along with it, but just barely.

***

It was hours in the cold, frigid air before we reached the second hot spot on our itinerary. Aranya held me close to her chest, keeping me warm with her body heat. The cold air didn't seem to bother her as it whipped against her, but without her heat, I would have died of hypothermia for sure.

We flew over the icy land until it turned into sea and then back to land again. Funny-looking monsters rose from the depths and snacked on each other. In the waves of the water, I recognized the vague outline of sharks and whales, alligators and turtles, but it was as if they were elongated and stretched from the pictures in my memory to fit onto this world.

The whales, for instance, were behemoths even on Earth, but on this planet, they were somehow even more immense. We glided past massive birds as we flew. Vultures and eagles still populated Earth, but nothing the size and shape of what I saw on this planet. They could shred me in half with one claw and gobble me alive while still having room for a dessert of Aranya.

Of course, that would never happen. Aranya would never let any injury befall me while she cradled me in her arms. She was a protector, first of Valhalla, then of the Godschurch, and now of me. I felt completely safe in her arms, in a way I had never felt before. I should have been on high alert. After all, she could have dropped me at any time, and if she dropped me, I would have surely fallen to my death on this weird planet that had no god to defend it, and thus no Heaven to speak of—yet, I knew she wouldn't. It surprised me to realize that I trusted her.

***

By the time we landed at the second site, I was frozen stiff. I couldn't fight if I wanted to. Luckily, the location was nothing but an active volcano, spewing lava all over the surrounding area and leaking in a near-constant stream. I sat on the edge of a lava rivulet and warmed myself on the heat coming off the molten rock.

Aside from warming myself, the second site was a bust. There was only one more to check out before we wrote off this planet. Before we left for the last site, though, Aranya insisted I slept. I hadn't slept since well before the Godschurch blew up, and I was running on pure adrenalin. I wanted to keep going, but she had the wings, so she made the rules.

While I huddled inside a cave, Aranya went and found firewood to construct a nice fire for us—well, really for me. She was perfectly comfortable and never needed sleep.

When she returned, I cuddled up next to her around the fire, and she draped me in her bear skin pelt for extra warmth.

"Tell me a story about your world," I said. "I know almost nothing about it."

"There's not much to tell, honestly. After Odin won the right to govern part of the universe as he saw fit, Zeus and his pantheon of old gods went away, confident we would destroy ourselves in a millennium, but we didn't. On the contrary, we thrived, mostly because we didn't try to build new civilizations, and we didn't try to conquer. We didn't have the power of creation—that right stayed with Zeus alone, so we had to live with the planets we had and split them up between us."

"How many were there?"

"About forty across a very small part of the galaxy, which meant we were never out of contact from the other planets for too long. That was always one thing I hated about the old ways. The planets were so spread out that once you left your friends, you never saw them again."

"But you did abandon your friends, didn't you? When you picked Odin and Thor over the pantheon?"

She stopped. "Yes, I abandoned them, and it still wounds me that I did it, but my heart was with Thor and his people, so I did what I must, and I have never regretted it. I found a family with Odin and the Norse—with Thor."

"Will you return to them when this is all over?"

"If there is anything to return to, I will. They will need me now more than ever."

I thought of everything Aranya had lost, how much I had lost. I didn't want to dwell on these things, but for the first time, I felt a deep wound at the idea of losing Aranya. It made me want to keep my distance . . . I was just so tired of the loss. I couldn't say anything to her about it. I was not selfish nor weak. I would carry on, whether or not we made it through this, but for now, I wanted to enjoy the fire and the company. I put the bear skin over my face and drifted off to sleep.

***

It was just before dawn when I woke, though I wasn't sure if I'd slept a day, a week, or longer. Aranya had not moved since I nodded off. She stared at the fire as if it held the long-lost secret to bring Thor back from the dead, but there was no secret. It was a foregone conclusion that Thor was gone, as were Persephone, Demeter, and all the other gods and officers who gave their lives in service to the Godschurch. Nothing could bring them back.

The sun crested over the volcano soon enough. Aranya went to find food and came back with a bushel of fish which she cooked for me to eat. It was the best meal I ever remember eating. The Godschurch had dreadful cooking, with premade meals and freeze-dried nutrient bars. Sometimes I got better food on an assignment, but those meals usually ended up being quick and dirty, consisting of whatever I could find on a street corner during a quiet moment.

After breakfast, Aranya scooped me up in her arms and started on the journey to the last location. It was not far from the active volcano, but with the wind whipping at my face, I was anxious for it to be over.

We flew above tundra and white-capped fields of the planet Eratus, with almost no life to speak of, except the occasional oversized polar bear. Eventually, the snow started to erode, showing the cracked ground underneath, and I knew we were close. A plume of green smoke shot into the air over the horizon, and as we neared it, we saw a massive, metal plant rising into the air, dwarfing the surrounding mountains. Staring out from every rafter and tower was an image I knew well—a plateau with a pillared temple on top, painted in red, and crossed out with a giant X. The symbol for the Godless.

CHAPTER 14

Whoever built the Godless chemical plant used the same blueprint as the Horde facility we just blew up. Aranya landed us on its spire just like she had done earlier. Knowing my way around on the inside was definitely going to work to my advantage.

"All right, just like before. You wait out here until I signal. Don't stay out of range of the earpiece, got it?" I blew into the earpiece to make sure it was still working.

Aranya folded her arms across her chest. "A lot of good not going in guns blazing did you last time. You almost got shot. I should come in with you, and we'll rough the Godless up. It'll be cathartic."

"I don't deny that, but if we go in there guns blazing, we'll never know if there are any more bases or not—and that's what matters. If we don't use every opportunity to find every Godless base, then this mission is a complete failure."

"Blowing up the armory of my enemy is not a failure, but I will do as you say."

I made my way down the spire's metal ladder onto the roof. The slatted grates beneath me revealed an ocean of green ooze, flowing in tubes along every wall. A scrawny boy, no more than fifteen, guarded the hatch that led inside the plant. Poor kid. He was barely able to hold the gun in his hands. I doubted he'd ever actually fired the weapon before, and I wasn't going to give him the chance.

I leaped forward and cracked his neck. He collapsed onto the metal grate, and I pulled him into the shadows. I pressed my finger to my ear, and my earbud popped to life. "I'm at the hatch. Going inside."

"Be careful," Aranya's voice crackled.

I turned the wheel on the rusted metal hatch and ducked inside. "No promises."

***

A combination of charred flesh and rancid meat rose into my nostrils and seeped into my pores. The Horde plant had smelled stale from the green ooze, yes, but the stench had been tolerable; this plant smelled so bad I could barely keep down my lunch.

Footsteps clomped across the metal stairwell, and I ducked away until they passed. Luckily, the ooze flowing down the hallway tubes was more muted than at the Horde plant, giving plenty of darkness for me to take cover.

I needed to locate the person in charge, the person who could give me the information I needed about the Godless—or die suffering. Following the green goop would take me to the center of the plant, but that's not necessarily where I wanted to go. I was going to have to pick off someone to send me in the right direction . . . someone along the periphery who wouldn't be missed.

Instead of following the green goop toward the reactor, I turned the opposite way and took a set of metal stairs down to a lower deck. I had a hunch that most of the workers were on the lower levels, near the ground floor, and I was right. The sound of workers gabbing away grew louder as I descended one floor and then another.

"I'm going to nab one of these worker bees to get some info," I said into my earpiece.

"I c—*sssfffzz*—hear—*sssfff*." I could hardly make out what Aranya said to me, and as I descended another flight, all I heard was static. I was on my own.

The lower I got, the worse the stench of rotting flesh. It wasn't hard to understand why every worker I saw wore yellow suits and gas masks, standard for handling waste and hazardous materials. No one could withstand these putrid odors for long.

I ducked behind the stairwell when I finally made it to the ground floor. A dozen furnaces dotted the room, and each funneled to a wide pipe which carried whatever they tossed into it throughout the facility. A team of two yellow-suited workers stood in front of each furnace, tossing material into the green fires inside the furnace. I crept into the darkness next to one of the furnaces, figuring I could peel off one of the more isolated workers.

That's when I saw what the workers were throwing into the furnace. I covered my mouth and focused on keeping my dinner down. Arms, legs, heads, and feet—human body parts. That was the decaying smell that overwhelmed every inch of the plant. They were burning human remains, probably trying to get the last essence of soul out of them. I stood in the darkness, panting, trying not to vomit, and watched the workers until one of them tapped their partner on the shoulder and pointed to the stairs. The yellow suit ambled away, down a dark corridor, perfect for me to follow.

I crept through the hallway behind the suit. It yanked the string on a shower to rinse away the human remains, then unzipped their suit, revealing a tall, lithe man with salty gray hair. After setting his helmet on a metal bench and hanging up his suit, he walked across the hallway into what I presumed was the bathroom. I snuck through the doorway before it shut, ready to confront him.

***

The bathroom was a standard affair, full of metal doors, toilets, and a trough along one wall where all the men pissed together like animals. It seemed like the salty gray-haired man was the only person in the bathroom, but I peeked under each stall just to be sure we were alone before I locked the door. I pulled out my revolvers and stepped forward.

"I need information," I barked.

The man stopped peeing into the trough and turned around. I smashed him in the nose with my gun. He screamed out, and I shoved the gun deep into his mouth.

"*Shh*. Okay. I don't want to blow your head off. I'm trying to be stealthy here, and a gunshot will draw everyone's attention. But if you scream, I'm going to blow your head off, got it?"

The man nodded, and I slowly withdrew my gun from his mouth. Just as I did, the door knob jiggled, and the door slammed twice from the other side. "What's going on in there!?"

I dug the revolver into the man's temple. "Tell them everything is okay. There's a leak. You are fixing it."

"Sorry!" the man shouted. "There's a leaky toilet in here. We're working on it. Use the one down the hall."

"Come on!" I heard the man on the other side stomp away.

"Good job," I said. "That wasn't so hard, was it?"

"What do you want?"

"Information. I need to find out where your main base is and have a talk with your leader."

"I have no idea—"

"I know, you're just a grunt. Nothing but a slightly useful and very stupid instrument. But you know who has that information and where I can find them, don't you? Where is your boss?"

"The—the boss. He's been overseeing everything. Comes and goes when he wants. Never know when he's going to be here."

"Is he here now?"

"I—I—I haven't seen him in a while."

"Good. Now, where is his office?"

The man pointed to the far wall. "It's at the end of the hallway. Two floors up, away from the smell. Says 'Superintendent' on the door."

"Good job. Now I don't have to kill you. Anything else?"

"That's all I know, I swear. What are you gonna do to me now?"

I slammed the butt of my gun into the man's head, and he collapsed.

***

I slid the man into a stall and pulled down his pants to make it look like he was taking a dump. I didn't have much time before he woke up and told everybody that I was here. Hopefully, that was enough time to find the boss's office and get the information I needed. I came to the door marked Superintendent. At least the man had given me good directions.

Of course, the door was locked.

I smashed the handle with my demon hunter, and the door swung open. Inside, the room was quiet. Deadly quiet. I stepped a foot inside, making sure there wasn't someone behind the door.

The walls were bare, except for a corkboard where the superintendent pinned notes. In the center of the room was a big metal desk cluttered with papers. I walked toward it and noticed an ID badge hanging from the lamp. When I looked at the photo, my jaw dropped to the floor. I recognized the foreman.

It was Dean—my old partner—working for the Godless.

I turned around just fast enough to see a hand come out of the shadows and knock me across the face. The earpiece fell out of my ear as I fell to the floor, unconscious.

CHAPTER 15

"You are an idiot, Rebecca," was the first thing I heard when I regained consciousness. Sometimes I wondered how much brain damage I had after being knocked out as many times as I had been in my life, but it wasn't a good time for that.

When my eyes refocused, I saw a dead man. Dean. The left side of his face was replaced with a metal exoskeleton and bright red eye—just like the one I used to sport before Velaska fixed me up.

"Dean?" I said groggily. "What is going on?"

"You could have lived out the rest of your life ignorant to the dealings of the Godless, and I would never have known you survived our attack, but instead you had to pull a Rebecca, get involved in things that don't concern you, and come half-cocked into this plant at the ass-end of nowhere, all by yourself, surrounded by Godless, to what, get revenge? That's very stupid."

Good. He didn't know Aranya was outside. He must not have seen my earpiece, which I couldn't feel in my ear anymore. With a casual scan of my surroundings, I saw it lodged under a small table in the corner of the room.

"You nailed me," I said, nodding. "I jump without thinking all the time."

"Yes, you do. It's what got me killed in the first place."

"No! You wanted to go into the house first. You demanded it!"

"Only because *you* nearly got yourself killed in that print shop. If you hadn't run off by yourself, who knows what would have happened!"

"I know what would have happened," I sighed. "I would have been first to that door, and I would have died. I'm sure that would have been preferable to you—and to the Godschurch. I've worked with them for months, and they still don't want me. Tress even accused me of betraying her. What do I have to do to prove myself to them?"

Dean pointed his crooked finger to his robotic face. "At least you still have your whole face. Look at me. I'm a monster!"

I looked up at his mutilated face. Even the half that wasn't robotic was covered in deep burn scars. "What happened, Dean? What happened after—"

"After the Godless took you? They found me . . . they found me smoking and charred. They saved me—no, *he* saved me. . ."

"Who saved you? The leader of the Godless? Who is he, Dean?"

"So that's what this is all about, isn't it? You want to know who is pulling the strings?"

"It's about more than that. It's about stopping you. It's about you killing gods, Dean. This is about you completely violating the mission of the Godschurch."

"It was *never* my mission! *This* was my mission. To lay in wait until the day that the Godless were powerful enough to take down the Godschurch, and then to destroy everything they built."

The implications of his statement flooded over me. He was a spy, a member of the Godless all along, and his job was to lay in wait. Every clone of Dean was implanted with his memories, including those of his betrayal, which meant…

"That's how Fezzick knew the codes," I said. "One of your clones gave it to him."

The scars on his face stretched when he smiled. "That's right, Rebecca. My handprint gave them access to the code banks, a perk of being the best agent in the Godschurch. I was to send them when the Godless were ready to come out of the shadows and carry out their mission, but I never got a chance. Luckily, one of my clones did. He provided the codes to Fezzick, who did his part to destroy you."

I scooted forward in my chair, trying to line myself up with the earpiece. "Why not just use Dimitri?"

Dean laughed. "Dimitri was an idiot. He brought you to the Godless and forced us to speed up our plans. He talked a big game but didn't know anything. We would have shot him for incompetence eventually if you hadn't arrested him."

"Why did it take you so long then? Why not just blow us up after you died?"

"We needed the location of the gods and your compatriots. It took six months for us to maneuver the pieces around, so we could destroy you and the god scum you work for."

"How did he know to betray us? How did the Dean clone know?"

"A word. A simple word. *Esperanto.* When the bomber whispered it to my clone, he knew it was time. Nobody knew the word except the leader, the bomber, and me."

It was time to make my move. I was close enough to my earpiece that one good hit would send me to the ground where I could grab it with my mouth.

"You son of a bitch! You killed so many people!"

Dean did what I thought he would do when insulted—what all powerful men do when insulted—and decked me across the face, sending my chair falling to the ground. I reached out my tongue and quickly snatched out the earpiece inside my mouth before he pulled my chair up from the floor.

"That was mean, Rebecca. I would rather us work together, truth be told. You and I could be very powerful together."

I stuck the earpiece inside my cheek. "And betray the Godschurch."

"There is no Godschurch, Rebecca. Not anymore. Don't you see that? We destroyed it. And now we will eradicate what remains."

I almost swallowed the earpiece as I gasped at the sheer bravado of his words. It was my idea to unfreeze the Deans to make more teams, and that decision may have doomed the surviving members of the Godschurch.

***

Dean typed furiously on his computer for another hour, watching me with the side of his eye as he input numbers into the computer. I leaned forward and spat the earpiece into my hand while he was distracted behind the monitor. I thought about pressing the button, but that would alert Aranya, and I needed him to keep talking if he was going to betray his master.

"What are you doing?" I asked him finally, tonguing the fat lip he'd given me.

"Calculating the launch, of course."

"Launch! You're launching another rocket?"

"Of course. The leader trusts only me to launch his payloads into the universe, and so far, I have never missed."

I felt the earth quake under me. "You don't have to do this, Dean. The gods, they did right by you."

He nodded, standing up. "Yes, they did right by me, but what about the rest of humanity? For too long, we have been nothing but the gods' playthings. Now, we take back what is ours."

Dean pulled a pair of handcuffs out of his desk and brought them over to me. He untied me from my chair and brought my hands in front of me, snapping the handcuffs onto my wrists and pulling me to my feet. "Come. We have a long trip ahead of us."

There were a dozen opportunities to snap his neck, but I turned them all down. I needed him to trust me if he was going to reveal the leader to me. "Where are you taking me?"

Dean smirked. "I've spoken with the leader and convinced him that you are valuable. He would like a word with you."

"At least you're not lying and saying there isn't a leader."

"I know better than to try lying to you, Rebecca. Our leader appreciates a good soldier. He won't take you for granted. He won't send you to die. Unlike the Godschurch. Doesn't that sound nice?"

I nodded. "Actually, it does."

He dragged me by the handcuffs out of the room and into the main reactor room. Now, the floor was cleared of people. A pool of green ooze seeped down into a massive hole in the middle of the room that hadn't been there before.

Dean dragged me forward and pushed my head down to look into the newly formed hole, where a massive missile, double the size of either I saw before, rose past me and up into the rafters of the building. As it rose, the roof of the building broke apart, and the rocket ascended into the sky, waiting to be launched into space.

Dean yanked me back by the hair. "This will take down Aphrodite and her ilk. It has enough payload to wipe out all of Mount Olympus on her planet and the fifty gods that live there."

"Dean, please, don't do this. You can change the universe without killing the gods."

"It is already done. One day, people will thank me for cleansing the universe of a plague. The leader will make you see the truth."

***

Dean pushed me down the hallway toward the exit at the end of a dark tunnel. At the end of that tunnel would hopefully be a shuttle to take me to the Leader. I only hoped that the beacon in the earpiece would show the Godschurch my location. I was risking my life to find the Godless base, but in doing so, I would be able to expose the leader and bring down the whole organization. If that wasn't worth risking my life for, I didn't know what was.

"You will like our leader," Dean said. "He will be very charming . . . right until the moment he kills you."

"I am not easily charmed, but I do look forward to meeting him, even if he intends to kill me."

Dean smirked, gliding his hand up my back. "Not easily charmed? As I seem to remember, that's not the case."

I slept with Dean the first time I met him, this was true, but I didn't do it because he was charming. I did it to release the emotions I was feeling—the anxiety of joining the Godschurch, coming back from the dead, and seeing the nexus of the universe. It was a way to regain some power over my life, nothing more, but that wasn't going to endear myself to him, so I couldn't say it.

"You were quite charming," I replied with a coy smile. "I was sorry we only got the one time together."

He chuckled to himself and pushed me toward the exit. "There will be plenty of time for that." We'd stepped onto some sort of loading dock. In front of us, a small two-seater ship hovered over a landing strip.

"It doesn't look like much. That's going to get us to the leader?"

Dean nodded. "It has a functional warp drive, and we use wormholes to shrink the distance we need to travel, circumventing a thousand light-years in a matter of moments. We may not have the power of the gods, but science has given us something better."

Dean pulled a clicker out of his pocket, and the doors to the shuttle opened for us. A great roar thundered from overhead as Aranya swooped down from the roof and tackled Dean.

"Murderer!" she shouted, raising her sword to deal Dean a fatal blow. I couldn't let that happen. He was our only shot at finding the leader, and we couldn't use him if he was dead.

"No!" I slammed my body into Aranya and rolled across the tarmac with her. I ended up on top of her, pinning her to the ground for a moment. She could easily have overtaken me, but she only lifted her face to meet mine.

"What are you doing?" she whispered.

"Punch me."

"What?"

"Punch me. Now."

Aranya swung her fist and clocked me. I fell off her, and she pounced on top of me.

"I have to go with him," I said. "He's bringing me to the leader."

Aranya struggled to pin down my arms. "That's suicide."

"That's the mission. You have to let me go. They're launching a missile to take out Aphrodite and fifty other gods. You need to get them to safety."

"Come with me."

"I can't." I looked over at Dean. "I have my earpiece. When we get airborne, I'll turn on the beacon. Save the gods, then follow me."

I kicked Aranya off me, and she tumbled away. I rushed back over to Dean. "Let's go!"

Dean's demon hunter hung loose around his belt, and I went for it. I grabbed it and fired at Aranya as she flew away, close enough to make it seem real but far enough to guarantee her safety. Dean wanted to react, but by the time he could, he saw I was helping him and let it happen.

I made my way to the passenger's seat of the ship and hopped inside. Dean jumped into the driver's seat, and the shuttle took off into the Heavens. I placed the gun on the center console, and he took it back into his belt.

"What changed your mind?" he asked.

"You are very convincing. The church has done nothing but take advantage of me. If there's even a chance the Godless will treat me better, I'll take it. Screw the church."

I watched Aranya fade into the distance, and then the planet fell away as Dean's shuttle rose higher into the sky. He flipped through a hundred switches, and we broke through the atmosphere into space.

"Hold on," Dean said.

And I did. I pressed the tracker on my earpiece and dropped it into the seam of my chair, then grabbed onto the center console with all my strength. Dean pressed forward on the thrust, and I slammed back into the seat. The stars turned a bright white, and then a rainbow of colors flooded over the ship as it shot through the Heavens.

As we flew away, I saw a streak in the distance and knew it was the bomb. I just hoped that Aranya could get there in time to stop it.

CHAPTER 16

"I don't want you to be afraid," Dean said when we came out of light speed.

"I'm not afraid of anything, Dean."

He smiled. "Good. Good."

The shuttle came to a stop in the upper atmosphere of the planet, a planet situated within a hundred thousand miles of a red, giant star. The star seemed to expand with every second I sat there, staring at it gape-jawed.

"What are you doing?" I said. "You're going to—"

"I told you," Dean said. "Just trust me."

I looked over at him. "No offense, Dean, but the Godless haven't been that honorable, so trust isn't really easy for me right now."

He turned to me as the shuttle jutted forward on impulse power. "I didn't say to trust the Godless. I said to trust me."

***

We landed on the tarmac outside of the sprawling ruins of a base. Only liquified remnants of the buildings remained, and then only as nubs, mere inches above the ground. I couldn't look up into the sky because it was on fire from the red giant. Even in the air conditioning of the shuttle, the heat was stifling.

"Did you just bring me here to burn me alive?"

"Interesting offer, but no."

The ground quaked under us and shifted to reveal that we were on a platform. Below us, a chasm opened deep into the underground, farther than I could see. The platform rose slightly into the air, then descended into the darkness. The opening above us closed, sealing out all lights except for those from the shuttle and tiny ones along the walls that flickered as we fell faster and faster into the cavern.

"We can't stay on the surface, obviously," Dean said. "The heat is too much. The base is far underground."

"And we can't trace your heat patterns because the sun interferes with our sensors. Smart."

"Also, because only a fool would set their base at the mouth of a red giant."

I looked over at him. "Only if they expected their base to be permanent."

He squeezed my hand. "You are much smarter than I gave you credit for."

It took everything in my power not to reach out and strangle him. I wondered if he knew just how much contempt I held for him and how close he was to being killed or if he was truly oblivious to my hatred for him. But how I felt didn't matter. I had to wait until I found the leader of the Godless and made sure he was on this base. Once that happened, it was going to be gratifying to pound Dean into a pulp.

He squeezed my hand again. He was getting more affectionate, and I was trying not to get more nauseous. His eyes fluttered as he looked at me, and there was a twinkle in them—well, the one that wasn't robotic. The sides of his mouth were shiny where the scars stretched into a smile.

"You're safe. Don't worry. I would never let anything happen to you."

I wondered if a power surge had fried his circuits. Why else would he be so nice and caring to somebody he slept with once and only knew for a couple of days? I wasn't particularly charming, or very nice. Still, I had an angle. I didn't want to overthink it. If he wanted me to coo for him, I would do so, right until the moment I slit his throat.

As we neared the bottom of the shaft, two metal bay doors opened for us. The platform lowered and revealed a hundred ships and thousands of workers bustling around a great hangar. On the other side of the building stood a gigantic monolith, haloed with a different colored ring every hundred or so feet.

It rose from a hole in the base of the hangar, reaching at least a hundred stories in the air. Even from my position across the hanger, it dominated my vision. An ominous green glow emanated from under the tower, which likely meant it was powered by the same human souls that powered the Horde weaponry and the Godless missiles.

"What is that?" I asked.

"The final solution," was all he said.

Those words have never been good, ever, in the history of the universe.

***

The platform came to a stop on the floor of the hangar. Dean lifted open the door to my shuttle and pulled me gently to my feet. I was less a hostage than a date at this point, and I got an eerie feeling in the pit of my stomach like we were going to meet his parents. He hadn't been nervous this whole ride, but as he grabbed my hand and pulled me forward through the maze of shuttles, sweat built up in his hand, making his palm slick with fear.

"Where are you taking me now? Prison?"

Dean heaved a guttural laugh from the depths of his belly. "Let's call it a holding cell, my dear. You won't be there for long. Soon, you'll meet the leader. Then, you will understand what we are doing, and you'll willingly join him."

The last time I spoke to the leader, he wasn't very convincing, but that might be because the Godschurch interrupted our meeting and destroyed the Godless base where he was broadcasting his image.

A shadowy figure in a black cloak stood in a glass-encased room above the hangar, looking out on the construction of the obelisk.

"Is that the leader?" I asked Dean.

He smiled excitedly. "Yes, he is thrilled to meet you. I've told him all about you."

"I didn't know you knew enough about me to get somebody excited."

***

Dean led me into a cell and took off my handcuffs. It was weird being on the other side of bars again, and it was weirder not having a forcefield to prevent me from escaping. Instead, the cell only had those rudimentary iron bars that fell out of fashion centuries ago, when technology made escaping from them easy. Of course, even if I were to escape, where would I go? Even if I somehow left these bars and made it to the hangar, I would have to climb up gods knew how long until I reached the surface, where I would be melted by the heat of the sun in moments.

I sat down and tried to ponder how I would escape but knew that I had to rely on Aranya and whatever gods remained to find me—if anything remained of them at all.

***

An hour later, Dean opened my cell door. He didn't look happy. More like a scolded dog after it just pissed on the carpet.

"What's wrong?" I asked.

"I'm sorry," was all he said.

He grabbed my hand and slammed on the handcuffs, then pulled me into the hallway, where he refused to say another word to me or even look me in the eye.

"Wait!" I shouted. I tried to stop him from pulling me forward, but his half-mechanical body was too strong for me. "Tell me what is happening."

"I lied to you," Dean said. "I didn't knowingly lie to you, but I lied to you all the same."

"What do you mean?" I said, pulling my arm away from him.

"I said you had nothing to fear, that you would be safe, but that's not true. There's every reason to fear."

Dean spun around. No longer was there a loving expression behind his good eye. It had been replaced with fear and panic.

I touched his arm with my handcuffed hands. "Tell me what's going on, Dean."

"I—" a light glowed hot pink in his mechanical eye as his head shook uncontrollably. "I can't."

He pulled me forward again, this time through a set of metal bay doors. Suddenly I was in the glass-enclosed room I'd seen earlier, looking out in the hangar bay, with the black-shrouded figure of the leader in front of me.

"Stop there." The figure had a posh accent I had only heard in rebroadcasts of old British movies from centuries before the Horde Wars.

Dean's feet stuck like they were suddenly glued in place. "Yes, my lord."

"Silence!" The accented voice boomed through the room. Dean closed his mouth sharply.

The figure turned on its heels and lowered the dark hood, revealing a face as rough as sackcloth and dark as onyx, like the edge of the universe, where light can't even escape. When he grinned, white fangs lit up his face. His blood-red eyes peered out like portals to another dimension, swirling in a pool of white pupils, untethered to their sockets.

"You have caused me much pain, Rebecca Lobdell, officer of the Godschurch."

I took a deep breath, trying to play off my nerves, but the truth was that I was frightened. "I can imagine."

"In fact," the figure said, pointing his blackened finger into the air. "You have caused me more trouble than every other member of the Godschurch combined."

"I'm honored you think so."

"If we had only destroyed you in the bombing, it would have been quite the feat, but instead, you were spared through some sort of magic."

"It wasn't magic. It was good luck."

A smile cracked the canvas face. "My dear, I know luck, and I know magic. Believe me when I tell you they are one and the same."

"Who are you?"

He floated toward me. "I shouldn't tell you, but since we are so close to the end and it is so dreadfully boring down here, I will let you in on my secret. I . . . am Dolos!"

It was obvious from his delivery that he expected the utterance of his name to be a great reveal, one that would leave me shuddering, but it did nothing. I blinked. "Who?"

His eyes narrowed. "You know, Dolos! God of trickery and guile, son of Gaia, and harbinger of doom."

I tried to look him directly in his eyes, but his pupils didn't stay in any one place for more than a second. Instead, they floated across his eyeball, dancing in every direction. They bounced off the edges of his lids before drifting off another way. "I know the words you said were supposed to be ominous, and doom is bad, but I still have no clue who you are."

"Fool!" he roared. "Never look a god in the eye!"

"You're a god?" I couldn't help myself anymore. I started laughing. The situation wasn't funny, but I couldn't help it. A whole big heaping bowl of irony fell on my lap all at once, and it hit me like a brick.

"Why are you laughing? Stop that! Stop that now!"

I wiped a tear from my eye. "It's just . . . hilarious. All this time, the Godless have been working to destroy every god in the universe, and they are run by a god—what, trying to take over the universe?"

"Fool!" Dolos shouted, slapping me across the face so hard I flung across the room. "Never disrespect a god!"

It wasn't funny anymore. My wits came back to me as I smacked hard against the metal door and fell to the ground. I stood and shook off the attack. Dean wanted to help. I could see it in his eyes, but he couldn't. Something prevented him from moving.

"How did you convince Dean to help you?" I asked, wobbling on my legs.

"It's not hard if you know what to say, my dear. Protect!"

Dean lunged forward, grabbed my arms, and locked them into place. I struggled but couldn't break free of him. His eyes said he was sorry, but his body was clearly under the control of Dolos.

"Much like you will be under my control before long."

"I wouldn't count on it," I said. "The Godschurch, even now, is on their way here."

Dolos laughed. "Are they? Why, of course, they are. Do you think I would let you keep that silly tracker in your pocket if I didn't want them to follow you? I wanted them to see my final solution first hand."

Dolos walked over to the console behind him and punched in a few buttons. Overhead a dozen monitors turned on, showing the surface. They triangulated a dot in the distance and zoomed in on it until it revealed Aranya, struggling to breathe on the surface of the planet.

"Even a Valkyrie can't stand the heat for long. This is all that is left of your Godschurch. All that came to rescue you. Pathetic."

"NO!"

Dolos stepped forward. "I have worked for this day for twenty thousand years. Nothing will stop me now, especially not you."

CHAPTER 17

I couldn't let Aranya die out in the sweltering heat of the planet's surface. I had to escape Dean's grip. Tipping my head forward slightly, I slammed it back into his nose. I leaned forward and lifted him off the floor with my powerful legs, swinging him around until he unlatched his hands from my chest.

I spun around and kicked Dean so hard he flung backward into the door and smashed his head into the metal. I used his arm and flung him into Dolos, and they both tumbled into the command console.

With the two of them in a heap, I rushed forward and slammed as many buttons on the console as possible. The obelisk swung and rotated around, knocking the workers on the platform into the green goop below. The bay doors of the hangar ceiling opened, and the pillar rose into the chasm above it.

"Fool!" Dolos shrieked, tossing Dean off and flying toward me at full speed. I raised my boot and dropped it into the console. The circuits under it sizzled and crackled as the buttons blinked frenetically.

"No!" Dolos shouted. "What have you done?" He threw me into the door and took over the controls. "Dean! Kill!"

Dean ran at me with all his might. I sidestepped him like a matador and tossed him into the glass wall, which cracked with the force of his impact. Dolos fumbled with the console as I rushed toward him. I was only inches away from him.

He saw me running toward him and called out to Dean. "Finish her, you fool!"

Dean was on me again. He tried to hurl me into the bay door, but I planted myself and swung him around using his momentum and flung him again into the glass.

I launched myself at him and swung again and again and again, faster than I ever thought possible, until Dean dropped, unconscious on the ground. Even then, I kept punching him. Except I wasn't punching his face, I was punching through his body without touching him, vibrating so fast I couldn't make out my own limbs.

"Marvelous," Dolos said as he turned to me. "Just look at yourself."

I looked down, and I could see streaks of gold where my arms should have been, but they were moving too fast to see anything except the gilded trails they left in their wake, just like the ones that followed me as I escaped the Godschurch.

"What is happening to me?" I started to hyperventilate.

"My child, don't you see? It was more than just dumb luck that caused you to survive. I suspected you were special, and here is the proof."

I looked behind him as the obelisk settled back on the ground. As it did, the hatch above it closed, and, almost imperceptibly, a little speck floated out of it onto the ceiling. It was Aranya, coming for me. I had to keep Dolos distracted.

"How am I special?" I asked. I was starting to be able to see my hands again.

"Did you know," he said, grabbing onto my arms, "that we are all made from the stuff of the gods?"

"Well, you specifically, yes, are made of god stuff, being a god."

"Not only me, everything, even humanity and the mythological creatures of old. We gods create life, yes, but every being in the universe is made from the same stuff as the gods. We simply harness that power more easily than humanity because we have a higher concentration of the god particle. However, some humans also have—they have something amazing inside of them—a gift from the nexus of the universe—waiting to be harnessed." He stopped staring at my arms and looked at me. "May I harness it for you?"

I didn't know what he was saying or what he was asking to do, honestly. I nodded toward the obelisk in the hangar. "Only if you tell me what you are doing with that thing out there."

"There is time for that," Dolos said, taking a step closer to me. "But first—"

"No," I said, jerking back, my whole body vibrating with exhilaration and fear. "You can't touch me until you tell me."

He smiled. "Very well. You are from Earth, correct?"

"Yes. That's right."

"A being your age would have gone through the black hole with the rest of your world, yes?"

"I did."

"And there you met my sister, Rhea."

The name sent shivers down my spine. Rhea was a name I tried to forget. While we were in the other universe during what we on Earth called the "Sun Incident," Rhea was our savior, our goddess, and our worst nightmare. She started benevolent, helping us make sense of what happened to us, but then she demanded sacrifices to keep protecting us. She wanted us to choose who would be eaten. Luckily, we were pulled out of the black hole before we had to sacrifice one of our kind, but since that day, her name has haunted my memories.

"I know of her," I said as calmly as possible.

"She has been imprisoned in that other dimension, the same place you were sent, by the gods, for eons. Several decades ago, she was joined by her husband, Cronus. This device will turn this star into a black hole and open the portal to bring them back into our universe. Then, we can destroy every god in our path. The only one who could defeat them was Zeus, and now that he is dead, Rhea and Cronos can join me in conquering the universe!"

"That's what this was all about?" Dean's words were slurred. The part of his face that wasn't robotic had swollen beyond recognition. "Everything I've done for you? It wasn't about humanity at all, was it? It was just your desire for revenge on the gods!"

Dean rushed forward and smashed Dolos into the console. At the same time, Aranya flew through the glass window behind us and sent the two of them flying to the other side of the room.

"Are you okay?" Aranya shouted to me.

I ran toward her. "I'm fine. Hold them off."

I couldn't read the words on the console, but one of them had to say self-destruct. Aranya pulled out her sword. She was ready to fight, but I thought she might be able to interpret the control panel better than me. "Any chance you can read this?"

Aranya looked down at the console. "As a matter of fact, yes, I can."

I grabbed the sword from her. "Find the self-destruct button. Smash it, and then destroy that console."

I turned to Dolos and Dean. Except Dean wasn't on Dolos's side, not anymore. He was screaming at Dolos with his back toward me.

"I trusted you!"

"Calm, Dean. Calm!" Dolos had his hands in the air. But the words didn't work. His betrayal of Dean had broken something in his slave's mind and made him free once again.

"I don't see one that says self-destruct!" Aranya shouted.

"Dean, keep him busy." I grabbed onto Aranya. "Take me to that weapon."

***

Demon hunter charges rang out from below as we flew through the hanger toward Dolos's final solution. Dozens of guards tried to bring us out of the air with their blasters, but they missed.

As we flew, Aranya stayed low to the ground so that I could swipe at their Horde weapons with her sword, slicing them in half and watching them blow up. Behind us, the explosions dotted our path and left charred marks on the ground.

When we reached the obelisk, a group of nerdy-looking men and women cowered in the corner near a guard rail overlooking a hole filled with the Horde's green goop. A dozen guards ran toward us, weapons drawn. There wasn't much time.

"Where is the self-destruct button?" I shouted to one of the frightened women. She looked at me, confused. I didn't speak their language, and they didn't speak mine. "Aranya, can you help me?"

"*Vlligim Nagiliat Foratum Ju?*" she shouted at the crowd.

"Zveliak!" the woman shouted back. "Nakualbrian iltobius mortunesil."

"What did she say?"

"She said there isn't a self-destruct button. They thought it would be stupid to build one in case somebody came to try and destroy it."

I couldn't argue. It was pretty stupid, though it would have come in handy right about now. I looked at the soldiers rushing toward us and got an idea. "Fine. We'll do this the hard way. Aranya, fly out there and bring me all the guard's weapons."

Aranya flew toward the guards and took their guns, just as Dolos threw Dean through the window of his observation room. Dean landed with a hard thud against the rocks on the other side of the hanger. I wanted to care that he was hurt, but the only thing I felt was fear as the hooded Dolos floated right toward us.

"Aranya! Hurry up!"

Aranya grabbed the last weapon from the guards and beelined toward me. "Now what?"

I looked down into the green ooze below the base of the obelisk. It was unstable, and when I blew it up, we would only have a few seconds to get out of the base. It wouldn't be enough time, but at least we would go down swinging.

I raised Aranya's sword over my head. "When I tell you, toss these weapons over the edge into that green goop, grab me, and fly to that shuttle. Got it?"

She made the same mental calculations I had, then nodded. "Ready."

I sliced through the weapons with her sword. "Now!"

Aranya flung the weapons into the base of the obelisk and grabbed me. She zipped us to the other side of the hangar while the explosions began to rock the ground and walls.

Dolos didn't try to stop us. He stared in stunned disbelief at the sight of his plans going up in smoke. The explosion cracked the base of the obelisk and sent it crashing to the ground, igniting explosions at the base of the green ooze at it exploded through the hangar.

I scooped Dean up from the ground as we passed over him. He was heavier than he looked, but I managed to lift him into my chest. When we neared his shuttle, I pulled his clicker from his pocket and used it to open the doors to his shuttle. Aranya tossed us both in the back and flew into the driver's seat. Behind us, the cascading explosions reached toward us. I caught a glimpse of Dolos just before he vanished.

"I hope you know how to fly this thing," I said, gripping the back seat tightly.

Aranya pulled a vial of glowing blue water from a string around her neck. "Don't worry. I have a plan."

She rubbed the blue vial and uttered a quick prayer to Odin. The whole shuttle glowed white. She muttered three more words under her breath, and we vanished, just as the shuttle bay collapsed upon itself.

***

"Is there any way to fix him?" I stood with Velaska in the bunker's sickbay.

Both of us looked down at Dean, resting mangled on a folding table.

"Maybe," she replied. "But why would you want to? He's responsible for all of this."

"I need to know why, Velaska. And we need to know what he knows. He worked with Dolos and knows more about his plans than anybody."

Velaska nodded. "We'll do what we can. Dolos is a powerful god. Maybe more powerful than anybody we have left. He is half Titan, you know, born of Gaia herself."

"If he's planning to unleash his sister from the other universe, we need to know how he's going to do it. The Godless are a secondary concern compared to the return of the Titans."

Velaska arched her eyebrow. "You sound like a leader."

"There're not a lot of other options," I said, walking away from her. "Besides, there's not much to be the leader of." I turned back. "Have you found out about anything more about me vibrating so fast I see golden streaks around me?"

"We're working on that, too."

I looked down at my hands. I didn't understand their power, and it frightened me. Dolos was a lot of things, but he didn't strike me as someone that got surprised easily. I'd seen his focused eyes when he studied my arms in that hangar. He was in awe of my power.

I walked back to the command center. More gods flooded in every hour from across the cosmos, but even with them, our numbers were piddly compared to the full strength of the Godschurch, and even at full strength, we could not stop Dolos and the Godless.

I passed by Aphrodite as I made my way to the consoles.

"Thank you," she said to me.

"It wasn't me. It was Aranya you have to thank."

She nodded. "I've thanked her too, but we wouldn't have known to evacuate if not for you. So, thank you."

Behind her, fifty more gods and a hundred cherubs crowded into the bunker. We had already outgrown this space, which was something. We needed a lot of people if we stood a chance at beating Dolos.

We certainly had our work cut out for us. First, we would need to rebuild somewhere the Godless couldn't find us.

I had failed to delete any information about where the gods were located, which meant Dolos still had it in his possession.

I thought maybe the destruction of the hangar meant the data died with it, but the next day three more attacks struck gods across the universe. Every hour the Godless went unchecked, more gods and Godschurch officers would die.

Hundreds of our men died making their way back to us. Our numbers had been in the thousands. We would be lucky if five hundred remained now.

There was a reckoning coming, and none of us were prepared for what would come next—but neither were the Godless.

They underestimated us. They doubted us. They hunted us. Yes, we were small, but we were also mighty. We would not let Dolos win, not until every one of us was killed . . . or he was.

BOOK 3

"The End Tastes Like Pancakes"

PROLOGUE

I pumped my legs until the muscles burned, and I couldn't feel my feet, but it didn't matter. The Godless were after me, and eventually, they would find me. There were too many of them and too few places for me to hide—and when they found me, they would kill me. Before they did, I needed to transfer the data on my portable hard drive to my handler in the Godschurch so they could decode it. If I did that, at least I would die a hero.

Stupid, Yvette. Stupid.

You knew you would get caught if you talked too much, and you just couldn't help it, could you? You spent too much time with them, and you got comfortable. Now you're outed as a spy and had to speed up your plans, move more quickly than you would have liked. If you could have just kept your mouth shut . . . you might've survived.

Sweat oozed off my palms as I ducked into a dark corner to catch my breath. My thumping heart echoed in my ears and pulsated through my hands. Still, when I listened for the pitter-patter of feet behind me, I didn't hear any.

I was quick—that was my one saving grace. I had always been quicker than anybody else, and that's how I let myself get sloppy. I figured my speed had saved me a dozen times before, maybe it could save me again. Maybe I could outrun the Godless and make it back to the church before they found me.

The hard drive slipped as I opened my fingers and looked at it in my hand. It lit up the darkness, and I quickly covered it with my free hand. I'd been running around the city looking for a signal. If I could find one, the Godschurch would have everything they needed to take down Dolos—the whole organization would tumble if I found a signal, but it wasn't that easy. The Godless jammed all transmission off the planet and blocked the Godschurch entrance—my only exit off the planet.

"Hey, Godschurch scum!" a shrill voice cut through the air. "We know you're hiding! You can't hide forever!"

Sandra. My best friend in the Godless. Or she thought we were friends. She brought me into the Godless, which meant she would be executed for her mistake. Signing the death warrant of people you betrayed was part of a spy's job. It wasn't hard to convince her that I hated the gods as much as she did—it was never hard to convince people you hate the same things they hate. Hatred is such an easy emotion to fake. People want to believe you, and Sandra was no exception.

I uncapped my hand from the transmitter and checked the coverage. No signal. I would have to get closer to the Godschurch to get a boost. Of course, the closer I got to the church, the more Godless I would find. They knew I had to end up there to get off the planet. All they had to do was wait me out.

The Godless were on my tail, jumping from roof to roof above me. I didn't see any on the ground, but I could hear them out there, hunting me. My lungs burned as I rushed across the street. The Godschurch wasn't far, but every inch I moved risked my capture.

"There!" I heard above me. Sandra spotted me, and soon enough, a dozen feet gave chase through the alley.

"She's over here!" a deep voice shouted as I bolted down the street. I wasn't going to lose them now. I could only hope to outrun them.

This was my fifteenth mission, and frankly, I wasn't that great a spy. It wasn't the first time I messed up by outing myself, it was just the biggest screw-up in a long line of them. I had no business being on this mission in the first place. If the Church knew the Godless on this planet had access to the plans for the Obelisk, they would have sent someone with more skill and experience.

Toni, my handler, told me this was a scouting mission—simple infiltration, nothing more. By the time we figured out the truth, I was already too deep, and they couldn't pull me out without setting back the mission by six months. We didn't have that kind of time. I had to succeed.

I stopped in a dark alley to catch my breath. I had lost my pursuers and hadn't heard anything from the rooftops in six blocks. The Godschurch entrance was straight ahead, lit up like a Christmas tree by multiple spotlights. Twenty Godless terrorists milled around with assault rifles between me and it, waiting for me to make a mistake and come closer.

I looked down at my transmitter. Still no signal. Behind me, the clomping of a dozen pairs of feet told me they were catching up to me. I had to get closer to the church, but I couldn't. Maybe, though, I could get higher. If I climbed to the top of a building, maybe I could rise above the jammer.

A rusty ladder leaned against the building next door to me, leading to a fire escape. From there, I could access the roof. I would be easily spotted, if not by the Godless members already running across the rooftops, then certainly by the ships flying overhead looking for me.

That's right, ships flying overhead. Dolos spared no expense in his quest to track me down. After all, what I had could destroy him; it could destroy everything. For the first time in our war, it could give the Godschurch the upper hand. I had the plans to take down the Obelisk.

I ran over to the ladder and started to climb. I thought of my family: my mother, my sister, and my father. They were back home on Epres, thinking I was a traveling spaceship salesman, making deals across the universe. They had no idea the danger I was in, though that was for the best. Toni would tell them I died in a spaceship accident or some other nonsense. That was the deal. I knew it when I joined, but it didn't mean I had to like it now, at the end.

"She's up there!" I heard from below as four Godless thugs came out of the shadows and started firing at me with their Demon Hunters.

The Demon Hunters were probably overkill. They were guns designed to take down gods and monsters. I was neither. Still, they used them. The charges from their guns blew up around me and disintegrated chunks from the ladder under me. I leaped from one floor to the next as the demon hunters melted away the walls around me.

"You're gonna die, scum!" Sandra shouted at me from a building across the street. It was true. I was going to die, but my life didn't matter. Not if I delivered the data to Toni and the Godschurch.

I pulled myself up to the final story and onto the roof before a Demon Hunter charge evaporated the ladder below. The Godless swarmed upon me from across the rooftops, and two choppers closed in with their mounted guns.

I looked down at my transmitter—two bars of reception. I could finally reach the church. Excellent. I typed out a quick message: "*Open ASAP*." Once I hit "send," I had done my job. Even if I died, I would die a hero . . . but that wasn't enough. I didn't want to die.

Now, I had to figure out how to survive. The Godschurch entrance was three blocks away, and every foot along the way was covered in Godless troops. More flooded into the square in front of the church with every passing second.

I had two options: wait to be captured or call for an evacuation and make a run for the church entrance. If the Godschurch sent the white beam of light down at just the right time, I could save myself. Of course, it was possible the Godless would jump inside as well and learn where our new base was located. If that happened, it could save my life while damning everyone at the church.

I should have accepted my death with dignity, but as the enemy closed in, I just . . . panicked. Pulling out my transmitter, I saw that the file had transmitted successfully. At least they had the information they needed—now to see if I could save my life. I flipped open the keyboard and wrote another short message. "*Open the portal in 3 mins. Leave it open 60 sec. Then abandon me.*"

I dropped the transmitter on the ground and smashed it to a hundred pieces with my boot. Then, I started running again. The Godless helicopters started firing on the roof just as I reached the edge, so I leaped for my life to the next building over, an abandoned gothic building with gargoyles on every ledge.

Charges from the demon hunters blew up behind me as I grabbed the head of a gargoyle and swung through the stained-glass window in front of me. I wished there was another way besides destroying priceless art, but I didn't have time.

I bounded down the stairs, the Godless shouting underneath me. The choppers shone their lights into the building, looking for me, but I managed to cling to the darkness and avoid them.

A dozen guns shattered more windows and peppered the ground around me. I swung over the railing and landed in the lobby, then took off in the opposite direction of the bullets. Seeing an old emergency exit, I crashed through it and found myself in a darkened alleyway. I thought I might get a moment's respite there, but a Godless terrorist was there in seconds, firing his machine gun at me. At least it was just a regular gun and not a demon hunter—it meant he had to reload often. As he was doing so, I rushed forward and knocked him over.

Across the square, the Godschurch beckoned me. If I reached the entrance in the next minute, I would be home free. If I didn't, I would be condemned to death. I sprinted toward it, running past the gunmen firing their demon hunters. Both choppers crested over the gothic structure and rushed forward with their guns blazing.

"You're dead!" Sandra shouted from the rooftop above me. "Come to terms with it!"

But I couldn't come to terms with it. I wanted to live. I needed to live. I deserved to live. A great white light signaled from inside the church. That was the beacon for the Godschurch. All I had to do was enter the church in the next minute, and I would return to our base. I would live to fight another day.

I had done enough. The Godschurch had all the information they needed to take down their greatest enemy, and it was time for me to rest. If I lived, I swore to the gods I would be good. I swore I would quit and go back home. My family would be so excited at my return, and I could tell them all about my adventures.

The bullets ricocheted on either side of me as I ran up the stairs and flung open the door to the church. I was home. I was done. I was—

—bleeding. Out of my stomach. I turned around to see the Godless firing at me. Another shot blew through my shoulder. I fell back into the whiteness, and it enveloped me. As I closed my eyes, I prayed to the gods that I would live.

CHAPTER 1

Dear gods, I was bored. It was my sixth meeting of the day. This has been my life every day since taking over as leader of the Godschurch two years ago.

After our base exploded and Tress died along with 90% of our agents, I was the only person left to assume command. Now, my whole life was one meeting after another—punctuated with short breaks to eat crappy food and sleep poorly—and staring at monotonous reports. Then there was another meeting and another.

I wasn't quite fat yet, but the thirty pounds I had packed on were completely attributable to my job. These days, I wasn't even walking Noodle as much, and my poor dog had grown fat and slow just like me. I was a horrible puppy parent.

"Are you listening, Rebecca?" a pudgy, garish god asked me from across my desk.

I perked up for a moment. "Yes. Sorry. I'm listening." I never thought that sitting could be tiring, but focused effort for so many hours straight was a grueling task. Honestly, it took a lot of energy not to look bored.

I was meeting with two gods, Meret and Osiris. The one speaking was Meret. "And that is why we believe that your continued use of this facility is not in the best interests of all parties involved."

At one time, he had been the Egyptian god of celebration, much like Bacchus was for the Greeks. However, once Osiris gave Meret his own planet to govern, he grew up and became an upstanding member of the Egyptian pantheon—unlike Bacchus, who took over Earth and was still the same drunk even thousands of years later.

Of course, I used the terms "Greek" and "Egyptian" colloquially as a way to remember the different sects of gods. They never called themselves that. They had long drawn out and elaborate names for their own pantheons that had existed long before they created Earth.

I was born on Earth, though, and it's where I went to school and learned about the gods, so that's how I categorized them. There were all sorts of gods across the universe. As director of the Godschurch, I protected them all. I had to keep them straight in my mind and extend them every courtesy, even when they were screwing me over.

"That wasn't our deal, Meret," I replied calmly. "You told me, not four months ago, that I could stay here as long as I needed. We haven't been able to put down roots in two years because the Godless have hunted us everywhere we've gone, but you told me to trust you—I did, and now …well, let's just say that I don't feel a lot of that trust anymore."

Two years earlier, a scumbag half-Titan/half-god named Dolos blew up the Godschurch, the only organization in the universe whose mission was to protect the gods—all the gods, no matter the pantheon. He ran a terrorist organization called the Godless, also known as the bane of my existence.

Humans from across the universe joined them in droves because they blamed the gods for their lot in life. I really thought that finding out that Dolos was a god would stop people from pledging loyalty to his organization—after all, the Godless were held together by their hatred of the gods. Their whole mission was to destroy gods, so it seemed hypocritical to work for one.

Lesson learned: never underestimate the ability of human beings to be hypocritical. They had no limit. None at all.

The Godless denied our claim. They said we were lying and that our facts—real, provable facts—were nothing but propaganda. If anything, Dolos's rampant denial caused more people to enlist, ratcheting up their numbers. This made the gods wary about letting us set up base on the planets they managed. The Godless attacks targeted them.

"We understand you might feel a little . . . put out," Meret said. "However, we feel that is not our problem."

He looked over at Osiris, an ornately dressed deity with painted eyes and dark skin. The Godschurch symbol for generations, the all-seeing eye, was based on the tattoo around his eye. It was ironic since Osiris never liked us— he hated us and the Greek pantheon at large, which accounted for most of our membership and revenue. To his credit, he never hid that fact. Contempt oozed out of every one of his perfect pores.

I crossed my arms. "And how do you expect us to move our whole organization off this planet?"

"We. Do not. Care." Osiris sneered through his thin lips and stroked his perfectly triangular beard. "We. Just want you. Gone."

"We can give you two weeks," Meret added with a smile.

"You don't want to do this, Meret," I said, leaning forward. "You know you don't. You're just doing what Osiris wants, but I think you still want to help us."

Meret's eyes darted toward Osiris, whose eyes narrowed at him. He broke out in a cold sweat. "No. That's not true. You took advantage of my hospitality, and you didn't tell me the scope of the situation. You lied to me, and I don't appreciate it."

I threw my hands in the air. "Lied to you? About what?"

Meret pointed his finger angrily as he stammered. "You—you told me the Godless were on the run, but they aren't on the run, are they?"

"They," Osiris added. "Are not."

"Maybe I embellished a little bit," I replied. "But the truth is, we've had more success in the past four months than we have in the past two years. Now that we have a base, we can recruit new agents and send them out on more missions. We've taken down more Godless cells since being here than we have in years. If you just—"

"Then why," Osiris bellowed. "Are gods. Still dying?"

He had me there. "I don't have an answer for you. We're doing our best."

"Which. Is clearly. Not good enough."

After splitting from Zeus and the Greek pantheon, the Egyptian gods controlled their own sector of the universe, free from the other gods' petty squabbles and neutral to every other conflict in the universe. As such, they had managed to avoid the Godless's wrath since Dolos targeted gods from the pantheons who worked with us. The Greek gods were our only true allies left. We used to have the trust of the Norse gods too, but . . . not anymore. They had abandoned us, too.

"I'm not saying it's good enough. What I'm saying is that we're making progress now. If you—"

"And," Osiris said, cutting me off. "Leaving a bullseye. On our chests."

"The Godless don't even know we are here!"

Osiris grinned a wide grin. He didn't say another word. He left that for Meret, who shook his head in disbelief. "Is that what you told the other gods whose planets you used? Every one of them turned up dead."

It was true. We'd had to move our base twelve times in the past two years, and somehow the Godless always knew where we were, no matter the extensive efforts we took to hide ourselves; they assassinated any gods who took pity on us.

"Is there anything I can do to change your mind?" I said to Osiris. It wasn't worth talking to Meret. He was just a puppet.

"Stop Dolos. Then, you may stay. Indefinitely."

That wasn't likely to happen, at least not in the next two weeks, but I couldn't tell him that. "Thank you for your generosity. I'll start the plans to vacate this planet. If you could give us a month, that would be much appreciated."

Osiris shook his head. "Even two weeks. Is generous."

***

After my meeting, I walked out into the third-floor hallway of Meret's building, which overlooked an atrium filled with exotic plants of all kinds. They all looked vaguely like what I remembered from Earth. That was the thing with humanoid planets, they all appeared similar, with just enough variations to make you know you're not at home. Like the palm trees that breathed fire every hour on the hour.

The atrium sat at the base of Meret's pyramid, a glass-enclosed structure he'd built to honor himself and to make a steady profit. He'd given us access to the first ten floors at an incredibly marked-up price. Gods didn't need money, but they sure liked sticking it to humanity any chance they got.

I craned my neck to stare up into the pointed glass pyramid that came to a tip a hundred floors up. Thousands of Godschurch agents and analysts bustled around the floors above me, and I was responsible for every single one of them.

When I fought in the Horde Wars, my fellow soldiers depended on me to take out a target, and it was a burden. I thought it was a burden when the Godschurch assigned me missions where my life and the life of gods and humans were at stake. But those things were nothing compared to the burden of thousands depending on me for their safety and security. That pressure weighed on my soul and never left. Often, in the dead of night, I woke up in a cold sweat.

My old boss, Tress, gods rest her soul, was crabby and sharp with everybody she met. I always thought she was a bitch, but now I knew she had a tremendous burden to carry—the burden of everybody in this building and every god in the universe—she was responsible for protecting them all. No matter what happened or who messed up, the responsibility fell on her shoulders.

The weight I carried was even greater. When Tress ran things, even she answered to the Masters of the Godschurch, three men who oversaw the spiritual side of the church. That eased her burden. When the Godschurch blew up, though, so did they. I haven't had time to find three new masters, not while battling the Godless and changing planets every couple of months.

Maybe Aranya was right. We should just move the whole operation into a ship in the sky, where we could travel the universe, moving as necessary. Osiris was right about one thing—we were sitting ducks on this planet. If the Godless wanted, they could destroy us at any time.

And yet, they didn't destroy us, even though they knew where we were—at least not this time. Up until now, we couldn't make it even a month before they obliterated the gods that helped us, forcing us to flee to another galaxy. Why were they leaving us alone now? Was it just to toy with us? Or did they have some other purpose? Whatever the answer, I didn't like the questions.

Dolos already had the coordinates of every god in the galaxy, and no matter how hard we tried, most of them would not leave their home, confident they could defend themselves where so many others had failed.

"Ma'am," I heard from behind me as I stared up into the pyramid, wishing I was anywhere else.

I turned to find my assistant, Angela, with her usual perfectly coifed hair, tailored and pressed suit, and manicured nails. I envied her for the time it must take to put herself together, that she had the time. My clothes fit poorly, and the best you could say about my hair was that it was still there, for the most part, even though it was thinning.

"Yes, Angela. How can I help you?"

Angela kept my schedule, and it was very detailed, down to the minute. She was very good at her job, which inherently made me despise her a little bit—after all, her job was keeping me in line.

"Your next meeting just arrived, and after it, you have the cabinet, and after—"

I held up my hand. "I can barely keep track of one meeting, Angela. That's why I have you."

She pressed her lips together and gripped her clipboard. "Yes, ma'am. If you follow me, I'll bring you to your next appointment."

Angela always seemed a bit skittish when we were together and stayed an arm's length away. I wondered if that was because she knew how often I fantasized about snapping her neck like a twig.

***

"We're broke," my CFO, Igbert, told me as I waddled to my desk.

"You've said that before, Igbert. In fact, you start nearly every conversation with that same line. Is that what they say on your planet instead of hello?"

He cleared his throat and started again. "Hello, ma'am."

"Hello," I replied. "That's better. Now, what can I do for you?"

"We're broke."

I shuffled some papers absently. "You've mentioned that before. What is it now?"

"The gods, ma'am. They have stopped paying their dues to the church. They don't believe you can protect them anymore, and without their dues . . . well, we rely on their dues to fund our operation."

"Have you talked to the banks?"

He nodded. "Of course, ma'am. And we've asked the few gods that remain loyal to us to float us by taking a loan from Plutus. But they won't—can't is more like it—not for this purpose at least. Even asking has caused many of the gods to drop their memberships."

To prevent corruption, the gods laid down rules for how the Godschurch could use the donated money. It had to be a special currency magically created by Plutus, the Greek god of wealth, in very limited quantities. He controlled all the godly wealth in the galaxy, and only he could distribute money to the gods to pay for the church.

"How many gods are still paying their dues?"

"One hundred and thirty-seven."

"And how many do we need to stay solvent?"

"Two thousand and fifteen."

"I suppose this is a bad time to tell you that we need to find a new planet, then? And that I was thinking of buying a ship."

"A ship? A ship?" Igbert made a sound like he'd swallowed a hairball. "We can't even afford a model ship at this point, ma'am."

"How much money do we have left?"

"None, ma'am. I have been trying to tell you for months that we were running out of money. Well, now we've run out. We have enough to make one more payroll and—well, that's it."

I looked up from the file I was pretending to read. "Thank you, Igbert. That will be all."

"There is much more to discuss if—"

"Leave."

"I really think it's more prudent if we—"

"You are aware I can kill you in over three hundred ways, right?" I said, smiling as sweetly as possible.

He stood and scooted out of the room. "Yes, ma'am. Thank you, ma'am."

I placed my hand on the intercom. "Angela, tell the cabinet I will be late and to start without me."

"But ma'am—"

"Don't argue. Just tell them."

I placed my feet up on the table and leaned my head back. At times like these, I thought back to my mantra:

The universe is cruel. It has always been cruel, and it will always be cruel.

I started to think that maybe that quote was inaccurate. After all, the truth wasn't that the universe was cruel. It was more . . . indifferent. Whether we lived or died, whether or not the Godschurch ceased to exist, was beside the point. The universe would keep on going either way.

The universe is indifferent. It has always been indifferent, and it will always be indifferent.

***

I hadn't been in my house for three days, but the moment I walked inside, I heard the distinct arooing of my excited dog, Noodle, as she wagged her tail from side to side, banging it against everything in her path, as she shook with excitement down the hall.

"Come here, girl!" I shouted to her.

Noodle was my miracle dog, and not because Velaska somehow saved her from the explosion of the Godschurch either. No, it was because whenever I was feeling bad about my life or ready to give up, Noodle was always there to lick my face and lie in my lap, lifting my spirits and proving I must not be so bad after all.

Noodle didn't care that I was a horrible boss or that I would be responsible for dooming the Godschurch. She just wanted to be near me, be fed, and be loved. It was a simple life, being a dog, and I often wished for it. Life would be simpler if I were simpler.

Noodle finished licking my face and snuggled into my lap. I pet her until she fell asleep, and though I felt marginally better, it didn't alleviate the massive weight placed on my shoulders. Noodle was a wonderful companion, but she gave terrible advice. I needed another opinion, and I was loath to get it, even though I knew it was the only way to ease my troubled mind.

CHAPTER 2

Meret not only gave us access to ten floors of the pyramid above ground but also complete control of the sub-basement, which had traditionally held his prisoners. Now, they held ours instead.

I took the elevator down from the Godschurch into the sub-sub-basement. There were only a few people with access to the jail cells under the Godschurch, and fewer than a dozen knew the jail even existed. Back when thousands of gods still paid their dues, we housed prisoners on planets in facilities across the universe, but with each cutback to our finances, we moved more and more into the basement.

We'd also started executing them outright, truth be told. It was easier on the budget. Most of the miserable jerks we captured would never talk, and if we let them go, they would just go back to the Godless. Seven test cases proved that, so now it was easier to arrest them, interrogate them, and execute them. Nobody was under any illusion that it was fair, but we didn't have time to be fair. At least it was efficient.

We didn't execute everybody, though. Some people we kept—those whose minds were too valuable to the Godschurch. People like my old partner, Dean Hendrix. He was a double agent for the Godless and my Godschurch commanding officer oh so many moons ago; Unfortunately, while he was our best agent, he had been working against us from the very beginning.

I was only his partner for one mission, and then, sadly, he died—or at least I thought he died. It turns out Dolos rehabilitated him and sent him off to work for the Godless yet again.

In its grief, the Godschurch made the mistake of trusting its Dean clones and using them for everything, even menial tasks like dishes. It was those clones that undermined us and destroyed the church, along with almost every man and woman on base at the time. I was one of the few that escaped.

I still don't know how I did it. My body moved faster than I thought possible. I could jump higher, run faster, and vibrate through things. It had only happened one other time when I finally faced Dolos and blew up his first Obelisk.

Dean was still on Dolos's side, clear up until those last moments before I blew up the Godless base. That's when he learned of Dolos's true motives. Dolos's plan, he revealed to me, was to bring his sister Rhea and her husband Cronus back into this universe to help him extinguish the gods.

Dean had no love for the gods, but he thought humanity should be responsible for destroying them, not the Titans. He turned on Dolos then, giving me the time I needed to destroy the Obelisk, and for that sin, Dolos nearly killed him.

I managed to save Dean right before we escaped the underground cavern that housed the Obelisk before it came crashing down, but he was badly injured and in a coma for three months. When he finally woke up, he helped us in every way he could. He was as high up an informant we could hope to turn. His intel led us to take down over a hundred cells across the universe and saved a lot of gods. Meret and Osiris liked to bring up how many gods have died on my watch, but they have no idea how many lived because of the information Dean gave us.

Still, we couldn't just let Dean free. He was a traitor to the cause. So, we left him in the sub-sub-basement, in an isolated cell only I had access to, and we squeezed every last ounce of information from him. Gods help me, we dangled the carrot of freedom, but we never intended to let him go. We dangled that carrot, but I think even Dean knew there was no way he would ever see the sun again.

I placed my hand on the sensor lock in front of Dean's cell, and the door cracked open. Inside, Dean was separated from me by a thick pane of transparent, bulletproof glass. Aside from his cot and a toilet, the only furniture in the room was the chair I sat on to face him.

"To what do I owe this unexpected visit?" he said, sitting on the floor, picking at his toes. "Need more information?"

"No," I said, shaking my head. "This is going to sound weird coming from me, but . . . I need a friend. Somebody who will tell it to me straight and isn't part of my inner circle. I already know what Velaska, Katrina, and Aranya will say. Mostly, I need somebody to listen."

He chuckled. "And you think I'm that person?"

I rubbed my head with my hand. "I don't know. Honestly, no, but we were friendly, at one point, weren't we?"

"We had sex once, yes."

"And we looked out for each other, at least for a little while, right?"

"Until I blew up, yes."

"I know this isn't ideal, but I don't have friends, Dean. I know how pathetic it must seem for me to ask my prisoner to be my confidant—"

"I don't think you could know how pathetic that sounds. Otherwise, you would never be here."

I looked up at him. "The Godschurch is broke, Dean. This whole thing is crumbling to the ground."

"Just like I wanted."

"Yes," I replied. "Just like you wanted. It seems that everything you ever wanted has come to pass."

"That's not true. Gods still roam free. Until that is no longer the case, it will not be everything I ever wanted. It's a good start, though."

"So, you think I should just walk away? Say that we had a good run and wash my hands of the whole thing? Let my gods, the ones I've risked life and limb for, be destroyed by the Godless, by Dolos?"

"I think the gods should be able to defend themselves if they are truly all-knowing and all-powerful."

"That's a fallacy born out of stupidity, Dean, and you know it. The gods are more children than omniscient beings, and they will be snuffed out of existence. Don't you care about that at all?"

He shook his head. "No. And I don't feel bad for not caring. The gods created us as their playthings, and now those playthings have risen up to destroy them."

"The things we create don't always rise up, Dean. We created robots. Are they going to rise up and destroy us?"

"Probably." He sighed. "But we can learn from all this, Rebecca. We don't have to be horrible like the gods. We can fight our nature and treat that which we create with respect."

I stood up. "Now you are just being an idiot, Dean. Have you seen the way we treat robots? Or the way we treat our own children? We are not better. We are just as horrible but in other ways."

As I walked toward the door, Dean eyed me up and down. "Look at what this church has done to you, Rebecca. You are a shell of your former self. Is it worth it to keep trying?"

"Yes," I said, grabbing the door handle. "It's always worth it to try."

***

Why did I think going to Dean would make me feel better? It made me nauseous and queasy as I sat down for lunch in the cafeteria. The cabinet meeting was underway, and they would be asking for me, but I didn't care. I wasn't ready to deal with them yet.

Katrina, Velaska, and Aranya could handle themselves until I showed up. They were gods, two of them, and a Valkyrie who'd fought in hundreds of battles. Hell, this whole place could have gone on without me. Anybody could have made this place crash and burn like I did. Maybe one of them could have even kept us afloat.

I sat down in the corner of the cafeteria, watching the smiling faces of my wards as they chatted away over green tea and salads. They had no idea the hammer was coming down on them soon, and I envied their ignorance. I envied them not knowing just how dire the predicament with the Godless had gotten.

More, I envied that they were laughing with friends and unaware of the great weight on my shoulders. I had been running at top speed for so many years now, carrying a burden that increased exponentially over time. Every time I thought I had some semblance of safety, it was taken away from me.

That was why I enjoyed eating in the cafeteria. Being around regular people allowed me a chance to eavesdrop on their conversations and study their sweet, oblivious smiles, smiles over the little things in life. I heard about dinner plans and weekend engagements, good movies, and bad plays; I heard about the minutiae absent from my life.

"Excuse me," said a voice next to me. I cocked my head to see a bright-eyed young girl with a huge smile and glistening white teeth standing next to me. "You're Director Lobdell, right?"

I wiped my mouth with a napkin. "Rebecca, yes."

"I—I—I heard you ate down here, and I just want to say what a big fan I am—all of us . . ." She pointed back to a group of children, twenty years old at best. The same age I was when my life was ripped away from me. They smiled giddily and ducked their eyes from my gaze. "I just wanted to say that I want to be just like you. I admire you, ma'am."

I gestured to the open seat across from me. "Sit down, please."

She bobbed her head from side to side, checking to see if I was talking to somebody else. When she didn't find anybody, she pointed to herself. "Me? Really?"

"Really."

She slid into the seat. "Thank you. Thank you."

"You know," I said, taking a bite of my chicken salad. "I was just thinking about how much I wanted to be like all of you."

She giggled. "Really? But we're just—I mean, you are *you*."

I pointed my fork at her. "That's right. I am me. I've been me for a long time now. I've seen war. I've seen death. I've watched countless people I loved taken away from me. Have you ever had anybody stolen from you as you watched them take their last breath?"

Her smile faded away. "No, ma'am. . . that happened to you? I never knew."

"Of course not. I wouldn't expect you to know any of that. What you know is that I sit up there, in that big office, and you want to be like that, right? Somebody important?"

"I want to help people."

"Of course you do. That's admirable. I never cared much for helping people—not until recently. I was always more interested in helping myself. I was selfish for a long time."

"That can't be true. You're being hard on yourself."

"Kindness will get you far in this world—I'm sorry, what was your name?"

"Zasha."

"Zasha. Kindness will get you far, Zasha, but watch out because people will take advantage of it at every turn." I pointed to the girls over at her table. "Do you see the girls over there?"

She nodded. "Yeah. They're my friends. We do everything together."

"And you all want to be me? Is that it?"

"Yes, of course. You're a legend. Who wouldn't want to be a legend?"

"Well, here is the fact. You can't all be me. Only one person in this whole place can be me. And you are kind, Zasha. I can see it in your eyes. You're gonna let the whole world step all over you. If you want to be me, you can't be kind, but do you want to know something?"

I could see the joy fade from her eyes. "I don't think so—"

"I want to be you, Zasha. I want to be kind. I want to have joy. I want to have friends. If I could go back and be you, I would never want to be me. Cherish that, Zasha. Cherish who you are and be you. Not me."

It was the advice I would have wanted to hear if I lived another life, one without war and terror. Without another word, I stood up and bussed my tray. Then I went to my meeting. As I left, Zasha remained where I left her, dumbfounded. I hoped she would never grow up to be like me.

CHAPTER 3

Clearly, I couldn't take a compliment. If I had just said "thank you," I probably wouldn't have ruined sweet, little Zasha's day. Of course, then I would be haunted by the idea that somebody would want to fall through a black hole, have their home world invaded by giant bugs, become a sniper, live on a planet overrun by demons, become a mercenary, watch their whole family die in horrific and miserable ways, get blown up by a god, watch their first partner die in an explosion, find out that partner was actually alive but a Godless double agent, barely escape from a firestorm after blowing up a Godless base, fall for a Valkyrie, break up with said Valkyrie, arrest their first partner, barely escape the wrath of a god, and become the leader of an organization about two weeks from going belly up.

That sounds terrible. I should warn people about that, right? Even if it meant destroying their day? At least they wouldn't destroy their entire life because that's what it meant to be me. Thirty years of horrible stuff happening to me, and somehow surviving despite my best efforts.

And now, I was walking into a cabinet meeting where I had to tell my three closest friends—though, in all honesty, I could hardly call them friends—that we were screwed, and no matter what we did in the next two weeks, there was nothing we could do to fix it short of destroying the Godless forever.

I pushed open the glass door to the conference room, and the violent shouts echoing off the walls immediately stopped. Sitting in front of me at a long conference table were Katrina, the god of Earth who vacated her position to help us take down the Godless, Velaska, a wandering god without a planet who introduced me to the Godschurch in the first place, and my ex-lover and ex-partner Aranya, a Valkyrie from Thor's planet who barely escaped Valhalla when the Godless blew it up. She had as much reason to hate the Godless as anybody, but the scorn ate away at her until I couldn't stand to be around her.

"About time!" Aranya scoffed. "Couldn't be bothered to show up to your own meeting?"

Every day since she watched Valhalla explode, she'd worked to the bone to get revenge on Dolos, but he always slipped through her fingers. She blamed the Godschurch's failure on me personally, which is what drove us apart in the first place.

I didn't hold it against her, though. She was right. It was my responsibility to find Dolos and the main base of the Godless. Despite my efforts, I failed time and time again, no matter how hard I tried. There are no medals for trying.

"I'm sorry," I said. "It couldn't be helped."

"We both know that's not true," Velaska replied, cocking her eyebrow.

Velaska was the closest thing to an omniscient being I've ever met. She swore she couldn't read minds, but she always seemed to know what I was thinking—and what I would do—even before I did it. Still, even she couldn't see what we should do, nor what I was about to tell them.

"You're right, of course," I said, looking into her deep blue eyes. "It could be helped, but I chose not to help it. I assumed you could carry on in my stead. I didn't realize you were children."

"We're not children, and we don't need you," Katrina said.

Katrina thought she should be the head of the church, and I didn't disagree, but the bylaws stated specifically that the gods cannot run the church—something about them being power-hungry and using the church for their own gains.

"I know you are capable," I said to her. "Which is why I don't feel guilty about being late. I know you have business to attend that does not require my presence."

"We have completed all that business, Rebecca," Velaska said. "Some time ago, in fact. Now, we've just been bickering at each other."

"Sniping is more like it," Katrina said.

"You have a little piece of lettuce on your shirt." Velaska gestured to me to brush it off.

"I hope you were having fun stuffing your fat face while we tried to find the Godless," Aranya said, every word dripping with scorn.

I brushed the lettuce off my shirt. It was true, I was much bigger than the last time I was in the field with Aranya, but I wasn't fat. I was more doughy and formless, like unmolded clay.

"You know I wasn't. I haven't had fun in a long time." I sat at the end of the table furthest from their scowling faces. "I have news from Igbert and the gods of this planet. There is no good news, so I will just come out with it. Meret wants us off this planet in two weeks."

"Come on!" Katrina said. "He's a feckless totem, and you know it."

I shrugged. "Very well, you are correct. Osiris wants us off this planet in two weeks, and Meret agrees with him. I should have been more specific."

"And what did you tell them?" Aranya said.

"There was nothing to tell. I asked them to give us a month, they refused. We have to be off this planet in two weeks."

The Valkyrie's armor clinked as she threw herself against the back of her chair. "Of course, you cowed to them. You would need to have a backbone to stand—"

"Enough!" Velaska shouted more sternly than I'd ever heard her speak before. "We'll deal with the fallout later. For now, I believe you have other news?"

"Oh right," I said, feigning a casual tone. "The gods have stopped funding us. We are out of money. At best, we have one more paycheck before we have to disband the church."

Velaska waved a dismissive hand. "If it's money you need, I can just conjure up—"

"You know that's not how it works. You might be able to fool the commoners with self-created gold, but you will never fool the gods."

"If we protect all gods," Aranya said, "why don't all gods have to pay?"

"Well, they do, my dear," Velaska said. "If they want protection. It seems, though, that the gods do not want protection."

"A hundred or so still pay, but that's not enough. We could ask them for more money, but it still would never be enough to fund this place. We need a miracle to survive into next month."

"So, what you are saying," Katrina leaned in closer, frowning, "is that you are a failure."

I threw up my hands half-heartedly. "That is what I'm saying. Unless we can somehow find a significant influx of money and a new place to house ourselves in the next month, the Godschurch will be no more."

"Thousands of years of noble existence, and it all blew up under your watch," Aranya folded her arms and glared at me.

"Technically," Velaska corrected, "it blew up under Tress's watch, not Rebecca's. She's just picking up the pieces." She turned to me. "Now, what do you suggest we do?"

I laughed. "Do? About what?"

"Well, about this situation, of course. How do we fix it?"

"I don't know, but I'm not giving up. Something will come through. It always does."

"Perhaps we can return to Odin—" Aranya said.

I didn't let her finish. "We've tried to raise money from the Norse gods, but they have abandoned us in droves since Sif . . ." I didn't want to think about Sif, our last patron, god of the Norse Odin line. I watched as the Godless shot her down in cold blood.

"Yes, her loss at the hands of the Godless was a great blow to my people," Aranya replied. "They will no longer support the church, no matter how much I plead with them."

"The same is true with every other pantheon," I replied. "The only one that still gives us the time of day is the Greeks, and even their patience is wavering. Only Aphrodite's support keeps them on our side."

"So, we're bones," Katrina said. "I just want you to say it."

I felt my temper welling up inside me. Katrina had a way of bringing it out of anyone she talked to. I stared at her for a few moments before I spoke. "We are all screwed, Katrina, if we don't figure this out. The minute the Godschurch disbands, there will be no stopping the Godless. I would suggest we all pray for a miracle. Of course, knowing gods, that will never work."

***

The bickering went on for another hour. It eventually rose to an ear-splitting volume, and I gave up. I left the room. The walls still shook with pulsating anger as I walked out, but there was nothing more I could do. I had tried everything and laid myself bare. Now was the time to look at every side of the situation and figure out what we missed. We wouldn't find out what it was by arguing.

That was what Katrina and Aranya didn't understand. There was honor in methodical planning, in studying every angle, and looking for the best way to proceed. I knew better than to rely on a hero to swoop in and save us.

I was a sniper, for the gods' sake. I was used to waiting for hours, sometimes days, for the perfect shot and studying every possible angle to make sure my target died. I hadn't gotten to assassinate anyone in years, but you can't take the sniper out of the girl.

There was a cold, calculating beauty in waiting. It was the opposite of being a warrior, and Katrina is a warrior. She does great things, but she is ruled by her heart. Aranya is the same way. When you have the lives of thousands on the line, you can't be ruled by your heart. Logic should prevail.

"They want to strike somewhere," Velaska said, walking out of the door.

"I'm not surprised. They are blunt instruments."

"Possibly, but they aren't wrong. If we are going down, they think we should go down swinging. I find it hard to disagree with them."

"Of course you don't. Katrina is great at speaking to a crowd. She can rile anybody up to do anything, but she can only see what's right in front of her nose. What if there's something we're missing? Some other way to save the church."

"There are many things we are missing, my love," Velaska replied, placing her hand on my shoulder. "But Katrina and Aranya are simply reacting to your words. You painted a bleak picture in there."

"And where should we strike, huh? Where should we waste our men?" I watched Zasha walk out of the cafeteria with her friends and cross the quad. "Where would I send them to die for our whims?"

"It's not our whims," Velaska said. "It's for the good of the church."

I brushed her hand off my shoulder. "This is what none of you can ever understand. These are not just chess pieces you move around a board. These are human lives, and if you want to strike somewhere, it means people will die. And if I'm going to send people to die, it better be for a goddamn good reason, not just some glorious last hurrah for a bloodthirsty cabinet."

"Is that what you think of us?" Aranya said, walking out of the room with Katrina.

"Yes," I replied, twisting my mouth with distaste. "I think Katrina has been detached from humanity for too long to understand it, and you and Velaska were never even part of it, so you can't possibly know the struggle."

"I'll have you know—" Katrina started.

"You let demons remain on earth after the Horde Wars, Katrina. Nobody who had an ounce of humanity left would have done that." I lowered my voice. "This is not the place to discuss this. We'll reconvene tomorrow, and you can berate me all over again."

"Whatever," Katrina said, walking off with Aranya.

Velaska smirked. "That is why the church is ruled by humans, Rebecca, because we cannot appreciate mortality. The Godless are horrific, but they are correct about that fact. We created humanity, so on some level, they will always be playthings to us, ones that we use for our own ends."

I opened my mouth to speak when I heard Angela's feet clopping up to me.

"Ma'am." She was standing with a rather tall, blonde woman I didn't know, who was clutching a manila envelope to her chest.

"What is it, Angela?"

With a gesture from Angela, the woman handed me the envelope.

"This is Toni. One of our handlers. She has something you need to see."

CHAPTER 4

I dragged Toni and Velaska into my office and sat them across from me. Pretty much my entire job consists of telling gods what to do, and gods don't like being told what to do—ever. Velaska didn't want to sit down, so she stood up and hovered around the desk next to me. "Explain to me what you have here," I said, looking down at a series of schematics and photos which looked remarkably like the black, ringed Obelisk I'd blown up two years ago in Dolos's base.

"My operative, Yvette. She was on assignment in a small Godless sect—or we thought it was small until she got to the planet and heard chatter about a new Obelisk. It wasn't much to go on, but we were suspicious they were recruiting workers for Dolos's massive construction project to rebuild the Obelisk."

"Why wasn't I informed about this?"

"I'm sorry, Director Lobdell," Toni said, "but it's not like we get to give good news often. We wanted to make sure of what we had before we showed it to anybody. Yvette spent six months making connections until her contact finally brought her to the base a week ago—right before she was found out."

"Found out? Like, exposed as a spy?" I asked.

"Correct. After she was found out, I told her to return to base, but she didn't. Against orders, Yvette infiltrated their base and retrieved the schematics on the Obelisk. She downloaded everything and sent them to me. We know exactly where they are constructing the Obelisk now—and we can analyze its weaknesses for an opening."

I turned the page of the briefing and read the numbers out loud. "Sector 47.974?"

"That's right, ma'am. A little planet called Niloria. It's perfect for the Godless. No god has protected it for generations. Close to a star that's about to erupt—"

"How sure are you that this is the right obelisk? We can't be wrong."

"These pictures were taken by one of our operatives on the planet this morning. We're very sure, ma'am."

"I want to meet this operative. Yvette, you said her name was?"

Toni bowed her head. "She's in a coma, ma'am. Critical condition."

I threw a look at Velaska. We didn't have to exchange words. She knew what she had to do. It was time to wake Yvette up.

***

Velaska placed her hand on Yvette's chest, just like I had seen her do a hundred times before—just like she had done with me so many years ago. Then, she lifted her hands into the air and beckoned water from a nearby sink to float toward her hands. The water formed into a large ball around Velaska, and she pushed it to cover Yvette, who floated in the air above her bed.

Yvette choked on the water, flailing against the sides of the water bubble enclosing around her.

"You're killing her!" Toni shouted. "Stop this, Rebecca!"

"Watch yourself!" I shot back. "I am in command here. Keep going, Velaska."

A moment later, the thrashing dropped, and Yvette laid limp. Velaska dumped the water back into the sink. Yvette floated back to the ground, her eyes fluttering open, and Toni rushed to her side.

"Hi, buddy," Toni said to Yvette.

Yvette smiled at her. "Did you get it?"

Tears welled up in Toni's eyes as she slowly nodded, and a happy smile overtook her face. It was a nice moment, but we didn't have time for nice moments. I stepped forward. "Agent, it's good to have you back."

Yvette jumped slightly but didn't have the energy for much more than to turn her head toward me. "Director? What are you doing here? Did you get the plans?"

I nodded. "Yes, I did. And I need to know everything that you know."

"I—I—I know we have to take down that base."

"How soon until they fire the weapon? How many men are there? How prepared is Dolos for an ambush?"

Yvette shook her head. "I'm sorry. I don't know. I'm sorry."

"This brief says he's planning to launch in two weeks' time. Is that accurate? Is that what you heard?"

"I don't . . . I'm sorry. I'm sorry, I was just trying to help."

Yvette's words faded to a murmur as she fell back into unconsciousness. Toni stroked her head. "Will she be okay?"

"She'll be fine, now. Let her rest and heal."

I pulled on Velaska's shoulder. "That is not good enough. If we are going to plan a strike, I need to know everything about that base and whether Dolos will be there when we attack."

I turned to Toni. "I need somebody on that planet right now—and don't send another agent that's going to get shot this time, okay? I want a video of Dolos and proof that he is there ASAP. Got it?"

Toni snapped back to attention at my curt tone. "Yes, ma'am. Consider it done."

"And nobody sees that file before me. Understood? Nobody."

"Understood."

Perhaps I should have given her more time to savor Yvette's recovery, but we didn't have time for that, and the wheels in my head were spinning. If this was the last stand of Dolos, then I could sell it to just about everybody to buy us a little more time. But I had to be sure before I risked everything.

***

I slammed my feet on the concrete sub-basement floor as I sprinted toward Dean's cell. Velaska was calling the cabinet together while I talked to the one person who would know whether this was a hoax or not.

I pulled open the door to Dean's cell and banged on the glass to rouse him from his sleep. He spun over, and I slammed an image of the Obelisk against the glass partition.

"Is this where he is, Dean? Is this where he's hiding?"

"Dolos? I don't know. Let me look."

Dean eyed the briefing page for a few moments before he moved back. "I don't know, Rebecca. It looks like that planet would be perfect for opening a black hole into

Cronus's dimension, but I just don't know. It's been two years. A lot can happen in two years."

"Will he be ready for us to attack?"

Dean bit his lip. "Unlikely. He's too proud to think that you would find out where he was hiding."

"What if one of our agents was outed and Dolos knew about it? Would he move or speed up his plans?"

"If he's been building for two years, then he must be almost done. He wouldn't move. He couldn't risk starting again. Besides, he knows how much you're struggling. I could see where he might move up his timeline, though, even if it was risky. The amount of planning necessary to speed up that kind of construction, even a single day, is astronomical."

"So, you think whatever it says in this brief is probably when he's going to strike?"

Dean nodded. "If I know Dolos—though I doubt anybody knows Dolos—that's what I would tell you."

"Then we have two weeks to prepare. Thank you."

I turned to leave, but Dean shouted out. "Wait! I want to help you take him down. You have to let me help you."

"And risk everything being destroyed by one of Dolos's informants? No thanks."

He narrowed his eyes. "If I know anything, it's that you don't have enough men to launch an all-out attack on Dolos. I can help you win this fight."

I twisted the door handle. "I'll think about it."

***

The conference room was already bursting with energy by the time I walked into the cabinet meeting. Velaska,

Katrina, and Aranya were in attendance, along with Igbert, who was there to ensure any decision we made was financially sound.

"You can't really expect to take down the entire Godless organization with the money we have in our coffers," Igbert said to Katrina. His pleas bounced off her.

"You're goddamn right we are!" Katrina said.

"All right!" I shouted over the din of the room as I found my seat. "No need to get pissy. Let's talk this out."

The room settled. The veins pulsed in Aranya's neck, and Katrina's face was flushed with anger, but they both seemed aware they were about to get their way, and that calmed their tempers. Igbert, on the other hand, sat on the edge of his seat. He was used to being an invisible face in the back of every room, not being screamed at by gods and Valkyries that could pop his head three times before breakfast.

"Thank you, Rebecca," Velaska said in a huff. "Trying to get through to these two is impossible. It is like they are two halves of the same, violent brain."

The comment wounded me. It was no secret Katrina and Aranya were sleeping together. I knew it, and Urania, Katrina's ex-lover and goddess of astronomy, knew it, too. That is what eventually broke up Aranya and me for good.

She claimed that my ideas of monogamy were outdated and "primitively human." I couldn't argue with her because I was a human. I'd spent my life hopping around from bed to bed, and with Aranya, I thought I'd finally found somebody worth settling down for. I suppose she didn't think the same about me.

"Can we just get on with this?" Aranya said. "Egghead over here doesn't think that we have enough money for a full-scale invasion."

"That is not what I said," Igbert replied. He looked like he'd summoned all his courage just to speak up. "What I said was that we couldn't launch a full-scale invasion and keep the church going at the same time."

I sighed. I knew it would come to this. "I know, Igbert, that is why this mission will be the last for the Godschurch."

"What?" Katrina shouted. "You're just folding up shop and admitting defeat?"

"I don't want to admit defeat, but there is no hope for the Godschurch if this mission isn't successful. Therefore, we must put every available resource into fighting it."

"It doesn't hurt," Velaska said, "that you'll be sending a lot of people to their deaths, and maybe payroll will be lighter afterward, does it?"

"That doesn't factor into my decision at all," I replied.

Her eyebrow shot up. "Funny. I seem to have had a conversation with somebody that looks just like you about not sending people off to their graves."

"I said we can't send them off to their graves foolishly. If Dolos really is overseeing construction on a new Obelisk, then we can destroy the Godless forever. That is a risk worth dying for, don't you think?"

"I'm not so sure," Velaska replied. "Have you been able to definitively prove that Dolos is on this planet in the hour since I saw you last?"

"No, I haven't," I admitted, clenching my fist. "But we are working on it."

"Until then, we are working on the assumption that this mission will be carried out—we're calling all our agents back, folding our forward bases, and preparing for a direct assault, correct?"

I nodded. "That's right. Until I find out otherwise, this mission is a go."

"And if it fails, that will be the end," Aranya muttered.

"Forget failure," Velaska said. "Even if we abandon the mission, there will not be enough money to keep us afloat, will there, Rebecca?"

I gulped loudly. "No. There will not be. I am not known for taking risks, but I see no other way."

"So, be honest," Velaska said. "No matter what, this mission will proceed if we approve it right now. No matter what."

"That's correct. If we vote to go to war, there's no turning back. Being on this cabinet is a messy business, Velaska. You knew that when you joined."

"Yeah," Katrina said. "And poor little Velaska's never had to run a planet before, so what would she know about tough choices? If we're voting, I'm in. It's the only move."

"I agree," Aranya said.

"I am voting against." Velaska folded her arms across her chest. "This is the kind of foolhardy move typical of Katrina and Aranya, but I expected more clear-headedness from you, Rebecca."

I rubbed my eyes. "It must be unanimous, Velaska."

"I know that," she replied. "But you haven't convinced me. I'm not going to risk the future of this church on your whim. If we don't attack, there might be some other way to save the church."

"There is no other way! The church is damned no matter what we do!" Aranya shouted. "At least this way, we go down swinging!"

"Igbert," I said. The little man nearly jumped out of his seat when I looked at him. "How much money would we need to stay solvent after this raid?"

"More money than we have, ma'am."

"I'm going to be honest with you," I said, staring at Velaska. "I am taking a risk that Dolos is on that planet and that we can stop him. There are no guarantees in the universe. Nobody knows anything. But I'm ready to take this gamble. If I'm right, the gods will come back to the church and keep us solvent. However, I have an idea for how we can stay flush even if we fail."

"I'm listening," Velaska said.

I inhaled deeply before I responded. I didn't want to say what I was going to say. "I'm willing to wager my soul with Meret. My soul against enough money to keep this church open for as long as I can. If we win this battle, and the church gets its money from membership dues, then he doesn't get anything. I pay him back, and we go about our lives. But if we fail, I'll trade an eternity as his slave for enough money to run this place for another month."

"That's a horrible deal," Katrina said, her mouth hanging open.

Aranya spoke in a low voice, "You can't do that."

Velaska, meanwhile, sat in silence, stroking her chin. She always loved a gamble, and she wagered souls all the time when she was the Devil.

"If I did that," I said, "and he gave us enough money to keep going if we failed, would you vote to move forward?"

"You are that confident?" Velaska asked.

I sighed deeply once more. "I'm confident this is the only way."

Katrina and Aranya turned their eyes to Velaska's coy smile. "Then yes, if you could make that work, I would vote to attack."

I stood. "Katrina. Aranya. Figure out how to make the numbers work before I get back. Come on, Velaska. We're going to make a deal."

CHAPTER 5

"That's the deal I'm offering you, Meret," I said, standing in the throne room of his opulent palace as he lounged on his gilded throne. He wore a flowing, purple toga which draped onto the ground, and his head was festooned with laurel.

Meret took a bite of a juicy grape. The liquid ran out the sides of his mouth and onto his chest, where a servant girl wiped it away.

"That is juicy," he said with a laugh. "Quite juicy."

"Are you talking about the grape or the offer?" Velaska asked. She stood next to me, stone-faced, while I made the worst deal of my life.

"Can't it be both?" he said.

"I don't have much time here, Meret." I sighed. "We're in a terrible rush."

"Fine," Meret said, brushing the girls away. He sat up in his chair and leaned toward us. "So, what you are offering is to pawn your soul to me, and if you win this battle, then you will come to pick it up in a couple of weeks. If you don't, what? I keep it forever?"

"Once I die, Meret. Let's not be hasty, all right? I don't plan on dying for a long time."

He leaned in even closer. "Do you know what I do with the souls that I've won? It's truly disgusting what I make them do."

I gritted my teeth. "I've heard stories."

Meret was legendary for sleeping with his indentured souls and forcing them to do unspeakable things. He contended that the men and women he kept as concubines enjoyed the process of being degraded and humiliated with every debauchery imaginable. I wasn't so convinced, especially as I watched the eyes of his servant girls turn from disgust to murder as they stood in the corner awaiting his next order.

"And you still wish to make this deal? Why? So that your precious church can last just a little while longer?"

I looked over at Velaska. "I am the last in a long line of directors of the Godschurch. I have taken over the role of steward, master, and director in my short time. If the Godschurch fails on my watch, it is on me and me alone. I do not wish that to happen. I will do anything to prevent it."

"Osiris surely won't like this. Not one bit."

"Let me deal with Osiris if he doesn't like it. You worry about what's best for you. I think this deal is more than fair."

"You're a little old for my taste, sweetie, I must say. My proclivities—they skew . . . younger."

I looked down at the skin sagging from the back of my hand. I pulled it back until its firmness took shape again. "This is what I have to offer you. Nothing more, Meret."

He eyed me up and down, then up again. "Very well. Your terms are acceptable. I've never had a Godschurch director before. I look forward to making you beg for mercy for eons to come."

"Let's not get too carried away now. I still have time. I might win yet."

He snapped his fingers, and we were gone. "You certainly might."

***

I tasted Flamin' Hot Cheetos as we reappeared back inside the Godschurch. It was no secret that every god had a different flavor to their beam of light. Meret's tasted like Cheetos. I hated Cheetos.

"Are you happy now?" I asked Velaska. "I didn't think you would actually go through with it."

"Well, this whole thing started when you bargained me to the Godschurch. It seems fitting that it would end with me bargaining it for the Godschurch."

I walked inside the meeting room, where Aranya and Katrina waited with Igbert. The poor man looked like he was sweating bullets just having to be near them.

"It's done," I said.

"Does that mean I can go?" Igbert asked.

I nodded, and he bolted out of the room faster than I'd ever seen him move before. The others turned to me and smiled. Katrina was especially tickled that I had just sold my soul.

"You know, I've done a lot of stupid things in my life," Katrina said. "But I've never sold my soul."

"You did bargain with it once, though," Velaska said. "I remember it well, and Hercules is at least as disgusting as Meret."

"Maybe," Katrina replied, standing up. "But that was on my own skill. The idiot over there bargained it on a series of chances. She's betting that Dolos will be at this Obelisk and that we'll be able to beat him, and then she's betting the gods will be so happy they'll start sending in money. That's a lot of betting for one poor, little soul."

"And it's my soul to bet!" I pounded my fist on the table. "It's my soul to bet. And it's done. So, let's get back to the matter at hand. A vote. We need a unanimous vote."

"I vote yes," Katrina shouted.

"Me too," replied Aranya.

"And you, Velaska?" I asked, gesturing across the table.

"How delicious would it be if I still said no, and you had to give your soul to Meret? Wouldn't that be exquisite? But I won't do that. I vote yes."

"I vote yes as well," I said. "There we have it, a unanimous decision. Katrina, find every god that's still paying us money and tell them we need their help. Velaska, call every agent back to the base. Aranya, I need you to convince the Norse gods to help us, however you can."

"I will try, but they are steadfast in their resolution to remain neutral. They haven't been attacked since Sif, and they don't want to start now."

"Tell them that Dolos plans to unleash Cronus and Rhea if we don't act quickly. Dolos may spare the Odin line, but Cronus will have no such grace with them."

Aranya nodded. "And if they still say no?"

I looked down at my poor, sagging hands. Meret would own them if we failed. "Either way, we continue."

***

Aranya grabbed me as I made my way out of the meeting. I spun around forcefully. I forgot how strong she was when she wanted something.

"You know the Norse gods are never going to help you, right?" she said.

"I know that unless you try, there is no hope at all. And if you can't convince them, we will have to move without them."

"Do you think we can win without more gods on our side?"

I shrugged. "There is only one god against us, Aranya. As far as I know, he has no other gods to aid him. There's a chance we can defeat him without their help, but I have nowhere near his manpower, and I'm worried that he'll be lying in wait for us. If you're asking whether we need those gods to win, then my answer is no. But my soul is on the line here, so barter with them as if that mattered to you."

Aranya looked me in the eyes. "It does matter to me, Rebecca. It's why I'm still here."

"Then, for once in the past year, act like it."

I pulled myself away from her and walked down the hall. I must be getting soft in my old age because I was on the verge of tears.

***

I stormed into my office, ready to cry, and pulled the blinds closed so I could have some privacy. I no sooner sat down at my desk than a flash of light appeared in front of me. When it dissipated, Osiris was sitting in front of me.

"I thought we told you to leave this planet," he said.

I frowned. "You sound . . . different."

He smirked at me. "Appearances, my dear."

"Good. I would think it really annoying to talk like that. In short bursts. All day. Every day."

"We are what people expect of us, Rebecca. I would think as leader of the Godschurch, you could appreciate that fact."

Osiris pulled a handkerchief from one of his pockets and handed it to me. I didn't even know tears were streaming down my face until he pointed to them.

"Thank you," I said, wiping them away.

"Appearances, as I said."

I finished wiping the tears from my eyes and placed the handkerchief on my lap. "If you don't mind, I'll keep this."

"Be my guest."

"Now," I started, clearing my throat, "what can I do for you?"

"You offered your soul to Meret earlier, and he rashly made a deal he had no business making. I am here to negate your bargain."

"If you take this back from me, we won't be able to fund the church if the attack fails."

He smiled. "I'm sure you will make that clear to your cabinet then. It would be a shame if they went to war under false pretenses."

"Why do you want us to fail?" I asked, finally. It was the question that had been on my mind for months. "What do you get out of it?"

"Nothing, except the pleasure of watching it. I have never been a fan of the pantheon; pompous, mean, and cruel."

"They don't control the church. We work for all the gods."

"Of course, you do. That must be why there are so many agents stationed across my planets."

"Our entire base of operations is here."

"Out of necessity. Tell me, out of curiosity, until you became director, did you even know our pantheon existed?"

I thought long and hard about my answer. "Yes. I did."

"How long before?"

"I assumed when I met Thor that the other pantheons existed, too. Aranya confirmed it."

"So, a short time before."

I nodded. "Not long before, yes."

"And it took the entire Godschurch blowing up for you to gain that knowledge. Now, how long would it have taken if the base hadn't blown up?"

"I don't—"

"Let me tell you. It would have been never. Despite my people contributing ten percent to the church, we got less than a percentage of their resources, while Zeus's line received eighty-seven percent of them."

"In fairness, they were the ones creating new worlds—"

"Exactly! Colonizers!" Osiris comported himself. "I'm sorry that I lost my temper. I feel very passionately about the subject."

"That's why you don't want us to stay here, isn't it? Because you have some stupid hang-up about the church?"

"That's correct. You know enough gods to understand how petty we can be. Now, I have given you back your soul and canceled your debt to Meret. What you do with that information is up to you."

I rubbed my temples. "Is there anything I can do to convince you to loan us the money we need?"

"Not unless you can go back and undo a million years of oppression."

He snapped his fingers, and he was gone, and my plans were gone with him. We didn't have enough money to survive without Meret, at least not if we failed. I couldn't hope to succeed without more gods backing us, and I wondered how many felt the same way as Osiris.

An uneasy feeling crawled into my gut as I planned the invasion, knowing I was about to lie to everyone that ever put their faith in me, especially Velaska. I trusted her with my life, but I could never trust her with the knowledge of Osiris's betrayal.

CHAPTER 6

The following week, the Godschurch filled with gods, angels, and agents. In all, only fifty-three gods came to fight by our side—out of just over three thousand that we knew were still alive. Along with them came fifteen hundred angels and cherubs, and just shy of five thousand members of the Godschurch, agents and analysts alike, some of them barely old enough to hold a gun.

The most heartbreaking moment was watching my new friend Zasha—all twenty years of her—smiling proudly during target practice with her friends. Too many of them would not be coming back, and I feared Zasha would be one of them. She was strong and fearless, but that's because she had no reason to fear. Her life was one of happiness. I knew the truth. There was every reason to fear.

The talk around the water cooler was how awesome it was that we were finally taking down the Godless, but I don't think many of the young soldiers could properly comprehend war. Some of them did, and when I locked eyes with them, I saw it there, stewing below the surface—the unspoken fear.

During the Horde Wars, nobody on Earth had a choice but to fight. The Horde, an overwhelmingly powerful species of bugs, invaded Earth and destroyed our entire world in less than a week. We had no choice but to fight back. None of us chose to go to war. We weren't career soldiers, but we suited up anyway . . . just like these poor bastards, suiting up for me without even knowing how to march in rank, completely ignorant to the fact I had no way to pay them for their sacrifice.

My betrayal ate at the lining of my stomach, but I kept my secret from everybody. Even Velaska, who seemed to know everything I was thinking before I did, couldn't detect my deception. Or maybe she wasn't looking for it. Every once and a while, I caught her looking at me, but then she would turn her head and go about her business.

The biggest help to our preparation was Urania. Katrina's old paramour came to us on the first day of our planning efforts. She fixed our transporters, so they were more accurate than ever. Part of our plan relied on the element of surprise. We needed to hit the Godless fast and with everything we had before they had a chance to counterattack or operate their weapon.

There was still a week until Dolos would be ready to fire, and we had to beat him before he knew what hit him. That was the key to my plan. Spies confirmed that Dolos was constructing the Obelisk a quarter-mile outside one of the biggest desert cities on Niloria. The plan was to unload our soldiers on the outskirts of the city and attack with everything we had—quickly and painfully.

Of course, Dolos might know we were coming, or at least expect an attack. Even if he didn't, this close to launch, he would be on high alert with guards stationed to protect his weapon. He must remember what happened last time when I managed to destroy all his work.

"Those calibrations are off," Urania said to one of the scientists. "If we land there, we'll be inside the Obelisk, not in front of it." She stared over the scientist's shoulder for another moment. "And we need the white light fifty yards wider to transport enough troops. We're not going to have a lot of time to get everybody through the door before they start firing. Wider is better."

"How is it coming along?" I asked.

She stood up when I approached. "It's fine. We should be ready by tomorrow. The specs you gave me weren't too difficult, so I think we'll manage."

"Good. I really appreciate—"

I watched as Urania's eyes drifted from my face up to the balcony, where Katrina stood arguing with somebody. Every time I saw her, she was arguing with somebody.

"Have you talked to her since you got here?"

Urania shook her head. "Except for a few words here and there, no. It's been awkward since—"

My eyes caught Aranya walking across the balcony toward Katrina. "Yeah. I know."

"Do you think they'll ever show any regret?" Urania asked.

I smiled an awkward smile. "Hopefully, before the end."

Katrina moved, and I finally saw who she was talking with—Toni, the handler that brought us the intel on Dolos and the Obelisk in the first place.

"Excuse me, will you?"

***

I ran up the stairs until I was out of breath, and then I kept running, hacking and wheezing all the way up to the cabinet room, where Katrina stood with Aranya, talking with Toni.

"Oh good," Katrina said when I reached the landing. "We were just coming to get you."

I took a minute to catch my breath and compose myself. "I thought I told you that nobody looks at this data before me."

"Well," Toni said, "we were coming to get you but didn't think you would mind—"

I snatched the folder out of Katrina's hand. "What were my orders?"

Toni ducked her head. "You see it first."

"Now, what did you find?"

Toni's face lightened as she delivered the news. "Our scout just got back from the surface. She took a dozen perfect images of the Obelisk." Toni pointed to a picture of a dark figure in a velvet hooded robe. "Take a look at that. We think that over there is—"

"Dolos."

"Yes, ma'am."

"You said 'think.' I need you to be sure. Are you sure?"

Toni nodded. "My agent heard him called Dolos, but every time she tried to take a picture of his face, it came out perfectly black, like his face absorbed all the light around it."

"Describe his eyes."

"The agent said they were blood red, and his pupils seemed to be detached from his eyeballs. They danced in his eye sockets around as if they had no anchor. She said he was unsettling to look at."

I clapped my hands together. "That's him. Katrina, go make the final preparations. Toni, thank you. How is Yvette doing?"

Toni's eyes dropped at the mention of Yvette. "She has returned to Epres. She told me she couldn't stand to see any more bloodshed or risk her life for the Godschurch again."

"She served us well. I wish her the best." The idea of losing another agent in our darkest hour was discouraging but not unexpected. Dozens of agents had abandoned us in the past week. Luckily, hundreds more stayed to fight. "You're still with us, though? Right?"

"Until the end, ma'am."

I gave her a brief smile and turned away. I was halfway toward my office before I noticed Aranya behind me. "What do you want?"

"I want you to know that I know," Aranya said as she closed the door to my office behind me.

"Know what?"

"Osiris talked to Odin. That's why none of them came. He told them all about your deal with Meret and how he reneged on it."

I placed the folder on the table. "And who have you told?"

She shook her head. "Nobody. I haven't told anybody. Because if I did, Velaska would fry you."

"Let's keep it that way. Hopefully, tomorrow we won't have to worry about it because we'll take down Dolos, the Godless, and that stupid Obelisk for good."

Aranya was silent for a moment. "You could have told me, Rebecca. I wouldn't say anything—"

I perused some papers on my desk. I didn't want her to see my face. "You haven't always had the best track record with my trust, have you?"

"I deserved that."

I looked up from my notes. "I know. Now get out of my office."

***

Over the next four days, Urania and Velaska dissected the blueprints of the Obelisk while I studied the imagery Toni's team brought back from the surface. Any hope of a surprise attack left me after I looked at those images. From the overhead shots Yvette took of the battlefield between the town and the Obelisk, it looked like the Godless were fortifying their base. They knew we were coming.

They placed sub-machine guns behind hastily built walls, and tripwire lined the sand from the town to the Obelisk. Two flanks lined the battlefield on either side of the Obelisk, with dozens of anti-angel demon hunters aimed at the sky. Troops were stationed along three sides of a desert field in front of the Obelisk to corner us in.

That was the bad news. The good news was that Urania found a structural flaw in the Obelisk—it still ran off human souls, just like all Horde tech. Human souls, and the green goop they turned into, were incredibly unstable. All we had to do was enter the Obelisk and set a few charges for the whole structure to explode. While we were destroying the Obelisk, a division of gods would track down Dolos and cut the head off the Godless organization. When Dolos fell, the rest of the compound would come down with him.

Once we had the plan, the rest of it fell into place. Katrina and the most experienced soldiers trained up the rest of the troops, and by the day of the attack, we almost had a functional invasion force. I would have liked a few more days, but we didn't have them.

***

On the day of the invasion, I took the elevator to the sub-sub-basement jail cell. It was almost time to give a final appeal to the troops. They were about to risk their lives, but before I left, I needed to do one thing. Whether we won or lost, we wouldn't be coming back, and that meant I had one last loose end to tie up.

My feet clomped slowly toward Dean's cell. We'd already emptied all the other cells, just in case none of us came back. None of the prisoners walked free.

Placing my hand on the biometric door lock to Dean's cell was one of the hardest things I've ever done. Yes, he was a terrorist. Yes, he was an enemy, but I had grown close to him over the past two years; he reminded me of a time in my life when I still had hope that things could be better.

I opened the door and a smiling Dean greeted me. He was doing jumping jacks on the other side of the door.

"Hey, Rebecca! I've been working out. Ready to kick Dolos's teeth in today!"

"Dean, sit down."

"Just a minute. I've got a hundred more jumping jacks to do."

"JUST SIT DOWN!"

Dean must have heard something in the timbre of my voice because he became somber. "What's wrong?"

"This mission, if it fails . . . we won't be able to come back here. We have to assume we won't be coming back."

"Well then, we have to make sure it doesn't fail, don't we?"

"We don't have to do anything, Dean. I have to make sure it doesn't fail, and I can't worry that some vengeful god is going to let you out into the world. Not with what you know. Not after what you've done."

"What are you saying, Rebecca?"

I pulled out my revolver, the one I kept by my side for so many years. The one I used to kill so many men. "All the other terrorists were executed hours ago. Except for you. It didn't seem right—"

"Right? You're going to kill me after everything I've done for you?"

Tears swelled in my eyes. "It . . . didn't seem right for somebody else to do it."

"So that's what this is about, Rebecca? You pump me for information, use me for years, and then you kill me. Is that what this is?"

"YOU KNEW THE COMPANY YOU WORKED FOR, AND YOU WORKED FOR THEM ANYWAY!" I lowered my voice. "You know what you did. You confessed. You knew the consequences. You helped us so you could unburden your soul as much as to take down the Godless."

Dean dropped to his knees. "Just make it quick."

"I can do that."

I flipped open a breaker box on the wall and pressed the big, red button inside it. The glass wall between us fell away. I looked into his eyes, right into his eyes, without a partition between us, for the longest second of my life. I raised my gun, just like I had so many times before.

"May the gods have mercy on your soul."

He may have tried to say something in response. I don't know because the bullets' echo drowned out his words. When the noise calmed, Dean was dead on the ground, two bullets through his brain.

***

The Godschurch soldiers were gathered in the atrium, humans and gods alike waiting patiently to be sent to their deaths in the hope that we could pull out a larger victory and save the universe. I had the entire walk back up to the third-floor balcony overlooking the atrium to get myself together.

Angela met me at the elevator. "Here is your speech."

She handed me a thick stack of paper. I looked it over quickly and tossed it in a trash bin we passed as we walked along. "I'm not saying that, Angela."

Her jaw clenched slightly. "Then what will you say, ma'am? We stayed up all night—"

"Go home, Angela."

"Excuse me, ma'am?"

I stopped walking and turned to her. "You've been a loyal friend to me these past two years, but there is nothing for you here."

"I can fight."

"You can die. I am sure of that. I can't save all these people, but I can save you. Go home. Be with your family. That's an order."

Tears welled up in Angela's eyes. "I want to stay. I can help!"

I placed my hands on her shoulders. "You've already helped. Now *live*. If nothing else, go live for everybody here that won't."

Angela stayed behind in the alcove, and I continued without her. Velaska, Katrina, and Aranya met me on the third-floor balcony in front of the conference room. Velaska was dressed in her most elegant attire, like she was going to a gala. She didn't have a role in the battle except to help Urania get our troops back after it was over or if we needed to retreat.

Aranya stood next to Velaska. Her full chain mail battle armor glimmered in the morning sun. Katrina wore her trademark gloves with a black leather jacket and held a long sword that was bigger than her. They were all somber, as were the collection of soldiers below us, holding their demon hunters, dressed in light brown desert fatigues, ready for battle.

As I looked out over the thousands willing to risk their life for the values of the Godschurch, I felt like a fraud for lying to them, but I knew that lying was part of being an adult—part of being a leader. It was part and parcel with responsibility.

Velaska placed her hand on my back. "Are you ready for this?"

"No," I replied, "but who else is going to do it? Let's end this."

I looked over to Katrina and Aranya standing on the other side of me and nodded to them. Katrina planted her sword into the ground. At the far end of the atrium, Urania gave me the thumbs up to show me she was ready.

"It's showtime," I whispered to Velaska. "I was never good at big speeches."

She smiled at me. "I'm sure you'll do fine, but first. This will just never do. You look like a bureaucrat, not a hero."

She snapped her fingers, and thirty pounds shed from me in an instant. Golden dust floated around me, and my loose muscles shrank tight. My sagging hands tightened, and the skin clung to my face again. When the dust finished glowing around me, I was no longer wearing a loose-fitting suit but a long leather coat, with two demon hunters packed in shoulder holsters on my chest. For the first time in months, I felt like myself.

"Now," Velaska said, straightening the collar of my jacket, "you look ready."

I smiled at her. "Thank you."

Velaska's kind gesture made me feel even more guilty about lying to her, but I had no choice. We were in it now, and I needed all my focus on the mission at hand.

"Friends," I shouted to the masses across the atrium, "agents, gods, angels, cherubs, and every one of you who risks everything today to save our universe from Dolos and the Godless—we are too brave to know how few we are. We are too strong to let the odds against us frighten us away. We are too loyal to turn our backs on the church in its moment of need. And for that, I commend you all.

"You could have run. You could have hidden. But you didn't. You came here to make our last stand, and I swear to you it will be a glorious one. We will not stop until that Obelisk is defeated. We will not stop until Dolos lies dead before our feet.

"If you are tired, know that you can be tired tomorrow. If you are hurt, know that pain doesn't last. Glory and honor. They are what endure. So today, leave it all on the battlefield! Today we stop running scared! Today we reclaim our universe!"

The crowd cheered as I threw my hands in the air. In front of me, a great white transport opened, and the first waves of troops ran through, carrying their demon hunters, ready to take on the world.

If only I were as confident in our victory as I made it seem. Still, sometimes lying is necessary—especially to yourself.

CHAPTER 7

After my rousing speech, Urania opened the portal to Niloria, and wave after wave of soldiers rushed through to their certain doom. I hoped for the best but knew in my gut they were fortifying the base, and our chances were slim. By opening the portal, I had signed everybody's death warrant. I only hoped we had enough troops to overtake the Obelisk before they all died.

I was the last one through the gate. By the time I arrived on the battlefield, whole squads of soldiers lay dead in front of me on the streets of the town. The air rattled loudly with the sound of Gatling gun bullets, and Demon hunter charges crackled through the air. A few of my flying angels disintegrated on contact with the charges.

The Godless were fortified behind four-foot-high walls and prepared for our arrival more than even Toni's imagery showed us. Their lines went on forever, stacked twenty deep, as far as the eye could see, surrounding our position on three sides, armed with machine guns, demon hunters, and cannons that shot a continuous stream of Horde charges.

"Get over here!" Katrina shouted as she pulled me into the cover of a building already riddled with bullets. Aranya cocked a demon hunter and fired it across the desert battlefield toward the Obelisk, which hung on the horizon, mocking us all.

"What happened?" I yelled over the crossfire. "We're supposed to be halfway through the desert by now."

"They were more heavily armored than we anticipated," Aranya said, waiting for her gun to recharge. "They must have brought in more troops since our last scout."

I pulled out my demon hunters and fired them around the corner of the building. Two of my agents fell backward, dead, right in front of me. I did my best to focus and not look at their lifeless faces, but then I saw her. Zasha, my young friend, lying dead on the ground next to my other agents. She was only a child.

"We're getting massacred out there," Katrina shouted. "We need to move forward or backward, but we can't just stay here."

"We were already supposed to move forward. What's holding us up?"

"Fear!" Aranya shouted. "Nothing can prepare you for war."

I surveyed the battlefield. Between the edge of the city and the Obelisk was nothing but desert. We needed trenches, and we needed them now.

"Katrina. Take Hephaestus and Aphrodite. Start building trenches along the route between us and the Obelisk. Make it quick but be careful. Those demon hunters can kill you, don't forget."

"Please. I've been dodging them since you were a baby."

Katrina flew across the bullet-ridden street to a cadre of Greek gods, including Aphrodite and Hephaestus. They were two of the stronger gods in the pantheon. I watched Hephaestus shake his head before Katrina flew off with Aphrodite. As the two of them crisscrossed the battlefield, Katrina shot fire out of her arms so hot that it melted the sand, and Aphrodite pulled up huge tracts of sand, tossing it toward the Godless flanks.

"That's enough!" I shouted to them as they neared the Obelisk.

"What about me?" Aranya asked.

"Get a squadron of angels and cherubs. Attack the right flank. I don't want any guns firing at my men on the ground, got it?"

Aranya nodded and took to the air. The ranks of angels and cherubs followed her. Only Velaska and Urania were with me now at the back of the battle. It was a coward's death to stay behind the fray, and I was no coward. There was only one thing left to do: lead the troops across the open desert toward the first trench Katrina created.

Urania was watching me. "What about me?" she asked.

"You and Velaska stay here in case we need to be pulled off this rock. You're the best one to do it, and Velaska, well, Velaska is worthless in a fight."

The two of them nodded without a word. I inched forward slowly at first, then sped up to a jog. Before long, I was sprinting through my troops, yelling, "CHARGE!"

Dolos once told me I had an inordinate amount of luck. I wasn't sure if that was true, but I hoped it was, for our sake. I needed every ounce of luck in my body to survive all the way to the first trench. I looked over my shoulder when I reached the sand, and my troops cascaded toward the first trench with me, firing at the Obelisk as they moved.

The Godless forces on the flanks were distracted by the angels and gods giving them Hell. They couldn't contain both them and our troops on the ground at once.

I jumped into the first trench and ducked my head low. Behind me, hundreds of agents flooded into the trench. Toni ran forward with the pack, along with hundreds more who had never seen a fight. They were pounding forward as fast as they could on my orders.

"Don't stop firing!" I shouted. "If you need to reload, tap out and let the person behind you take your place. I want a continuous stream of bullets firing at them."

I looked back at the edge of the city, where we'd begun our attack. We hadn't moved as far as I would have liked. Hundreds of bloody and broken angels, agents, and gods lay behind us, but we were only a quarter of the way to the Obelisk.

"Hephaestus," I shouted, rushing to him. He was one of the few gods not in the air. "Why didn't you go off with Katrina?"

"I would be better deployed as a weapons expert who can—"

"We don't have time for who can do what—take any remaining gods. Attack the left flank with Katrina and hit it hard. If you can break through there, then my troops can work our way toward the Obelisk."

"Yes, ma'am."

Hephaestus scuttled off, and I scoured the lines for any angels or gods I recognized. There, I saw him. Michael, an angel from Katrina's planet, fired demon hunters with his Archangels at the right flank of the battle. He was one of Katrina's best angels, or so she said.

"Michael!" I screamed his name until he turned around. "Get the rest of the angels into the air and take down that right flank. Draw their fire, and we will cover you. We'll deal with the Godless in front of us."

Michael nodded to me and got the attention of Samael and Dennis, two more of Katrina's angels. They gathered some more angels, and then together, the three of them flew into the air with a battalion of other angels. The air was a light show with cannons, lasers, and gunfire going off in every direction. That firepower would soon descend on us when I gave the order. No more gods or angels were left in the bunker. It was just humanity, defending the gods and risking our lives for them.

"All right," I shouted to the troops in the trench with me. "Every third soldier follow me! The rest of you, cover us!"

The word spread down the line, and every third soldier rose to a crouched position, ready to move. The fear shone in their eyes, and it was warranted, but they held their emotions in check. This was a fool's mission, and I was a fool for leading them on it.

"Now!"

I went up and over the bunker just as the gunfire from the Obelisk descended upon us. There was no longer any air support. We were on our own, but at least we were only taking fire from in front of us now. Still, the agents next to me fell in droves on our way to the second bunker.

While I was pressing forward, my hands started to glow gold. My heart thumped louder and faster in my chest. Instead of a body, I became a golden streak zipping between the trenches, moving faster than human eyesight could comprehend. I had hoped that my strange power to turn into a golden streak would return before I ran to my doom. I could not predict when it would come or will it to do so. My power had been dormant for the last two years, but now it was back, and this time I didn't freak out about it. This time, I used it to avoid the bullets zipping across the lines.

I slid inside the second trench just as a demon charge whizzed overhead. Half of the troops with me died in no man's land between trenches, but those of us remaining were almost to the Obelisk now. Toni wasn't there anymore, and many of the faces I recognized were gone.

Our lines were thinning, but there was resolve in my soldiers' eyes.

"Fire at those Godless guns!" I shouted. "Don't stop until every one of our men is safe and sound!" I turned around to the first trench. "All right! Now! The rest of you! Come to me!"

The rest of the agents jumped up and over the first trench, firing as they went. I hadn't seen such bravery since the Horde Wars. They dropped like flies, but their valor never wavered, not until those who survived slid into the trench next to me and realized what they had done.

There were no more trenches between us and the fortified Godless troops, safe behind their walls. Between us and them, razor wire lined every inch. We needed the angels to break the lines before we could move forward again.

But the skies were filled with fewer flying figures than before. At the beginning of the battle, their troops had nearly blocked out the sun. Now, there were far more gaps where the sun peeked through. No, the angels couldn't help us. They had their assignment, and we had ours. We would have to do this on our own.

I grabbed the demon hunters from my shoulder holsters and started firing across the battlefield. Even when I hit the Godless walls, my charges didn't disintegrate them. Somehow, the Godless created tech resistant to the Horde weaponry.

"Damnit!" I shouted. The ground kicked up dust in front of me, and it gave me an idea. I fired my demon hunters at the ground, and the sand exploded on impact, sending plumes of dust into the air and evaporating the razor wire in our path.

"Fire at the ground," I shouted. "Break up the tripwire."

A great hail of dirt came from the desert as hundreds of demon hunters fired into the ground at once, blocking the Godless and sending a cloud into the sky a hundred feet high.

"Enough!"

And the field went silent. When the dust settled, and the Godless guns started again, the ground was clear of razor wire. All we had to deal with was the army of Godless scum guarding the base, and I had an idea as to how to do that.

"Everybody reload!" I ducked down into the bunker, the bullets from the Godless zipping over our heads. "When I tell you, shoot at the ground and wait three seconds. Then, jump over this bunker and run like the wind!"

The message was carried down the lines, and after a minute, I was confident everybody had heard me.

"NOW!"

The dust blew up around us, and I jumped over the bunker. A thousand troops rushed forward with me, and we didn't stop until we saw the whites of the enemy's eyes staring wide-eyed at our brazen bull rush of their defenses.

"Shoot!"

The Godless scum were completely taken off guard when we emerged from the dust storm, firing directly on them. No one could expect us to be so stupid as to rush their lines, and when we jumped over their barriers and started taking them on in hand-to-hand combat, they couldn't do anything but welcome death.

My agents dealt death blows to Godless scum after Godless scum. At a distance, the Godless had the advantage in battle, but up close, my Godschurch training overwhelmed the ineptitude of the terrorists. I ducked under one of my agents, gouging out the eyes of his enemy, and ran toward the angels at the right of the battle.

"Aranya!" I shouted, "Aranya!"

A blur turned to me and stopped. It was Aranya, barely out of breath. "Our battle is won!"

"Here as well!" I replied. "Any sign of Dolos?"

Aranya picked up one of the battered Godless soldiers, bleeding out of his mouth, and gave him a violent shake. "Where is he? Where is Dolos?"

The terrorist didn't say anything. He just pointed his finger, and we turned to see a black hooded figure crest over the horizon. It was Dolos, but he wasn't alone. A hundred soldiers flew behind him. They weren't Godless.

"Who are they?" I shouted to Aranya.

She squinted her eyes to get a closer look, then I watched her face transform into a furious sneer like I'd never seen before on her. "Meret, Osiris, Odin. The Egyptian and Norse forces . . . turned against us."

At that moment, I knew why we couldn't get any other pantheons on our side. I couldn't believe I was so stupid. The Egyptian gods screwed us.

CHAPTER 8

"You are a fool," Dolos said, floating in front of his throng of gods, angels, and Valkyries. His voice boomed over the battlefield between us.

The bearded faces and axes of the Odin line merged with the sleek, gilded elegance of the Osiris line as they headed toward the battlefield. Valkyrie and Egyptian angels decked out in golden armor and carrying scythes flew behind them in a secondary formation. Godless scum rushed toward Dolos from their positions around the Obelisk. All of them marched toward us.

"Make ranks!" I shouted. The Godschurch troops formed into rows behind me. "Prepare to fire!"

"It won't matter," Dolos said. "This whole battle was designed to get you here at this exact moment, for this exact reason. Everything we've done for the past two years has led to this."

I thought back to Meret allowing me access to the pyramid, his wager with me, and how Osiris called it off. Dolos knew, the whole time, what we were planning and when we were planning it. He had all the intel he needed to defeat us, so there was never a need for him to attack.

"I knew you would force an attack if we pushed the limits of your finances," Dolos said.

"Then why play the game?" I asked, walking toward him with Aranya floating behind me. Katrina came to my side and we trudged through the sand together, joined by the angels and the Greek gods. "Why not just destroy the Godschurch once and for all?"

Dolos laughed. "I had to be sure you would all be here. You have a habit of sneaking away from me when I try to kill you, Director Lobdell. Besides, your little organization had cells across the universe, operating without you, which would still be determined to take me down if I simply destroyed you. That would not do. Now, here, on this planet, I can take you down for good, all at once. Gods, angels, and agents alike."

"And what did they promise you?" I said, pointing to Osiris. "What could they have said to make you turn against your own people?"

Osiris laughed, wrapping his arms around his wife, Isis. "He promised me clemency, Rebecca. Clemency for me and my people against the Titans. Something you never offered."

"I didn't need to offer clemency. I offered protection. Protection from the god who's trying to destroy the church, and the universe."

The ground quaked under us, and a great crack in the sand grew beneath Dolos and his gods. From it, a giant Obelisk arose, twenty times bigger than the one from our plans.

"Now, you will see what true power is," Dolos shouted. "I will use this to bring back my sister and make the universe tremble."

"If you do this," Katrina said, "you doom us all. You doom the whole universe to extinction."

"You think that," Dolos said, "but the gods are not the whole universe."

"Screw that!" Katrina shot back. "Who cares about the gods? I'm talking about everything. Twenty years ago, when Urania and Apollo eliminated every black hole in the galaxy, we trapped a universe filled with a creeping whiteness behind these stars. It's already destroyed everything in Cronus and Rhea's universe. If you open the portal and let them through, you will also let in the creeping whiteness. It will destroy this universe."

"Fool. Do you find me so stupid that I would be swayed with something so childish and idiotic?"

"It's not childish," Katrina replied. "Cronus decided to destroy this whole universe and everything in it—all because we annoyed him. He thought it was too much of a bother to keep this universe. Trust me, he was going to kill everything, including you. I saved us with the help of Apollo and Urania."

"Never! He would never kill me. Not when I've worked so hard to free him."

The bigger Obelisk wobbled for a moment, and when it locked into place with a loud click, the ground stopped grumbling. The massive object dwarfed everything around it, casting a shadow across the entire battlefield.

"Please," I said. "Don't do this."

Dolos laughed, his red eyes bouncing across his pupils. "It is already done."

Green energy bolts pulsated from the base of the Obelisk and inched toward its tip. With every passing second, the energy reserves crept further up the base toward the imminent destruction of our universe.

"I won't let this happen," I growled.

"Idiot," Dolos laughed. "Do you think I would have brought you here if there was any chance you could stop me?"

"No, but you underestimate my ability to destroy you." I raised my fist in the air and began to run. "NOW! CHARGE!"

What remained of my army fired at Dolos and his army, and the Godless troops returned our volley with one of their own. Gods and angels from every pantheon clashed in hand-to-hand combat. The sky lit up with demon hunter charges, fireballs, and every manner of magic as I scanned for an opening to the Obelisk from across the new battlefield.

"Aranya," I said, "we have to get to the Obelisk and shut it down."

Aranya picked me up and flew me toward the entrance inside the Obelisk. The sky cracked with bullets, but Aranya navigated through it deftly. As we passed into Godless space and the Obelisk grew in front of us, the Egyptian gods took notice.

"Get her!" Osiris shouted.

Meret stopped tossing lightning at my men and gave chase to us. I turned and fired at him. The first charges missed, but he was fat and slow. My second barrage clipped him on the shoulder, and he slowly blinked out of existence.

"Fool!" Dolos shouted from his coward's perch at the back of the battle. The other gods were engaged in the fight, but Dolos did nothing except watch the action. "I've waited for this day since our last meeting! The day where I could crush the Godschurch, and you, once and for all."

Dolos lifted himself into the air and gave chase as we neared the Obelisk. I thought he would be slow and lumbering, but the old god surprised me. He swerved to avoid every shot I fired, and he was fast—faster than Aranya. Within seconds he was right on top of us. Green electricity covered his arms as he charged up to take us out of the air.

And then *slam!* Dolos was gone, crashing down to the ground. Katrina dropped him to the earth with a shot of fire from above us, and he slammed into the sand, kicking up a torrent of dust in his wake.

"Figure out how to destroy that thing!" she shouted at me before flying down to the ground. "I've got Dolos."

The last time Aranya and I destroyed one of Dolos's Obelisks, we'd targeted the green goop under the Obelisk. The green goop was a product the Horde made from human souls. Souls were powerful killing machines. However, they were also highly volatile and unstable, especially in large quantities.

If we could enter the Obelisk and cause an explosion near that green chemical compound, the entire vat of goop would explode instantly. That's what saved our asses last time, and according to the new schematics, it was a design flaw we could still exploit. However, we had the schematics of the decoy Obelisk, not the real one, and something told me Dolos had learned from his mistakes in the new design. If the army he brought to destroy us was any indication, he learned plenty from our previous encounter.

Aranya flew us into the crack in the sand created for the Obelisk, which was more than half charged with green energy bolts, and into the belly of the facility a hundred feet below. We didn't make it far before the flood of demon hunter charges put a stop to our descent. Thousands of Godless terrorists fired at us from every floor of the underground facility.

"We're not going to make it down there," Aranya said. "I can't avoid that many weapons."

"Drop me," I said.

"Are you crazy? I'm not going to drop you!"

"I am still your superior, and this is still a battle! Now, drop me."

Aranya sighed. She couldn't argue with a direct order. "Goodbye." She let go of me, and I dropped toward the ground below as wave after wave of demon hunter charges fired at me from every direction.

I had a theory about when my new powers kicked in, and it had to do with how much adrenaline coursed through my veins. "Please, please, please . . ." I whispered under my breath. My suspicion was that the closer I was to death, the more likely my abilities were to activate.

Of course, I had been in high-stress situations before—often open combat—and this new power only presented itself three times in my entire life, and all of them recently. Why now? Honestly, I didn't know, and I didn't care. I just hoped that it would work. Otherwise, I would be vaporized or end up as a stain on the floor of the Obelisk.

A Horde laser cut through the air right above my head. Startled, I lurched forward past the charge in a streak of gold and ended up on the other side of the cavern. I turned my head to see a golden streak following me from one side of the cavern to the other. It looked like my hunch was correct.

Another bullet came by, and I disappeared once again. And again. And again. I jumped down the cavern walls, leaving nothing but golden streaks in my wake, until I reached the bottom of the cavern, next to the base of the Obelisk, unharmed.

Just as I thought, Dolos had learned from his mistakes. While the schematics we'd studied showed a giant vat of green goop, the base of this Obelisk was surrounded by a metal barrier that extended to the edges of the room. There were no controls to destroy, only guards at every door firing at me. The Obelisk was locked in place, with no way to move it, and this planet's star was straight in its path. Worse yet, the Obelisk's charge was almost at the tip. When it charged completely, it would fire, and our universe would be doomed.

My hands still vibrated too fast for me to see. The last time it had happened, I could punch my fist straight through somebody's head as if their skull wasn't there. If I could do the same with the Obelisk's casing, maybe I could get to the wiring and dismantle it from the inside. I punched at the casing repeatedly, but my hands only bounced off it. Dolos must have figured out how to block my powers.

Because, of course, he had. He had seen my powers firsthand and was both fascinated and terrified. He must have prepared for even this eventuality that I would break through and reach the Obelisk. The moment when his guards encircled me. The moment when all hope was lost, and we were defeated.

Then again, Dolos could not have known me very well. For me, hope was never completely lost. As long as I drew breath, there was always a chance to survive. The guards squeezed in around me. They thought I was trapped, but they were wrong. With my body still vibrating faster than I could see, I rushed up the side of the Obelisk. I needed to escape, and I needed to take down the Obelisk from the tip before it fired.

The vibration from the Obelisk hummed under my feet, charging ever hotter as I hurried along its side. Normally, an incline like that would be too steep, but with my lightning-fast speed, I reached the top with ease.

In mere moments, I rose from the crack in the sand. The lightning power was about to hit the tip of the Obelisk. I looked to my right and saw Katrina winning her battle with Dolos, smashing his face into the ground again and again.

"Katrina!" I shouted. "Bring him up here!"

Katrina nodded to me and punched Dolos in the face one last time. She scooped him up into her arms, limp, and flew toward me.

"I'm not going to ask what you are doing," she said, "but it looks like it's gonna be awesome."

"I know, right?" I replied. "Get him on the tip of the weapon, right in its line of fire."

I met her there. The energy to fire the weapon was inches from the tip as I smacked Dolos awake. Katrina held him a foot from the great weapon, right in its path, while she hovered a safe distance above the Obelisk.

"Wake up!" I spat. "You don't get to sleep. Not now."

Dolos groggily opened his eyes. "What—what is happening?"

"Look in front of you, asshole. If this thing goes off, you die. Tell me how to turn it off and make it snappy."

Dolos kicked his legs to get away, but Katrina held him tightly. "You fool. Let me go! Don't you know there's no chance of you winning this battle? Even if you—"

"You can pontificate some other time," I said. The heat was right under my feet. In less than a minute, it would be fully charged. "Tell me how to shut it off, now!"

"You can't shut it off! Don't you know that? I made it perfect so that my plans could not be thwarted. God-resistant metal covers every inch. You can't change that."

"Then I guess you'll be dying now."

Dolos dangled in front of the Obelisk. The green energy sparked under my feet, and I jumped into Katrina's arms just as the device crackled to life. A green laser shot out into the star above it.

The energy vaporized Dolos immediately. Finally, the Godless were done for, but another problem loomed on the horizon—bigger than the Godless. Bigger than anything else in the universe. Katrina landed us on the ground just as the laser hit the star.

"What now?" she asked.

"Get everybody you can off this rock," I replied. "Godless, god, angel, or agent. I don't care what side they were on, just get them all out of here!"

The battle lines were no longer destroying each other. Instead, they all looked up into the sky as the great, green laser beam shot out across it. I hoped it dawned on Dolos's minions just how screwed they were and that they were responsible for the end of everything.

"Listen up," I shouted across the battlefield. The Obelisk crackled behind me. "Dolos is dead. There is nobody to protect you from Cronus now. There is nobody to speak for you. Cronus hates gods and humanity more than anything. Now is your chance to run. The Godless are no more. Any deal you gods made with Dolos will not be honored by Cronus. No clemency, I can assure you of that. The Godschurch will offer you sanctuary, but you must go now!"

It was too late, though. The Obelisk stopped firing its green laser. For a moment, all seemed to be well. Then, the star popped like a balloon, and we were all royally screwed.

CHAPTER 9

I had felt the intense pressure built from a black hole before. Twice actually, since the first time I went through a black hole, I had ended up in Rhea's universe, then a black hole pulled me back again to our universe.

So, I knew what it felt like to be in the presence of a black hole, and the feeling wasn't the same. Instead of a sensation of the universe being sucked into a vacuum, it felt like the puncture of a balloon, with all the air escaping into our universe from another one.

Except that all the air was escaping with a whimper and not a scream. It was like a slow leak as if a tire wasn't completely filled, and then you poked a hole into it. The last time I was around when a star collapsed, I couldn't move, think, or talk, but this time I was able to walk around as if nothing was the matter. I even heard the panicked screams behind me, which would have been impossible in the vortex of a black hole.

"Get everybody back!" Katrina shouted. "No matter what you do, don't stop moving!"

She was right, of course, but I couldn't help but stop and look up. From the puncture, pure whiteness spiraled its tendrils out into the universe, wrapping itself around the puncture and easing itself out like an octopus escaping a fishing boat through a narrow hole.

"Shit," Katrina said, flying toward me. "That whiteness is what Cronus is gonna use to destroy our universe. I contained it twenty years ago, but now it's here, and it's going to destroy everything."

"So, this is what the end of the universe looks like. I never thought I would live to see the day or have a part in its destruction. It's kind of bland, isn't it? I always thought it would be more like an explosion and less like . . . an eraser. Do you think it will hurt?"

"Let's not stick around to find out. Come on."

But I couldn't move. I stood transfixed. I had worked so hard to prevent the universe from ending, and yet here I was, staring down at imminent destruction, and I couldn't shake the feeling it was my fault.

I looked back at all the other gods, Godless, and agents of the church rushing back toward the portal. The wind from the puncture helped move them along, but they would never make it in time, no matter how long Urania left it open.

"What was it like?" I asked. "Watching that other universe die?"

"It was like a big bowl of nothing. Endless nothing, as far as the eye could see."

"That actually sounds nice. Nothingness. Very little to protect in nothingness."

"Prepare to be surprised then. It was bland, like hummus, except that it tasted like pancakes. Now can we go?"

"It tasted like pancakes?" I asked, my eyebrow raised quizzically.

"Yes, you know how every god has a different flavor to their light. Well, Cronus's white wave of destruction . . . it tasted like pancakes."

"So, the end tastes like pancakes?"

"You are taking this very well."

A tiny object fell out of the puncture in the sky, illuminated by the tendrils waving out in the universe.

"What is that?" I asked.

"I don't know."

A high-pitched, whining sound howled louder as it fell toward us. Katrina grabbed me and flew me away before the object crashed into the ground, sending sand careening into the air out of the crater it made. Its shockwave felled all those who were running toward the light.

When the dust cleared, a huge beetle dressed in the finest accessories of an Egyptian Pharaoh lay beaten and bruised on the ground below us. Katrina floated closer to look at the bug oozing its green blood all over the sand around it.

"L'l'itoh," Katrina whispered under her breath.

Before I could ask any questions, the sky quaked and a great hand ripped open the puncture. A massive, hairy, and decidedly human-like leg stepped through from the other universe into ours. I didn't have to ask who was on the other side of that foot. I knew. It was Cronus, and he was coming for his revenge.

Moments later, a second hand came through the expanse, followed by the rest of an arm, and then a big, bald head. Even from miles away, I could still make out the whites of his eyes scanning the horizon in front of him.

"Cronus is not going to be happy with me," Katrina said, staring up at the puncture.

"Well, you are a god. He isn't happy with any of you."

"That's true," Katrina said, nudging the dead bug with her foot. "But I sent that thing in there to kill him."

"Why would you do that?"

"It was the only way to end the Horde Wars. L'l'itoh used human souls to become a god and was too powerful for us to defeat. I figured it was easier to have Cronus take care of it than try to take it down myself."

I looked back at the other gods and humans crawling onto their feet and rushing toward the escape light that Urania set up. The first wave had disappeared, but there were still thousands that would die if we didn't stall Cronus.

"Can you use that?" I asked her. "His hatred of you?"

"To what end?"

"To keep him busy until we can get everybody off this planet."

Cronus was now completely through the barrier, and another pair of hands pushed out of the puncture. They were slighter than his, with less hair on them, but they still filled the sky. I knew before her head popped out of the puncture that it was Rhea. My hands began to sweat, and my gut tightened at the thought of seeing the evil Titan again after so many years.

Katrina watched them make their way onto our planet with more fascination than fear. "I suppose I could try. Although, risking my life for a bunch of ungrateful assholes isn't really my idea of—"

"You signed up for the Godschurch, too, Katrina, and that means protecting all gods, even those that want us dead."

"It's a stupid mission."

"Be that as it may, it is our mission."

Cronus finished pulling Rhea out of the puncture. Naked as babies, they looked around with furrowed brows until Cronus locked onto our position. His lip curled, and he stomped toward us.

"This isn't good," Katrina said.

"Katrina!" Cronus shouted. "We had a deal."

He lunged forward until his face came within inches of the planet's surface. The force of his movement sent the desert sand into the sky and shot us into the air. When we crashed back onto the planet's surface, Urania's escape light no longer shone brightly. I tried to scramble to my feet, but my body was plastered to the ground. The gravitational force of Cronus's body was too much.

Katrina struggled against the new weight in the air as she rose to her feet. "Cronus. What brings you out beyond the stars?"

"I wanted to see how the destruction of this universe was progressing, and I come to find that you have been living quite comfortably for all this time."

"It's really not that much time, dear," Rhea said behind him, crossing her arms.

"Has it not been?" Cronus responded. "I'm not quite sure. Life in the utter whiteness of space is timeless and eternal."

Katrina's knees buckled as she fought against the incredible power of Cronus's gravitational force. "You told me that you would let this universe live if I could find a way to close the black holes and prevent the whiteness's ability to destroy us."

"Did I say that? It doesn't sound like me."

"I believe you did say it, dear. But I doubt you meant it," Rhea said, pointing to Katrina. "That one has a way of manipulating your words."

Rhea's eyes fell on me then, standing next to Katrina. I felt them bore into me. My breath shallowed, and my eyes pressed closed tightly. She was going to eat me, and I knew it. I just knew it in my bones. I had never been more petrified than when she was planning to eat us after Earth was sent through the black hole to her universe, nor felt more relief than when we were pulled back from the brink, which prevented it.

"Cronus," Rhea said in a whiny voice. "I'm cold. This hole is making a draft."

"Ah yes," Cronus said. "Let us find a warmer area of the universe."

He grabbed the edges of the planet, knocking us every which way. "I'm not done with you yet, Katrina."

With his hands firmly around the planet, Rhea latched onto Cronus's arm. He closed his eyes and vanished with us. Katrina was right. His white light did taste like pancakes, with warm, gooey maple syrup.

CHAPTER 10

We reappeared in darkness, most assuredly millions of miles across the universe from where we began, but I didn't know how far. While I could see the stars in the sky, I couldn't feel the warmth of one near me. There was no moon, and no light bounced off Cronus or Rhea, meaning there probably wasn't one on the far side of the planet either.

"Cronus," Rhea's voice carried in the darkness. "I thought you said it was warmer here."

"I'm sorry, my love. I thought it was. Forgive me. It has been a long time since I walked through this universe. Let me fix that for you."

The planet shook as Cronus shifted his hold on it. He lifted one hand into the air, where a small ball of light appeared, casting light on the planet and Cronus's face.

"Grow, my sweet. Grow."

Cronus blew lightly on the ember, and it expanded, spinning and rising into the darkness on its own.

"What is he doing?" I pushed myself to my feet. The gravity was lessened now that we were away from the puncture.

"He is creating a star," Katrina answered, watching the ball of light. "Only Cronus has the power of creation. He is tied into the Source, which emanates from the Nexus."

I hadn't thought of the Nexus since the Godschurch base blew up, and now wasn't the time either. All around me, my troops intermingled with the Godless. All of them ran, trying to leave the planet, but I realized now that we couldn't. If we left, Cronus would be free to conquer the universe again or destroy it—but now, right now, we had a chance to stop him in his tracks. There would never be a more formidable collection of gods and humans in one place.

I turned to run away. "Aranya! Scoop me!" I called to Katrina over my shoulder. "Keep him distracted!"

"And how am I supposed to do that?" Katrina replied.

"I don't know," I said, reaching for Aranya. "You're really annoying, though, so maybe play into that."

Aranya flew me toward the city. "What do you want? I'm trying to get everybody to safety."

"No. Take me to Urania. We can't leave. We have to stay and fight. This may be our best chance to defeat Cronus. He seems weak from the other universe, and the longer he stays here, the more powerful he'll become. If we let him escape, then we spell doom for the whole universe."

"What about the whiteness seeping into our universe that is going to wipe us out of existence?"

"We have two problems right now, and neither of them is going to be solved by running away. I need you to take me to Urania. If I know her at all, she's already working on a way to get us off this planet."

"Fine. You're the boss."

Aranya flew me past the Godless and Godschurch soldiers running below us. Cronus's light was getting brighter, and I could see that even while they ran to escape, the Godless and Godschurch were trampling each other. The fighting got worse the closer we came to Urania and the Godschurch portal. Fistfights broke out as the men from both sides crammed together.

"Urania!" I shouted, flying above the tangle of limbs. People were jammed ass to ankles in the streets, pushing each other to get through to the portal entrance—or where the portal would be if it was operational.

Urania's slight frame was barely noticeable in the throng of people encircling her, but Velaska had created a sort of forcefield around them to fend off the masses. I pointed Aranya to it.

Velaska lowered her forcefield just long enough for Aranya to land us inside, then raised it again before any soldiers could penetrate it.

"Thank the gods you've come," Urania said, wrapping her arms around me. "It's been a non-stop onslaught since the grid went down."

"Can you get it back up?" Aranya asked.

"No," I replied. "We don't want it back up. We need these men to fight."

Urania's eyes darted from Aranya to me and then to the mass of people behind her. "I don't think we should talk about it here." She led us into a tall, bullet-riddled office building. Velaska moved the bubble with us until we were safely inside the complex while the angry mob screamed at us outside.

"We can't go back to the Godschurch base," Urania said to me.

"I know," I replied. "We have to fight."

"No. I mean, even if we got the transport working again, I wouldn't know where to send them."

"We can go back to Meret's world."

"To get anywhere in this universe, you need to know where you are and where you want to go."

"We're here," Aranya said. "We want to go there."

Urania was getting impatient. "That's not how it works," she said. "I have no idea where we are right now. Cronus jumped us halfway across the universe. I can't even see the puncture right now. It might take years for the puncture to be visible to us, so I can reorient myself. If I were to just punch in the old coordinates, we could end up a million light years from our desired destination. I need to know where we are in the universe first, and then I can know where we are going. Space is infinite, and we don't want to get lost."

"And that's not what I'm saying. Even if we could leave, we have to stay," I replied. "We have to stop Cronus and Rhea here."

"Oh, that sounds like a swell idea." Velaska rolled her eyes. "Just swell."

"I know it's going to be hard to defeat Cronus, but we can't let him leave this planet. Katrina's keeping him busy for the moment, but that won't last long. He wants to kill the gods, and I think we send him a message that the gods won't go without a fight."

"And what about the whiteness?" Aranya asked.

I nodded. "That's where you come in, Urania. You closed the black holes once. Can you do it again?"

"Maybe . . . maybe. But I can't do it alone. We would need—"

"Apollo," Velaska said. "I thought I would be able to go my whole existence without seeing him again."

"Do we know where he is?"

Urania bit her lip, thinking. "I think so. I know where he was, at least."

"Fine, then we'll go find Apollo and close the portal while Katrina leads everybody here into battle."

"Aren't you forgetting something?" Aranya said. "These people all hate each other. How will they ever fight together?"

"One thing at a time," I said, turning back to Urania. "Can you figure out where we are?"

"Possibly."

"It doesn't matter where we go, we just have to get somewhere that you know. Work with Aranya." I turned to Velaska. "Let's go try to fix this situation outside."

She smoothed out her elegant dress. "Oh, goodie. Nothing I like more than stopping a riot."

***

I stepped back outside the building, where the sounds of explosions filled the air and drowned out the screaming of humans and gods trying to get to safety. In the distance, a small speck that must have been Katrina flew around Cronus's laser beam eyes. He swiped at her with his great paws. Rhea joined him, grabbing at the air for the tiny speck, and I could tell Katrina wouldn't last much longer.

"Does anybody in the universe like Katrina?" I asked Velaska.

"I like her," she replied.

"Anybody else?"

"Urania tolerates her sometimes . . . she did for a while, at least."

"I actually feel a little bad for her, alone and neglected. Everybody needs friends."

"Many people rely on Katrina," Velaska replied.

"That's not the same."

She chuckled. "You two are very similar."

"Yes, I suppose we are," I agreed. I looked at the mayhem around us. "Can you lift me above all of the people?"

Velaska's bubble expanded below us, and we rose into the air. Sparks shot out of her eyes as we flew above the crowds of humans, angels, and gods alike.

"Wish me luck," I whispered to Velaska.

"People!" I called down to the masses of people and gods. "Gods, Godschurch, and Godless. We are at a crossroads!" Their eyes darted between me and Cronus's hulking figure. I was asking them to participate in a suicide mission, for sure, but it was the only chance we had to save the universe.

"Let us out!" one woman shouted.

"Open the gates!" screamed another.

"The portal back to the Godschurch is broken," I admitted. "And even if I could release you back to safety…we need you here."

"To die like dogs!" Osiris shouted, flying through the air toward us. "Like Meret!"

"No!" I replied. "To fight like heroes. Those titans out there, they mean to destroy you—all of you. Katrina cannot fight them alone. Even with all of us together, there is hardly a chance. But think of the consequences of letting them roam free."

"They will destroy all the gods!" one of the Godless terrorists said.

"Yes! Yes, they will!" Velaska responded. "But they will not end there. They hate the gods because once we fought against Cronus's cruelty—we fought for you and banished Cronus because he wanted to destroy all of you."

"I don't believe you!" another Godless woman said. "You have every reason to lie."

"Ask Osiris, who fought alongside you and Dolos," Velaska replied. "Do I speak false?"

All eyes turned to Osiris, who floated beside us. "No. You have spoken the truth. The Titans wish to destroy you all."

"Then why did you work with Dolos to free them?" I shouted.

"I thought it a foregone conclusion that the Titans would return, and I wanted to be on the winning side—I . . . I hoped they would show us mercy."

"That is unlikely now, is it not?" Velaska asked.

Osiris nodded. "Yes. It is unlikely they will show any mercy now that Dolos is dead."

"Then you have a choice!" I addressed the crowds again. "You can hide like cowards and let Cronus leave this planet, or you can work to contain him until we find a way to put him back in his place. What will you do?"

Osiris's eyes narrowed. "My duty is to my people."

"Do you truly think there is any hope to defeat Cronus unless we fight together?" I asked.

Osiris took a long second to look back at Katrina, clearly fighting a losing battle against Cronus.

Cronus's eye beam struck Katrina, and the little dot grew as the beam shot her toward us at an incredible speed. Velaska closed her eyes and expanded the bubble to envelop Katrina and protect her. The eye beam flung all of us in the bubble backward against the wall of a building.

"I can't hold it much longer!" Velaska screamed. The power was fading from her eyes.

Katrina was bleeding on the bottom of the bubble. This looked like the end for us all. We couldn't carry on, and without the three of us, the resistance to Cronus would crumble. He would rip through the planet with Rhea and move on to the next, killing every god and human as he went.

Osiris floated in the sky above, watching us with an angry grimace. He turned to the side, and I thought he was leaving us to our doom, but he was just gaining momentum. In a miraculous display of selflessness, he launched himself in front of Cronus's eye beam, deflecting it away from us.

Velaska could no longer hold us in the air. Her protective bubble disintegrated when we crashed into the ground. It shielded us from the main force of impact, but my head still bounced on the concrete. Above us, Osiris turned into a glowing ball of yellow energy and burst apart in front of us all. The beam dissipated, and there was a chilling silence.

All eyes turned from where Osiris had been to his wife, Isis. She had raced toward him when he imploded, and now she hovered silently, biting her lip and fighting back tears.

"For Osiris!" she shouted as she flew forward. The rest of the gods flew forward, followed by the legions of men below them. I watched the glorious onslaught for a few seconds before I fell unconscious.

CHAPTER 11

I woke up to the sound of explosions in the distance. Next to me, Aranya rang out a towel and pressed it against my head.

"You should be in the fight," I told her.

"There are plenty of soldiers giving their lives out there right now, and I'll have plenty of time to get myself killed once you are up and walking around."

I pushed myself up onto my elbows. Velaska and Katrina were nowhere to be found, but I hadn't moved from where we had crash-landed. "Where are—"

"Velaska is with Urania, trying to figure out where in the universe we are. Katrina is on the front lines, fighting Cronus and Rhea. It's not going well."

I stood up. "I doubt it would—" I started to speak but stumbled back against the wall, my head still woozy. I needed to rest, but every moment wasted was a moment we weren't turning the tide of battle—a moment more people died.

"You shouldn't be walking around yet," Aranya said.

"Can you—can you just help me?"

I wrapped my arms around Aranya, and she enveloped me in her wings. I felt her heart beating in her chest, and for a moment, I felt safe. It wouldn't last, but I wanted to savor it.

"Come," she said. "We should get you to a bed."

"No. There isn't time. Take me to Urania."

"If you insist."

Aranya's great wings unfurled, and as we ascended into the heavens, I watched the massacre below. Cronus smashed his hand down on a battalion of troops, killing them instantly. Rhea swatted at a group of angels like mosquitos on a hot July eve.

"How did they ever win last time?" I asked. "How did the gods ever beat the Titans?"

"It was a final battle just like this—an alliance of man, gods, and angels. We came after them for so long, and so many of us died at their hands, but eventually, they became weary, which is when Zeus landed the final blow. If they can survive long enough, we have a chance, but we had many more troops last time. So many more."

The air thinned, and the bright blue sky turned black as we crossed out of the atmosphere.

"Cling tight to my chest," Aranya said. "Let my heat warm you."

We rose over the planet and out of sight from the battle. The star that lit Cronus and Rhea faded, and all we had was the darkness—it was peaceful. Peaceful and cold. Aranya wrapped me with one of her wings and used the other to steer. In the distance, surrounded by the twinkle of stars, two figures came into view.

By the time we reached Velaska and Urania, I was frozen stiff, lips blue and teeth chattering. Velaska took one look at me and created a protective bubble around the four of us.

"What are you doing bringing her here?" she asked Aranya.

"It was her idea. And it didn't seem much more dangerous than being in that battle, really."

"I'm fine," I said in a weak voice. I kneeled on the bottom of Velaska's bubble. "How are we doing up here?"

"Better than down there," Velaska replied.

"Good, actually," Urania said, smacking Velaska on the shoulder. "After Cronus jumped us across the universe, I lost track of where we were among the stars. However, I've been able to pinpoint where we are down to the quadrant of space and think I can move us to where Apollo is drinking his troubles away."

"That's a lot of 'I think.' How confident are you?"

"Seventy-five percent?"

"That's like a C, Urania," I said. "I need a little more confidence than that."

"Confidence starts with a C, and it takes time," Velaska said. "Time we do not have. Are you willing to risk the lives of everybody on this planet—everybody in this universe—for a little bit more confidence?"

"I suppose not," I said. "After all, if we die, it's only us, right?"

"Most likely, it will only be you," Urania said. "We can survive in the vacuum of space if necessary."

"And without food and water even longer," Velaska said.

"Perfect," I replied. "Well, I am willing to risk my life for all of those on the planet, so let's do it."

"Katrina waits for us with her sword, which will open a rift in space and lead us across the universe."

"Then let's go to her."

"It is done then," Velaska said, snapping her fingers. We disappeared.

***

We reappeared on top of the tallest building in the city, overlooking the battle before us. Cronus clapped his hands together and slaughtered a battalion of angels in an instant. I couldn't turn my eyes away from the carnage and found myself drawn to it. I wanted to help. Aranya spun me around.

Urania was holding Katrina's sword. "Once I cut a hole in the universe, Rebecca, you'll come through with Velaska and me."

"What about Aranya?" I asked. "She's coming too."

Aranya shook her head. "You don't need four people to bring Apollo back here. I'm needed here. I have fought in many battles. I will be an asset."

For the first time in months, I finally felt close to Aranya again, and she was being taken away from me. I knew she was right, she was needed in battle, but my heart broke at the thought of losing her.

"Don't die," was all I could squeak out.

"You either."

I reached out and kissed her. I kissed her hard, and I kissed her long. This wasn't a kiss of arousal or passion, it was one of longing. It was one of regret. It was one of goodbye. Aranya and I fell into each other like we had when we first fell in love, and for a second, there was no battle—but that second couldn't last, and as quickly as I started it, she pushed me away.

"Goodbye," she said.

Without another word, she flew off into battle. I wanted to believe it was because she was too choked up to watch me go. After all, I didn't want her to see the tears in my eyes.

"It's time to go," Velaska said to me. "We can get sappy later."

I wiped the tears from my eyes. "You're right. Open the thing already, would you?"

Urania gripped the sword tightly and closed her eyes. After a moment, she swung the blade into the air. A million lights twinkled and dashed where she'd cut away the fabric of the universe.

Velaska grabbed my hand, and we jumped into the hole, and Urania fell in behind us. The three of us drifted into space.

***

I expected to be transported through the interdimensional cut just like I'd been transported through so many white beams of light before. All I had to do was close my eyes and disappear into the ether, then I would come back a few seconds later, millions of miles away.

That was not how this portal worked. Instead of traveling straight through a white beam, when I opened my eyes, I saw the entire universe, from the smallest star to the biggest galaxy, all around me. It reminded me of the old Godschurch base, where I would stand in the hallway and stare into the Nexus of the universe.

Nothing came out when I opened my mouth to speak. I wasn't even sure what to say, anyway. Velaska smiled at me. This kind of thing must have been normal for her. She wasn't looking out at the expanse around us. Instead, she looked directly at me as I stared wide-eyed into space.

A comet appeared, and I watched it soar further into the nothingness until we zipped past it. I knew we were going incredibly fast because the stars stretched behind us, but it felt like I was standing still, suspended in jelly as the universe whooshed by.

Ahead of us, another white light appeared. My gut told me it was the end of our journey, and as the ashen planet grew larger in my view, I was not afraid. I felt only exhilaration that I had survived—though there was still a long way to go.

CHAPTER 12

Both Urania and Velaska rolled out of the hole perfectly coifed, but I fell and then stumbled across the ground for a good hundred feet before slamming into the side of an apartment complex.

"You need to prepare yourself better next time, my love," Velaska said, floating over to pick me up with the elegance and grace only a god trying to prove a point could manage.

While I brushed myself off, I looked up at the amber sky raining ash down on us and knew something was wrong with this planet. Most planets the gods created had blue skies in the morning and black skies at night. Every once and a while, you found one that had a slight reddish hue to the daytime, but I had never seen a sky the neon orange of this planet, nor one that rained ash like the days of Hellfire on Earth.

During the Horde Wars, the sky was often burnt, but that was because embers emanating from Hell rifts scorched the planet. The ash rained down across the planet from the deep vents of Hell rising up onto the planet's surface.

But this planet had no demons. In fact, it had nobody or nothing around for as far as I could see. The planet's vegetation worked hard to reclaim its land, with long vines gobbling up what used to be sleek, expensive buildings. Cracks had formed in most of them, their roofs long ago collapsed from the constant heat of the planet. Something like a park in front of us had worn down to nothing but a field overrun with verve, dotted with rusted, old monkey bars and jungle gyms. Boy, was it hot. Hotter than any planet I ever encountered.

Urania stepped across the cracked pavement, wrinkling her nose. "What is that smell?"

"Sulfur," Velaska and I said in unison.

"It smells like rotten eggs," Urania replied.

"That's sulfur," I said. "Why is it up here on the surface, though? Did they have an Apocalypse?"

"Yes," Velaska said, "But not like the ones you had on Earth. Here they dropped bombs on each other until they burned the sky."

"Wait. Like, nuclear bombs?" I said. "Shouldn't I be in a suit?"

"That was thousands of years ago." Urania waved a hand.

"It's quite safe now, but you can see that the world never recovered. Humanity went extinct. They thought they could weather the nuclear storms—but they couldn't."

"Why would Apollo come here?" I asked.

"I haven't talked to him much since the Horde Wars," Urania said, stepping over a broken bottle, mostly liquefied now from the heat. "But he said he needed quiet. Peace and quiet."

"There's not much more peaceful than this planet," Velaska said.

"Peaceful?" I replied. "It looks like a warzone."

"Perhaps to you," Urania replied, "but to me, I see a place where people would never come. The Godless and Horde would write it off as a barren wasteland. Even

Cronus wouldn't waste his time here until well past the end of the universe."

Cronus. My thoughts drifted back to Katrina and Aranya, fighting against the end of the universe while we walked around looking for a destitute god. I shouldn't have come. They didn't need three people to find Apollo.

"Where is he?" I asked. "We don't have all the time in the world after all."

"I don't know. He just told me he would be here if I ever needed him. I don't think he expected me to call in a favor from him, though I suppose time makes fools of us all."

"Let's just hurry up and get off this desolate rock before we miss our chance to save everybody."

"Well," Velaska said, "I think it's already too late to save everybody since most of them are dead, but your point is taken."

"No pressure, though, right?" Urania said. "I mean, we only have to search the whole planet and hope he's around here somewhere."

"One thing I know about Apollo. He's all flash," Velaska said. "You can't take that out of him, no matter how hard you try."

"So, just look for the most garish thing left standing is what you're saying?" Urania said.

"That's where I would begin," Velaska replied, shrugging.

***

I was never big on reading, but most planets had some sort of book repository that banked a civilization's knowledge. On Earth, they were called libraries, but every planet I've ever been to has somewhere they keep the collected knowledge of their people, and this planet was no exception.

The towering pillars of the city's most monumental library were cracked and crumbling down on every side. However, the structure itself was fully erect, including the roof, which wasn't common among buildings on this planet. We ambled up the stairs and into the main entrance. As we crossed the threshold, a light blue hum came from the middle of the room.

"*Jilforgian Mon Colbrino*," the projection of an old, bearded man said from the middle of the room.

"Man," I said. "I don't have my translator."

Velaska snapped her fingers, and a universal translator appeared in my ears, glowing blue just like they have done in my ears a hundred times before. "He said welcome to the central library of Birjac."

"If you are listening to this message," the recording continued, "it's because we have destroyed our civilization. The last thing that we did before the bombs hit was to make sure our knowledge was recorded for future explorers, should they ever come. We knew that our technology would die with us, so these books were preserved with the hope that new people could rebuild. Please, be better than us."

The hologram cut out. I looked over at Velaska and raised an eyebrow. "I don't think he figured we'd be looking for the biggest house on the planet. He probably thought we would want to know about like, history . . . science."

"Maybe," Velaska replied, "but he should have known that humanity never changed. Big, beautiful houses will always be more entertaining than a book about science."

"Not to me!" Urania insisted.

"Fine," Velaska replied, rolling her eyes. "But to most of us. Now, let's split up and look for anything travel-related. Books, maps, newspapers. Anything that could give us a place to start."

***

After an hour of searching, we all met back in the middle of the library with stacks of books. I had no idea if any of the things I brought back would be helpful since I didn't read the language they were written in, but a picture was worth a thousand words, so I grabbed the ones with the prettiest houses.

Urania and Velaska got to work looking for clues about the history of the planet, to see whether there was anything to be gained by staying here any longer. Their magic allowed them to flip through whole books in a couple of seconds.

"Found something!" Urania stood up.

"Me too!" Velaska said.

"What is it?" I was eager to get out of the dusty library with its eerie silence. All I'd heard for the past fifteen minutes was the flipping of book pages while I kept lookout, protecting the two gods from nothing. I felt inadequate knowing my friends were waging war while I was waiting for something to pop out of the bushes on a planet that had long ago lost any sign of life.

"The biggest house on this planet is one called Intrepid. It's not very far from here," Urania said. "It was built to withstand an atomic bomb."

"That jibe with what you found, Velaska?" I asked.

She nodded her head. "Absolutely. Apparently, the threat of nuclear war was prevalent for several hundred years. It was just a matter of time before people destroyed themselves. The architect capitalized on that and built all sorts of homes for the rich and powerful that would survive, well, forever, apparently. Intrepid was his crowning achievement."

"Great. Let's go there and find Apollo."

"If he's there, that is," Urania said.

"If he's not, at least we won't be here."

Velaska grabbed our hands, closed her eyes, and vanished with a snap. I still couldn't believe that her light tasted like nothing. I wondered why I had never noticed it before.

***

We reappeared in front of a house blaring loud, instrumental music. It was like the death metal on Earth, except there was more harp. Too much harp for my taste, but even a little harp is too much harp.

"That's unbearable!" I shouted as we walked to the front door.

Velaska snapped her fingers, but the music didn't turn off. If anything, it got louder with each snap of her fingers as we walked toward the house.

"Stop right there!" a drunken vagrant slurred from the roof. He was a long-locked, blond man holding a jug and staggering around. His hands weren't flesh but instead made of gold that glinted off the light from the sky, blinding me every time I looked up.

"Apollo!" Urania called out. "Come down here!"

"Or at least turn off that blasted music," Velaska added.

Apollo tried to snap his fingers, but the metal on his hands wouldn't let him. "There. Are you happy now?"

"Well, no," Velaska yelled over the blaring harp, "because the music is still on."

"You turn it off then!" Apollo shouted.

"I work with bickering children." I stalked toward the front door. "I'll just do it."

Apollo wound up his fist and flung a fireball down at me. Velaska lunged and knocked me out of the way.

"Stay out of there!" Apollo shouted. "I don't go inna your house and piss on your sheets."

"And I appreciate that," I replied.

Urania floated up to Apollo and looked him in the eyes. "How are you, Apollo? You have looked better."

He smiled at her. "I have never felt better, Urania. Look at me. Doing what I love with what I love—booze!" He took a swig of the bottle. "I'm protecting this planet, you know. Nothing is gonna happen to it while I'm here."

Urania smiled at him. "That's good. It's nice that you've found a purpose."

"Not that you would ever know. Never come visit."

"That's not true. I'm here now."

Apollo collapsed into Urania's arms. "Yeah, right. You probably just need something."

She nodded. "I do need something, but there can be two reasons for my visit, can't there? Come on. Let's go inside, huh?"

Apollo nodded his head slightly. "Yeah, okay."

CHAPTER 13

"I don't want to go," Apollo whined, sitting on a big leather couch across from the three of us. Even with his massive frame, he looked like a child slouching inside the overstuffed cushions.

"I don't want to go either," Velaska said. "None of us want to. None of us wanted Cronus to come back at all, but he is back."

Apollo shot us a scornful look. "And how is that my problem? I did what I was supposed to do. I paid the price for it. Look at my hands!" He held up the golden hands. "I lost them, and I'll never get them back. I can never do that again."

"Yeah," Urania cut in. "But you lost them well before you closed all of the black holes—to be fair."

"That doesn't matter! They are gone, and I'm useless now. I can't do anything to help you."

"Yes, you can." Urania walked over and kneeled in front of Apollo. "Don't you see that your hands weren't what allowed you to close all the black holes in the universe? It was all in your mind. You did it, don't you remember? You did it on Earth without any hands. You and I sent L'l'itoh into the black hole together without your hands."

"I can't—don't you understand what it did to me the last time? Don't you get it?"

I tapped Velaska on the shoulder and pointed her into the kitchen. She followed me until we were out of Apollo's line of sight.

"This isn't going to work," I said.

"Just give it some time, all right? We just got here."

"Right now, that creeping whiteness is destroying the universe. We don't know how big it is or how long it will take to get across the entire expanse, but I have a feeling that if it gets to the Nexus point, we're all toast."

"Why there?"

"Because that's our connection with the Source. And if the Source goes, there's nothing to feed energy back into the universe, which means no new life. Every second we spend here isn't just giving Cronus longer to destroy the gods, it's giving the whiteness more time to destroy the whole universe."

Velaska grabbed my shoulder forcefully. "There is no other option. Those two in there are the only two gods who can close a black hole or a puncture, or whatever that thing is that Cronus crawled through. If she can't convince Apollo to close it, we are all done for. Got it?"

"Then let's hope that she does her job and gets Apollo on our team."

As if on cue, Urania rose to her feet with a heavy groan. "He will help us."

***

There wasn't any water left running through the sewers of the city, so Velaska resorted to pulling what little dew remained out of the air to wash off Apollo and sober him up. However, her efforts were in vain. Even after another hour, Apollo staggered from one room to the other and smelled like a wet sock.

"We can't wait for him to look presentable," I said. "We have to go now."

"Where are we going?" Apollo asked. His voice was a croak.

I lifted him from the bathtub and opened my mouth to speak, but the truth was I didn't know where we were going. I was just kind of making it up as I went along—which wasn't normal for me—and trusting Urania to guide us where we needed to go.

"Back to Aphrodite's planet. That was the last place I brought the weapon we used to close the black holes."

"But the Godless nuked that planet," I said. "The gods were lucky to get away with their lives. I've seen what happens when a Godless bomb goes off. There is nothing left."

Urania picked up Katrina's sword and swung it into the air, cutting open a hole in space. "Then, let us hope you are wrong."

I dove into the hole first this time, anxious to lose myself in the grandeur of the cosmos. Except, the grandeur was no longer there. All that remained were the tendrils of the whiteness expanding out in every direction and gobbling up everything in their path. We had been on Apollo's planet for less than a day, but the whiteness had expanded a million-fold since then.

It was a scary sight, being in the presence of your doom. Even if we got the puncture closed, it would only slow the crawl of the universe-ending chasm. It wouldn't stop it, not for long at least. If our efforts failed, we would have to come to terms with the fact that our extinction was upon us.

***

We rolled out onto a pillow of clouds that, on a different day, would have been Mount Olympus. And on a different day, I would have been ecstatic to be in the home of the gods. After all, I'd been fighting for an invitation to Heaven for many years—I joined the Godschurch for the chance to live among the gods instead of ending up in Hell.

But there was no joy as we rolled out of the hole and onto the clouds. Not today. In fact, there wasn't much of anything aside from the embers of a long-destroyed castle and char marks where gods and angels once stood.

I placed my hand on Urania's shoulder. "I'm sorry. I told you this is what we'd find, but I'm sorry all the same. We can't wait here, though. We have to move on to the next plan."

"Next plan?" Urania said, shaking me off. "This was the only plan. The next plan is to let everything fall apart."

"That's not good enough," I replied. "There is always a next plan."

The whiteness lit up the sky brighter than the closest star and loomed over us. "Do you see that?" Urania said, pointing up. "That's doom, right there. I have no way to fix it. I'm just an astronomer!"

"Ladies!" Apollo said, holding his head. "You both need to shut up."

"The universe is ending." Velaska shot him a dirty look while she spoke to him. "And you want us to quiet down?"

"No," Apollo said. "That's not—no. But I'm sure there's something more productive to do than bicker at each other like children." He turned to Urania. "Think, Urania. Think. There must be something."

Urania stayed silent for a moment, then spoke in a hushed voice. "There is one other option. The device, I made two prototypes. They're much smaller sizes since they were just a test. Maybe we could use them to amplify…they might do the trick."

"Where are they?" Velaska asked.

"In Hera's dungeons."

I had never been to Hera's dungeon, and from the way Velaska's eyes went wide when Urania said the words, I wasn't jumping out of my seat in excitement. Still, if there was no other way to get what we needed, then that was where we had to go.

***

By the time we exited the sword's hole onto Hera's world, I was a pro at interstellar space travel. I rolled onto the ground and hopped back up with ease. In front of us, a collapsed castle stood on a wasteland, looming above everything around it, the single totem in another dead planet.

"Follow me," Urania said, walking toward the gates.

I yanked Apollo to his feet and pushed him forward. "What happened here?" I asked as we walked.

"There was a great battle," Apollo said. He leaned his heavy body into me for support. "It was the last time we were here and the first defeat of the Horde in memory."

"I thought Zeus kept them at bay," I said. The threshold of the moat bridge creaked and snapped with every step.

"True," Velaska said. "Zeus was responsible for protecting us from the Horde, but in truth, they were too scared of him to attack until Katrina killed him."

"Of course. Katrina brought all this on."

"Don't complain, Rebecca," Urania snapped. "She saved you from the black hole in the process and brought a million planets back from the other side of the universe."

"Is that what you did last time you were here?" I said, looking over at Apollo. Velaska came to help lighten the load as we trudged through the arid hallways of a prison, but even between the two of us, Apollo was quite the burden. "Were you and Urania responsible for destroying the Horde here?"

"It—broke me. And my will to go on," Apollo dropped his eyes. "So many souls . . . crashing upon me. I still see them in my dreams." He fell to his knees, crying. We tried to pick him up, but he waved us off. "Stop! Leave me!"

Velaska looked from the fallen god to me. "Go. I will take care of him."

I ran ahead with Urania, leaving Velaska to deal with the broken god that was Apollo. "He was a pretty pathetic god, huh?"

Urania shook her head. "You know nothing about Apollo. He was Hera's favorite. In his day, he commanded respect from all the gods. We all feared and loved Apollo."

"And you . . . you loved him?"

"Of course not, except as a friend and warrior. He carried out Hera's will across the universe. Each of these cells was filled with a god who disrespected the covenant between god and man."

Urania pointed to the cells on either side of us, cracking and empty now, with their bars rusted. I had more questions, but she clipped forward too quickly for me to ask them. So instead, I followed her silently through the chambers and past a fifty-foot-high gilded door that swung from its hinges.

"This used to separate the prison from the palace. It was so grand. If you could have seen it, you would have known our power."

"I'm sure it was great."

"It was great, Rebecca. We were great . . . once. Before Zeus died . . . before the Horde . . . before Cronus returned.

Before the Godless. We were envied and feared throughout the universe."

She stepped through the doorway, and we entered a palace which would have been impressive if not for the thick layers of cobwebs and dust on every wall. Faded paintings depicted a lovely looking woman, beautiful really, with deep, lustful eyes and long, elegant hair. She radiated grace even through the dust that covered her.

"Who is that?"

"That is my queen—Hera, eaten by Cronus after Katrina brought her to him." Urania squinted at the painting, remembering. "That was after she cut off Apollo's hands."

"Man, she really did a number on the pantheon, didn't she?"

Urania quickened her pace again. "She had her reasons, and she has made amends."

"How do you make amends for all that?"

"Slowly. Just come along."

We passed through a circular room with a tipped-over golden throne in the middle of it. Five hallways radiated out from its center, and Urania ran toward one directly across from us.

Above the throne, the blazing light singed everything in the room, giving it all a burnt smell and hurting my eyes with its brightness. I ran down the hallway and came to a stop behind Urania. In front of us stood two faded blue bay doors.

Urania pushed them open and let out a gasp. "What? It's all—It's all gone!"

I stepped around her and saw the remains of an observatory. A slotted hole for a telescope sat empty across the domed roof, as did every desk and wall in the room.

"There used to be computers and telescopes, maps, and charts everywhere. They are gone."

Urania dropped to her knees just as two human-sized Horde flying ants flew in from a window and fired at us. I whipped out the demon hunters from my jacket and returned fire, easily killing both bugs with two well-placed shots.

"Are you okay?" I ran over to Urania.

"Yes! Yes! I'm fine! What is happening?"

A ship came into view above the slotted roof. I recognized the gnarled hull of the ship, composed of a hundred different pieces from a hundred different ships, stuck together with no rhyme or reason other than they happened to fit.

"Junkers," I whispered.

CHAPTER 14

The junker ship hovered above the observatory. Its undercarriage opened, and three figures flew down to the surface in jetpacks. I recognized their silhouettes immediately.

"Januz," I grumbled under my breath. "And his cronies."

I'd worked with a lot of horrible informants to get intel for the Godschurch, but the worst by far was Januz. He didn't care who he hurt to make a dollar. To him, the universe was all just one big shitshow, and he was out to make money from it any way he could.

"Rebecca!" Januz's gruff voice called out from under his thick beard. "I thought I left you dead on Manij."

"And I thought I left you dead on Algor. I guess neither of us got what we wanted."

His two fire ant bodyguards held up their demon hunters on either side of him. Januz was the only human I knew who employed Horde soldiers. He learned long ago that the Horde doesn't speak through words. They speak through scents and ants most of all. He released a pheromone that made them think he was their queen, and because of that, had an army of willing slaves.

"Horde lackeys still the only recruits dumb enough to work for you?"

"Cheap and efficient. I don't need to pay them or feed them. They work 'til they die, and then they're replaced. The perfect slaves. Humans . . . they're so messy."

"And they know you're full of crap, Januz. What are you doing here?"

"We've been raiding this castle for ages. No matter how much I take, there's always more. It's like my own private bank account. This time we're back for Hera's throne. It's worth a fortune."

"You leave that alone!" Urania shouted.

Januz raised his arm, and the ants powered up their guns. "Easy, little lady. Easy. I'm not here to cause trouble. I just want what's mine."

"None of this is yours."

"Well, finder's keepers."

"I don't care what you do with this place," I said, pulling Urania back. "I just want . . . well, what is it we want?"

Urania sighed, swallowing her anger. "I made two prototypes of my telescope—long cylindrical tubes about a meter long. Lots of old Greek writing on them, I'm sure you wouldn't understand."

Januz thought for a moment. "Did they have a red core in the middle?"

Urania nodded. "Yes. So, you've seen them."

"Yeah, I remember it. Sold those off a couple of years ago to a trader. Said he was gonna use them to build a superweapon."

"Dark cloth, black face, eyes bouncing every which way?" I asked.

"That's the one."

"That was Dolos," I said. "He must have used those prototypes to build his Obelisks."

"That's impossible," Urania said. "Only a god could... oh my god—Dolos was a god. He could have used my prototypes . . . he could have used them to destroy the universe."

"It's a bummer, huh?" Januz said. "I really wish I could help you, except that I don't. Now, you'll die."

"Oh, shut up, will you?" Velaska said. She'd finally caught up to us, walking into the room carrying Apollo.

She snapped her fingers, and Januz exploded, along with the ants behind him. Another snap, and she blew up the cruiser above the castle. With a wave of her hand, she pushed the smoking ship to the planet's surface, and it crashed on the ground. "Now," she said, patting her hair back into place, "what was that all about?"

"The answer. It's been in front of us all along," Urania said. "The core of Dolos's device is the same as the telescope Apollo, and I used to close the black holes all those years ago."

"Then it's an easy fix," Velaska said. "We get to that core, and we use it to send them home."

"It's not so easy as that." Apollo shook his head. "Even if we send Cronus and Rhea home, and even if we close the portal to the other universe, the whiteness will still destroy us. Only Cronus can stop that."

"There's a chance we close the portal without actually going back to that planet," I said.

"How?" Velaska said. The gods looked at me.

"Do you remember where you sent me, on Persephone's planet, where I got kidnapped and brought to Dolos's first base?"

"It's hard to forget."

"There. If we go to that planet, we might be able to find the original Obelisk and pull out the core."

"Wasn't that planet consumed by a red giant?" Velaska asked, scratching her head.

"Last I checked, it hadn't been. But it will be pretty hot."

"It's worth trying," Urania said. "If we can get that core, then we can close the puncture before going back to Cronus's battle. But if we don't get it . . . well, we'll have a much tougher row to hoe."

I grabbed the sword from Urania and handed it to Velaska. "Do you know where we're going?"

Velaska nodded. "This is stupid, but follow me."

***

I knew it was a bad idea before we even reached the planet. The red giant was only miles from the planet's surface, and it would consume the planet before long. Velaska formed a protective bubble around us before we exited the portal and filled it with cool air. However, even with the bubble, the heat was stifling. I had never seen Velaska sweat, but even she was dumping sweat into the bubble.

"Can—you—find it—?" I spoke through gasps.

Urania stomped her feet and felt the ground. "It's right under us. There is no way—it's all collapsed. We can't—"

I choked out a few more words. "Then—no choice. Return—to battle. Take our chances—cut it open—"

Velaska barely got the sword upright through her pained sweat. She swiped up to open the portal, and we fell inside, away from the planet that almost killed us. We were heading back to where Cronus waged war with the gods, and he would most assuredly kill us.

***

We rolled out of the sword's tear onto Niloria amid the battle against Cronus and Rhea. The gods and soldiers were engaged thoroughly in combat, but they were tired—it showed in their faces. The few remaining Godless and Godschurch troops fired in small bursts because they were running out of ammo. In the air, the cadres of angels were barely a nuisance to Rhea and Cronus, as their numbers were a hundredth of their former strength.

While I stood surveying the battle, a shadow rose above me. Cronus's hand blotted out the sun and smashed down toward us. I thought I was dead, and my mission to save the universe had already failed, but in the last second, a whoosh grabbed me and sprung me away from the battle toward the town surrounding it.

The blue streak dropped me off at the tallest building in the city, where I'd left the planet in the first place. In a flash, Urania and Velaska appeared on either side of me, holding up Apollo between them. When my senses caught up with me, I recognized Katrina as the one who'd saved me.

She didn't look at me or say anything, though. She took two giant steps toward Urania, and they kissed passionately. Katrina was not one for emotions or displays of affection, I knew, but in certain moments that sort of control goes out the window.

"Ahem," Velaska said after a moment. "I appreciate you are happy to see her, but we do have a job to do."

Katrina let up from Urania and comported herself. "Of course. Did you close the puncture?"

I shook my head. "No. By the time we—no. The answer is no."

"Then what have you been doing out there?" Katrina shouted. "Huh? I thought we had a deal? We keep Cronus busy. You close the puncture."

"Yes, we had a deal," Urania said, pointing to the Obelisk. "But it turns out Dolos bought the equipment we need years ago. It is inside that Obelisk."

"You are getting massacred," Apollo said, looking out at the battle. "I just thought you should know. Can I go now?"

"Nice to see you, too."

"Aranya?" I asked, fearful of the answer. "How is she?"

Katrina didn't say anything at first. Then she looked down at her feet.

"Gone."

Tears filled my eyes, but I refused to cry for her. She died as she lived.

"I'm sorry, Rebecca," Katrina said. "A beam from Cronus's eyes. There was nothing we could do. She—she died valiantly."

"She would have appreciated that."

"It was—"

I held up my hand. "Later. Right now, we have a mission. Urania and Apollo need time to reach the Obelisk and reconfigure it. That means we need to make sure the battle goes in the other direction to give them time. If that Obelisk shatters, so do our plans."

"You need to cause a scene?" Katrina raised an eyebrow. "Because I can cause a scene."

"I'm with you." I turned to Velaska. "Anything that tries to stop Urania—you stop it first."

"I'm not much of a fighter," Velaska replied, "but I will do my best."

"You are the best god I have ever known," I said, pulling the sword from her hand. "Remember that. If it weren't for you, I would be nothing."

She smiled. "Well, you also wouldn't be here, fighting for the fate of the universe."

"No. I suppose I have you to thank for that as well." I handed Katrina her sword. "Here you go."

Katrina gripped it tightly. "Let's go save the universe." She picked me up and flew me toward the battle.

As we charged forward, the shadow of Cronus's hand fell over us. Katrina swerved and maneuvered around it but carrying me slowed her down. She tried to dive down and drop me off, but it was too late. The great paw of Cronus enclosed around our bodies.

"Ah, Katrina," Cronus said. "I have been waiting for this day a long time."

I watched through the cracks in his fingers as Velaska, Urania, and Apollo disappeared from the side of the building and reappeared on the battlefield below us.

"No! No! Leave us!" I shouted.

"You'll die!" Velaska said.

"Then I'll die. Make sure the universe carries on!"

Without another word, the three vanished again. Cronus opened his hand and studied the two of us.

"Oh-ho, it looks like we have a bonus. I don't eat much human—very unsatisfying—but since you are friends with Katrina, I will make an exception.

Cronus opened his mouth and tossed us in. I tumbled toward his slimy throat while Katrina fought his wet tongue. We struggled against the saliva and the giant tongue pushing us back, but it was no use. The muscles on the sides of his mouth tensed, and with one gulp, he swallowed us whole.

CHAPTER 15

"Hold on!" Katrina shouted. She was trying to get a good grip on her mucus-covered sword. I latched myself onto her leg. Below, a bubbly cauldron of stomach acid waited for us, and I didn't like the idea of burning alive in the stomach of a Titan.

Katrina reared back her sword and jammed it into Cronus's esophagus. His blood spurted out and oozed over us as she cut through into the digestive tract. Viscera poured over us, sliding us gradually down the digestive tract.

"It's working!" Katrina said.

And it was working . . . until it wasn't. I don't know if her hand slipped or the sword jerked, but Cronus's throat fixed itself faster than she could cut through it, and when the hole closed around her sword, Katrina lost her grip, and we tumbled down Cronus's long throat.

"What's happening?" Katrina shrieked, flailing in the air as she nosedived toward the acid below. "I can't fly!"

We exited the esophagus and slid into the stomach cavern, where moans echoed through the air, bouncing off every side of the stomach lining. For the first time I'd ever seen, panic set in Katrina's face. We were heading right into the stomach acid, where I would surely die. The only upside was that I would die quickly.

At the edge of the acid lake, there was a shore of some sort, where bones and half-digested debris had washed up. Katrina saw it too, but we couldn't both get there if she couldn't fly. She shoved me hard, sending me as far from the center of the lake as possible.

I flew until I smashed against the gooey lining of the stomach and slid down it toward the lakeshore below. There was a splash, and I knew it was Katrina falling into the acid lake.

As I settled on the edge of the lake, I looked for anything I could use to help her, but there was nothing except the wailing bones of decaying corpses that wouldn't die. Thousands of them—the gods from our battle no doubt among them.

Katrina screamed from the river, splashing in a frenzy while she attempted to swim for the side. With every stroke, the acid burned more deeply into her skin.

"Here!" I said, holding out my hand.

"No!" she shouted. "Don't touch me."

She rolled out onto the edge of the lake. The left side of her face had burned to the bone. Her eye hung out of her head and dangled from the socket. Her hair fell out in tangled clumps, and the skin on her limbs was slowly being eaten away. Whimpering, she tried to pull off her leather coat, but like her gloves, it was seared to her body.

"It looks worse than it is," she said. "I will heal in time."

A laugh sounded next to us and rippled across the lake. A meek, shrill voice said, "You—will never heal. Gods have no power here—except to suffer—forever."

Katrina crawled forward, and together we made our way over to a gooey skeleton lying on the shore, casting off a putrid smell. One of its legs was still blistering in the lake, but the skeleton didn't bother to move. Maybe it couldn't.

"What do you mean?" I said. "Gods are immortal. They always heal."

"Immortal, yes," the gaunt figure said. "But healing—no healing here. That is our punishment."

"Who are you?" Katrina asked.

"You know who I am," the voice replied.

Next to the gaunt figure lay the remains of a bearded man in a tattered toga. At the sight of him, Katrina's face showed a spark of recognition.

She looked back at the skeleton that had spoken to her. "Hera," she muttered under her breath.

"Yes—it is funny," she said. "Only in here—were Zeus and I—able to find our love—our love was the only respite—for our pain."

The emaciated figure beside her muttered, barely more than a whisper. "Who—is it—dear?"

"Katrina—the horrible—woman—who damned us—"

"Tell her," the voice said, "I hate her."

"You can—tell her—Zeus," she said. "For the—rest of eternity."

"That's how long we will be here?" I said. "Eternity?"

Hera flopped to her side and looked at me with her terrible, half-dissolved face. "Not you, my dear. You—you will die. There is something—something about you—different than just a human. What is it?"

I shook my head. "I don't know. I don't know. I can sometimes run so fast that I look like a blur. I can punch through things like they weren't there."

Hera tried to smile but winced instead. "Golden—streak?"

"Yes, that's right. Do you know what it is?"

"We—liked to play—sometimes. Zeus and I—created non-humans—orcs—demons—pixies—"

"Pixies?"

"We—liked them—most—" Zeus said. "Beautiful—creatures—but humanity—hated them—"

"Bring it—back around—to us. Hera—you said—eternity?" Katrina said, suffering with every word.

"Hang on," I replied. "Where else do you have to be?"

"Pixies—could fly—move faster than the eye. Faded into memory—but some—maybe some lived on—"

"So, you are saying I'm a pixie?" I said, looking down at my hands.

"Not full. A millionth—of one, maybe more." Zeus said. "Bred out—but still a spark remains. I see it—in you."

Hera took a deep breath. "We created—the pixies—not Cronus. If it's in you—you could—use your magic. I can—unlock it."

"You can do that?"

"Possibly—" Zeus said. "If our magic works."

I knelt in front of them. "At least some piece of your magic must work because you're still immortal."

"Because—it helps—our suffering—" Hera said, turning away. "He—took away—everything—that could—help us escape."

"He—didn't want—us defeating him—again," Zeus added. "It is—hopeless—"

"You can at least try," I replied.

"What—is the—point—," Hera said.

Suddenly Katrina's working eye got very large. "To see—Apollo."

"Apollo?" Hera said, suddenly interested.

"He—is outside this stomach—right now—fighting— for the universe," Katrina said, falling to the ground. "Your—most loved—god. He needs you."

Hera's bloodshot eyes, caved into her skull, looked at me. "You—Apollo?"

"Yes," I nodded. "I could bring you to Apollo. If you help me."

Hera lifted a shaky arm. "Come—"

I leaned forward and let her place her melting arm on my head. For a moment, nothing happened, and then, with a shot of electricity, golden flames emanated from my fingertips and made their way up the sides of my arms and into my stomach. A warm glow filled my chest and rose into my head. In another burst, it shot out through my eyes, ears, mouth, and nose in a luminous array as I rose into the air.

Pressure built in my back until what felt like two baby's arms broke through, sprouting from either side of my spine. I was confused, surprised, but there was no pain. In another second, it was over, and when I looked down, I was still hovering above the ground.

"What is happening?"

A cool breeze whipped from behind me. I looked over my shoulder to see golden wings, like the wings of a dragonfly, fluttering behind me.

"What's going on?" I asked, amazed. "I have wings!"

"Yes," Hera said. "Now—use them—pixie."

"To do what?"

Hera pointed up. "The sword—get the sword."

I wobbled through the air, trying to get a handle on my newfound powers. Much like driving a car, the wings were part experience and part technical prowess. I figured out how to float forward, but I needed to go up, not sideways.

I looked up into the esophagus and willed myself upwards. I jerked and jimmied but only moved up a little at a time. Eventually, I had ascended through the hole in the Titan's throat. The sword was buried about halfway between the stomach and the mouth. When I finally reached it, I grabbed tight onto the hilt with both hands and yanked hard.

The titan's whimper thundered through his throat as the sword dislodged and fell into my hands. I gripped the sword tightly in my hands, determined not to let it go.

I willed my way back down to the stomach lake and landed near Katrina. She was in bad shape. The acid had eaten down to her bones. She looked the same as Zeus and Hera, even though she hadn't been there more than a few minutes.

"Katrina!" I said, trying to pick her up.

"Stop. Stop," she whispered. "Don't—touch."

"I need you," I said. "I need your help. I can't get us out of here alone.

"You have to," she replied, sliding back down to the ground.

"The—sword," I heard Zeus say. "The sword—"

"This sword?" I said, pointing to it.

"I—I used to—to cut open—Cronus before—it can— destroy a titan—"

"How?" I said. "How can I do that? How can I cut open his stomach when it regenerates all the time?"

Zeus held out his hand, and I placed the blade into it. "If Hera can—then maybe I—have magic—too."

The sword lit on fire, a rainbow of colors glinting against the slimy walls.

"It—cuts—deeper—longer—now," Zeus said, collapsing back to the ground.

"All right, you old piles of bones," I said, gripping the sword, "prepare to be saved."

CHAPTER 16

I held on to the glowing sword, hovering above the stomach acid lake bubbling and popping beneath my feet. I wondered what was going on outside of Cronus's accursed stomach. With any luck, Velaska, Urania, and Apollo had reached the base of the Obelisk and re-engineered it to send Cronus and Rhea into the abyss. If they could do that, then it wouldn't matter what we did in here.

Then, a thought occurred to me. What if my soldiers had already won outside of Cronus's stomach? What if Cronus and Rhea were on the other side of the universe, wishing they could get back, and we popped out of their belly there? How would we get home? Could we even survive?

I shook the thought off as quickly as it came. There wasn't time. I had to believe we were able to beat the Titans. All right, I told myself. Make a beeline for the lining. Swing in one smooth motion. Use your momentum to burst through the stomach. Let the other gods ooze out behind you, and then rebuild your troops.

Flying was still new to me, and I was nervous about rushing toward the stomach lining at full speed, but there was no more time to spare. I had to hope I'd figured it out.

Closing my eyes, I flapped my wings faster and faster until the golden streaks shimmered around me. I stared at the gooey lining of Cronus's stomach and then flew toward it as fast as I could.

The stomach wall came up quickly, and I lowered my sword as I neared it. When I was close enough to smash into the lining, I slashed the flaming sword up, hard and fast. An explosion of goo and viscera spewed onto me on my way through the guts and muscles of Cronus's insides. I popped out on the battle-torn planet of Niloria covered in innards, but the remaining gods and soldiers didn't seem to see me. They were busy firing the last of their bullets toward the Mad Titan.

Cronus let out a deep, guttural moan and slumped onto the ground as gods, humans, and angels alike bounded away from him, dodging the weight of his limbs as he crashed forward.

"My love!" Rhea shouted. She dropped Aphrodite and rushed to him. I flew down to the ground and watched Katrina, Zeus, Hera, and a hundred other gods ooze out of Cronus's stomach back into the world.

Katrina's body was goopy and disgusting, but she could fly, and so could Hera and Zeus. Even though they were merely skin and bones, they joined the fray. Cronus had tortured them for too long, and they would take their revenge, even if they only had a fraction of their powers left.

Before Cronus's stomach could close up and regenerate, Katrina flew to the skin flaps and held them open, shaking with every ounce of her zapped strength. Zeus spun thick metal chains to bind Cronus's arms and legs, just as he had millennia ago. However, he was weak, so a collection of gods flew to his side to aid him.

"Help me!" Katrina shouted. As gods slid out of Cronus's stomach, they joined in to help her. They were at a fraction of their full strength, but together they still had incredible power.

"Get off him!" Rhea tried to swat the gods away.

"No!" I screamed, holding out the flaming sword. "You have seen this glowing sword before, so I assume you know that it vanquished you once. *Velaska!*"

Velaska appeared in front of me with a flash. "Oh, you're alive, and you look gross."

"Is it ready?" I said, ignoring her.

"Yes, Urania and Apollo are prepared."

"Did you hear that, Rhea?" I said. "We will send you back to your universe to live in the whiteness, forever. We have done it before."

"I don't care," Rhea said. "I don't like this universe anyway. It bores me."

The sound of her voice sent chills through my body, and I found myself trembling, but I was not the child that I was during our last encounter. "Possibly. Though it raises the question why you would bother to come here then if you were so happy in the other universe."

She sighed and folded her arms like a child. "*Fine!* It was boring, all right? Is that what you want me to say? Cronus, I love him dearly, but he is a bit of a bore."

I flapped my wings and flew up to confront her eye to eye. "Then I have a compromise for you."

Cronus moaned, trying to speak, but the open wound in his stomach prevented him from giving more than a light, pained whimper.

"I do not compromise with your ilk," Rhea said.

I shrugged. "Then we will send you back to your dimension, where you can live out the rest of eternity. *Velaska!*"

"Wait!" Rhea said. "What is your compromise?"

"Twice you have fought us, and twice you have failed, so can we assume that if you fight the gods again, you will fail a third time?"

"I don't think that is fair. After all—"

I held out my sword inches from her eyeball. "What you say is yes, and only yes, if you do not want to be sent back."

"Fine! Yes!"

"We do not wish to fight you. So, I will offer this one-time-only deal. If Cronus stops the whiteness from creeping across this universe, and you both agree never to bother the gods again, you will be able to live in peace at the Nexus point, near the Source of all things."

"You can't do that!" Katrina shouted.

"You do not speak for the gods," Zeus replied.

"Yes! I do!" I said. Authority boomed from my voice. "I am the head of the Godschurch, and as such, it is my duty to protect the gods. We cannot stop the whiteness from infecting our universe. Only Cronus can. And if he does save the universe, then we can be fair to him and Rhea."

"He will never live up to his side of the bargain!" Zeus said, flying toward me, his thick beard growing more glorious with each second as his skin repaired itself. "I know him. I have fought him. If you listen to me and—"

"You left, Zeus," I replied. "You were defeated by Katrina and fed to Cronus. In your absence, the universe continued without you. The Godschurch continued, with me running it."

"And a fine job you have done!" he shouted. "The gods Cronus ate in this battle told me of the Horde, how they nearly destroyed the Gods. And the Godless? A group of humans nearly took us down! You are weak."

"I am stronger than you know. Back down, or I will feed you to Cronus again."

I held up the sword and stared Zeus down. Velaska flew up behind me, as did the Odin line and the Osiris one. Soon, almost all the gods not holding open Cronus's stomach were behind me.

"You can fight us all," I said. "Or you can shut your mouth."

Zeus snarled and threw up his hands. "You are making a big mistake." He turned back to Cronus.

"And it won't be the last time, I'm sure. But we don't run from our mistakes. We fix them." I turned back to Rhea. "I will let Cronus heal if you agree to my terms. You will not attack the gods, or humanity, ever again. You will live in peace with us at the Nexus point. If you maintain that pact, there will be no war, and with the gods and Titans back, there will be harmony in the universe."

Rhea looked down at Cronus, who had no choice but to give a weak nod of approval.

"Very well," she said. "We accept your generous proposal."

"Excellent," I replied.

***

Katrina begrudgingly released Cronus, and we let his stomach heal—after getting every god out of his stomach, of course.

"This is a very rash decision you made, entreating with me," Cronus said, studying me. "Have you thought this through?"

"Not really. You didn't give me much choice, though. There was no other way to stop the whiteness. That power rests solely with you."

"Still, very rash." He pointed at Katrina. "It is the kind of thing I would expect from her."

I chuckled. "I've heard we are a lot alike."

"Annoyingly so," Rhea said, standing behind Cronus.

"It is time to do your job," I said. "Repair the universe."

"You know, I could just go back to destroying you."

"I know, but that would be a really terrible thing to do, wouldn't it?"

He chuckled again. "Yes, it would."

Cronus placed his hands on the sides of the planet, and we vanished. The taste of warm maple syrup slid down my throat. We reappeared in front of the puncture, which continued to leak out little bits of whiteness, consuming the universe in every direction for miles.

"I can't do anything to close up the puncture," Cronus said, pointing to the gash in space. "There is a gap in my knowledge about interdimensional travel. Otherwise, I would have come back much sooner."

I held up my hand. "We have that covered. Velaska, fire the thing!"

The great Obelisk spun upward and the green energy filled to its tip. Once again, the great, green laser shot toward the sky. But this time, it worked in reverse: This time, it mended the puncture, returning the star to its rightful place in the cosmos.

I looked up at Cronus once the puncture was sealed. "We've done our part. Now, it's your turn."

Cronus lifted his arm and snapped his fingers loud enough to quake the ground underneath us. As he did, the whiteness receded from across the galaxy into his fingernail as if it was sucked up with a vacuum. In less than a minute, the Heavens were once again filled with stars.

I nodded to him. "Thank you."

"Now," Cronus said, "I suppose we will adjourn to the Nexus."

"Can I ask you one little favor before you go?"

"Have you not asked enough?"

"This is not part of our deal. You are free to say no."

Cronus narrowed his eyes, considering this. "Interesting. Continue."

"You exist outside of any pantheon, above even the powers of the gods, which means you have power the gods do not, yes?"

He nodded. "That is true. Though they continue to defeat me."

Katrina rolled her eyes. "Be bitter about it on your own time."

"Enough." I shot her a glare before returning to Cronus. "The Godschurch base will take untold amounts of money to rebuild by ourselves. However, I was wondering if you might be able to speed it along as a favor to me?"

"I could help you. It would take a fraction of a second. But why would I want a place where the gods can congregate together and be protected? They are my sworn enemy."

"Because the church will rotate around the Nexus point, where you can keep an eye on it. And it will protect gods, titans, and humans alike."

"That's really not its mission," Velaska said.

"Well, it is now," I replied. "Will you help us?"

Cronus smiled. "Yes, very much alike, the two of you." He touched his finger to my forehead. "Think of the church. Ah yes, there it is."

He opened his eyes, and his fingers quaked the ground a second time. "It is done. Now, I will leave you in peace. Or, I guess I should say that we will meet again soon."

With a third quake, Cronus snapped his fingers, and he and Rhea were gone. I turned to the gods and soldiers who remained. I was still responsible for helping them. We had recovered most of the gods from Cronus's stomach, but the angels and humans were gone, including Aranya. I would mourn for her later, in private.

"That was a mistake," Hera said.

"I agree," Zeus added.

"I can't believe I'm going to say this," Katrina said, raising her eyebrows, "but I agree with them."

"We'll see," I replied. "We defeated Cronus for a second time, and we can do it a third."

Another flash of light and Velaska appeared next to us with Apollo and Urania. Urania's eyes sprung tears at the sight of Hera, and she rushed over. "My queen."

Hera brushed her out of the way, instead galloping toward Apollo, ragged and weeping. She wrapped her arms around him. "Apollo! My love! What has become of you?"

Urania looked on with jealous contempt. Katrina slid her hands around Urania's waist. "Let's go home, baby. We can drink wine and complain about Hera."

"I'd like that." Urania wiped her eyes and addressed Velaska. "Can you get them home?"

"You taught me enough that I can manage."

Urania took a deep breath and turned to Hera. "Just so you know, your castle is nothing but rubble and ash now. I hope you rot in it."

Katrina took the sword from my hand and cut open a hole in the universe. She stepped through it with Urania, and they were gone.

"No thanks from her, I see," I said.

Velaska walked up to me. "No. There never is." She gestured to the bands of gods, Godless, Godschurch agents, angels, cherubs, and all manner of ruffians spread out before us. "What will you do with them?"

I flapped my pixie wings and flew up into the sky. "Listen up, all of you!"

The crowd hushed and looked toward me. "This is the dawning of a new day. If you were against us before, I will not hold your past against you. However, you must join us now. It's time to wipe the slate clean and try again.

"All here will be welcome at the Godschurch. From here on out, we will not merely protect the gods. Our mission will be justice and balance for everybody in the universe. We will open the portal to the Godschurch and let you enter. If you still oppose us, know the Godschurch will not cower to you. We will fight, and we will beat you into the ground."

I floated back down to the ground and smiled at Velaska. "That should do it."

Velaska placed her hand around my shoulder. "I think so."

"And what about me?" Zeus said. "What will happen to me?"

"The same thing that happens to us all, my friend. We will live to see tomorrow." I stuck out my hand. "I would like to offer you and Hera a place on the inner council of the church, where we will make decisions together."

Zeus glanced back at Hera, who gave a slight nod. "You know I will vote for you to be replaced as director," he said.

I smirked. "Do you think I would complain? I hate this job. However, my last act is asking you to allow Odin and Isis onto the board once I am gone."

Zeus nodded. "Agreed."

With that, I started walking. The sea of gods and people parted, allowing me and Velaska to make our way to the portal.

"So, you know how to work this thing now?" I asked her.

"I can figure it out."

"That's all I ask. We work together to figure things out."

***

You just finished reading *Doom*. If you liked this book, transport backward in time over thirteen centuries and visit the past with *Hell*. Here's a preview of that book.

HELL

Book 7 of The Godsverse Chronicles

By:
Russell Nohelty

Edited by:
Leah Lederman

Proofread by:
Katrina Roets & Toni Cox

Cover by:
Psycat Covers

Planet chart and timeline design by:
Andrea Rosales

CHAPTER 1

"Then I ripped his leg off and beat him to death with it!" A fat, square-jawed ogre shouted to his monstrous friends.

They were all drinking ale inside the tavern they had occupied for the last ten days and nights. The innkeeper paced back and forth, a tall, lanky man with dark bags under his eyes. His body twitched with every word from the horde's mouth.

I had been eyeing them closely the whole of the night. Over the past few months, King Odgeir had sent a dozen of his best men to deal with Bjarngimur's monsters and expel them from the tavern, and twelve times all that made it back to the king were the heads of his soldiers, eyes cut from their skulls.

That would not happen a thirteenth time. The people of Odgeir's kingdom would not have to endure the tyranny of this menace for one more night. That was why the king's herald summoned me in the dark of night to deal with them. I never failed.

"Ha! That's a great story!" an orc shouted back. It was green-skinned and sported a mohawk down its lumpy head. I enjoyed killing all manner of vile beasts that strayed beyond the Veil, but orcs were my absolute favorite.

An orc was responsible for killing my father before I was born, so I had no love lost for them. I was only a few days old when a troll killed my mother. I had never met either of my parents, yet the memory of their deaths haunted me every day of my life. It was the reason I became the best monster hunter in King Odgeir's kingdom.

"Human!" a fiery-haired goblin shouted. "More ale! And be quick about it!"

The knock-kneed innkeeper shot straight up to full attention before spinning on his heels and hurrying to the spigot. He poured the ale into thick, metal steins and placed them on a wooden tray.

I counted twenty of Bjarngimur's men lining the wooden tables that stretched from one end of the tavern to the other. Bjarngimur and his monsters had menaced the countryside for years, but they usually disappeared into the trees before anyone could catch them. This was their boldest attack yet, and it would be their last after I was done with them.

Before Bjarngimur's monsters invaded, the tavern was quaint, sleepy even. I often drank there on my way through the deep forest. It was not so sleepy today, though, not with ogres, orcs, and goblins running amok. I would return it that way, in short measure.

"Don't be so scared, human," the fiery-haired goblin said with a fiendish grin. "I won't hurt you or your family unless you spill my ale, of course. Do that, and I'll cut off your kid's pretty, little face and feed it to you!"

The tavern burst with laughter. That kind of heartless cruelty was to be expected from monster kind, and it was what I was hired to stop. And I was a pixie, one of the fairy folk, which meant I was a monster, just like them. I might not look like a monster, but people lumped us into the same category. If you weren't a human, you were a monster. It was my greatest advantage and greatest burden all at once.

To catch a monster, you need a monster.

That's what King Odgeir had said to me ever since I started hunting monsters for his kingdom, back when he was just a prince, and his father, King Odgeir I, sat on the throne. Technically, my brother was King Odgeir II, but he hated to be called that. He never liked not being the first in anything.

After monsters slayed my parents when I was a baby, the royal family took me in. They should have left me for the wolves. They should have burned me at the stake, but they didn't. They kept me and raised me. I had been repaying that debt – gladly – ever since I could fend for myself.

The innkeeper stepped carefully to avoid spilling a single drop of the beer. I could tell by the fear in his eyes he fully understood the goblin would cut off his child's face. From the timbre of the monster's voice, I knew he meant it as well. That was the kind of thing monsters did, after all. They were callous, cruel, and mean.

"Hurry up!" the goblin shouted.

A visible shiver went up the man's spine, but he didn't spill a drop. He took another deliberate step forward and let out a deep sigh. In front of him, a short, fat orc with a pocked face chuckled to himself and stuck out his leg as the innkeeper went past.

The beers flew into the air and rained down on the monsters in the hall. Several of them stood from their seats and grabbed their weapons, but the goblin hopped onto a long bench and held up his arms.

"Wait!" the goblin shouted. "Don't be so hasty. I claimed this one fair and square. Go back to your drinks, boys."

The monsters grumbled and wiped themselves off before returning to their beers, annoyed and soggy. There was honor amongst thieves and monsters as well—though the code of ethics monsters followed was not one I'd call based on honor.

"That wasn't very nice," the goblin said, sauntering toward the innkeeper. I had been crouched in the bushes, waiting for the right time to strike, but I feared I didn't have time to wait any longer. "I thought I asked you not to spill my drink."

"Well…I…" the innkeeper stammered, turning back to see his wife and child huddled in the far end of the room. His wife had big, round, beautiful brown eyes. She ran her rough hands through their child's curly hair. "Please, don't hurt them."

"I warned you!" The goblin lunged forward. "But since you asked so nicely, I won't hurt your kid. I'll just kill you instead."

Another goblin piped up, "I want the kid, then!"

"Be my guest," the red-haired goblin said with a smile. He held a knife against the innkeeper's face. "I'll take care of you once you watch your kid get gutted."

"Please don't," the innkeeper sobbed, struggling to break free. He couldn't. Monsters were much stronger than humans, which gave them an unfair advantage in any fight. The only advantage that humans had was me, their secret weapon.

I couldn't hide in the bushes any longer. I wanted to wait until the crowd of monsters thinned out, but I would have to take my chances fighting against all of them. I would gain nothing from stealth. Frankly, I preferred a clean fight out in the open to hiding in the bushes. Most rangers didn't and relied instead on their bow, but I enjoyed watching the life drain from a monster's eyes. Up close.

"Don't squirm, human!" the goblin shouted as I sprinted toward the door. "Just enjoy the show!"

"Remember," the second goblin said, inching toward the little boy and his mother. "Your father's failure is what brought this on, not—"

I kicked open the door and flung a throwing dagger through the air. It whizzed past the monsters with deadly precision, borne from decades of practice, and embedded into the back of the encroaching goblin, who fell to the ground at the feet of the mother and her child.

"You're beyond the Veil, monsters." I lowered my voice as I stood at the front door of the tavern.

An ogre turned to me, and its eyes narrowed. "It's the pixie!"

I might have been as much a monster as they were, but I was nothing like them. They lived in the muck and the mire. They killed for fun, pillaged for sport. Unlike them, I chose the side of righteousness and defended humanity from their hatred.

"Ylfingur has a price on your head, pixie," a goblin with a protruding forehead growled at me.

"There is one on yours as well," I replied. "The king does not take kindly to monsters in his kingdom. Take me to Bjarngimur, and I won't collect on them, as long as you leave this place and return beyond the Veil, never to return."

King Odgeir's father, King Odgeir I, had established the Veil as a safe haven for monsters, where they could live their miserable lives for as long as they were able, without being hunted by humans. It was a magnanimous offer from the king, whose ancestors had battled with monster hordes for generations.

King Odgeir I could have wiped monsters from the world for good but instead chose to end the bloodshed and come to peace with them, as long as they left us alone. It worked for a while, but lately, more and more monsters were emboldened to cross the Veil and attack humans.

"You're outnumbered twenty to one," a pudgy orc said.

"Yes," I replied. "And I have beaten worse odds than that. In fact, I hardly think it a fair fight. You don't stand a chance."

"You won't beat those odds today!" An orc with a spiked, leather pauldron raised its club and shouted, "Get her, boys!"

The key to fighting a group of monsters was knowing that they were impulsive and irrational. They did not coordinate with each other, and their movements were sloppy. They'd knock into each other like stooges. It was just a matter of biding your time and letting them do your work for you.

However, I didn't have a lot of time, so I pulled out two ivory-handled daggers and threw them through the eyes of the closest attacking monsters. They fell to the ground in a heap as one of their orc brethren ran at me with a knife. I sprinted forward, dodging his swipe, and stuck him in the gut with one of my daggers.

I spun around to face the monsters creeping toward me. "Where is Bjarngimur?" I shouted. "This is your last chance."

The monsters laughed. They would have had the upper hand in any other situation, but they had never met me before or seen me use my pixie dust. Most monsters who have met me fell under my blade; few lived to tell the tale. Maybe they'd heard of the golden-winged fairy who could disappear in a puff of purple smoke, but I had never met a monster who believed the whispers about me. Much to their detriment, of course. The stories were all true.

I took off my cloak and tossed it across the room. I unfurled my hidden wings, which lit up my face with a faint glow.

"What're you gonna do?" A yellow-skinned orc with rotten teeth chuckled. "Fly away?"

"No."

Without another word, I reached into a blue pouch with stars on it that I kept held tightly around my waist. I pulled out a pinch of what looked like pink, shimmering, rock salt, the fine crystals just big enough to not fall through my fingers. This was my pixie dust, the magical powder that let me disappear in a puff of smoke.

Clenching a fistful of the dust, I raised my hand high in the air, then hurled the dust onto the ground. With a puff of purple smoke, I disappeared from the bar and reappeared in the middle of the monster pack, stabbing two of them through the throat before I dropped another handful of dust and disappeared again. This time I reappeared by the front door, where I ripped the sword from a goblin's hand and used it to cut him in half.

"Where is Bjarngimur?"

A massive ogre with rippling muscles swung a two-handed broadsword at me. I leaped backward into the air to avoid it. When the ogre swung again, I dodged it easily, then wheeled on him and cut him from naval to sternum with my dagger. I kicked him back into his friends.

"Tell me now!" I vanished again and reappeared to slit the neck of an encroaching orc. "And I will end you quickly!"

I disappeared to dodge the club of another ogre. When I rematerialized, I roundhouse kicked him into the wall and stuck two daggers through his chest.

"Refuse, and you will suffer greatly." I landed on the top of the bar. "Now, where is Bjarngimur?"

The ground rumbled beneath me. Something was approaching, and it was massive. In another moment, a hulking figure smashed through the door. A behemoth Cyclops towered over me and roared, his great, red eye staring at me with fury and rage. Smoke billowed from his nose, where a bull ring dangled. Two huge fangs protruded from his bottom lip, and when he opened his mouth to growl at me, I saw three rows of spiky teeth.

"I am Bjarngimur!" The Cyclops raised his massive, spiked club, the size of an oak tree, into the air. "And you will die, pixie!"

The huge lug must have expected me to be intimidated by his huge frame and deep, booming voice, but I had vanquished worse than him dozens of times in my life.

"Tell your men to leave, and I will spare them," I replied, floating down from the bar. "My quarrel is with you."

"Never!" Bjarngimur glared at me. "Attack!"

Half a dozen of his men still lived, and they ran toward me at his command. I dropped a pinch of pixie dust and disappeared behind their ranks, stabbing one in the brain before taking its sword and using it to stab another one in the gut.

Bjarngimur was strong, but he was lumbering. He didn't have a good turning radius. When I disappeared again, he couldn't stop himself or recalibrate his position, which sent him crashing into the wall of the tavern.

I reappeared between two orcs and stabbed them both through the ears with my ivory-handled daggers. They fell on either side of me. All that was left was the red-headed goblin, cowering before me, as frightened as he had made the innkeeper just a few minutes before.

"Leave this place," I said. "Tell everyone what you saw here. Never step beyond the Veil again."

The goblin didn't hesitate. He sprinted out of the hole Bjarngimur made in the wall and disappeared into the woods behind the tavern. He would not be back, at least not for a long time. Maybe I should have killed him, but I needed enough tales of my deeds to spread through the monster realm that they would never dream of stepping beyond the Veil again.

"Akta of the Forest," Bjarngimur shouted. "We have unfinished business."

I turned to see Bjarngimur smashing his hands together, growling. The great Cyclops lunged and swiped at me with his club, and I flew backward to avoid him.

"You are slow and dumb," I said to him. "Just like all the others."

His anger bubbled over into rage, and he swung his club wildly at me. The biggest ones were always the sloppiest, relying on their great strength to save them. It never does, at least not when I was involved. If I weren't so quick on my feet, I would have likely succumbed to one of Bjarngimur's blows. However, his brute force could never match my skill and determination.

I waited for Bjarngimur to lift his club over his head, so I could get a clear shot at his eye. The small tavern could not take much more abuse before it collapsed upon itself, and I couldn't let that happen.

Finally, the Cyclops lifted his arm. His club slammed down upon the ground with a great, thunderous crash, and I floated back again to avoid it. There was only an instant before Bjarngimur picked up his club again, and I had to capitalize on it. I only had one shot at his eye, the only place on a Cyclops that wasn't covered in a hardened, impenetrable skin.

I flung my dagger through the air just as Bjarngimur looked up. He didn't even have time to flinch before the dagger lodged into his eye, and he collapsed on the ground, dead.

"The biggest always fall the hardest," I said, walking up to Bjarngimur's dead body. The king demanded proof of my success in the form of the Cyclops' head. It was a messy business but using a broadsword I pulled from an orc's belly, I severed Bjarngimur's head after several chops.

When it was all over, I made my way toward the door, dragging the head behind me. I looked through the debris for my cloak along the way, and that's when I saw the innkeeper and his family huddled in the corner, shaking with fear.

"It's okay," I said. "They will never bother you again."

"Th-th-thank you," he stuttered. "How can we ever repay you?"

"The king is very kind to me." I picked up my cloak from where I'd flung it on the floor. "I apologize for the mess. The gold, weapons, and armor should be more than enough to cover the damages and live the rest of your life in peace."

CHAPTER 2

Hogarth's caravan rolled through the woods every evening, carrying food and water from the countryside into the city. It was a favorite target of bandits, especially monstrous ones, so half a dozen guards protected the caravan at all times. Hogarth was kind and gave me a ride whenever I needed it.

"It's a nice evening," he said from the front of the caravan. He pulled the reins of his horse slightly to make her slow down. Cherry liked to strain ahead, even in her old age, but Hogarth was happy to ride leisurely through the woods, ensuring that everything made it safely to its destination.

"It is at that," I replied, pulling my cloak hood up over my head. "A bit cold, though."

Hogarth nodded. "It's getting to be fall soon, then winter after that."

"That is how the seasons go, my friend."

"Predictable," he said. "Just how I like it."

I could have transported myself to town in an instant using my pixie dust, but I enjoyed the slow, plodding progress of a horse-drawn carriage. It yoked me to the earth and reminded me how privileged I was to vanish in an instant and reappear a thousand miles away.

That was not the only reason, though. I started traveling by horseback long ago, even though I could easily fly because me being a pixie scared a whole lot of people. In the end, I was a monster, even though I looked human, and seeing me fly around and then disappear without a trace…it frightened folks. King Odgeir thought it would be better if I blended in as much as possible to avoid terrifying his wards, to avoid reminding them that their greatest savior was a monster.

The citizens of Odgeir's kingdom were nice, but they were fearful as well. They didn't like things that were different from them. My skin was already darker than theirs, and my ears longer. Flying over them would push them past their breaking point.

I mostly liked to travel by foot or horseback, so people could see I was on their side and not a monster like the others. Odgeir called it "public relations", but I just wanted people not to hate me. Most of my life was about convincing people not to hate or fear me.

It would have been so easy for them to hate me like they hated the other monsters, but they were all so kind and let me into their lives. I like to think that was because I made sure to meet and greet them as much as possible. I walked among them. I bought from their shops. People saw me more than they saw the king. Despite the fact that I lived in the castle with him, I wanted people to know I was one of them, even if I looked different.

So, I decided not to show my wings unless it was essential. I still wasn't sure exactly how they worked, even after all these years, but my wings could appear like magic when needed and disappear just as quickly when I didn't want to cause a scene.

That was usually the case—I didn't like to draw attention to myself. Even though I had killed over a hundred monsters in my twenty-six years, most of my life was filled with the banality of everyday existence, just like everyone else. On those days, it was nice to blend into the scenery to avoid being gawked at, or worse, threatened.

Yes, sometimes a new monster hunter, trying to make a name for themselves, would threaten me. The people of King Odgeir's kingdom loved me, and they kept me safe from those attacks.

"Did he put up much of a fight?" Hogarth asked.

"Excuse me?"

"The head, sitting next to you, oozing on my wagon. Did he put up much of a fight?"

"Oh," I replied. I had been lost in thought and forgotten that Bjarngimur's head sat next to me. "No more than usual."

"How is the king these days?" Hogarth asked.

"Regal," I replied curtly.

I didn't like speaking about my brother's business, as it was his own and not mine. At one time, we walked the streets of the capital together, cavorting with the townsfolks. He was the first to introduce me to his people, and I owed him a great debt. That seemed like a lifetime ago, now.

On the day of his coronation, he stopped being my adopted brother and started his life as the king of his people. On that day, we stopped spending time together. He stopped laughing. He didn't call on me unless it was to give me a mission. The only other time I saw him was when I returned with news of my conquest.

I wasn't sure why King Odgeir I adopted me when I was a baby. I liked to think it was because I was so young, and he was kind. However, it's hard to believe that he didn't see the potential in my pixie lineage for something greater, something he could mold to a higher purpose, just as he had his son. His son would become a great king under his guidance, and I would become a great monster hunter under the tutelage of his greatest knight, Sir Cleybourne. The two of us, working together, could offer his people lasting peace.

His whole life, my father was consumed by his pursuit of peace. He had only known war, and he worked relentlessly to end it. I wished my brother felt the same way, but our troops had fought six wars since he took over and always seemed on the go. He was never satiated with the size of his land or the scope of his power.

"I didn't mean to pry," Hogarth said.

"No," I replied. "I'm sorry. It has been a very long day, and you are very kind to offer me a ride."

"It's my pleasure, my lady. Having you in my caravan means I don't have to worry about marauders or monsters, at least for a night."

"Well, I appreciate it," I said. "The truth is, I'm not sure how my brother fares these days. He spends most of his days locked in the tower and most of his nights huddled away with his generals. I haven't had a chance to see him in weeks."

"Planning something, is he?"

"I'm not sure," I said, smiling. "I don't really care about any of that. I am excited to bring this home to him, though, because it guarantees me an audience with his majesty. This Cyclops terrorized his countryside for far too long."

"He sure did," Hogarth said. "I look forward to the peace…while it lasts."

"It will last as long as I draw breath."

"We both know that's not true," Hogarth said. "Soon, another will band together the monsters from the Veil, and they will be back."

"Then I will be ready for them, friend. We all will be ready for them."

***

By the time the sun crested over the horizon, Hogarth's caravan was nearly at the walls of Odgeir's castle fortress. A one-hundred-foot-high wall spanned the outer perimeter of the city, which could keep out most any monster. Once, an ice giant nearly destroyed the town. It was only at the last moments that I was able to send it to the depths of Hell. After I defeated the massive beast, King Odgeir demanded that his best mages construct an impenetrable wall around the city that not even a giant could destroy.

Of course, that didn't apply to me. I could still come and go as I pleased through the wall, as could any who used pixie dust, but there were so few of us anymore that it was almost as if pixies no longer existed. I had never met another fairy in my whole life, no matter how far my travels took me. I have heard rumblings of another pixie in the woods, one with a scar on his face and a patch over one eye, but I have never seen it myself, no matter how many hours I wandered there.

"Hope the ride was okay," Hogarth said to me as he stopped his horse and leaped down from the caravan.

"It was excellent." I hopped down from the back of the caravan and pulled Bjarngimur's head from the bed of the trunk, noticing the thick goo it left behind on the wood. "I'm sorry about that."

"It's fine, Akta," Hogarth replied. "Seeing that thing, well, it makes me feel safer going into the woods. You did a great service to me and my kin by killing it."

"Still," I replied, "go to the stables and have Paget wash it off and give your horse a nice meal for your troubles."

Hogarth replied. "Thanks. I'll say high to Magpie while I'm there, too. She and Cherry always get along like old friends."

I smiled. "That's kind of you. I plan to take her for a run myself soon when I'm able."

I wished that my pleasantness was because of my innate goodness, but it was truly a survival mechanism. I needed these people to like me, to love me even, and they would only do that if I were kind to them. I suppose I could have chosen to be ruthless to the point of cruelty and forced their respect, but I had no interest in fighting a violent coup or ruling with an iron fist over villagers who hated me.

Besides, the truth was that I loved this kingdom and all its citizens. They took me in as a child, and they treated me like their equal. They chose to let me walk among them and smiled when I did.

"Oh, my gods!" I heard as I dragged the head of Bjarngimur through the town. "Is that—"

"It's the head of Bjarngimur, the terrible," one of the fruit vendors shouted out.

"He's dead!" a priest said, covering his mouth in shock.

Dragging a giant cyclops's head through town wasn't a daily occurrence, even if the townsfolk in Odgeir's capital had seen plenty of monster violence. People stared, mouths agape, as I passed. For my part, I wanted to show them that I was once again victorious. If I could show my worth, they would see the value I brought to their lives and know their king would protect them.

A little, freckle-faced boy ran up to me with his little red-headed sister. "Can we touch it?"

"Quickly," I said, chuckling to myself.

"It's squishy," the boy said. "Ewww!"

"It's cool," the little girl said. "I can't wait to hunt monsters like Akta when I grow up."

I sighed a deep, contented sigh. I was an idol to somebody, to many people in this village, at a time when my kind was seen as evil throughout the land. The effort I put into earning and keeping their respect was paying off.

"Bucket!" a shrill voice cut through the air. "Hope! Let's go!"

"Mom!" the little girl shouted. "You'll never guess what we just did!"

The little boy and girl ran off to their mother, who smiled and gave me a slight nod of approval. I had made her children's day. Most every day was the same around the village, and they would surely talk about the head of Bjarngimur for weeks to come.

"That's unsanitary, you know," an old man said as I turned back toward the castle. His name was Edwin, and he was a widower who ran a small tavern in town.

"I know, but how else will people know how great I am?"

He grinned. "You could just tell them."

"Words are my brother's business. I prefer actions."

"It's very gross," he replied.

"Luckily, you just have to watch it pass by. I had to cut it off from between two very ugly shoulders, then travel with it from deep in the woods."

"Yes," he said, eyeing the blood on my shirt. "Well, you can't see the king looking like that. Let's fix you up with a meal and some clean clothes, so you don't drag blood into the castle."

***

While the castle made delicious feasts the likes of which were beyond compare, I preferred to eat in the town, among the people I protected. The castle was majestic and enormous, but it was also lonely. Besides my brother-king, whom I never saw, the castle was filled with servants, guards, and nobles. None of them had any time for stories of adventure.

Most days in the castle were filled with loneliness and solitary contemplation. I did not like being alone with my thoughts or hearing my footsteps echo off the stone walls. I wanted to be amongst the people, listening to the hustle and bustle of city life.

Perhaps it was because I was surrounded by silence during the long months of a mission that I longed for human contact when I returned. Often, I'd live in the wilderness for days on end, hunting and tracking my targets without coming across another living soul—and when I did, it was only to kill them. It didn't make for very good company.

"Tell us about the great dragon Aziolith again, Akta," the little boy pleaded. We were seated at the table eating his father's stew, which oozed off my spoon and down my gullet in a rather pleasant manner. It wasn't like any other soup I have ever had, and I wouldn't call it good, but I still enjoyed its interesting texture.

"I don't think your father wants to hear that again, Michael. He's heard that story since before you were born."

"It's fine," Edwin said, shoveling a spoonful of soup into his mouth. "I've heard all your stories a hundred times, except maybe this last one." He pointed to the head of Bjarngimur, sitting on the stoop outside his tavern. "That, though, might be a little close for you to tell."

I nodded. "In time, I will regale you with the story." I stood up. "But for now, I must be going. I owe the king a bounty. Thank you for the lovely meal, the lovely company, and the clean clothes. I appreciate them all."

***

I had taken most of the morning and much of the afternoon wandering through the city, meeting many old friends along the way. Each of them wanted a bit of my time, which meant I made it through the gates of the castle just as the sun fell over the horizon.

"You're late," Tilda scolded as we walked through the high-ceilinged halls. She was made up in white powder and held together with a tight corset, as was the style among noblewomen in the capital. I thought it garish and foolish to wear something that restricted your movement, but not having to worry about such things was one of the benefits of being rich. While the citizens of the town accepted me as one of their own, the nobility eyed me with much suspicion, and Tilda was no different. "He has been waiting all afternoon for you."

"I'm sorry," I replied. "I got carried away and a little nervous. I haven't seen my brother in—"

"The king. You haven't seen the king. He hates when you call him your brother."

"Don't you mean *you* hate it?"

The nobility resented the fact that their king and I were related by law, and they worked to downplay it at every turn.

"I am here at the behest of my king, not your brother, and we both expect you to treat your meeting with the reverence it deserves."

"Of course," I replied, tired of fighting. "That is what I meant. I haven't seen the king in many weeks."

"Yes, well, he has been busy running an empire while you were off galivanting around…" Her voice trailed off as her eyes landed on the rotting head I was carrying behind me.

"Protecting his kingdom." I followed her eyes and gave her a cold smile. "I think those are the words you are looking for."

"Yes, quite." She snapped her fingers at two palace guards standing on either side of the door. "Let her in."

"Nice seeing you again." I pulled Bjarngimur's head behind me, making sure to drag it over her opulent, white lace dress as I passed her. The goop would take days to wash off, and she would likely never rid herself of the smell.

No doubt, I had ruined her day. The thought of it brought me endless joy.

***

If you enjoyed this preview, make sure to pick up *Hell* today!

ALSO BY RUSSELL NOHELTY

NOVELS
My Father Didn't Kill Himself
Sorry for Existing
Gumshoes: The Case of Madison's Father
Invasion
The Vessel
The Void Calls Us Home
Worst Thing in the Universe
Anna and the Dark Place
The Marked Ones
The Dragon Scourge
The Dragon Champion
The Dragon Goddess
The Obsidian Spindle Saga

COMICS and OTHER ILLUSTRATED WORK
The Little Bird and the Little Worm
Ichabod Jones: Monster Hunter
Gherkin Boy
How NOT to Invade Earth

www.russellnohelty.com

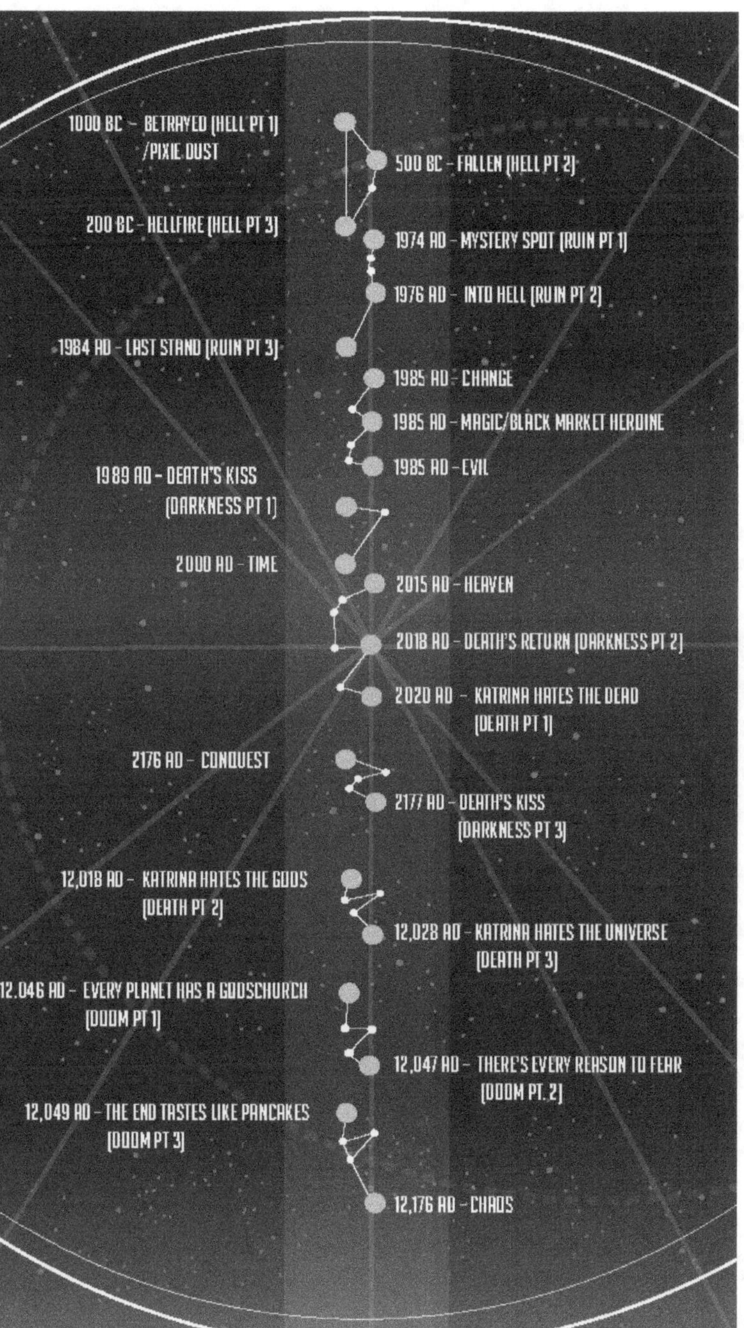

1000 BC – BETRAYED (HELL PT 1) /PIXIE DUST
500 BC – FALLEN (HELL PT 2)
200 BC – HELLFIRE (HELL PT 3)
1974 AD – MYSTERY SPOT (RUIN PT 1)
1976 AD – INTO HELL (RUIN PT 2)
1984 AD – LAST STAND (RUIN PT 3)
1985 AD – CHANGE
1985 AD – MAGIC/BLACK MARKET HEROINE
1985 AD – EVIL
1989 AD – DEATH'S KISS (DARKNESS PT 1)
2000 AD – TIME
2015 AD – HEAVEN
2018 AD – DEATH'S RETURN (DARKNESS PT 2)
2020 AD – KATRINA HATES THE DEAD (DEATH PT 1)
2176 AD – CONQUEST
2177 AD – DEATH'S KISS (DARKNESS PT 3)
12,018 AD – KATRINA HATES THE GODS (DEATH PT 2)
12,028 AD – KATRINA HATES THE UNIVERSE (DEATH PT 3)
12,046 AD – EVERY PLANET HAS A GODSCHURCH (DOOM PT 1)
12,047 AD – THERE'S EVERY REASON TO FEAR (DOOM PT. 2)
12,049 AD – THE END TASTES LIKE PANCAKES (DOOM PT 3)
12,176 AD – CHAOS